UNDER THE HARVEST MOON

UNDER THE MOON SERIES
BOOK TWO

TRACIE PROVOST

MIDNIGHT
CONFESSIONS
PRESS

Print ISBN:978-1-955168-01-4

Ebook ISBN:978-1-955168-00-7

Editing by Mert Gareis

Cover Design by 100 Covers

❀ Created with Vellum

For my mom,
thanks for believing in me

CHAPTER 1

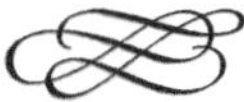

I have seen my fair share of dead bodies. I have even caused
a few, but this one was just *wrong*. It wasn't the gore
although that was certainly present. My magical shields protected me
from the worst of the malevolent energies washing over me, but they
were so strong that I could still feel them. Josh, who could feel magic
though he couldn't use it, shuddered next to me. When I instinctively
reached for his hand to comfort him, something completely unexpected happened. As soon as our skin touched, my magical shield
flowed through me to him, protecting both of us. I felt Josh tense at
the unexpected sensation and then relax.

"Is that supposed to happen?" Josh asked me quietly.

My eyes were wide with surprise at what had happened before I
dismissed it with a shrug. As fascinating as this particular develop-
ment was, there were far more pressing matters to attend to: namely,
the nude female body splayed, Vitruvian Man fashion, on a blood
pentagram.

Detective Mike Angelletti stood well away from the body and the
blood. "I didn't touch anything, just called you right away," he said,
shifting his six foot three frame from one foot to another. Even he,

who was not magically sensitive, could feel the wrongness of the scene.

"Who reported it?" Josh asked as he let go of my hand and began walking the perimeter of the large room, his cowboy boots echoing on the hardwood floor. Despite the gruesomeness of the scene before me, a part of me couldn't help admiring my lover's tall trim form as he paced the room running his hand through his shaggy blonde hair. I pulled my attention away from him and focused on the task at hand.

"An anonymous call about screams came into dispatch. It was a slow night, so I offered to check it out. Found this." He gestured to the scene in front of us. "I radioed dispatch that the homeowner had been watching a war movie and the screams reported were on the TV." It was part of Mike's job to keep human members of the police department as far away as possible from supernatural crime scenes. This was not always possible, but he did the best he could.

"Good," I said. The last thing we needed was NOLA's finest investigating this. We had been busy enough these last three days trying to keep the supernatural presence—vampires, werewolves, and mages, along with a number of summoned demons—hidden from the human population, and I did not want to have to try to hide things during an active murder investigation. "Do we know who the victim is?"

"The house is owned by Gina Breslin," Mike consulted his notebook. "I assume that's her."

"Oh, shit! Gina?" Josh's head whipped around to look at Mike and then the victim.

"Yeah, you know her?" Mike asked.

"Yes. She's been dating a coven member, Eddie Sykes, and we've been looking at turnin' her," Josh said. As the second in command—the lieutenant—of the Sylph coven here in New Orleans, Josh knew all the members and possible initiates. Composed mostly of artists, writers, and musicians, the Sylph were the largest of the five vampire covens.

"Ugh. Could Sykes have done this?" Mike asked.

"No," I answered definitively. "Neither he nor Gina had any magic. This really doesn't make sense." Most vampires outside of my own coven, the Aether, did not have magical abilities. There were some few that did but neither of these two.

"How do you mean?" Mike asked, clearly curious.

"This room is set up for two very different rituals. The murder is dark blood magic. It may even be necromancy. Over by the bed, that is set up for sex magic." It was a large room, taking up most of the second floor. An unmade bed flanked by two nightstands was positioned against one wall. The nightstands had obviously been recently moved because they were not by the head of the bed but midway down each side. Guttered red candles sat on each.

"So the perp sets up for sex magic, rapes her, and then does the dark blood magic?" Mike hypothesized.

I shook my head, walking close to the bed. "No, this is a consensual act configuration," I said, examining the candles arrayed in power positions around the bed.

"There are different ritual configurations?" Mike asked, dismayed.

"I don't think I wanna know how you know this is a consensual configuration," Josh said dryly.

I ignored him. Turning to Mike, I said, "Many, but the big clue is the color of the candles. Had this been rape, the candles around the bed would've been black."

"I don't see Gina cheatin' on Eddie," Josh said as he rifled through the pockets on a pair of pants he'd found on the floor. Pulling out a wallet, he quickly examined the contents. "These are Eddie's pants. This is his wallet."

"So where is he?" Mike asked. "There is no vamp dust in the circle that I can see." With all the blood, I was not sure how he could tell. It obscured many of the markings of the elaborate pentagram.

"Here, on the bed. I'm pretty sure this is vamp dust," Josh said.

I turned from the candle configuration I was studying and looked at the bed. After inspecting the rumpled sheets, I nodded. "Definitely vamp dust. My guess is that Eddie was killed first, and then the murderer took his time with her."

"So we have a double murder, and at least one of them has a ritual component. Is it the Rogue Aether?" Mike asked. Three days ago, almost all of the members of my own vampire coven, the Aether led by Honore Rochon my arch nemesis, had unsuccessfully rebelled against the city's leader, Grandmaster Marc Gautier, and been declared Rogue as a result. Any Rogue Aether was to be killed on sight.

I stopped for a moment and dropped my magical shields to see if I recognized the magic. To my surprise there was none. None. Nothing. This room should've been teeming with it, but there was not one trace —just the overwhelming presence of evil that slid over my skin like oil and tried to worm its way into my essence. I shuddered and threw my magical shields up again.

I turned to Mike. "I would love to lay this at Honore's feet, but I do not think so. The magic has been drained from the room, but there is an evil here that I have not felt before."

"Demonic?" Mike asked as he ran his hand through his black curly hair in frustration.

I shook my head. "No sulfur, but perhaps something adjacent. A dark summoner, maybe? Once I read Eddie's dust and Gina's body, I might have a better idea."

"Is that safe? Reading the body and dust, I mean. Mrs. Deroche never did. She'd read anything else, but never bodies," Mike said uncertainly.

Frederique Deroche had been the New Orleans Aether coven mistress for centuries and my close friend until she'd been killed less than a month ago. I wasn't surprised that she never read a body. Reading a body was dangerous. There was always the chance that the reader could become trapped in the memory. Frederique was probably right to avoid it, but I didn't think that I had a choice. There seemed to be a dangerous new player in the New Orleans supernatural community, and we needed to know who it was.

"All magic has risks. I am willing to take them to get answers," I said.

"Are ya' sure, Juliette? That sounds mighty nasty," Josh asked, his concern clear.

I smiled and touched his arm. "It will be nasty, but I have you to return to."

As much as I didn't want to, I knelt by the bed and placed my palm on top of the rumpled sheets. I opened my third eye and was flooded with images and emotions of Gina laughing and happy as Eddie lit the candles. I knew I needed to go deeper into the vision, so I moved my hands slightly and brushed some of Eddie's dust. Suddenly, I was viewing the scene through his eyes, but there was a second consciousness in Eddie's mind with me. Eddie was more than Eddie, as if someone was controlling him. Murmuring incantations, he lit the candles and undressed Gina. Heat, passion, thrusting, pleasure, lust. Then his hand closing around Gina's throat, choking her into unconsciousness while she fought him. Eddie's essence tried to fight this action. He did not want to hurt Gina, but the other presence was too strong forcing Eddie back down. Suddenly, I was shoved from the scene and fell back hard on the floor. I sat for a minute, needing to regain my bearings and composure.

"Are you alright, darlin'?" Josh asked as he knelt beside me concern shading his green eyes.

I nodded. My stomach roiled, and I was glad that I had not fed before coming over. "I just need a minute. It was . . . powerful."

"I don't think you oughta touch Gina," Josh said quietly.

"I probably ought not," I agreed "but I need to. I only got part of the story. I still do not know who was responsible for this."

Josh grimaced but didn't argue with me.

I took a deep, steadying breath, and walked to the pentagram with Gina's body inside. I sat cross-legged, just outside of the blood circle. Suddenly I was glad that Josh had insisted I change into jeans and sneakers before coming to the crime scene. Steeling my nerves, I swiped my index finger through the blood and touched it to my tongue.

I let the blood tell me its story. As before, I saw the events unfolding through Eddie's eyes. There was definitely someone very powerful and very evil controlling him. I could feel the two battling for dominance, but the evil entity was much stronger. Eddie continued to struggle, but the Other was firmly in control of his body. Eddie slit his wrists and drew the elaborate pentagram with his own blood. He then moved the still unconscious Gina to the center of the pentagram. The image faded, and I could learn no more from the blood.

As much as I did not want to, I knew that I needed to read Gina's body. I reached out and placed my hand on her forehead, immediately regretting it. No longer was I seeing through the killer's eyes, but through Gina's. Her panic and pain flooded me. I heard his whisper, tauntingly telling her everything he was going to do before he did it. There was a sob, and I realized that it was my own. I held on for as long as I could, hoping the villain in Eddie's head would tell me who he really was, but he never did. I heard his rhythmic chant, and then the worst pain I had ever experienced caused me to wrench my hand from Gina's body.

The images were so powerful that I could not tell where Gina's terror ended and mine began. Shaking and crying, I curled into a tight ball trying to protect myself. I heard Mike and Josh asking me questions, but it was as if I was underwater. They were muted, and I was alone with my terror. Slowly, I came back to reality and away from the horror that I had witnessed. I tried to sit up and gather my thoughts, but it was too much, too soon and nausea wracked me. Leaning over, I heaved, but there was nothing in my stomach to vomit.

I lay sobbing for several more minutes. Josh finally ventured forth and touched my shoulder, but I recoiled. My third eye was still open, and his feelings of fear and concern flooded me as well.

"Juliette, darlin', what can I do?" He asked as he knelt next to me.

Squeezing my eyes tightly shut, I choked out, "I just need a minute."

"Mike, could you see if you can find Juliette some whiskey or somethin'?" Josh asked.

Mike hesitated, "Um . . ." obviously worried about compromising a crime scene.

"For Pete's sake it ain't like Gina's gonna mind, and we need ta call

Vinny in to clean up anyway," Josh snarled. Vinny Carlucci was our vampire "cleaner," a function he had carried out in life for Al Capone. He disposed of the messes that needed to remain hidden from the human world.

"Yeah, I guess you're right," Mike reluctantly agreed.

"Fuckin' Dudley Do-Right Boy Scout," Josh muttered after Mike had left the room.

It took me several more minutes to gain control of my emotions and order my thoughts. I was seated upright, leaning heavily on Josh when Mike returned bearing a bottle of Glenlivet and a glass. Ignoring the glass, I took the bottle from him, un-stoppered it, and took a long pull. I let the burn of the scotch chase away the lingering coldness of death that had nearly paralyzed me.

"Can you tell us what you saw, darlin'?" Josh asked gently.

I nodded and told them, careful not to leave anything out.

"Holy hell," was all Mike had to say when I finished.

"Far be it from me to tell you what to do, Juliette, but . . ." Josh started.

I held up my hand. "No need. I will not be doing any more readings, at least for tonight," I assured him.

Josh nodded grimly. "Mike, I want to get Juliette fed. Can you take care of telling the Grandmaster?"

"Yeah, I'll call Vinny to clean this up and then stop by the Gautier House," the detective said. Another part of Mike's job was keeping Marc Gautier apprised of all supernatural crime activity.

"I called Jaime. She is supposed to meet us here," I said absently. Jaime Sprenger was a Gatekeeper—a member of a secret order of mages who were charged with keeping the paranormal world hidden. Her insight might be vital to this case.

"I'll take care of briefing the Gatekeeper when she gets here or tell Vinny to do it," Mike said.

I didn't really like the idea but was too drained to argue. I needed vitae, the blood that sustained me, soon. I wasn't one to shirk my duty as coven leader, but right now, I did not want to face Marc Gautier, Grandmaster of New Orleans and ruler of the vampire community that resided here. I had been avoiding him and his temper since the coup attempt three days ago, and I was decidedly not up for dealing with his open hostility to me. Even though I had not rebelled against him, the rest of my coven had. That was enough cause for him to mistrust me. In addition, I was not dressed for an audience with the Grandmaster. Josh could get away with wearing jeans to meet with Marc, I could not.

"Maybe I should text Jaime and have her meet us at your house," I said.

"She'll probably want to view the scene," Josh reminded me.

I nodded. She might see something in the ritual that I had missed.

"I'll take care of this, and you go take care of yourself. If you think of anything else, just call me," Mike said.

WE HAD JUST EMERGED from the house into the courtyard when I felt Jaime's aura. I put a hand on Josh's arm to halt our slow progress and said, "Jaime's here."

"Where? I don't sense her," Josh asked.

"Over by your car," I said.

"Juliette . . ." Josh cautioned.

"Wait," I stopped suddenly, "I should not be able to feel her this far away," I whipped my head around to look at him. I detected a subtle difference in the tang running through her aura that had not been there before and should not be there now.

Panic propelling me, I hurried to the courtyard gate with Josh right behind me. Jaime, dressed in her typical all black tee-shirt, cargo pants, combat boots, and trench coat, but without her normal heavy make-up, had stopped to rest next to Josh's parked car on the street. She held her hand up in weary greeting. She slumped heavily against the red Mustang, looking as exhausted as I felt.

"Come on, let's go face this," Josh said taking my hand. Together, we walked the short distance to the ailing Gatekeeper. Jaime appeared even more pale and gaunt in the streetlight than her normal Goth look. Her red-tinged dark hair hung lank on her shoulders. I knew even before I touched her, she would be cold. I felt tears well in my eyes.

"I don't suppose you could use some of that magic mojo healing power on me, could you? I haven't felt right since I took that hit during the coup attempt." The young woman tried to smile but failed.

Summoning strength I didn't know that I had, I took her arm and opened the heavy car door. "Let us get you back to Josh's, and I will fix you up."

Josh stepped up and assisted Jaime into the back seat and tucked me into the front. The grim expression on Josh's face told me he knew what had happened.

"Wasn't there some sort of murder scene back there that I needed to look at?" Jaime asked as we pulled away from the curb.

"I will tell you all about it after I fix you up," I promised.

"I got pictures," Josh said. I hadn't realized that he'd taken them. He probably did it while I was in one of my trances.

"God, I feel like death warmed over. It isn't Demon Fever, is it? Like the Master Gatekeeper had?" Jaime asked. Nicholas Remy, head of the Gatekeeper Order of Mages in New Orleans, had contracted Demon Fever several weeks earlier after nearly losing a fight with one of the Hell minions. The fever, contracted by a demon bite or scratch, normally resulted in death. Renowned for my healing abilities, I had been summoned as a last resort to treat him. His successful recovery had allowed for a tentative friendship to form between the two of us. The malady that Jaime currently suffered from might well destroy that relationship.

"No, there is no fever. You are as cool as a cucumber," I assured the young woman.

"Or as corpse," Josh said too quietly for Jaime to hear, or so I hoped. I shot him a warning glance. I wasn't sure how attuned her senses were, especially since she obviously hadn't had her first feeding —the one that would complete her transformation—yet.

I had no idea how to tell Jaime that I had accidentally made her into a vampire three nights ago. I leaned my head against the window, going over in my mind the events of the coup attempt. I had found Jaime laying in a pool of blood in the Gautier's foyer. One of her attackers was dead a few feet away. While Josh went after the other, I tried to use my inborn magic to heal Jaime, but I had expended too much of it fighting Honore and banishing demons, and the girl was losing too much blood too quickly for conventional human methods, so I used my dagger to cut my wrist and feed her my blood. That should have healed her and made her my human servant. But Jaime must have been much closer to death than I knew. Instead of healing Jaime and theoretically making her my servant, my blood healed her and made her my vampire childe instead. It was the sire bond that had allowed me to sense her at a distance.

I still had reached no conclusions about what to say by the time we pulled into Josh's courtyard.

"Can you manage on your own while I get Jaime? I don't think she can manage the stairs herself," Josh said. His house was a traditional Creole townhouse with the primary living areas on the second and third floors. The street level door opened to a small entry hall. To the right was a door that led to what had once been a business area and to the left, a steep, narrow set of steps led up to the expansive living room.

"I will be fine," I assured him.

Josh carried Jaime upstairs and deposited her carefully on the couch while I went into the kitchen. Once there, I pulled four bottles of neatly labeled blood from the refrigerator with shaking hands. One of Marc Gautier's human servants delivered several bottles every evening. While I preferred fresh vitae, this was an expedient solution to our current problem. Opening one bottle, I drank it cold. I pulled a large coffee mug from the rack and poured two bottles into it. Once it was in the warmer, I drank the other cold bottle. Cold blood was vile, but I needed the nutrition in it in order to clear my head.

I pulled two more bottles from the refrigerator and poured them into another large mug. The second mug was in the warmer when the true gravity of what I had done occurred to me. I had turned Jaime Sprenger into a vampire without the Grandmaster's permission.

Normally, as a coven leader, this would not have been an issue, but Marc had specifically forbidden any new Aether be created in New Orleans the day after the aborted coup attempt. I rather doubted he would care that technically I had already turned Jaime at that point or that I had not been trying to turn her at all.

The timer on the warmer buzzed, and I took the two mugs into the living room.

Jaime smiled weakly and said, "You got some nasty voodoo stuff in there, Juliette?"

I laughed despite the situation. "No eye of newt or bat wing, I promise. This should restore your strength." Cradling her head with my hand, I put the mug to her lips. At first, she grimaced, but then greedily drained the mug. I switched the empty vessel with the full and helped Jaime drink that as well.

Josh handed me a third mug that he had warmed in the kitchen. I took it gratefully. "Thank you."

"You gotta tell her," Josh said.

"I will."

"I'll leave ya alone for it. You need to tell Marc too."

"Tell me what?" Demanded Jaime after she finished her third mug of blood.

I ignored Jaime's question for the moment and said wearily to Josh, "I guess I'll be meeting with the Grandmaster tonight after all. Could you call Sophie and set up an appointment for me?"

Josh brushed a kiss across my forehead, murmuring, "Of course," before leaving the room.

"Tell me what?" Jaime demanded again.

"How are you feeling?" I asked, again ignoring her question.

"Better" she said, a hint of suspicion in her tone, "I'm not queasy anymore, and I can mostly think clearly. Are you going to tell me or not?"

"Can you sit up?"

Jaime frowned but pushed herself into a sitting position. "Wow, Juliette, what the hell did you put in that concoction? It's amazing. I didn't feel you do magic on me. Did you? Wait, that tasted like blood. Did you give more of your blood, like the other night?"

I sat back on my heels, shaking my head. "No magic, Jaime, and no more of my blood either." I hesitated, not really knowing how to break the news to her.

"Whaddya need to tell me?" she tried again.

"I . . . you are a vampire now," I blurted out.

Jumping from the couch, Jaime yelled, "What the fuck did you do to me, bitch? I came to you for help, not so you could turn me into a monster!"

I stood and faced her. "Your becoming a vampire did not occur this evening. It happened when I gave you my blood during the coup attempt."

Jaime violently shook her head. "That healed me, and at worst, it should have made me your human servant, but I shook that off."

"That is what I thought as well," I said with forced calm. "I never intended to keep you as my servant in any case. I only fed you to save your life. Unfortunately, you were much closer to death than either of us realized. In fact, you must have briefly died. The reason that you felt ill these past few days is that you had no vitae."

"Human blood? Is that what you just gave me?"

I nodded. "Human, Type O."

"Fuck! Fuck! Fuck! I can't believe this!" she screamed, fists balled at her side. I wondered if she would take a swing at me. I'd let her if she did. Just this once.

"I am so sorry, Jaime. I did not mean for this to happen."

Josh chose that moment to walk back into the living room. Glancing between Jaime and me, he said, "Marc can see you in twenty minutes."

CHAPTER 2

I stood in front of Marc's large mahogany desk and waited for him to say something—anything. The silence stretched between us uncomfortably. I shifted from one foot to the other, vividly reminded of our first meeting barely two months ago after I was awakened from my two hundred yearlong enforced slumber. I was at least wearing appropriate clothes and shoes this time instead of a torn, mud-crusted eighteenth-century gown with bare feet. *Had it really only been two months? It seemed so much longer.*

Finally, the Grandmaster of New Orleans spoke in a low hard tone. "Mistress Grammont, did I, or did I not expressly forbid you to create any Aether childer?"

I looked at the floor. "Yes, you did, my liege," I said softly.

"Yet tonight you appear at my home with a fledgling in tow."

"Yes, my liege." I felt distinctly like I was six years old again, and Papa had caught me doing something that he had forbidden. Unlike Papa, Marc Gautier did not dote on me, and my punishment could be much worse than a switch across my backside. Judging by Marc's dark mood, I would be lucky to keep my head.

"Please explain to me why you defied my order and turned a Gatekeeper—a Gatekeeper for Christ's sake—into a vampire," he demanded.

"With all due respect, Your Grace, I did not defy you," I said carefully.

"What?" Marc asked sharply, and his glower deepened if that was possible.

I cleared my throat and gathered my thoughts. "I gave Jaime my blood on the night of the coup. She had been attacked by a succubus and was near death. I had expended all of my magic fighting Honore, so I used my blood to heal Jaime. It was not my intention to turn her. I told you what I had done when we met later that evening." I reminded him, "And technically, I was not yet under interdict when she was turned."

Marc jumped from his seat and placed his fists on the desk, leaning towards me. "You. Dare. Defy. Me?" Each word was louder than the last, and his intense blue eyes blazed with a cold fire. I shivered. It was all I could do not to cringe and cower in front of him. Force of will kept me upright.

"Marc," Gabe Gautier's calm voice came from across the room. In addition to being the Grandmaster's brother, Gabe also served as his second in command, the city's lieutenant. "A word, please."

"Get out!" Marc snarled at me. Without another thought, I fled the room leaving the Grandmaster to his brother.

I was shaking so hard that I could barely close the door behind me. I stood for long moments in the foyer, trying to control my quivering body.

"Um, Juliette?" Jaime asked tentatively. She sat in the same chair where I had left her before going into the Grandmaster's office, but now she was huddled, knees drawn up to her chest and coat wrapped around herself in an attempt to become invisible or at least as small as possible.

I took a deep breath and ordered my body to stop shaking. "It will be alright," I tried to reassure the young woman.

"It didn't sound alright. It still doesn't," Jaime said.

"What do you mean?" I asked, but then heard it as well. The sounds of angry voices coming from the office. Voices that I should not have been hearing. I sent a tendril of magic through the wall, and where it should have been stopped by a magical ward, my magic passed easily through.

"What's going on, Juliette?" Jaime asked.

"The ward on the office is down," I said, worried that the rest of the wards were similarly not in place. Josh, with his impeccable timing, strolled down the hall from the kitchen, sipping a beer.

"So, how'd it go? Marc wasn't too mad at you, was he?" Josh asked when he was close enough.

Another burst of angry voices erupted from the office. "The only reason you are defending her is because Bouchard is fucking her!" Marc yelled.

"What the . . ." Josh said with rising anger before I put a restraining hand on his arm.

"You are being completely unreasonable, Marc. You have been for days. You're like a bear with a sore paw, snapping at everyone. Hell, you had Sophie in tears earlier," Gabe's voice was quieter but still quite distinct.

"Something is very wrong," I said.

Josh cocked his head and went quiet for a moment. "I didn't notice it before, but none of the wards are up on this house," he said.

"How could this have happened?" I asked.

"Maybe during the coup?" Jaime suggested.

That jogged a memory, and I nodded vigorously. "Marc told me that Honore had re-warded the house not that long ago. Probably the first thing she did the other night was take down those wards."

"There's a lot of magic in this house, but somethin' in there is bad magic. It's givin' off some nasty juju," Josh said, indicating the office.

Abruptly, the office door opened, and Gabe stormed out, slamming it closed behind him. He stamped his foot, swearing violently in French before noticing the three of us. Immediately, he straightened. "Um . . . sorry about that. Marc hasn't been himself since the coup attempt."

The pieces of the puzzle began assembling themselves in my mind. "Gabe, was the office breeched during the attack?" I asked.

"Briefly. Still can't figure out how Louis got in, but he did. We grabbed him before he could do anything though," Gabe assured me. Louis Pontbriand had been the Aether lieutenant under Honore Rochan.

"I am not so sure about that," I said.

"Whaddya mean?" Gabe asked.

"The wards around the office are down," I said urgently.

"Actually, they're down around the house," Josh clarified. "And I can feel some seriously nasty juju comin' from the office."

"I wonder if Louis might have placed a poppet in the room and that is what is causing the Grandmaster to act in this strange manner." I said.

"Puppet? What in the world does a puppet have to do with anything?" Gabe asked.

"A poppet, not a puppet. It is a doll, a representation of an individual that can be used to cause harm," I explained.

"You mean a voodoo doll?" Gabe asked.

"Yes. Voodoo can be used to harm the individual by inflicting damage on the representation. Both Honore and Louis were skilled practitioners."

"Can you stop it?"

"Once I have the poppet, it is not difficult to break the hex," I said nodding.

"And you think this thing is somewhere in the office?" Gabe asked Josh.

"That's where I'm feelin' the bad juju common from," Josh said.

"Can you narrow it down? Like you could tell the bullets in my gun were magiked?" I asked. I had discovered Josh's magical sensitivity when he'd sensed bullets I had magiked and asked about them.

Josh nodded. "Yeah, I got a real good sense for it."

"You have magic bullets?" Gabe asked with interest.

"Yes. I promise I will explain later, but I think that fixing Marc is more important right now," I said.

Reminded of his primary duty, Gabe said, "Of course. Let's go find this thing."

Without saying another word, Gabe turned and walked back into his brother's office without knocking.

Marc was still at his desk and came to his feet snarling obscenities at the intrusion. The uncharacteristic outburst convinced me more than anything else of the correctness of my assumption. "What is the meaning of this?" He demanded.

"We're here to save you," Gabe said simply.

"I don't need saving!" The Grandmaster growled. "Get out!"

The two began arguing while Josh, Jaime, and I searched frantically for the poppet. "It's somewhere over here," Josh said, indicating a tall bank of built-in bookshelves.

"Probably behind the books. Look for something small, maybe about the size of your hand," I said and began pulling books out from a lower shelf.

"Ouch! Goddamnit!" Josh cursed. "Sorry for the language, Juliette."

I looked up to see Josh holding a bunch of nettles in his hand.

"Let me see that," I said and rose to take the bundle carefully in my hands. I carried it back to the Grandmaster's desk and laid it down. The leaves had been tied to keep them together. I unfastened the knot, trying to touch as little of the stinging bundle as I could. Peeling back the layers of nettles, I revealed the poppet. Made from burlap and grey suiting material, it bore a crude but unmistakable likeness to Marc Gautier.

"I need water and salt," I said.

"I'll get some from the kitchen," Josh offered.

"No need," Gabe said and briskly walked to the sideboard bar. He took the ice bucket from the top of the bar and reached into an underneath cabinet for a saltshaker. "Will these work?" He asked.

"What the hell is going on?" Marc demanded, obviously not used to being ignored.

"I believe Honore has hexed you, my liege. This is why you are so angry and irritable," I said as I took the top off the shaker and poured the salt onto the mostly melted ice. I stuck my hand into the cold water and swirled the contents to mix them completely.

"Impossible! This house is completely warded. There is no way I could be hexed, and I am not irritable!" Marc roared.

"Who warded your house the last time, my liege?" I asked without looking up. I carefully unwrapped the poppet fully from its nettle enclosure and dropped the leaves into the salt-water mixture.

"You!" Marc exclaimed.

"No. I did not ward the house, remember? You ordered me not to because you wanted to be able to meet the werewolf alpha here if needed," I reminded him. I had set up an elaborate matrix of magical wards last month to stop a series of vicious werewolf attacks. We initially feared that these attacks were being carried out by members of the local werewolf pack led by alpha Beau Roulet. It was quickly apparent that the New Orleans pack was not responsible for the killings but instead a group of Strays—werewolves without a sanctioned pack—were to blame. We had worked with the New Orleans pack to end the danger to the city's human population.

"Eh, you're right. I guess that Honore was the last one to ward," he sat back down, starting to calm a bit.

"Currently, there are no wards active in the house. I think that Honore disabled them during the coup attempt, and I did not think about it until I realized I could hear you and Gabe arguing from outside the office. I am sorry, I should have thought of it sooner," I said as I added the various components of the poppet into the icy water, one at a time. Hair, fingernail, cloth, string, a coin, and something I could not identify, all were put into the ice bucket and immersed in the salty water. As the last piece went in, I thrust my hand into the bucket to submerge all the components. The angry fire went out of Marc's eyes, and he shook his head as if to clear it.

After a moment he said, "I really was hexed, wasn't I?"

"You feel different now?" I asked.

"I'm not angry or uncomfortable anymore, so yes, I do feel different. A bit foggy though," Marc said.

"Perhaps some blood would help," I suggested, and Gabe walked back to the bar and poured a pint of warmed vitae into a beer glass before bringing it to his brother.

"Thanks," Marc said taking the glass from Gabe. "I think I owe you all an apology."

"You were not yourself," I said. He obviously still was not himself if he was apologizing to us.

"Still, I said some very unkind things to you and Gabe," Marc said.

"And Sophie," Gabe reminded him.

Marc groaned loudly and put his head in his hands. "I am in such trouble."

It surprised me to see the Grandmaster so open and, well, so human. I was fairly certain this wouldn't last. The vampire mask would soon descend, and we would once more have our inscrutable Grandmaster.

"I suggest a lotta flowers for Sophie," Josh said.

Marc groaned again before draining the pint of blood. When he finished, he ran his hand through his dark brown hair and asked me, "Did I really hand you the broadsword in the Council Chamber and command you to behead Louis and his accomplice in front of the Undead Synod?"

"Yes. Are the events hazy?" I asked, suddenly worried. In the aftermath of the coup attempt, Marc had called a meeting of the Undead Synod—the Master or Mistress of each of the five vampire covens, along with their lieutenants, and three coven Elders. An impromptu trial had been held for two Aether coven members, Louis Pontbriand and Edward King, who had been apprehended during the insurrection. Both had been condemned to death, and I had carried out the sentence.

"No," Marc sighed. "Everything is in very clear focus; I just can't believe I did and said those things." He sat up very straight and smoothed his suit jacket. "Well, I cannot sit here and bemoan what I've done. We need to get back to business. Madame, I believe you brought me your childe for introduction?" Marc said and stood, once again and every inch the Grandmaster of New Orleans.

"Yes, my liege. As I explained earlier, I had not intended to change her, only to save her life," I said.

Marc nodded. "Would you give me a few minutes alone with Jaime?"

"Of course, my liege," I said, and Gabe, Josh, and I filed back into the foyer.

After closing the door behind us, Gabe turned to me and asked, "How long will it take to ward the house again?"

"Alone?" I thought about it, considering the level of difficulty as well as the rather large size of the house, "In a few hours, I can have the preliminary wards up that will cover the house and property. To do it properly? All tonight and at least part of tomorrow," I said. "Part of that is variable depending on the wards Grandmaster wants on his office. That room alone may take several hours."

"And if the girl helps?" Gabe asked.

"Working together, we should cut the time nearly in half."

Gabe nodded. "Can you start now?" He asked.

"Of course."

"Why don't you do that, and I'll have the girl join you once Marc is done with her. At some point, we all need to discuss this occult murder as well. I suppose it was too much to hope for some recovery time after the coup attempt. It seems our enemies are continuing their assault," Gabe said. Indicating the ice bucket he had carried into the hall, "What should I do with this?"

"It would be best if it could be disposed of down by the river. The tide will take it out to sea."

"Okay, I'll take it down to the harbor and dump it."

"Why don't I do that?" Josh offered. "Juliette and Jaime got wardin' to do and Gabe, you should probably stick close to Marc. I'm as useless as tits on a boar right now, so it'll give me somethin' to do."

"Thanks," Gabe said and handed Josh the bucket.

"I'll be back for you and Jaime before sunup," Josh said to me.

"It might be better if we stayed here for the day. That way we can work until dawn and finish up after sunset."

Gabe said, "I'll have Sophie arrange rooms for you."

"Thank you," I said.

"Ya sure?" Josh asked.

"It makes more sense this way. I will call you tomorrow evening when we are done," I said. I did not want to spend the day at Gautier House, but it was the best option under the circumstances.

Josh leaned in and kissed me. I drank in the scent of his cologne as he pulled me close to devour my lips. I nearly told him to come back and pick me up later, but I kept my libido in check. The Grandmaster's safety was more important than my sex life—at the moment.

I walked with Josh through the house, into the back courtyard, and through the ornate iron gate to the side street where he had parked the car.

"Be careful tonight," he said before kissing me again.

"What could go wrong? I'm at the Grandmaster's house." I asked sarcastically, and he rolled his eyes.

"Go easy on the kid, too. She's had quite a shock tonight."

"And I haven't?" I asked.

"Just sayin'."

"I will find a way to smooth things between Jaime and me," I promised before Josh got into his car and drove away.

CHAPTER 3

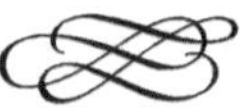

I had a very basic ward up around the main house by the time Jaime joined me about an hour later. She looked the worse for wear—pale and shaky, but I could not tell if it was the after-effects of the change or her meeting with Marc causing it.

There was no point in her helping with the wards if she wasn't up to the task and it would actually take longer if she couldn't keep focus. After ingesting several more bottles of blood to help me regain focus after the draining readings earlier this evening, I could manage on my own if I needed to. "Do you think you can help me with the wards, or do you need to rest?" I asked.

Jaime shrugged and ran a hand through her dark hair. "I can ward. It'll probably do me good to focus on something other than vamping out."

I nodded. I wanted to talk to her, to explain what had happened or at least what I assumed had happened, but now was not the time. The house and grounds of Gautier House—a three story, nineteenth century Greek Revival—took up almost the entire city block and warding something that large took a great deal of concentration. We warded, mostly in silence, for the next several hours. We only spoke about the invocations and where to go next. It was not uncomfortable, and Jaime and I worked well together.

Shortly before sunrise, when the basic warding was done, I suggested we retire.

"I secured us accommodations upstairs," I told her.

"Um . . . we're staying here?" Jaime asked tentatively.

I nodded. "Traveling this close to dawn is dangerous, especially with you being a fledgling. You may go into torpor at any time."

"Torpor?"

"That is what we call our daytime sleep. Older vampires can sometimes push to dawn and occasionally beyond, but new vampires are often awake one second and asleep the next. Now that you have had your first feeding, your transition is complete."

"As a Gatekeeper, I got reports of vampire behaviors and such, but sometimes it's kinda unreliable and usually didn't include the terms y'all use," Jaime said.

"Maybe your reports were not so much unreliable, but did not consider the fact that, like humans, every vampire is different and can change over time."

"Change?"

"It is a very slow change," I assured her.

"So . . . I'll have my own room upstairs?"

"Of course," I said. The poor girl looked decidedly uncomfortable, and I quickly added, "But only if you want. If you would be more comfortable staying with me, that is fine."

Jaime's relief was palpable. In a low voice she said, "This house is full of vampires."

It took every ounce of reserve not to laugh. "Jaime, *you* are a vampire now," I said in an equally low voice as I led her up the grand staircase to the family quarters. I stayed here so often that I had my own suite.

"You don't mind me staying with you, do you? I mean, if it was Josh's house that would be one thing, but here . . ." she let her voice trail off as I led her into my room.

I tried to remember what it had been like as a new vampire and smiled. "It is fine."

Jaime gave a low whistle as she surveyed the sitting room with its richly appointed furnishings. "Nice digs."

Having seen how spartan the Gatekeepers accommodations were, just about anything would've been luxurious. Jaime prowled the room like a restless cat picking up throw pillows from the cream taffeta sofa, transferring them to one wing-backed chair, and then moving them back again. I went to the mahogany bar and poured myself a glass of wine.

"Would you like something?" I asked.

"Nah, I'm good," she said and continued her pacing across the Persian carpet.

I wasn't sure she would tell me, but I thought that I would ask. "May I ask what Marc said to you?"

Jaime halted her pacing and raised an eyebrow, "Considering how he'd been screaming at you just a few minutes before, he was surprisingly nice. He said how lucky I was that you had made me even if you hadn't meant to and that you would be a good sire. But, damn, he scares me. I mean Josh is powerful, and when you don't shield, you have some mad wicked mojo, but Marc Gautier, well let's just say that he makes me want to piss my pants—even—as a vampire."

"Marc is powerful but also merciful. If you give him no reason to harm you, he will not. If you are loyal and prove useful, he will protect you."

"What if I'm not?"

"We will both pay the price," I said matter of factly.

"Both?" She stopped pacing and looked at me, clearly confused.

"As my unreleased childe, your actions reflect directly on me. I will be punished for any misdeeds you commit," I said.

"Look, I'm no kid. I don't need anyone to take responsibility for me. I don't need a mom. What you mean 'unreleased childe'? Like you own me or something?" Jaime declared suspiciously.

"No," I hastened to reassure her. "I do not own you. I do not mean childe in human years, but as a newly created vampire. Perhaps fledgling is a better term. Think of me as your mentor, your teacher, your protector. A bit like Yoda to Luke Skywalker."

Jaime smiled slightly. "I think you're bullshitting me."

"You have significant power and potential but are very raw. It is our tradition to nurture a fledgling or unreleased childe until certain basic skills are mastered. It makes the transition into vampire society much smoother. I do not own you. Although I have known sires that treat their childer in that manner, I do not hold to such ways. I am responsible for you, for your actions. We will decide, you and I, what our relationship is to be, but I think that we should put off that discussion until tomorrow. We are tired and shocked by tonight's occurrences. I promise to explain things better and more thoroughly then."

"Yeah. I need some time to wrap my brain around this," Jaime said.

"I will take the sofa, and you can have the bed," I suggested, finishing my wine.

"No, I'll take the sofa or the closet."

"The closet?"

"Dark. Secure. Safe," she paused. "That thing about no sunlight?"

I smiled. "That is true. We burn terribly if exposed to it, and too much for too long can kill us. However, do not worry about darkness or security in this house or Josh's or mine. That is taken care of. There is no need for a closet or coffin."

"Oh. Okay. I guess you would want to live in luxury. I'll take the couch," Jaime took a pillow off the bed and went to the sofa. "I like the Jedi thing. Not fully buying it, but I like it. So you're gonna show me some stuff? Teach me spells? I'll be like your apprentice?"

Thank God for Josh and Chris Gautier. Between the two of them, I'd had quite a course in pop culture over the past month. At least it let me communicate with my new childe in a mostly non-offensive manner.

"I will teach you everything I know in time. My skills lean towards rituals and research. As a Gatekeeper, you have the fighting skills well mastered. If you feel you need more work in that area, I can easily find someone to further your training. And of course, I will show you *stuff* as you say. I will show you how to use your enhanced senses to their full ability–to read people's auras. Later to touch objects to see the user's intent. There are spells that I can teach you, if you wish, as well as certain useful rituals."

"What sort of rituals?" Jaime asked, clearly interested.

"How to darken a room so that no light can penetrate it or how to scent for a werewolf. I will give you free rein of my library. It is not as large or extensive as I would like, but I am steadily adding to the collection."

"Okay, that sounds pretty useful," Jaime conceded as she settled onto the sofa.

"I am also hoping that you will help me learn things," I said.

"Huh? Oh, like technology and stuff?" Jaime brightened.

"Yes. I missed so much while I was staked. Josh is wonderful about filling in the gaps, but two hundred years is a long time," I said. Both my sire and I had been staked in 1797. Contrary to lore, a wooden stake through the heart does not kill a vampire, it only immobilizes him or her. My sire, Andre de la Croix, was lucky. His body was recovered quickly, and he was un-staked. I had been lost for over two centuries until about eight weeks ago. Needless to say, my transition to modern society had not been smooth and was ongoing.

"I did not mean for this to happen," I said. "I did not intend to make you a vampire that night. I only wanted to save your life."

Jaime shrugged and looked uncomfortable. "I know. I said some really nasty things to you at Josh's house earlier. Sorry about that. It wasn't like you took any blood from me before you gave me yours. I remember that much. I just never thought I'd be a bloodsucker."

I nodded. "How is this going to affect your status as a Gatekeeper?"

"I don't know. I've never heard of a vampire being a Gatekeeper, but maybe Nicholas won't kick me out," Jaime said uncertainly.

"I will see if I can meet with him tomorrow and explain the situation. He was here that night, so he knows how badly you were hurt and that I gave you my blood." I could feel dawn coming on, so I slid my shoes off and walked to the bed. "Are you going to be alright on the sofa?"

"I've slept on a lot worse. I'll be fine," Jaime said.

"I will see you at sunset then," I said and crawled into bed.

JAIME and I finished warding Gautier House shortly before midnight the next evening. I left my protégé in animated conversation with Chris Gautier in the family's Media room. The two were nearly the same age and had struck up an instant friendship when I'd introduced them. Chris, as Marc's nephew and heir, knew all about vampire culture and society. I hoped that Chris, even though he had not yet been turned, would help ease Jaime's transition to being a vampire.

I plodded down the stairs to Marc's office, apprehensive about the mood that I would find the Grandmaster in. I knew the destruction of the poppet had defused his anger and belligerence but was unsure how much of the ire directed at me in the wake of the failed coup attempt resulted from magic and how much was distrust because of the situation. Trying not to cower in the face of danger, I squared my shoulders and knocked on the office door.

I opened the door at Marc's invitation and entered the room. The Grandmaster stood and walked around the desk to greet me. I took this as a good sign that perhaps we were back on a more solid footing.

"Were you able to finish the warding?" He asked.

"Yes, although I would like for Jaime and me to come back later in the week and put down another layer of warding. It might be a good idea to have another mage come in and lay down a third layer. Maybe someone from out of town–Paris or Montréal, perhaps," I said.

"Please, have a seat. Can I get you a glass of wine?" Marc asked as he indicated the seating group in front of the fireplace.

"Wine would be nice," I said, and sat on the couch.

"Why several layers?" Marc asked as he poured two glasses of wine at the sideboard bar.

"Safety and peace of mind. One reason Honore and the Rogue Aether breached your defenses so quickly was because Honore was the one who warded your house last. All she had to do was take down the wards she had in place. They had problems in places where Frederique's wards were still active. As it stands now, I have warded half the house and Jaime the other half. Both of us would need to work together to bring down all the wards in the house. After we put on the second layer, neither of us will be able to bring down all the wards ourselves without a huge expenditure of magic, if then. If you have a third mage come in and overlay what Jaime and I have done, it will be exceedingly difficult to breach this house magically," I explained, sitting back in a more relaxed posture.

"I see. And you suggest that I get someone from out of town so the chances of the three of you coming together to overthrow me are minimal and thus put my mind at ease?" Marc suggested with a slight smile.

"Exactly. By having an outsider come in, you can rest easier," I said, sitting forward to take the glass of wine he offered before leaning back once again.

"It isn't that I don't trust you . . ." he trailed off.

"You do not," I said as he sat down. "I will not lie and say that it does not hurt that you no longer trust me, but I am rational enough to understand. Honore violated your trust, and it is going to be awhile before you can trust another Aether because of it."

"You seem to understand my feelings better than I do," Marc said wryly, his inscrutable vampire leader mask slipping a bit.

I took a sip of wine, savoring its richness. "It is not so much that, as I know how I would feel. I never liked nor particularly trusted Honore, but even I feel betrayed by what she did. You must feel it more. After all, she was a Coven Mistress, if only briefly, in your city. She swore oaths to you, pledged fealty. It is a betrayal beyond measure."

"Thank you for understanding," Marc said.

"And I complicated the problem by creating a childe without your permission."

"I am not sure why I made that decree. I'm going to blame it on the poppet. While I do not wish for you to create a legion, as Coven Mistress, you do not need my permission to create childer. I only ask that you be judicious in your choices. As for my demand that you not invite foreign Aether to settle and add to your coven numbers . . . ." Again, he trailed off but did not break eye contact.

"I would greatly value your input on those choices," I said leaning forward.

Marc nodded. "Good. I'm glad we're on the same page with that."

"I want to go slowly and build carefully," I said. "Being a coven of two is not sustainable, but creating a lot of new vampires or bringing in unknowns from other cities are not good choices either."

"Well, all things considered, you aren't off to a poor start. Jaime is an excellent choice, even if unintended," Marc said.

"I admit to thinking that Jaime would make an excellent Aether Initiate at some later date when I initially met her, but this is a mixed blessing."

"She would have died without your intervention," Marc reminded me.

"I know, but she is so young."

"This is true, but she is a trained Gatekeeper and, from what I have seen, a talented mage."

I took a sip of wine and nodded. "I asked Jaime what her being a vampire meant for her role as a Gatekeeper. She said she did not know. "

"I expect we will have that answer soon. Master Remy called earlier and requested an urgent meeting. He specifically asked that you and Josh be there."

"Does he know about Jaime's condition already?" I winced. Nicholas Remy was the Master Gatekeeper here in New Orleans and Jaime's direct superior.

"I don't think so. He also requested Gabe and Sophie be at the meeting." Marc sipped his wine.

"Could it have something to do with the coup?" I asked.

"That is my guess. Nonetheless, there are a few things we ought to discuss before the others arrive."

"Of course."

"The first is the matter of your personal security. As Coven Mistress, you need a bodyguard."

"Josh and I have discussed the problem," I sighed and slumped slightly.

"I know that you have been staying with Josh since the coup," Marc said.

"Yes. As you know, Josh has been acting as my unofficial bodyguard for a while now, but it cannot really continue. He has his responsibilities as Sylph lieutenant as well as his business concerns. I am reluctant to turn someone just for him to become my bodyguard. Also, I think that being so new would make him too weak to be effective," I said.

"That is a valid point. I might be able to spare one of the house guards. Any of them would be perfectly capable," Marc offered.

It was a kind offer, but Honore had been able to magically remove the guards at Gautier House before the coup attempt. I was still working on how to prevent that from happening again. Even so, I could not in good conscience deprive the Grandmaster of even one of his guards. Plus, after what just happened, I wasn't sure I wanted guards loyal only to him watching over me.

"Josh suggested that, as he put it, I go outside the box. I am not completely sure I understand this box thing, but his suggestion that I use Pack members has great merit."

"Pack members? He suggested hiring werewolves as your bodyguards?" Marc sat forward so suddenly that some wine spilled over the rim of his glass.

"While they would not have coven loyalty, they certainly would have the supernatural strength to defend me, and they don't have the daylight prohibitions that vampires do," I pointed out.

"But the entire city is warded against werewolves," Marc countered.

"True, but since I created the wards with my magic, I can produce a talisman that will nullify the wards' effects," I said.

Marc looked concerned. "What stops someone else from making one of these nullification talismans?"

"Nothing."

"But . . ." he started.

"They can make as many talismans as they wish," I clarified, "but they will not be terribly effective. Only *my* magic can completely nullify *my* wards using talismans. At best, someone with powerful magic could produce a talisman that would allow a werewolf in human form to walk the city. The wards would need to be taken down or destroyed before a werewolf in wolf form could enter the city or transform out of human form," I assured Marc. "Beau could not even break the wards. They are solid."

"That is actually a good idea, then," he said nodding, "Can you produce a talisman that will allow for transformation?" Marc asked.

"Yes, because it is my magic in the wards."

"I see," Marc said.

"What was the other thing you wished to ask about?" I prompted.

"I would appreciate your discretion about the breech in our security and the poppet. I think the fewer people who know I was hexed, the better." While politely phrased, this was an order, not a request.

"That goes without saying," I said. "If you would like, I can make you an amulet or magic something you regularly wear to protect you from most attacks. It may take several days, but it will add another layer of protection. Regardless, if another fetish is left in the house, the wards will trip and alert me."

"That would be very useful. Thank you. Could you do the same for Sophie and Gabe? It might be a good idea for Chris, too."

I nodded. "It will take time to create that many, but I can certainly do it. I will speak to each of them." My magical expenditure was going to be astronomical. "I'm going to need extra vitae. That much casting will drain me."

"Not a problem. Just let Sophie know, and she will arrange the delivery of extra bottles."

"Thank you." I said.

"Would my signet ring be appropriate to magic?"

"Your Grandmaster signet?" I asked. All vampires in the city's ruling hierarchy wore signet rings as signs of power. As Mistress of the Aether coven, I wore one. Marc had at least two—one as Grandmaster of the city and the other as the Master of the Gnome coven.

"No, my personal signet," he said, twisting a small gold ring off his left pinky and handing it to me.

"This is perfect," I said taking it from him.

CHAPTER 4

There was a light tap on the door. "Come in," Marc ordered.

Sophie, the city's steward who doubled as Marc's executive assistant, poked her head inside and said, "Josh and Nicholas Remy are here."

"Let them in, and please let Gabe know."

"He's on his way."

"Please send Jaime down as well. I believe she is upstairs with Chris," Marc said looking to me for confirmation.

"I left them in the Media room," I said.

"I'll get her," Sophie said and admitted the New Orleans Master Gatekeeper and the Sylph coven lieutenant into the office. Both Marc and I stood as the two men entered the room. Marc stepped forward, extending his hand to the distinguished, white-haired man.

"Thank you for convening this meeting," Master Remy said as they shook hands.

"I was on the verge of calling you when you contacted my steward," Marc said. "Can I pour you some wine? Juliette and I have been enjoying a new Chilean Malbec."

"When in Rome," Josh said. He typically drank beer, but I knew he liked a good red on occasion.

"I'd love a glass. Is this about the coups?" Nicholas asked as he shook my hand.

"Yes," I said. "Or at least an after effect of it."

"Here or in one of the other cities?" Nicholas asked as he sat in the chair Marc directed him to.

"Other cities?" Marc asked quizzically.

"Perhaps we should wait until the others arrive," Nicholas suggested. Marc did not look like he liked that suggestion but was enough of a statesman not to argue.

Turning back to me, Nicholas said, "I'm glad that Jaime finally sought you out. While initially she felt fine after you healed her, by the next day she looked and felt horrible. I thought it might be an aftereffect of the altercation with the succubus, so I suggested that she see you. Your healing abilities are legendary."

I squirmed uncomfortably in my seat but was saved from formulating a response by a knock on the office door. We all rose as Gabe, Sophie, and Jaime entered the room.

Nicholas smiled as his protégé joined us. He stepped forward to take her hand. "Ah, I see that Madame Grammont has worked her magic. You look much better, my girl. Still a bit pale but . . . ." the Master Gatekeeper stopped speaking abruptly, dropped Jaime's hand, and whirled towards me. "How dare you turn her into a vampire!" Fire blazed in his blue eyes. Josh shifted next to me, ready for a fight if necessary.

"Wait and hear Juliette out. It isn't what you think," Marc said quietly. The Grandmaster could rage at me all he wanted, but for an outsider to do it was unthinkable.

Nicholas Remy stilled for a moment at the command and then demanded, "Explain your actions, Madame. Why did you turn my protégé into a vampire when I sent her to you for help?" His voice dripped with venom.

I explained quickly, "It did not happen last night, or even tonight. Her transformation began the night of the coup attempt. The illness you saw was her body changing and at least partially her hunger for blood."

Nicholas's eyes widened in remembrance. "You gave Jaime your blood when you ran out of magic."

"Yes. My thaumaturgy, magic from within me, can heal. Between banishing demons in the courtyard and battling Honore, I had exhausted that. While I could still draw magic to fight with if I needed to, I did not have the magic left in me to heal Jaime, so I fed her my blood, hoping to stabilize her," I explained. All vampire blood has healing properties to it. Given to healthy humans in the correct amount, it binds them to us. The blood not only makes them our servants, it also imbues them with enhanced strength, stamina, and agility. While it does not make them as strong or as quick as vampires, it makes them stronger and faster than other humans. However, blood given to humans at the moment of death begins the transformation to vampire. This is what had happened to Jaime.

"She was much closer to death than we suspected, then," Nicholas said quietly.

"I knew she would die without intervention, but I did not realize she was already slipping away," I said.

Nicholas did not look pleased, but his anger dissipated. "Now what?"

"Well, that is what we need to decide," Marc said.

"Don't I get a say in this?" Jaime demanded. She stood outside our grouping, arms akimbo. "It's my life, after all."

"Come sit down. If we were not going to give you a voice, we would not have invited you to the meeting. That having been said, there are certain protocols that must be followed that limit all of our choices," Marc said kindly.

Chastened, Jaime sat in the seat farthest from Marc. I sat back down on the couch next to Josh, and the others found their seats.

"He is right, my girl," Nicholas said. "There are protocols to be followed."

"What sorta protocols? I really don't like the sound of that," Jaime said uncertainly.

"I doubt you will like it," Nicholas sighed. "You are out of the Order, I'm afraid."

Marc and I shared a look. We had both been afraid of that. In some ways, it made my life easier, but it made my relationship with Jaime even more difficult. She would certainly blame me for losing her status.

"No vamps allowed?" Jaime remarked bitterly.

"I'm afraid not. No werewolves either. The Gatekeepers are very clear on this. It is a humans only organization," Nicholas explained.

"That's discrimination!" Jaime said.

"Those are the rules, and they have been in place for millennia," Nicholas said, sadness tingeing his voice.

"This sucks!" Jaime exploded. "This isn't fair!"

"No, it isn't fair, Jaime," I said, "But life rarely is, even for those who cheat death. Maybe even more so for us since nature tries to balance things out. The pretty life that movies portray us as having is a fantasy. Yes, some of us live in beautiful houses, drive fancy cars, and have lots of money, but that isn't the reality for most. Many vampires live a modest existence. The wealthy have accumulated the money and property over several lifetimes of hard work and skilled investment."

"You're telling me you're not rich?" Jaime asked sarcastically.

"Oh, no. I am, as you say, filthy rich as are the Gautier's. But where does that get us exactly? I am still out dispelling demons, and Marc is still putting down coups. Problems don't go away when you become immortal; they simply change."

"Now you tell me," Jaime collapsed back into her seat defeated. "Well, shit. Where am I gonna live? I'm guessing that I'm out of the church." I could understand her pensive look. All the Gatekeepers lived at St. Cecilia's, a de-commissioned Catholic church in the Bywater.

Nicholas nodded a confirmation.

"You can live with me at least for a while. There is plenty of room," I offered.

"Aren't you living with Josh?" Jaime asked.

"Not a regular basis," I said, a little embarrassed. While I'd spent the days since the coup with him, I had moved none of my things into his house, nor had we discussed making my residence there permanent.

"Plenty of room at my place too," Josh said. "You and Juliette can discuss your livin' arrangements in private later."

"Well, what am I supposed to do now that I'm not a Gatekeeper anymore?" Jaime asked, unwilling to let her tantrum end.

"Perhaps now that you aren't my protégé anymore, Madame Grammont might have some suggestions," Nicholas said.

"First and foremost, you are my padewan, and I will train you," I smiled as I spoke, drawing on the *Star Wars* reference again. "Because of unfortunate circumstances, I am also going to ask you to take on responsibilities reserved for much older vampires. I need a lieutenant. Normally, I would not ask, but your magic and your fighting abilities were excellent as a human, and they will only become stronger now."

"You really want me to be your second in command? This isn't just a bone you are throwing me?" She asked eagerly.

"No bones. I hate to even ask because it is a tremendous responsibility and more than a little aggravation," I said.

"I'm there!" Jaime declared with an enthusiasm reserved for one who had no idea what she was in for.

I smiled softly. She would not be half so eager if she knew the headache she was facing. At least Josh should be able to give her some guidance. Although with Josh, I wasn't sure that his guidance wouldn't be more like corruption of a minor. I liked Josh a lot, but he had some novel ideas to say the least.

"Wait! We're like a coven of two, right? Since all the other Aether in the city have been declared Rogue?" Jaime's enthusiasm dissipated as she began to realize what she'd agreed to.

"Yes, we are a coven of two for the moment," I answered. I had no idea what that meant for me politically, and I wasn't sure I wanted to know.

"I also have a task for you, if it is permissible to both your sire and the Master Gatekeeper," Marc said.

"Um, what task?" Jaime asked in a far less eager tone.

"If it is alright with both Mistress Grammont and Master Remy, I would like you to act as liaison between the vampires and Gatekeepers. I sincerely wish to keep the lines of communication open between the two groups, especially as December draws nearer," Marc said. December 31 was when an old, apocalyptic prophecy could be fulfilled: *One with magic in blood and bone will come forth on the Cold Blue Moon, and with willing sacrifice, open the Gates of Hell. Angels will weep and Lucifer will reign on Earth. Only another with magic in bone and blood can stop this.* This would be the first time in over 200 years that there would be two full moons in December. All of us—Gatekeepers, vampires, and werewolves—were united in preventing this prophecy from happening. While we did not yet know who would be trying to open the Gates—one of which was here in New Orleans—we did know who could stop it. Me. My thaumaturgy could close the Gates as long as I was willing to sacrifice myself.

"I think that is an excellent idea," Nicholas said, and I nodded my agreement. Jaime looked relieved and even slightly excited about the position.

"Thank you for your understanding about this matter," Marc said to Nicholas.

"I cannot say that I'm happy to have lost Jaime as a Gatekeeper." He reached over and gave Jaime a fatherly pat on the shoulder. "I was grooming her to be my successor. However, I realize that I would've lost her that night, no matter what. At least she is still with us. I think in the coming days that will be even more important," Nicholas pronounced.

"I will take care of her," I promised.

"I know you will try to, and that is all I can ask," Nicholas said.

"You asked that we all be present at this meeting; have you learned something about the coup?" Marc prompted the change in topic.

"Have you heard anything from other Grandmasters?" Nicholas asked. A Grandmaster governed every city or territory with a sizable vampire population in conjunction with the council of coven leaders. There were dozens across the globe.

"Things have been a little unsettled here since that night," Marc said.

"I called Paris and Montréal saying that we were fine, but we have spent most of our time trying to track down the Rogue Aether," Sophie said.

Josh leaned forward and broke into the conversation. He looked at me and Marc, "After I left here last night, I started hearing disturbin' rumors from other cities."

"What rumors?" Marc asked.

"Rumors of attempted coups in other cities and Hunts bein' called out on the Aether," Josh said. Hunts were the vampire version of the ancient Wild Hunt where the accused were literally hunted down and killed. "I've been tryin' to verify if there is any truth or if the news of the New Orleans coup attempt got corrupted and mis-attributed to other cities."

"They are true," Nicholas said. "I have heard from Master Gate-keeper's in Mexico City, London, Vienna, Jerusalem, and Memphis. All had Aether lead coups in their cities. London and Jerusalem were unsuccessful. The others were. I've only been in contact with a handful of the Master Gatekeeper's, and I know nothing about the cities that don't have Chapter Houses," Nicholas said.

"Chapter Houses?" I asked.

"They are Gatekeeper residences overseen by a Master Gate-keeper. St. Cecilia's is our Chapter House here in New Orleans," Nicholas clarified.

"How many Chapter Houses do you have?" Marc asked.

"Over fifty, one in each city that has a Gate. We also have Sentries, mainly retired Gatekeepers, living in other cities to keep an eye on the supernatural community and report problems to the Mother House— the Order Headquarters in Rome," Nicholas explained.

"There are fifty Gates to Hell?" I gasped.

"No, no. We guard Gates to all the different realms. There are only thirteen Gates to Hell," Nicholas clarified.

"Only thirteen," Marc mused wryly.

"At least it isn't all of them," Nicholas said.

"Are we sure about that?" Marc inquired.

"I think the Aether just targeted cities with Hellmouths. It is too much of a coincidence with the prophecy time so close," Nicholas assured him.

"I can try to call Diana Langdon in London," I offered. I had few contacts with members of my coven in other cities, but London was where the ultimate head of my coven was located. Diana, as Aether legate, had traveled to New Orleans last month to give official sanction to my regency after the fire that killed our previous coven mistress and the disappearance of the rest of the members.

Marc held up his hand. "While I do not wish to make light of these other coups, we can't go down this rabbit hole. By all means, check on your friends in other cities, but we can't help them. We have our own problems. The Hunt for the Rogue Aether here in New Orleans is ongoing, and we may have a new problem. Last night a potential Sylph Initiate and her lover, a Sylph fledgling, were found ritually murdered in the Treme. Juliette, could you please tell us what you found?"

"Of course," I said. "Josh, do you have the photos?"

"Yeah. They're on my phone," Josh said as he pulled out his phone and tapped the screen a few times. "They're pretty graphic."

"The room was set up for two separate rituals—a consensual sex magic ritual and a death magic ritual, but all the magic had been drained from the room," I explained.

"Were the rituals not carried out?" Marc asked.

"No. They were carried out, and then the magic was drained and, I believe, saved for later use."

"Do you have any idea what happened?" Marc asked.

I explained what I saw and felt when I read the blood. It was almost as bad in the retelling.

"So someone was controlling Sykes?" Gabe asked.

"Yes."

"How is that even possible?" Marc asked.

"Very dark magic. I think it was Necromancy," I replied.

"Necromancy?" Marc sounded as horrified as I felt.

I nodded.

"That makes sense," Nicholas said. "Technically, vampires are dead, and Necromancy controls the dead."

"Wait, you mean somebody using Necromancy could take control of us? Any of us?" Gabe asked.

I held up my hand, "In theory, yes. In practice, no. I've been thinking about this since I read the blood. Generally, Necromancy animates the dead. Vampires are already animated. The necromancer would have to be very strong to overcome a sentient being. However, I am not entirely sure what I felt was necromancy. I have never dealt with it before." I looked to Nicholas. "Have you?"

Nicholas nodded. "I have—many years ago. I should look at the murder site."

"I'm afraid that it has already been cleaned," Marc said.

"Then, if there is another murder or set of murders, I should be called," Nicholas said decisively.

"I'll let Detective Angelletti know," Sophie said.

"So we think there will be more murders?" Gabe asked.

"Honestly, I do not know. I could not read his thoughts. I could just feel his presence," I said.

"Do you have any idea who did this? Was it one of the Rogue Aether?" Marc asked.

"I do not think so. When I was in Eddie's mind with the intruder, he did not feel like an Aether. He felt human. He had a magic user's tang but, it was different from the Aether tang—it was . . . cold." I unconsciously shuddered.

"You've said *he* and *him* several times. We are looking for a man?" Gabe asked.

"Yes. That much I am sure of," I said.

"Should we be letting the covens know what has happened?" Sophie asked.

"Y'all let Toussaint know that one of our own was dead and the circumstances? That'll be enough," Josh said dryly. Toussaint Dubriel was the Sylph Master and a notorious gossip. Not much happened in New Orleans without him knowing about it. "Every vampire, Sylph or not, will know by morning. Besides, we don't know if this is a serial or not. There's no point in panickin' people."

"Is there anything else we should know?" Marc asked.

"I don't think so," I said. "If I remember anything else, I'll call Sophie."

"What about Convocation? Are we still holding it?" Gabe asked.

"What is Convocation?" This was something that I had never heard of.

"Every year on Halloween, all the city's vampires gather to renew their fealty to their coven leaders and to me as Grandmaster," Mark explained. "With the recent coup attempt, the renewal of vows will be more important than usual, so I am disinclined to cancel it."

"It may be an enormous security risk, and as your lieutenant, I am bound by oath to point that out," Gabe said.

"Duly noted." Marc paused for a moment. "Let me think on this. We have time, and I may want to discuss this with the Undead Synod. Please call if anything further happens. Thank you all," Marc dismissed us.

CHAPTER 5

osh drove Jaime and me back to my house. During the short trip, he broached the subject of our staying with him.

"I know you have a security system and all, but with Honore and her crew runnin' round, I'm not sure it'll be enough," he said as we neared my house.

I could not argue with his logic. Plus, I liked sleeping with Josh. He made me feel safe.

Before I could say anything though, Jaime interrupted, "Have you got a PlayStation?"

"And a Wii," Josh answered with a grin.

"I'm good with staying there then." My childe could be bribed by video game systems. Great.

"I'll run back to the church and grab my stuff," Jaime said as she pushed the back of my seat forward to climb out when we stopped.

"Give me a minute, and I will let you out," I snapped and opened the passenger door. I was not a fan of two door cars when there were backseat passengers.

"I can drive ya," Josh offered.

"Nah. I don't have that much stuff, and I kinda want to be alone for a bit. No offense," Jaime said climbing out from behind me.

"I get it," Josh said. "We'll be here for a while packing up Juliette's stuff. If you make it back before we do, the guards'll let you in."

"Guards?" Jaime and I asked simultaneously.

Josh shrugged as he admitted, "Well, I called in daytime security right after the coup attempt. Even though vamps can't run around durin' the day, that don't mean they can't hire somebody else to do their dirty work for them. Then, when I got home last night and started hearin' rumors about coups in other cities, I decided round-the-clock security might be in order. I might be jumpin' the gun, but until we know what's goin' on, I'm not takin' chances. I know Marc said we can't do anything about what's happenin' in other cities, and he's right, but we do need to stay informed. What is happinin' else-where might spill back to New Orleans."

"I'll see if Master Remy has heard anything new when I clear out my stuff," Jaime offered.

"Please be careful," I said.

"Don't worry about me. Nobody knows I'm a vampire yet," Jaime said disappearing into the night.

"It's gonna be interestin' raisin' a teenager," Josh said in amuse-ment, then turned to go into the house, "Let's go get your stuff. I'll make some calls while you pack."

Josh had contacts all over the country and worked them in an effort to find out what was truly happening. His friend in Nashville had heard nothing, but the Sylph lieutenant in New York confirmed a failed coup in London, and Los Angeles verified the same for Kyoto. Both mentioned Aether unrest in their own cities. I found all of this very worrying but was not sure what, if anything, could be done about it. It seemed as if the Aether, or at least some of its members, had declared war on the other vampire covens. The bodyguards I had resisted getting now seemed of pressing importance. The Rogue Aether would come for me, and I needed to be prepared.

"Did you call Beau?" I asked Josh as I set my rather ample suitcase by the front door next to the assortment of small tote bags.

Josh ignored my question. He just looked at the luggage with a raised brow and asked, "You leave anything behind?"

"Ha! It is not full at all," I retorted, but it was the only sizable valise that I could find other than an old ship's trunk of Andre's, which was even larger. This was his as well. I had not had reason to purchase luggage since I'd been back. "My magic implements are in the smaller bags. I do not wish to leave them behind."

Josh threw his hands up in surrender, "I was just kiddin'. Bring whatever ya need. I'll come back with a couple of guys to get the Aether cabinet from the library."

I cocked an eyebrow, surprised. "How do you know I have an Aether cabinet that needs moving? Or even what an Aether cabinet is?"

Josh laughed. "You forget I can sense magic. That big old cabinet radiates it; plus, I've been around long enough to have learned a few things."

I stroked his stubbled chin with my hand. "You are a sweet man, Josh. Do you really not mind me bringing the big cabinet?"

Catching my hand in his, he brought it to his lips and kissed it gently before saying, "Don't let that sweet thing get out. It'll ruin my reputation. But no, I don't mind. You need a safe place to store magic stuff. It can't just be left out. I know not to touch things, and I'm sure Jaime does too, but we'll have human guards who might get curious even after they're warned."

"Or especially after they are warned," I said.

"True dat."

I smiled and repeated my earlier question. "Beau?"

"Yeah, I left a message. Probably has a gig if he isn't answering."

"Do you think he will be interested?"

"Providing you with bodyguards? Sure. He is always interested in furthering pack interests, and I know he has ex-servicemen looking for work. Come on, let's get loaded up and get home."

It did not take very long to put the luggage in the car or drive the half block down Rue Burgundy to Josh's house.

I noticed three obvious guards when we pulled into the courtyard.

Looking more closely, I noticed one more in the shadow of the carriage house. "How many guards did you hire?" I asked as we got out of the car.

"We have five guards per shift. On this shift, three of them are servants, so while they aren't as strong as vampires, they are stronger than normal humans," Josh said as he retrieved the bags from the trunk. "All the daytime guards will be servants."

"Do we really need five guards?" I asked.

"I figured with you bein' Aether mistress and me bein' Sylph lieutenant that we warranted extra protection," Josh explained. "We ain't quite the target Gautier House is, but we're close—especially if the larger Aether coven has something hinky goin' on."

I sighed, "Even more since I officially named Jaime as my lieutenant."

"Are you sure that's wise?" Josh said uncertainly, "her bein' a newborn in all?"

"It's either that or not have one. Certainly, it is not optimal, but at least I know she is trustworthy and a good fighter. I think it will also take the sting out of her losing her place as a Gatekeeper."

"That makes sense," Josh said. "What about creating other members? Are you still under moratorium?"

"No, it seems that decree was the result of the poppet. I will move slowly to bring in new members, however. For the moment, they will all be native New Orleanians. I cannot trust those from the outside."

"What about those who will come in and challenge ya?" Josh asked as the guard at the door let us in.

"Reign fiery death upon them?" I said, only half joking. "No. Seriously. I know that there are those who will try to usurp my position, but Marc will not accept them, and I will fight to hold it. I took Aether leadership by force of arms, and if necessary, I will hold it by force of arms."

"That's my girl." Josh winked and carried my bags down the hall to the master suite. "I cleared out some space in the closet and dresser for you. I hope it's enough room. If it ain't, let me know, and I'll shift more stuff into one of the spare rooms."

"When did you have time to clear space?" I asked.

"I did it when I got up tonight," Josh said a little sheepishly.

"But I had not yet agreed to move in," I said, arching an eyebrow.

"Well, I was kinda hedgin' my bets on that. Really hopin' you'd say yes. I wasn't all that sure about Jaime though, so I still got some stuff to do in the guest room," Josh said after he deposited my bags on the bed. "I'll leave ya to get settled in. Come find me when you're done. I got a surprise for ya,"

"Thank you, Josh," I said and raised up on tiptoes to kiss his cheek.

He left the room whistling a cheery tune. I unpacked my clothes and began settling in. Despite Josh's joke about the size of my suitcase, there was not a lot to put away. There were three small tote bags that held some of my ritual magic components and my grimoires. I took those with me, hoping to store them in whatever room Josh planned to have the Aether cabinet moved in to. He had several empty guest rooms that would be just fine.

I found Josh talking to Jaime in the large living room. It was obvious that the young woman had just arrived because two small duffel bags rested at her feet. I joined them, my magical implement tote bags still in my hand.

"Why don't you both leave your bags here, and I'll take you around and meet the guards," Josh suggested.

As Josh had told me earlier, there were five guards on each shift. Night shift had two vampires and three human servants. At first, I wasn't sure how I felt about having non-Aether vampires guard me, and then I realized I was being ridiculous. I would be no safer with my own coven members, and considering my thaumaturgy, I might be a good deal less safe. My own grandmother had been hunted and bled of her thaumaturgy before being killed.

The two vampires were stationed at the front and courtyard doors. They were members of the Salamand coven, the warriors among vampires, and Josh had known each for years. Human servants would replace them during the day.

"No use trying to use Sylph. None of them can fight worth a tinker's damn."

"How did you become a Sylph? I am not questioning your musical talent, but you seem more suited to one of the other covens," I asked as we walked through the house.

"I blame all this on Em," he said.

"Your sister?"

"Yep. She'd been turned for a while, and I knew. I wasn't wild about her choice, but she said she'd done it of her own free will, and I respected that. Well anyway, I was a Ranger, she was a traveling musician, and we finally managed to be in the same city at the same time. Unfortunately, a smalltime bank robber by the name of Frank Carlson was also in town and gunning for me. I'd put away his brothers a couple years earlier, and he wanted revenge. Caught me backstage visitin' Emma. It was a good news, bad news situation. He shot me, and I'd be six feet under if not for Em. She turned me."

"I did not realize she was your maker."

"Yep. Always thought it was my job to protect her, and she ended up saving me," he said dryly.

"Did you mind? Becoming a vampire, I mean," Jaime asked. She was so quiet as we walked through the house, I had forgotten she was there.

"Beat the hell out of the alternative."

I had to agree. Josh had more in common with Jaime than I realized.

"Thanks for telling me . . . us. It helps," Jaime said looking at her black combat boots when we stopped at the base of the stairs.

"My turnin' story ain't a secret. I say I blame Em, but really, I'm damn thankful to her. Or at least I am when I'm not stuck doin' coven shit," he laughed. Opening the back door, he said, "Come on, let's meet the guys."

The three human guards were Josh's servants. "I use them as bouncers at The Cowboy," he explained. Two were in the courtyard, and the third was on the roof with a sniper rifle. "Another five-man team will replace them just before dawn. I'll introduce you to them when we get up tonight."

"And you know all the men personally?" I asked.

"Yep."

I decided that was good enough.

"I'm also going to talk to Beau about getting some weres to come and fill out the house guard," Josh said as he led us back inside.

"In addition to my bodyguards?" I asked. "Is that really necessary?"

"Honore and God knows how many other of her people are still out there. Plus, this thing just seems to keep getting bigger. I can't always be usin' my bouncers." He said firmly. I knew firsthand just how busy and rowdy The Cowboy, Josh's bar on Bourbon Street, could be.

"He's right," Jaime pointed out.

I nodded, knowing that they were right.

Josh showed Jaime to her room saying, "Redecorate however you want."

It was a large room, easily three times the size of the Gatekeeper bedroom I had seen. Simply furnished with a queen-sized bed, two nightstands, a huge armoire, and a dresser with mirror, all in light pine, the room was almost a blank canvas for Jaime to work with. There were two gray overstuffed chairs situated under a heavily blinded and draped window, but the exposed brick walls were bare except for three framed music posters.

"Wow, thanks Josh," she squealed twirling around in the middle of the room.

"Let me know if you want different furniture or different color bedding. I'll order it," Josh offered. There was a crimson comforter folded at the foot of the bed.

"This is awesome!" Jaime exclaimed before retreating to unpack.

As he led me down the hall to the living room he whispered, "I really hope she doesn't paint the walls black."

I laughed and poked him in the chest. "You gave her free rein."

"Well, I figure she's had enough upheaval. She needs somethin' she can make her own. A bedroom is a small enough price to pay."

"You seem to know the adolescent mind quite well."

"Emma'd say it was because I never grew up. Grab your magic stuff. I'll show you where you can store it."

Josh took me back downstairs. Instead of opening the door leading to the courtyard, he led me through a second door into a sort of storage area. Josh walked me past Christmas and Mardi Gras decorations to a short hallway. There was a set of double doors on each side. He indicated the set on the left. "I used this as an office for a while. There's a computer, phone lines, a couple of tables, and a desk, plenty of room for your Aether cabinet, and we can get you anything else you need," Josh said.

"You do not use it?" I asked.

"Not anymore. It's just easier going into The Cowboy and dealing with stuff there when I need to. It's a big room, and if you're gonna be coven mistress, you're going to need a private space for the Aether stuff," Josh said.

"Are you sure?" I asked.

He nodded and opened the door. It was a sizeable room, about half the size of the upstairs living room. Part of it was outfitted as an office with a desk, file cabinets, and several bookcases while the rest of the space was empty. I could easily convert the area into a stillroom and ritual area. I didn't even have this sort of space in my own home. If I wanted to do a ritual there, I needed to move the furniture in my study to accommodate a circle. This would be an unaccustomed luxury.

"Thank you," I said and not for the first time, thought just how lucky I was.

Josh dug in his pocket and pulled out his keyring. Flipping through the assortment, he removed two keys and handed them to me. "This one is to the outside door. With the guards here, you probably won't need it, but here it is anyway. This other one's to this room. I expect you'll want to mage lock it as well."

"I trust you," I said.

"It ain't me ya got to worry about, darlin'. Or Jaime. You got enemies out there. Honore, other former New Orleans Aether, and maybe this new outside threat. You need to keep your magic stuff safe, and I respect that."

"You are a very special man, Josh," I said and kissed him passionately. He backed me up against the desk and returned the kiss. Josh tugged at the hem of my shirt and slid his hand up my side.

It might have gone further than that if Jaime had not chosen that moment to find us. "I was wondering where you two had disappeared to," she said merrily causing me and Josh to jump apart.

"Josh was just showing me this space for storing my magical implements," I said as I straightened my skirt, deeply embarrassed at having been caught in a compromising position.

"Is that what you're calling it now?" Jaime snickered.

I gave her a dark look.

Josh asked, "You all settled in?"

"Yeah," Jaime said enthusiastically, "I really like the concert posters on the walls of my room. I don't think I want to change much, not that I have anything to change it to anyway," she added.

"I got other posters if you wanna trade those out. I think I've got just about everybody who's played this city in the last 50 or so years."

"Wow. I might want to look through those some time."

"No problem. Seriously, if you want new stuff, just ask. Don't worry about the cost. It's a help to me. I never got around to deco-ratin' the guest rooms, except the one that Em uses. Anyway, I'm gonna head back upstairs and call some more contacts. See if anything else has shaken loose," Josh said and kissed me again. "Take as much time as you need down here."

After Josh left, Jaime shifted uncomfortably from one foot to the other. "I'm sorry about interrupting you two. I'm not real good with this whole parent thing, I guess,"

I smiled softly. This was hard for her. For all of her knowledge and bravado, she was still so young—I guessed 17 or 18, but I was not really sure. Every time she irritated me, I needed to remind myself of that. I did not know very much about this woman I had made my vampire childe, and I needed to remedy that—but carefully. Jaime did not seem to trust easily, and I had already violated that trust by turning her without her consent—no matter how much of an accident it was or how pure my motives were.

"Neither am I," I answered, "but we will figure it out together. What do you think about this as a ritual space?" I asked.

"Once it's clean, it'll be sweet," Jaime said while surveying the room. "Where you gonna store stuff?"

"Josh said he would bring my Aether cabinet over, and I will talk to him about procuring a workbench and shelves." I leaned against the desk, noting the layer of dust on it.

"Aether cabinet? What's that?"

"It is a cabinet that has been specially created—magically—to keep magical items in and the unauthorized out," I explained.

"That's cool!" Jaime's eyes were bright with excitement.

I thought to myself, "Perhaps now would be a good time to begin her training." Then I thought, "No. The first thing that needs to be done is a thorough cleaning of this room, and I will not make her do that. Maybe just an overview of vampire culture then." I turned to her.

"Jaime, since you are now my lieutenant, I need to make sure you understand vampire hierarchy. I know that as a Gatekeeper you observed us, but by your own admission some of your information was not complete."

"That's true," she admitted. "Why don't I run upstairs and get some cleaning supplies. Then, you can tell me all the stuff while I scrub the floor."

My mouth dropped open, and I gaped at the young woman. *Had she really just offered to scrub the floor? Without me asking?*

"I do not expect you to clean," I said hastily.

"Why not? I'm your apprentice, right? Isn't that what apprentices do? All the dirty work?" It was Jaime's turn to look at me oddly.

"Yes, you are my apprentice, but that does not mean that I intend to use you as a scullery maid."

"Not sure what a scullery maid is, but with the Gatekeepers, apprentices scrubbed floors and did general scut work. Plus, we can't safely cast in here until it's done."

I still did not feel comfortable making her to do all the work alone. "Alright, but I will help you," I said.

"Don't you trust me to do it properly?" Jaime asked quietly, her lower lip quivering slightly.

"What? No. It is not that at all. I just do not wish to be the sort of mistress that forces her apprentice to do all the menial labor that she does not wish to. Besides, if we both scrub, it will take half the time," I explained.

Mollified, Jaime nodded. "That makes sense. So should I get two buckets?"

"I will come with you. I expect it will take both of us to carry everything."

Once back upstairs, Josh cheerfully pointed out the supply closet to us.

"You know, I can have someone come in and clean that for you," he offered.

Jaime and I both shook our heads.

"Ah, it's a magic thing then. OK. Have fun."

Armed with brooms, buckets, scrub brushes, and other cleaning supplies, Jaime and I attacked the disused and dusty room.

As she swept, Jaime said, "So, I know that each city with a sizable vampire population has a Grandmaster, and he rules over everyone."

"Sort of. He, or she, since there are Grandmistresses, governs in conjunction with the Council of Five. The Grandmaster or mistress does have final say, but they are not an absolute ruler."

"Council of Five?"

I quickly ran through the who's who of vampire society. "The Masters and Mistresses of the five vampire covens. I am the mistress of the Aether. Marc Gautier is technically the master of the Gnome coven, but Jerome Livaudais runs the day-to-day coven matters. The Undine mistress is Collette St. Pierre. Tousaint Dubriel is Sylph master, and Paul Barthelmy is Salamand master."

"Why exactly are they split into different covens? The Gatekeepers figured it was because different covens do different things and maybe have different abilities."

"They are correct in that. The covens do have different abilities and responsibilities. Aether are chosen for their magical abilities. It is rare to find an Aether who did not possess such ability and practice magic before being turned. Sylphs tend to be musicians, artists, or writers. Gnomes are vampire aristocracy. They usually hold positions of power. Most Grandmasters are Gnomes. They also have a talent for organization. Undines excel at spying and gathering information, and Salamands are our warriors."

"So like Hogwarts without the sorting hat," Jaime said as she industriously scrubbed one corner of the room.

I laughed, again thankful that Josh regularly made me read current literature and watch movies. I actually understood the Harry Potter reference. "A bit. Although only the Aether have magic usually," I clarified.

"How do you know which coven someone is in? Do we have house colors or something?" Jaime asked jokingly.

"We do have colors and crests," I informed her.

"Seriously?" She looked incredulous.

"Seriously. It all relates back to the pentagram and the five elements."

"Five elements? Oh, you mean Earth, Air, Fire, Water, and Spirit," Jaime said.

"Yes. Our covens take their names from the elemental spirits—Gnome, Sylph, Salamand, Undine, and Aether—and our colors correspond," I explained.

Jaime stopped scrubbing and looked at me. "Dude. I never put two and two together. I had no idea why the covens had those weird-ass names!"

"Do not feel bad. Most vampires do not know the origin either. It is not as if we have a vampire academy to teach history," I said. "It is generally a sire's duty to pass down this sort of information, but even in my early years as a vampire, the lore was being lost."

"Ok, so we've got the Grandmaster, the five covens overseen by masters and mistresses, the Council of Five," Jaime said, ticking off the things we had discussed. "What is the Undead Synod? Grandmaster Gautier mentioned it earlier."

"Each coven generally has a master or mistress, a lieutenant and three Elders who make coven decisions. Those five from each coven come together to form the Undead Synod," I explained.

"There is a ridiculous amount of hierarchy in vampire society," Jaime said as she tossed her brush into the soapy water. "I think I shoulda been takin' notes."

"It is a lot to take in," I commiserated. "But fledglings are not expected to know everything right away. Although since you are now my lieutenant, you will need to be proficient at this quickly."

"I guess it's a good thing that I'm a quick learner, then," she quipped.

"Yes, indeed. I actually have a question or two for you."

"Shoot. I'll see if I have the answers."

"Earlier this evening Master Remy mentioned there are thirteen Gates to Hell. I know there is one here in New Orleans. Do you know where the others are?"

"Oh sure. We have to memorize all the locations when we join," Jaime paused and then recited as by rote. "Delhi, Fargo, Jerusalem, Kyoto, Lima, London, Mecca, Memphis, Mexico City, New Orleans, Rome, Vienna, and Ulara."

"I am not even sure where all those places are," I confessed. Fargo and Ulara were complete mysteries to me, and I could only guess at some of the others.

"I'll pull up a map later and show you. The one here in New Orleans has been real active lately, as you know, and Master Remy mentioned there's a lot going on with the one in Vienna, too."

"There were coups or attempted coups in a couple of those places that I know of," I told her.

"Do you think they're going to try to open more than one set of gates?"

"I do not want to even contemplate that. Even if they are, Marc is right. We need to concentrate on what we can control here in New Orleans. We know Honore intends to try to open our gate, and stopping her needs to be our focus," I said and sat back to survey our work. The floor gleamed under our ministrations. "I think that is enough for tonight. The floor is clean, and your brain is full. Why don't you head upstairs, and I can finish up here."

"OK." Jaime readily agreed before I changed my mind.

It took me longer to put away the cleaning implements than I anticipated, and it was nearly dawn when I stumbled upstairs to find Josh and my bed.

CHAPTER 6

I had barely pried my eyes open that evening when my phone rang. I briefly considered letting the call go to voicemail but reasoned that anyone calling at this ungodly hour would have a good reason. Picking the phone off the bedside table, I frowned, seeing a number that I did not recognize.

"Hello?" I answered carefully.

"Juliette?" asked a poshly accented British voice.

"Diana? Is that you?" I asked as I pulled myself into a sitting position and arranged the pillows behind me.

"Yes. I am sorry to call so early. I was finally able to retrieve the messages off of Victoria's phone and got yours," Diana said. "I am sorry to inform you that Victoria Mountbatten is dead."

That explained why I had not heard back from her. I had called Victoria, the worldwide leader of the Aether coven three nights ago to report what had transpired in New Orleans and that I was now coven mistress in the city. Aether masters and mistresses in major cities reported directly to Victoria. While we all owed fealty to the Grandmaster in the city we resided in, our first loyalty was to the head of the Aether coven which was based in London. It was all very feudal, and loyalties sometimes conflicted.

"What happened?" I asked. "Who is in charge now?"

"There was an inter-coven coup, and Victoria was assassinated. The man who killed her and tried to assert control was also killed along with the Aether lieutenant and three of the Elders." That was most of the order of succession dead. No wonder no one had called me back. "I, as the next ranking Elder, am now in charge." Diana did not sound happy about it.

"Congratulations?" I offered tentatively.

"I believe that my ascension to Head of Coven is as welcome as your own elevation." Meaning not at all. I remembered something that Diana said to me at our last meeting, *We do not look for leadership; it is thrust upon us.*

"What do you need from me?" I asked.

"Just some information at the moment. Your message to Victoria was a little vague. What has happened in New Orleans that you are now coven mistress?"

I gathered my thoughts, "Four nights ago, Honore Rochan, as Mistress of the Aether coven, led an unsuccessful coup against the New Orleans Grandmaster for control of the city. To my knowledge, all of the New Orleans Aether and several from outside the city followed her—except for me. During the attempt, they raised several demons."

"Demons?" Diana interrupted in shock, "Good God, I thought what happened here in London was bad. How were you able to dispel them? You were able to dispel them, weren't you?" There was a worried edge to her voice.

"Yes, all the demons were sent back to Hell where they belong," I assured her. "I had a great deal of help from the Gatekeepers."

"Who are the Gatekeepers? I've never heard of them." There was uncertainty but also curiosity in her voice.

"Apparently, they are a secret order of mages that are charged with keeping the supernatural world hidden from humans. They also guard Gates to other realms."

"Are they just in New Orleans?"

"No, they are in all cities with Gates."

"So they are in London? I know there is at least one Gate out on Glastonbury Tor."

"Yes," I confirmed. I did not know about other Gates, but there was definitely one to Hell in or near London.

"How can I find them?"

"I am not sure. They found me. Do you want me to . . . ?" I trailed off unsure what I could really offer her. Have Nicholas Remy contact the London Gatekeepers and have them contact Diana? The New Orleans Gatekeepers worked with us, but I knew the organization being outed had caused political problems for Nicholas.

"No, at least not now. So, are you the only non-abjured Aether in New Orleans at the moment? I assume your Grandmaster called out the Hunt on the rebellious Aether and declared them Rogue."

"He did, but there are actually two of us that are still non-abjured. My newly created childe and me."

"Congratulations on your progeny! You'll have to tell me all about them later," Diana sounded genuinely happy for me for a moment but then became serious again. "Have the Rogues been killed yet?"

"A few. Honore is still at large."

"Are you both safe?"

"As safe as we can be," I assured her.

"Stay that way. There is a lot of Aether unrest in other cities right now."

"Yes, I have heard rumor of that. It may be related to why Honore staged the attempt here."

"I'm not following. Isn't it obvious why Honore tried to seize power?"

"I think it is bigger than just grabbing control of New Orleans. We know she intends to open the Gates of Hell to fulfill the Blue Moon prophecy," I explained.

"Bloody Hell. Are you sure?" I could tell by her tone she hoped I was wrong.

"Absolutely. We captured Louis Pontbriand during the attempt, and he confessed their plan. I think we'll find much of the unrest took place where the thirteen Hellmouths are located."

"You may be right. If you are, this is much worse than I thought. I have a number of other calls I need to make before the sun comes up, so I need to go. I'll be in contact in a few days with more information," Diana said before ending the call.

I was greatly troubled by what Diana had told me. I had so many questions. Were these coups and other Aether unrest related in the way I thought? Was the ritual murder we found last night connected, or was it just a coincidence that a vampire fledging and a possible recruit were the victims? Was that damn prophecy at the root of all this? I was still struggling with these questions when Josh sauntered naked into the bedroom from the adjoining bathroom.

I had quickly found out that nudity did not phase Josh—his own or other people's. He seemed to understand my own modesty, but now that we were lovers, he did not always bother to wear clothes when we were at home. I assumed with Jaime in the house that Josh's naked wanderings would be confined to our bedroom suite. This saddened me slightly.

"I was hoping you'd be up," Josh said as he dropped the towel he'd been using to dry his hair on the floor and joined me on the bed.

"I thought about joining you in the shower," I said in between kisses.

"You should have," he said as he caressed my right breast. "I might need another one here in a bit."

I temporarily forgot all about Diana Langdon and the trouble within the Aether coven as Josh's magical mouth paid homage first to my right breast and then my left. I was wet for him by the time his fingers found the curls hiding my core.

I moaned as he slid two fingers inside me, and suddenly it was not enough. I wanted him now. Hard and fast. I flipped him onto his back and straddled him. Josh seemed surprised but willing to go along with my newfound aggression. Not that I'd been a passive lover up until this point, but now I was letting my passion and need rule me. Josh smiled up at me and didn't try to reassert control.

Afterwards, Josh lay stunned. Finally, he asked me, "Juliette, was that a stress fuck?"

"Pardon?" I was not offended by the question, just not familiar with the terminology.

"A stress fuck. When you are really stressed out or something is really heavy on your mind, you have really strenuous sex to try to get it off your mind," Josh said.

I hope I managed a sheepish look. "Um, I think so. Sorry," I said.

Josh drew me into his arms, and I could feel the low rumble of laughter in his chest as he held me close. "I didn't say I minded. What's happened that's got you so worried?"

I told him about my conversation with Diana. He was quiet for a long time after I had finished, just holding me and stroking my hair. "I ain't gonna tell ya that it'll be all right, as I'm not sure it will be. But I will tell you that I'm gonna be right by your side to help you with this and that we face this together," he whispered and, in that moment, I knew that I'd lost my heart to Josh Bouchard.

JOSH HAD ARRANGED for us to meet Beau Roulet in Baton Rouge to discuss hiring werewolf bodyguards for me and the house. With New Orleans closed to the pack, Beau was playing gigs in Baton Rouge. I wondered how much the closing of the city was costing the werewolves monetarily. While they avoided cities as a rule, many members were musicians and traveled to New Orleans, Baton Rouge, or Lafayette to perform, going home afterwards to the quiet of the swamp. Beau had readily agreed to my warding New Orleans against werewolves to stop the Stray attacks on humans, but I doubted he'd taken into consideration lost revenue. Then again, Josh said that there were plenty of clubs in Lafayette and Baton Rouge, so they should be able to find work. I was also sure that once the crisis was over Josh would book the various musicians to play in his many clubs. I had discovered that Josh not only owned The Cowboy, but several other bars in the Quarter and the CBD. His newest, Chintz, was scheduled to open later this month. In addition, he had controlling interests in many other city businesses. I hoped that hiring pack members as my bodyguards would also offset the loss of income.

The drive to Baton Rouge took just over an hour. I had the impression the trip should take longer, but cars went at speeds so much faster than I was accustomed to that I was not a very good judge. This was the first time I had ventured out of New Orleans since my return, and it disappointed me that the countryside passed in a high-speed blur. Josh apologized for this and promised that as soon as the Rogue Aether, the Stray werewolves, and the latest crisis were over that he would take me on a leisurely drive.

"It just ain't safe to be out and about right now. Plus, if we wanna hear the band play, we gotta get the lead out," Josh explained.

While I conceded the point that tonight we had little time, I disagreed about the danger. "Is it any safer in New Orleans?" I asked.

"Darlin', you're a big target right now," he said glancing over at me.

"From my point of view, I am safer out of town," I said. "In New Orleans, Honore can pretty much guess where I'll be. There may be more security at the locations I am at, but I am easy to find. If they stumble across me while I'm out of town, I'm less guarded, but they do have to find me first."

"I can see where you're coming from, but I ain't sure I totally agree," Josh said. In the end, we agreed to disagree.

"So tell me how you know Beau," I prompted.

"I ran into him about twenty . . . no twenty-two years ago, over in Texas. We were at one of the smaller music festivals, and luckily, I was the only vamp, and he was the only werewolf there. We sensed each other right off. Even though he wasn't Alpha yet, I could feel his power. At first, I figured he was just a local Texas werewolf, and it wouldn't be a problem. There was a vamp/were war that had been goin' on for decades—one of those we don't even remember why it started, that's how long it'd been goin' on—but it was confined to Louisiana and Mississippi at the time. There weren't enough werewolves in Texas for the Grandmasters over there to bother with. Then I got a whiff of him. Pure Louisiana swamp. I was a brand-new Sylph lieutenant and the last thing I wanted was an incident. I figured I'd better have a sit down with him."

"I am guessing that it went alright since you are both still alive and are now good friends," I said.

Josh winced. "Not initially. He didn't realize I was from New Orleans and had wanted to extend an olive branch. Come to think of it, I should've sent an actual olive branch. It might a worked. He thought I wanted a fight, I sure as hell didn't. Anyway, in the end we cleared up the misunderstanding—no fangs or claws involved—and found out we weren't all that different. We drank a whole lot a good bourbon and talked a lot. Nathalie was just a little thing yet, and the apple of her daddy's eye. The boys were taken their time showing up, and Beau thought Nathalie might be an only child."

"That's rare in werewolf families, is it not?" I asked.

"Very. Multiple births are more the norm. Both Beau and his wife come from big families, so no one could understand it. And it wasn't like they could consult a specialist or anything. The pack has a doc, of course, but he's just a GP and was baffled. Anyway, that's another story. Beau and I decided the whole vamp/were war was a bunch of bullshit, and we'd be friends anyway."

"That was rather dangerous, was it not?" I asked.

Josh shrugged, "As soon as I got back to New Orleans, I talk to Marc and Gabe about it. It opened kinda a back channel of communication, and when Beau became Alpha, he met with Marc and formally buried the hatchet."

I now understood more clearly why Marc hadn't asked Josh to scent the werewolf that had attacked his nephew a few weeks ago. While I did not doubt for a moment that Josh would have been honest with Marc no matter what he had smelled, Marc had not wanted to put Josh in that sort of awkward position.

We pulled up in front of the club and immediately found a parking spot. Josh had the devil's own luck. I once commented on his ability, and he told me that his grandmother had blessed him on the day he was born. I knew one of his grandmothers had been a thaumaturge and wondered if she was the one who had blessed him and if this was a heretofore-unknown capability that I might have. One day I would gather the nerve to ask. However, I was raised in an era where the accusation of witchcraft could get you burned at the stake, and deeply ingrained fear held my tongue even now. I was taught not to speak of magic amongst the non-initiated, but I was much more liberal about this than most mages, recognizing that some non-magic users, such as the Grandmaster and his heir, needed a working knowledge of magic. Still, I was hesitant to ask Josh, fearing that I would cross an unspoken line and break the fragile trust that existed between us. We might be lovers, but it was a new relationship, less than a week old. I was not ready to push boundaries yet.

As Josh, being a gentlemen, helped me out of the car, he looked down at my feet. "Are those the boots I gotcha?" he asked.

"Of course." I pulled up the hem of my jeans to show off the red cowboy boots that had been on the bed when I'd emerged from my shower with the note, *Welcome home*.

"I wanted a housewarming gift for you, but it was kinda short notice," Josh said.

"It was very sweet. How did you manage?"

"The Internet is a wonderful thing, I ordered them last night, and they arrived just after dark. They fit okay?"

"Like they were made for me," I said.

"I'm glad," he said as he led me to the front door of the club.

Once inside, we found a table with an excellent view of the stage. A perky, brunette server in tight jeans and an even tighter white T-shirt took our drink order and bustled away.

Josh leaned in and said close to my ear, "We'll listen to Beau's first set and then meet with him back in his dressing room."

"Did he seem favorable to the idea?"

Josh nodded. "He wants to forge closer ties between vamps and weres. Beau's spent the years since endin' the vamp/were war consolidating his power base and creatin' nonofficial ties." He gently squeezed my hand and leaned back slightly. "Looks like the band's about to start."

Beau and four other musicians took the stage and began a lively

Cajun tune. Eventually, the server brought us our drinks and Josh wisely ordered another round before we'd even started this one. As slow as the service was, we might only get two rounds.

I knew little about Cajun music, but I liked what I heard. Josh had been working diligently to fill in the two hundred-odd year gaps in my knowledge, but there was so much that I had missed. With everything else going on, my music education was generally on the bottom of the list of things to catch up on, but I hoped there would be some time when things settled down to explore more fully all I'd missed.

After the fourth song, Beau called Josh up on stage to join the group. Although Josh tried to demure at first, pointing to me, the lure of the stage was too much for him. I'd heard Josh play the guitar any number of times at home, but this was the first time seeing him perform. I was not disappointed. He sat in with the band for the next few songs with his normal hundred watt smile amplified three-fold before rejoining me in the audience, and he exuded extra energy when he took his seat. It was easy to see that he loved performing, and I wondered why he didn't do it more often. I gave him a quick welcoming kiss and reminded myself to ask him later.

When the band finished the set, Josh and I followed them back to the dressing room area. It was one big room with numerous lighted vanities and chairs with two curtained alcoves serving as private changing areas. As Josh and I took seats, Beau asked what we were drinking.

"Just a Dixie for me. Juliette's shooting whiskey—Jack, straight up," Josh said.

Beau gave me an appreciative smile. Turning to his accordion player, he said, "Jean Philippe, do me a favor and get me a Dixie and another round for our guests."

After the young man left, Beau joined the rest of us. "Jean Philippe is a good kid, but not pack, so we need to watch what we say around him. Josh, I think you know everyone in the band. Juliette, may I present my daughter, Nathalie, on vocals and fiddle, Adrien is our bassist, and my nephew, Gaetan, is our drummer. Everyone, this is Juliette de Grammont, Aether coven mistress."

"It is nice to meet you all," I said nodding to each one in turn. The others murmured polite acknowledgments.

"Josh says you need a couple bodyguards, Juliette," Beau said.

"Yes. As you know, members of the Aether coven mounted the recent coup attempt against Marc Gautier," I explained. "With them now avowed traitors, I am coven mistress. Normally, I would choose members of my coven to protect me, but there are just two of us who have not been abjured," I said.

"That does pose a problem getting guards," Beau commented crossing his arms in front of his chest as he settled back in his chair

"There is a lot of Aether unrest in other cities, so requesting help from them is not an option." I absently rubbed my palms on my jeans.

"What's up the Aether's ass?" Beau asked.

"It is unclear at this point. All I know for sure is that the overall coven leader based in London was assassinated four nights ago. I resisted getting guards while I acted as Regent, but that is no longer possible."

"Well, I got a two-man team . . ." Beau said before Natalie clearing her throat loudly interrupted him, "um, a two-person team that can act as your bodyguards starting tomorrow, but the city is still warded against werewolves. Are you takin' down the wards?"

I shook my head. "No. Until the pack of Strays is killed, we cannot risk opening the city back up. I will provide the guards with amulets that will allow them to pass unharmed through the wards and even to change form. The amulets will be particular to each guard, so if they are lost or stolen, another werewolf cannot use them to gain access to the city."

"We can help you then. My daughter, Nathalie, and my nephew, Gaetan, both have security training and would be excellent choices."

I had given each a cursory look when we were introduced, but now I studied them closely for the first time. Nathalie had the look of her father with the same aquiline nose and dark coloring. Her long, brown hair had more curl, but she was tall and willowy like Beau. I still had trouble judging the ages of women in this time as women seemed to age more slowly now, but I thought she might be in her mid-twenties. She was definitely older than Beau's two boys that I had met. Nathalie also had a powerful aura. Not as strong as her father's, but respectable in her own right. Gaetan was a powerfully built young man in his late twenties. His hair was a lighter shade of brown, but there was a pronounced family resemblance.

"How do you feel about it?" I asked them leaning forward.

"It would be a very valuable experience for me," the young woman said meeting my eyes. "I actually like the city. I graduated from Loyola last spring, and I've been thinking about going back for law school. But don't think that I'm some helpless girl who cries over a broken nail. I'm a practitioner of jujitsu, and I am more than proficient with a handgun."

I nodded and turned to Gaetan.

"I joined the Army when I was eighteen and became a Ranger. I came home about a year ago. After a couple tours in the desert, I missed the swamp," the man grinned. "And my family."

"You won't have much time for the swamp or to visit family. At least initially," I warned.

"Oh, I've had enough of family, at least for a bit," Gaetan said.

"His mama is trying to marry him off," Beau clarified.

"She's paraded every girl in the parish past me and had most of them over for Sunday dinner," Gaetan groaned his shoulders slumped. "You'd be saving me. Really."

I laughed. I could appreciate trying to avoid well-meaning but unwanted matchmaking. "I will need samples of your hair to make the amulets. Beau, if you give me some of yours, I'll make you an amulet as well. I should have done this before, but . . . ."

"Everything went sideways so fast that you're still trying to catch up?" Beau finished for me.

"I may never catch up," I confessed.

"How long will it take you to make the amulets?" he asked.

"I can probably have them done by midnight tomorrow, barring any emergencies," I said.

"Maybe we should plan on two days from now," Josh said.

"Things that bad?" Beau asked.

"You have no idea," Josh answered and fell silent as the accordion player returned with drinks for everyone.

After passing them around and snagging a bottle of Dixie for himself, Jean Phillipe said, "I'm going out for a smoke. Unless you need me for something?"

"No, go enjoy your cancer stick," Beau said and checked his watch. "We're back in twenty."

"No problem," the man said and left the room.

After the door closed, Josh turned back to Beau. "Last night there was a ritual murder in the Treme. Actually, two murders. A Sylph fledgling and his human girlfriend. Juliette's been asked to investigate."

"I'm not much for occult knowledge–unless it pertains to were-wolves–but my degree is in criminology from Loyola. I might be able to help." Natalie leaned forward in eager anticipation.

"Whoever did this used dark blood magic—possibly necromancy. This may be very dangerous," I warned, wondering if it was a good idea to employ Beau's daughter as my bodyguard, not that I doubted her ability, but I worried about the political ramifications if she died protecting me.

She seemed to understand my hesitation and sought to reassure me. "Ms. Grammont, I know that guarding a coven leader is dangerous work in the best of times, and these are pretty much the worst of times. This is why you need Gaetan and me. We can protect you around-the-clock, if need be, and no one will expect werewolves. Plus, necromancy won't have any effect on us."

Beau broke in, saying, "We have discussed this at length. They guard you with my full blessing and no reservations. If something should happen to either of them, there would be no repercussions on the vampire community as a whole. I will hunt down those responsi-ble, but since they were gunning for you, it shouldn't create an inter-species incident."

"Fair enough," I said.

Josh jumped in, "When I initially contacted you, I thought we were gonna just need guards for Juliette, but I'm not sure that they'll be enough. I've engaged humans and servants to guard the house around-the-clock, and I'd like to hire at least four weres to fill out the contingent."

Beau looked thoughtful for a moment. "I've got twelve, maybe thirteen pack members who are qualified, so getting you guards won't be a problem. Are they for your house, Juliette's house, or both?"

"I persuaded this lovely lady to move in with me, so it will be at our house," Josh said with a smile.

"Coven leader and lieutenant in the same house? You'll be a big target." Beau mused.

"Two lieutenants. Juliette's childe, Jaime, is living with us too."

"I'll send you six pack members," Beau said tipping the neck of this beer bottle toward Josh. "You got room to house them, right?"

Josh nodded. "The carriage house is partially renovated, and I'll get a contractor in to add some more interior walls."

"I'll need hair samples and some extra time to make the amulets for the other pack members," I said standing up. While I understood the need and indeed the wisdom of having extra guards, I wondered when I would find the time to make the amulets as I still needed to make magic protection items for the Grandmaster and his family. And time was not my only obstacle. Creating all of these would take a great deal of magic.

"I'll bring the crew with me when we meet up in a couple of days. You can get your samples then."

I nodded and, taking three glass vials from my purse, collected hair from Gaetan, Nathalie, and Beau. I carefully labeled each vial so I could return the correct amulet to its proper owner.

"We will be able to shift when wearing these amulets?" The former Ranger asked.

"Yes, I will make sure that the leather cords are long enough so they don't break during your transformation," I assured him.

"And no one else can use them?" Nathalie further clarified.

"Only you. However, you will need to be careful not to lose it, or I will need time to make another," I warned.

"Don't worry," Nathalie said with a smile. I could tell that she was looking forward to this.

"Have you got everything you need?" Josh asked me.

"Yes."

"We should get going then," Josh said draining the rest of his beer.

"You aren't staying for the rest of the show?" Nathalie asked.

"I wish we could, but we gotta get back. Juliette needs to make the amulets, and I've got a new club I need to check on."

"I'll get in touch with packs in other cities—see what I can find out about that Aether unrest. If it's anything important, I'll call you," Beau said.

"We appreciate that," I said. "This guard duty won't harm your music careers, will it?"

"Gaetan and I aren't professional musicians. We just sub in when Dad needs extra bodies, Mrs. Grammont. You aren't messing with our careers," Nathalie assured me.

"Good," I said. "If you're going to guard me, we need to be on a first name basis. I am simply Juliette." Nathalie nodded in agreement.

Josh stood and, placing his hand on the small of my back, ushered me from the room.

CHAPTER 7

*J*osh waited until we were in the car on the way back to New Orleans to ask, "So, whaddaya think?"

"Honestly, I have no idea how to assess the capabilities of a bodyguard, but Nathalie must know what she's doing if Beau is sending his daughter to me. She is his heir, correct?" I answered, angling my body in the seat toward him.

"Yeah, it's kind of unusual. The eldest son usually inherits, but neither boy has exhibited more than modest power. Nathalie, on the other hand, has exuded confidence and strength since she was a toddler. I know that Beau had hoped that the boys might develop or come into their powers at puberty, but that didn't happen," Josh explained as he looked over at me.

"Beau has trained her?" I asked.

"Oh, yeah. Even though he hoped one of the boys would take over, he's smart enough not to neglect talent and power. He trained her to lead a pack: either his or to be a strong alpha female to her husband."

"She isn't married, is she?" I had a flash of panic. She would not be leaving a husband behind, would she? Nathalie hadn't been wearing a wedding ring, but as a musician she might have taken it off for the performance.

"Naw. Says she ain't ready to settle down and start squeezin' out pups yet–her words, not mine. She's got ambition and the smarts to back it up."

"She said she was thinking about going to law school."

"She'd make a hell of a litigator, but what she's really doin' is positioning the pack to move into this century." Josh smiled at the thought.

"A little too insular and old-fashioned to compete?" I asked.

"Yep. Beau has done a great job with the pack, but he knows he's just the transition guy. He ended the vamp/were war and is preparing his kid to take the next step."

"He's taking a large gamble sending his daughter and heir to protect me," I observed.

"Yeah, but the payoff is huge if it works. It strengthens the ties between the two supernatural groups and earns her a powerful ally once she becomes Alpha."

"Strong political motivation to keep me alive works," I said wryly.

Josh laughed. "It's a bit more than that. Beau really likes you."

"He's only met me a handful of times," I scoffed.

"True, but he likes what he sees. He's a leg man, and you've got great legs." He took his right hand and ran it across the top of my thigh for emphasis.

I rolled my eyes and groaned at his blatantly sexist comment, not sure if Josh was being serious or not.

"No, really. You're a straight shooter, and he respects that. He's Alpha and can strategize with the best, but he'd rather just have a straight up conversation." Shifting the subject suddenly, Josh asked, "Makin' those amulets won't be a problem, will it?"

"They should not be. I have some good samples, and the spell is not overly complex. It will just take a few hours with no interruptions," I said shrugging my shoulders.

"A few hours without a crisis might be the hardest thing," Josh said.

"I know," I agreed in frustration. "I feel as if we lurch from crisis to crisis. As soon as we solve one problem, another one appears," I paused and then added, "I do not wish to invite trouble, but I wonder what happened to the Stray werewolves. They are no longer hunting in New Orleans, so where did they go?"

"That's a damn good question. Beau thinks they dispersed into the outlying communities and are feeding on the marginal—the homeless, vagrants, runaways. It won't take long before the attacks are noticeable again. Beau's got the pack out looking for 'em. They found a couple, but there're still more out there," Josh said.

"And then we have my lovely coven," I said, voice dripping with sarcasm.

"That is a much more pressing problem," Josh said. "I'm guessing they went back to whatever hidey-hole they were at after the fire and are waiting."

"Waiting for what though?" I asked.

"Well, darlin', that's the $64,000 question, isn't it?" Josh asked.

I sat back and pondered his words for the rest of the trip back to New Orleans.

"I HATE LEAVIN' you but the grand opening date for the new club has to be pushed back, and I gotta change all the promotional materials," Josh apologized pulling up to the house.

"Why has the opening been changed? Because of what's happening?" I asked.

"Naw. There's another club, Den of Iniquity, opening up in the CBD on the same night. They dropped their promo material last night. I thought about going ahead anyway since we're goin' after way different types of people, but it just ain't good business. We hadn't announced anything, so it's easy to move it one week. Maybe we can get all duded up and go check out the place."

"That sounds nice," I said.

"It's a little outside our norm, but it could be fun."

"How so?"

"It's a Goth club."

"Oh, like Jaime." I had once asked Josh why the young woman

dressed as she did, and he had very briefly explained Goth culture to me. "Well, I can, what is the phrase? Rock some black?"

Josh laughed. Then he leaned over and kissed me hard. "I'll see you when I get home."

As much as I did not wish to, I got out of the car and went into the house. There was too much work to do to moon like a love-sick schoolgirl. I walked through the storage area to my new ritual room. Unlocking the door, I marveled both at the space and that Josh had given it to me. Still, there was much to do.

Giving myself a little shake, I got to work. First, I ritually cleaned and sanctified the space. Even though Jaime and I had scrubbed the room the previous night, it still needed to be purified. I was eager to get to work on the amulets, but I worked slowly and thoroughly to make sure that the purification was complete. It was better to do it right the first time rather than waste energy needing to do it again later. Once done, I turned to amulet making.

I drew a warding circle on the floor with chalk and charged it with a drop of my blood. As soon as the ward flared with power, I felt oddly drained. I wondered if I needed more vitae. Josh and I had fed before going to Baton Rouge, but I was still recovering from the immense power drain I'd experienced when the other Aether attacked the Grandmaster.

I sat for a minute wondering if I should break the circle and go to the kitchen for a bottle of blood. After debating the merits, I kept working. I was not sure if the vitae would help, and if it did not, I might not be able to recharge the circle and do the amulet work that I needed to get done.

I pulled the box of trinkets I'd brought into the circle to me and began sorting through the baubles. These were things I had collected in the years before my staking that had been stored away in the hope of my return. I chose a slender, clear crystal for Nathalie's amulet, an intricately carved wooden wolf's head for Beau, and a round, metal disk for Gaetan. Retrieving the three glass vials from my pocket, I set them next to the trinkets. I pulled a long strand of Nathalie's hair from her vial and carefully wrapped it around the thin crystal. I tried to spool my power to bind the hair and the crystal together, but utterly failed. It was as if I was trying to grab smoke, and the harder I tried, the wispier my magic became. Frustrated, I stopped for a moment. This was not working. Clearing my mind, I stopped trying to use my inborn power and instead called magic to me. While I could not invoke the amulets with drawn magic, I could create the outer shell.

This time, I called the magic, and it came in a rush. I spooled it and pushed it into the crystal. I am not sure when I lost control of the magic, but suddenly the crystal shattered, sending shards throughout my circle. I stared stupidly at my hand for a minute. I was not all that sure what had gone wrong. I had made amulets like this before and never, ever, had one shattered.

I did not have time for this. I searched through the trinket box again, this time choosing a more substantial blue stone. Stopping again, I centered myself and cleared my mind. No good magic came from frustration or anger. I pulled another strand of hair from Nathalie's vial, glad that I'd taken several samples from each of the werewolves. Again, I carefully wound the hair around the new stone.

I pulled the magic to me again and allowed it to spool for several minutes. Then, with infinite care, I fed the magic into the stone to bind the hair to it. At first, the stone resisted the binding, but gradually, under the steady pressure of my magic, the two became one. I smiled with satisfaction as I set the partial amulet aside.

Centering myself, I took a deep breath. I followed the same careful steps to create Beau's amulet. I let the magic spool for quite a while to make sure that I had good control of it. Handling drawn magic was harder for me than using my inborn skill mostly because I did not do it that often. My inborn magic was so much more powerful and versatile than what I could draw. I must have pushed the magic too far and too fast into the first crystal, causing it to shatter, I reasoned. I did not want to repeat that with wooden shards. Beau's hair fused with the wooden wolf's head beautifully, and I was quite proud of my accomplishment.

Two down, one to go. I uncorked the stopper on Gaetan's bottle and withdrew his hair. Then my vision blurred. Blinking hard, I sought to focus. Nothing like this had ever happened before. Panic rose in me, but I refused to give in to it. By feel, I put the hair back in the vial and recapped it.

When I tried to stand, my knees gave way, and I sprawled across the crystal shards in the circle. I laid there for a long time, shaking. Finally, I tried again raising myself to my hands and knees, the crystal biting into my palms. I made sure I was steady before getting to my feet. This feeling of helplessness scared me. I swayed a bit when I took down my circle but managed to stay upright. My vision swam as if I were drunk. *Could vampires even get drunk?* I was not sure, but I knew that even if we could, this was not an alcohol induced stupor.

Cautiously, I made my way upstairs and collapsed onto the nearest sofa. That was where Jaime found me when she came home twenty minutes later.

"Juliette, are you okay?" Jaime bent to look at me when I didn't even raise my head at her entrance. Concern laced her tone.

"No," I croaked. Even speaking took more energy than I thought I had.

"Do you need blood? Should I call Josh or get the guards?" she asked urgently.

"Blood. Don't call. I don't want anyone to know."

My childe scampered to the kitchen and returned a few minutes later with two bottles of warmed blood. Jaime helped me into a sitting position and held one bottle to my lips as though I was a baby. I certainly was weak as one and gulped the blood greedily.

"What happened? Did the incubus come back?" Jaime asked.

"No, it was not the incubus," I said. "I'm not sure what happened. I was making the amulets for the werewolves, and I felt weak. More than weak. I lost my vision for a minute."

She handed me the second bottle. "Is that normal?"

I looked at her. "No. It started as soon as I set my circle—the weakness, not the loss of vision. That came after I made Beau's amulet."

"Do you think it is residual from your big boss fight?"

"Boss fight?" I asked, unfamiliar with the term.

"The big fight with Honore," Jaime explained.

"I'm sure that didn't help, but there were two demons in the court-yard before that when I wasn't at full strength."

"Because the incubus had drained you."

I nodded as I finished the second bottle.

"Is the blood helping?"

"A bit." I could now sit and drink unaided, but I didn't like my chances of walking very far.

"Do you want another bottle?"

"Yes, please. How is our supply?" I asked.

"We have plenty, and I can always call Sophie and ask for more," Jaime promised.

"And explain the consumption how? I do not want anyone to know about this," I said.

"I'll take the blame: growing girl and all, or I'll say that I was clumsy and dropped the bottles when taking them out of the fridge."

"Thank you," I said.

"Um, why don't you want anyone to know? I mean, they all knew about how the incubus drained you. Why the secrecy now?" Jaime asked as she walked to the kitchen.

"I was attacked, and it was unavoidable—that they know. It is different now. I'm the Aether Mistress. I cannot afford to show weak-ness," I explained.

"But . . ." Jaime clearly did not understand my reasoning, and if I was honest, I didn't fully understand it either. All I knew was that it would be very dangerous for me if anyone besides Jaime found out I had become so weakened. I had to hope that Jaime wouldn't take advantage.

"This stays between us, Jaime," I said firmly.

"Josh is gonna be pissed when he finds out, and you didn't tell him," she warned.

"So be it. I do not wish anyone to know: not Josh, not Marc Gautier, not Nicholas Remy. Do you understand?" I said forcefully. I could not put magic behind my words to compel her silence, but she got the message just the same.

"Alright," she said sullenly. "What else can I do?"

"Can you help me into the bedroom? I think it would be best if I just went to bed."

Jaime was a strong woman and had no problem guiding me down the hall to the master bedroom. My memory is blank after that.

CHAPTER 8

osh was still in bed when I awoke the next night. He had
drawn me into his arms and held me close as I slumbered
the day away. I drank in his scent, a masculine mixture of
musk and hoppy beer.

"Mornin' sleepyhead. How're you feelin'?" He asked low in my ear.

I panicked, wondering if Jaime had broken her word and told Josh
what had happened, but then realized it was simply a wake-up greeting. Even after all these years as a vampire he still said 'good morning'
upon rising, even though it was now night. Old, ingrained human
habits were hard to break.

"I am fine. How are you?" I inquired.

He nuzzled my neck and playfully nipped my ear. "Enjoying snug-
glin' with you."

"You normally don't stay in bed this late," I said, snaking my arms
around his neck.

"You were already asleep when I got in last night, and I wanted to
spend at least a bit of time with you before I run all over hell's half-
acre for Toussaint tonight."

"Sylph business?"

"Nothing so glorified. I'm his errand boy, it seems, for his protégé's new show."

"I'm sorry."

"Eh, I'm combining it with stuff I've got to do to get Chintz opened anyway. I'm just grousin' because I don't wanna get out of bed."

"We could just stay in," I suggested.

"Woman, you could tempt a saint, and we both know I ain't no saint. Nope. Gotta get up and get stuff done." He kissed me playfully and then pulled away. "I know better than to start anything, or we won't get out of bed."

I pouted a bit. I was feeling much better this evening, and I craved his touch. "Spoilsport."

"Ha!" He said as he slid out of bed and offered me a view of his magnificent backside. "You could join me in the shower."

I did not give another thought to my previous evening's weakness as I lost myself to the sensual pleasures of Josh's mouth and hands under the hot spray of the shower. But I should have. Just as our love-making was becoming truly passionate, my vision again blurred, and my knees buckled. Josh was not so lost in his own pleasure that he didn't realize that something was wrong, nor did he mistake my clinging to him as spent passion. He knew my body and me well enough to understand that there was a serious problem.

"Juliette, darlin', what's wrong?" Josh asked, clearly concerned.

"I'm not sure. Very weak and dizzy," I managed to say.

Josh held me tightly with one arm while he fumbled to turn the water off. He then set me gently down on the built-in shower bench. "Let me grab a bunch of towels. Are you okay to sit?"

"Yes," I promised, although the world spun around me in a kaleido-scope of colors that had me worried about my ability to stay conscious.

Josh was back in a moment, wrapping me in a thick plush towel. With infinite care, he carried me back to bed and tucked me in. "Let me get you some blood," he said after he gently kissed my forehead.

"Pants," I mumbled.

"What?" Josh said as he started to open the bedroom door.

"Put on some pants or a robe. You don't want to scare Jaime."

Josh gave a startled laugh as he remembered his other houseguest. "I guess runnin' around nekkid ain't appropriate with a teenager in the house."

I closed my eyes and leaned back against the pillow. I heard him pull the robe from the back of the bathroom door before leaving. I drew deep, unnecessary breaths, trying to calm myself. While not quite to the level of the incubus draining me of both my life force and magic, the panic I now felt was paralyzing. I did not know why this was happening, and perhaps that was what scared me the most. At least I knew why I was weak after the incubus attack; this had no discernible cause. I had not even been using magic this time.

The bedroom door opened, and I cracked my eyes open a slit. Josh was blurry but recognizable as he hurried towards me. Cradling my head in his hand, he held the mug of warmed blood to my lips with the other. I gulped the contents, and finally, my vision cleared. My limbs still felt like jelly, and I knew without a doubt that magic was beyond my current capability.

There was a knock at the door, and Jaime let herself in. She carried two more mugs of warmed vitae. Josh wordlessly took one mug from her and held it to my lips. I managed not to gulp its contents. After I'd finished the third mug and Jaime had taken the empty containers back to the kitchen, Josh climbed into bed next to me.

"Feeling better?" He asked.

"Yes."

"Do you want to tell me what's going on?"

"I am not sure. Suddenly, my vision blurred, and I got weak-kneed," I answered.

He shifted to look at me. "Is this the first time it's happened?"

I briefly debated lying but decided on the truth. "It happened yesterday as well. When I was making the amulets," I admitted.

"Why didn't you tell me?"

"I felt fine when I woke up, so I thought it was an aberration."

"You can't keep stuff like this from me! What if we'd been out somewhere and it had happened?" He sounded as panicked as I felt and maybe a little angry too.

"I did not think it would happen again! When it happened yesterday, I was casting. I thought that I had used too much magic too soon after dispelling the demons, fighting Honore, and re-warding Gautier House. I thought that if I did not use magic for a day or two, it would pass."

"You weren't gonna tell me, were you?" Josh sounded hurt.

"I did not think it was a big deal, and I did not want to worry you." I lied now not wanting him to know that I hadn't told him because I didn't wish to reveal a weakness, even to him.

He gently took my face in his hands and looked me straight in the eye. "Juliette, you've gotta tell me when this sorta stuff happens."

I looked sideways, not wanting to meet his gaze. "There is no reason . . ." I started to say.

"Don't you get it yet? I love you, Juliette." He cut my excuse off.

My eyes swept back to his and locked. I could see the truth of his declaration there. It was like gazing into his soul and seeing mine reflected back. The revelation shocked me to my very core, as did the realization that I felt the same.

I open my mouth to say something, but suddenly knew that I didn't need to. He had seen the same thing. Still cupping my face, Josh gently brought his lips to mine. The moment they touched, I experienced a connection unlike anything I had ever felt before. Magic cracked between us forging a bond that alternately thrilled and terrified me. I was flooded with disjointed images and emotions from Josh —his sister as a child, his grandmother, his parents, the man who shot him, good times and bad. I felt an all-encompassing love, passion, deep longing, and boundless joy.

I leaned into him, unwilling to break the connection. Power and magic flowed from me to him and back again. Then, in an instant, the thinking part of my brain flashed panic and I abruptly broke the kiss.

Afraid that I might have drained his energy, I asked, "Are you alright?"

Josh drew a ragged breath and leaned his forehead to mine. "What just happened?"

Panic rose higher. "I don't know," I admitted.

"I felt you. Everything about you. Your fears, your desire. I even got memories."

"It was the same for me, but I also felt a transfer of magic and power."

"Yeah, that was intense. How are you? I felt your power bleed into me. Did you lose more?"

"No. Yours flowed into me. I thought that I was draining you somehow without meaning to."

Josh paused for a moment and furrowed his brows as if taking inventory. "No, I'm good. Actually, better than good. I feel energized. Are you sure you didn't transfer your power to me?"

"No" I insisted shaking my head, "I am much better than I was. Much stronger, at least, than after the incident in the shower." I was deeply confused and more than a little scared. A transfer of information such as that should not be possible without casting powerful magic or sharing blood. I had not cast, and while Josh was sensitive to it, he could not cast. Neither had we shared blood. In truth, it had been the lightest of kisses that had unleashed this storm.

The phone rang, snapping me out of my thought train. Breaking contact with me, Josh picked up the phone and answered it. "I can't tonight, Toussaint. Sumthin's come up," he said.

Whatever the Sylph Coven leader said was disagreeable, and Josh frowned. I lightly touched his arm to gain his attention.

"Go," I mouthed, unwilling to verbalize, lest Toussaint hear me.

"Look, the soonest I can get there is in an hour," Josh said. He winced as he powered off the phone and placed it back on the nightstand. Turning back to me, Josh said, "I don't want to leave you alone. Not like this."

"I will be fine. I am feeling much better. I am more worried about you."

"I'll take one of the house guards with me. Don't worry." He took me by my shoulders. "No magic while I'm gone, ya hear?" he said firmly, looking me in the eye.

After what happened in the shower without casting, I was willing to accede to his wishes. While I needed to finish those amulets, they would simply have to wait. I could not afford another debacle such as last night.

"Go. I'll be fine and I promise, no magic tonight," I said.

Josh looked like he didn't believe me.

"Really," I promised.

He grumbled, but then dressed for the evening. I lay in bed and watched him. I was so lucky. I loved him, and he loved me. I allowed his fine physique to distract me for several minutes and temporarily ceased musing over my problems.

When Josh finished dressing, he returned to the bed and sat beside me. "Are you sure?"

"Go!" I said and pointed towards the door.

Josh sighed and kissed me gently. "I'll be back as soon as I can."

I smiled. "If you see Jaime, could you please send her in?"

Josh left, pulling the bedroom door shut behind him. I debated getting out of bed and dressing but decided to wait. A moment later, Jaime knocked on the door and let herself in.

Jaime sat down on the foot of the bed, "Are you okay?"

I nodded. "I am now, but we need to sort this out before it happens again."

"Alright." She looked thoughtful. "The first time this happened you were downstairs working on werewolf amulets, right?" Jaime asked.

"Yes." I began to relay what led to the previous night's episode. "I noticed the power drain as soon as I cast my circle. I could not spool my inborn magic, so I called magic to me. The first bit I used was much more powerful than it should have been, and the crystal exploded. I was very careful the next two times and completed the amulets for Nathalie and Beau. I had just started on the last amulet when my vision went, and my power drained to nothing."

"You were in a protective circle when the magic went wonky?" Jaime asked. I nodded. "How is that even possible?"

"Magic can always be miscast, circle or not."

"But this wasn't really a casting problem, was it?"

I knew what she was trying to say, but her logic was slightly off. "No but remember that circles just keep cast magic inside them and others' cast magic out. The essence of magic, the aether flows freely through the circle."

"So it couldn't have been an attack?"

"No," I said and stopped. "At least . . . not a direct one."

Jaime frowned. "What do you mean? Someone indirectly attacked you?"

"Honore and Louis left a hex bag in Marc's office. It made him irritable, caused him to make poor decisions and snap judgments. What if they left one for me as well?"

"One that drains your power instead of making you cranky?"

"Well, I would not say this one is not making me cranky, but I am fairly certain that we will not find nettles in it when we take it apart. We need to find that hex bag and destroy it."

"Where do we even start?" Jaime said looking around the room.

I had no idea. "It works best when in proximity to the victim, so we should search around here."

"How would they even know to leave it here? You moved in after the coup attempt."

"That assumes both bags were created and left at the same time. Remember, I was to have been one of their first sacrifices." Just prior to the coup attempt, Honore and her followers had ritually killed several people to summon a number of demons. Jaime had noticed something was off and stopped me from going into the house where the slaughter would take place.

Jaime countered, "I still feel like your house is a better bet, especially since it's unguarded. The distance might also explain the odd power drainage patterns."

I nodded in agreement, "My place is only four houses down the block. We will check both places, but there is something else that happened tonight. After I passed out in the shower and fed, there was a moment that Josh and I connected."

Jaime held up her hand to stop me. "Juliette, I really don't wanna hear about your sex life."

"This was not sex. At all. We were looking into each other's eyes, and he gave me a chaste kiss, but suddenly I got a flash of his memories and his feelings. It was as if we had shared blood, but we had not. He felt the same thing. There was a power transfer, too. At least mine regenerated. He said that he had no drain on his."

"Now that's some crazy shit right there. Are you sure the power drain and power transfer are connected?"

I shrugged. "What are the chances that these are two completely unrelated magical incidents?"

"In New Orleans? Completely possible," Jaime assured me. I was not convinced.

"All right, let me get dressed, and we will search for this hex bag," I said.

WE SCOURED Josh's house for the offending item, going room by room, drawer by drawer, my power and energy constantly draining. Exhausted, I collapsed on the sofa. This was what it was like to be human, and I hated it.

Jaime brought me a mug of warmed vitae before I even asked.

"Thank you," I said, gratefully taking it from her.

"If you give me the keys to your place, I'll go search over there."

I hated sending her alone, but I was too tired to accompany her. Moreover, Josh would have a conniption fit if I left the house.

"Take one of the guards with you," I urged.

That earned me an eye roll. "I can take care of myself," she huffed.

"Of that, I have no worry. It is just that is a big house, and two sets of eyes will see more than just yours," I reasoned.

This mollified her, but she still argued, "But he won't know what to look for, and it will actually take longer than if I go alone. Besides, Josh took one of the house guards with him, and if I take another, that only leaves you with three. Normally, I wouldn't be concerned but with you like this . . . ."

I relented. "Do me a favor and check the courtyard here before you go. The hex bag might actually be outside."

I was still reclined on the sofa when Josh returned an hour later. I had stirred enough to make myself another mug of warmed vitae and pick up my oldest grimoire, the one that had once been my grandmother's, it's familiar worn leather cover giving me comfort. The book contained not just spells but also her observances of magical rituals and stories now consigned to folklore. I diligently searched for any mention of odd energy and memory transfers, but to no avail.

"You're actually resting." Josh sounded surprised.

"I do occasionally do what is good for me," I said.

Josh harrumphed.

"How was your evening? Did you get everything done that you needed to get done? How are you feeling?" I asked in quick succession.

Josh sprawled on the couch next to me. "I missed you too, darlin'."

I playfully punched his shoulder. "Dratted man, you know that I missed you. Now, answer my questions."

"Alright, alright. First off, I feel fine. No weakness, lightheadedness, or loss of vampiric skills. I got all Toussaint's errands done and in much less time than I expected. Anne is far more organized than him and a lot easier to work with. She had actually taken care of most of it, so I was just support staff. Anne's gallery openin' is all set for next week. So, all in all, it wasn't a bad evening. Although I much would've preferred spendin' it with you," Josh said.

"You are sweet," I said as I snuggled against him.

"What about you? Did you rest?"

"Sort of . . ." I said.

"Juliette."

"Jaime and I thought we figured out what was causing my weakness," I explained.

"What?" He was suddenly very interested.

"A hex bag, like the one that Louis left in Marc's office."

Josh jumped off the sofa, dislodging me from my comfortable position. "We gotta find it!" He looked frantically around the room.

"Jaime and I have already searched this house. We did not find it. I'm afraid we were very nosy. Normally, I would've waited, but I believed that time was of the essence."

"That's not a problem. I don't have any secrets from you. Although . . . ."

"Yes, Jaime found your porn stash," I said.

"Well, that's kind of embarrassing," he said sheepishly. "Uh . . . she find anything else?" He added hesitantly.

"No. I was the one who found your sex toys," I assured him.

"Um, Juliette, how do you know what sex toys are?"

I smiled. "The addition of batteries is brilliant, but other than that they have changed little in three hundred years."

Josh's mouth dropped open.

"Have I shocked you?"

"But, but you're a lady," he sputtered.

I thought about further scandalizing him by laying my knowledge at my sire's feet or some other sundry anatomical parts but decided to be kind and tell the truth. "You know that I was a healer in my human life, and sometimes as part of my duties I would see to the girls working in the brothels. They gave me quite an education."

"Seriously?"

"Oh, yes. Some of the girls didn't have money to pay with, so they imparted knowledge instead."

Josh grinned, "I wondered where you learned some of those tricks."

I laughed. "Anyway, back to the hex bag. We did not find it here, so I sent Jaime to my house to look for it."

"Alone?" He asked.

"I tried to send a guard, but she said a non-magical guard wouldn't know what to look for, and I had to agree," I admitted.

"Well, I do know what I'm looking for, so why don't I mosey on over there and give her a hand?"

"Would you? Thank you. I wanted to go, but just didn't have the energy."

Josh looked at me seriously. "We need to find that thing and quick," he said, and I didn't argue.

I AWOKE the next night in our bed with no memory of how I'd gotten there. Josh was already up, dressed, and pacing the room.

"What has happened?" I asked groggily.

"You wouldn't wake up, and it's after ten already."

I blinked and tried to clear my head. I felt mussy and sick. "You did not find the hex bag, did you?" I asked unnecessarily. I would not feel this bad if they had found the bag and destroyed it.

"Let me get you something," Josh said and hurried from the room to warm me some vitae.

I struggled to sit up, weak as a newborn kitten. I hated this. Josh found me expending what little energy I had crying out my fear and frustration.

Setting the mug on the nightstand, Josh gathered me in his arms. "Shh, shh. It'll be alright," he cooed as he gently rocked me. My tears eventually subsided, not because I felt better but out of exhaustion.

"I am sorry," I apologized.

"None of that. Here, drink this before it gets cold," Josh said as he handed me the mug. I gulped it, and he went to get me another.

After the second mug, I felt better, but by no means restored. I was fading fast and feared that if the hex bag was not found soon, I would slip back into a torpor state. I had spent two centuries in that stake-induced state, able to hear, but not see or communicate. I desperately did not want to return there. I did not think my sanity would hold if I did.

"Let's try to re-juice your power and energy like we did yesterday," Josh suggested.

"No. We do not know what that does to you," I protested.

"Darlin', it didn't do anything to me. I was thinking about it earlier and figured it was like jump-startin' the car. Jumper cables from my battery to yours."

I had no idea what he was talking about and told him so.

"Do you trust me?" Josh asked.

"I do," I assured him.

"Then let me do this," he said, cupping my face in his hands and looking deep in my eyes. I think the energy transfer began even before he kissed me this time. A warmth suffused my body while magic and energy cracked through each of my cells. When he broke contact, I felt energized and invigorated.

"No ill effect?" I asked.

He kissed me again. "Nope," he promised. "I'm gonna head back over to your place and help Jaime look for this thing again. Have you got any sort of amulet or charm that can counteract this hex?"

"I found a reference to a protection amulet in my grandmother's grimoire yesterday. I will go downstairs and make it."

"Is that wise?" He asked.

I shrugged. "Will making the amulet drain more energy than it prevents being leeched from me? I have no idea, but it is better than sitting here becoming weaker by the minute."

"Be careful," he said before cupping my face and kissing me gently. "We'll be back as soon as we can."

After Josh left, I quickly dressed, collected my grimoire and several bottles of blood, then went downstairs to the ritual room. As I gathered the ingredients needed to make the protection amulet, I very briefly considered taking the ingredients for the werewolf pendants as well but knew better than to push my luck. Making the single protection amulet would be taxing enough in my condition. With a bit of trepidation, I stepped into the circle I drew two nights ago, closed it, and invoked it. Nothing unusual happened. I felt no discernible power drain. Certainly, nothing like I had experienced the last time I'd been here.

Taking my time, I created the protection amulet following the instructions in my grandmother's grimoire. I had chosen red jasper, a stone renowned for its protective properties. I further enhanced these protective attributes with spell-work stopping numerous times to gauge my power levels but continuing when I found them to be fine.

As soon as I finished, I invoked the amulet and put it on. I immediately felt better although I wondered if it was simply a case of putting my mind at ease rather than any real spell effect so quickly.

I felt the first signs of fatigue as I dropped my protective circle, so I gulped a bottle of vitae. It was lukewarm and tasted disgusting but immediately revitalized me. Taking the amulets, I went back upstairs, hoping to hear good news from Jaime and Josh, but they were not back yet. I settled on the sofa to wait for them.

CHAPTER 9

I managed to craft Gaetan's amulet the next night without incident as well as charge Nathalie and Beau's. Josh had already called the werewolf alpha to change our meeting day. As anxious as he was to move my bodyguards into the house, it simply could not be done until the amulets were complete. I had been resistant to hiring guards, but after the strain of the last few days, even I could not wait for their arrival. Finally with everything done, Josh and I arranged to meet Beau and several other members of the pack at a drive-thru daiquiri stand close to the city two days later than originally planned.

"Do you think it's safe for you to be going?" Josh asked before we left the house. "What if you have another episode?"

I had woken up from my daytime slumber more or less at my regular time and feeling more or less as I normally do. The amulet seemed to be working, and I was anxious to get things back to normal.

I had considered this, "I should be safe since we are leaving the city. It should take us further from the hex bag and lessen its effects. Besides, you will be with me if anything happens."

"I can go alone," Josh insisted.

"And if there is a problem with the amulets?" I asked.

"Do you think there will be?"

"No. I am confident that they are properly crafted and will work." And I was. I had felt the magic course through me and take hold of each piece of jewelry.

"Then you don't need to come along," Josh said firmly crossing his arms.

"I need hair samples to make the amulets for the house guards." I picked up my purse. "I am coming with you."

Josh sighed and fished his car keys out of his jeans pocket.

When we arrived, Gaetan and Nathalie sat together in a smart, red convertible, Nathalie in the driver's seat. Beau and several other pack members that I didn't know were in a large, black Suburban. Everyone seemed to be in high spirits.

Beau made introductions in the parking lot while Nathalie went to get drinks for Josh and me. The four men and one woman that Beau had brought along with him would form the cadre of our house guards if we approved them. Josh had met them all before, and since I had no objections, it was decided. I took hair samples from all the werewolves, putting them in carefully labeled vials, and hoped that I wouldn't have any difficulties making this set of amulets. Even this far out of the city and with the protection amulet on, I started feeling drained. This worried me. This far from the city, the hex bag should have little effect. I quietly mentioned it to Josh before I gave Beau, Nathalie, and Gaetan their amulets. Worry creased his normally happy face as he hurried us to our cars.

"I thought you said you'd be fine outside of the city?" he snapped, worry making him angry.

"I should have been!" I insisted throwing up my hands in exasperation. "I feel fine now."

"This doesn't make any sense."

"No, Josh, it does not," I sighed wearily.

Nathalie and Gaetan followed us home, and while I'd had a moment of unease, second guessing my magic, they had no problems passing through the wards at the city's perimeter. The real test would come when they tried to shift into their werewolf forms, but I could deal with any problems at home—or at least I hoped I could.

We showed the pair their quarters in the old carriage house and let them settle in. Servants had once lived on the upper floor, and with minor renovations, it would serve as a bunkhouse for our guards. There was one bathroom for Nathalie and Gaetan to share for the moment, but three more and a state-of-the-art kitchen were due to be installed in the coming weeks. Josh seemed to know everyone in the city, and most seemed to owe him favors. This worked to our advantage to get things done quickly.

Jaime was waiting for Josh and me in the living room.

"Did you find out anything?" I asked as I sat in one of the club chairs. Before leaving to pick up my guards, I asked Jaime to discreetly check the Gatekeepers' files to see if there was an explanation for the odd power and energy transfer that occurred between Josh and me.

"Nothing that's gonna help. Unless Josh here is a closet thaumaturge," Jaime said gesturing to him.

Josh and I exchanged a look. Josh wasn't a thaumaturge, but his paternal grandmother had been, and she'd gifted him with magical sensitivity. Perhaps there was something in the bloodline.

"Just tell us what you found," I said, not willing to give up Josh's secrets even to my childe.

"I found a couple references to Thaumaturges sharing energy in our files. These were pretty old accounts, and they typically occurred between family members," Jaime explained as she sat forward in her seat.

"At least we know it ain't unprecedented," Josh said.

"You two ain't kin, are ya?" Jaime drawled jokingly.

I laughed. "Highly doubtful. Although I'm sure that your extensive files on me would be a better source."

She shrugged. "I looked," she admitted "but didn't find any blood connection. Most of your family died in the French and Haitian Revolutions." Frowning she said, "These energy and power transfers shouldn't be happening between you two."

"The files didn't say anything else?" Josh asked.

Jaime shook her head. "Not really. Remember that Gatekeepers observe and only step in when necessary."

"Well, y'all have managed to fly under the radar until now," Josh said.

Jaime winced. "Yeah, well, I probably would've gotten tossed out of the Order for breaking protocol even if Juliette hadn't turned me into a vampire. There are a whole bunch of Masters in other Chapter houses that are pretty pissed that I let the cat out of the bag on our existence."

"I hope that we have ushered in a new era of cooperation between our groups now that we know about one another," I said.

"We have a veritable supernatural United Nations right here in this house," Josh quipped.

"So the werewolves didn't have any problems getting through the wards?" Jaime asked changing the subject.

"The amulets seemed to work just fine although neither has tried to shift yet," I said.

"Are you worried?" Josh asked.

"Not really," I said. "Normally, it wouldn't even be a question, but those magic fluctuations do concern me."

"I got faith in your magic even if you don't," Josh said, but was stopped from further comment by the arrival of Nathalie and Gaetan.

I looked up, surprised. "Unpacked already?"

Nathalie shrugged. "I pack light."

Gaetan chortled. "What she means is that the trunk of her tiny car wouldn't hold more than one of her bags along with my rucksack."

Nathalie shot her cousin a dark look. "That damn pack took up the entire trunk. It's big enough to carry a body!"

"Kinda the point. I promise to bring back all of your bags when I take the amulets back to the pack and pick up my Jeep," Gaetan said sweetly.

Nathalie rolled her eyes. "You're lucky I'm low maintenance."

"You've got more shoes than Imelda Marcos," Gaetan ribbed.

Josh laughed. "I'd think you two were brother and sister with the way y'all bicker."

"He's kind of a stand in for my two brothers, to keep me sharp," Nathalie said dryly.

"Let's show you two around and introduce you to the house guards. Some are human by the way." Josh said.

"Are they 'in the know'?" Gaetan inquired.

"Yeah, they're all human servants of mine. They're up on the recent disturbances in the city. Not fair to employ them without letting them know the score," Josh said.

Gaetan nodded. "You said there was third vamp in the house?"

"Yes. Juliette's childe, Jaime, lives here as well."

On cue, Jaime uncurled from the couch and extended her hand. "Jaime Sprenger, Aether lieutenant." Jaime barely came to Gaetan's shoulder, and her hand was tiny in his large paw.

Jaime and Nathalie regarded one another warily but must have decided that the other would do because they also shook hands. I breathed a silent sigh of relief. It had not occurred to me that Jaime might clash with my guards. From the look on Josh's face, it wasn't a possibility that he had considered either.

"Let's show y'all around," Josh said.

LATER, after familiarizing Nathalie and Gaetan with the house and grounds and making the proper introductions, we sat them down and explained why we had been unable to bring them into the city when originally planned. Both were alarmed about the hex bag and eager to help. All five of us searched both houses again but still found nothing.

"Josh, can't you sense it, like you did at Gautier House?" Jaime asked.

"Even when I open myself and actively search for it, I detect nothing malevolent in either house," Josh explained. "Could you be wrong about it being a hex bag?"

"I don't think so," I said. "As soon as I started wearing the protection amulet, the energy drain diminished."

"So it hasn't totally stopped?" Josh demanded.

"No, but it is minuscule. I started to feel drained when we were at the daiquiri stand but once we were in the car, it stopped. When we got home, it started again but it is—I'm not sure how to explain it—like a drip every now and again instead of a constant stream."

"We gotta find that bag." Josh ran his hand through his hair in irritation.

"Okay, so if the hex bag isn't in either house, where is it?" Jaime asked.

"The caster might still have it," I said.

"Well, shit. We might not get it then. Nobody has found Honore's hidey-hole," Josh said pacing back and forth.

"So we stop looking?" Jaime asked.

I thought for a moment. "No. While we know that it is not in either house, the grounds and outbuildings have not yet been systematically searched."

"You're right. I only did a quick search of the courtyard before heading over to your house, and I didn't go into the carriage house at all," Jaime said.

"That needs to be our next area of concentration," I said.

"There isn't enough time to do it before dawn. It'll have to wait until tonight."

Nathalie looked at Gaetan and said, "We don't have daylight prohibitions. We can keep searching."

I thought about it but shook my head. "I think I would rather you both be well rested at sundown. We will resume then."

"If you're sure."

"I am." I was not sure what nightfall would bring, but I knew I wanted my guards at their best.

THE NEXT EVENING, I rolled over when I woke to find a steaming cup of coffee on my bedside table. Josh spoiled me, and I loved it. I pulled myself into a sitting position and reached for the mug. I did not hear the shower, but I knew that Josh was not far.

He returned to the bedroom a few minutes later, looking pensive.

"What is wrong?" I asked as he perched on the side of the bed.

"There's a problem at the new club. We've been hit with a stop work order. I gotta go take care of this," he apologized.

"So go," I said, not seeing the problem.

"We haven't found that hex bag yet. We're supposed to search the yard tonight." Worry once again etched his handsome face.

I reached up and caressed his cheek. Smiling, I said. "Jaime, Nathalie, Gaetan, and I can search. It will be a chance to see if the werewolves are attuned to that kind of magic and see what kind of vampire abilities Jaime is manifesting."

"I hate leaving you alone," Josh said raking his hand through his hair.

"I will hardly be alone. You need to take care of this. The opening of Chintz has already been pushed back once. You can help search when you get back."

"Are you sure?" He looked me straight in the eye.

"Yes." I met his gaze and put my hands over his.

"I should be back by two." He kissed me passionately and disappeared out the door.

After Josh left, I rose and showered quickly, then went to the kitchen and found Jaime, Gaetan, and Nathalie sitting around the sturdy oblong table. Jaime stared longingly at Gaetan as he worked through a series of cheeseburgers. I was not at all sure if the longing was for the sandwiches or for the handsome werewolf who ate them. I would need to inquire tactfully later in order to head off any possible complications. Nathalie took notes on a yellow legal pad and occasionally stole a fry from the mound in front of Gaetan.

Jaime looked up as I entered the room and retrieved a bottle of blood from the refrigerator, "Morning, Juliette. What's on the agenda since Josh ain't here?"

Dropping the bottle in the warmer, I replied, "The agenda has not changed. We will search the courtyard and carriage house here, and if we find nothing, then we will go to my house and search that courtyard."

"But without Josh . . ." Jaime began, but I cut her off.

"Josh would be of minimal help when we search outside other than another set of eyes. There is too much ambient magic in New Orleans for him to notice anything specific until he is right on top of it—unless it is very strong."

"It's certainly that way with us," Nathalie chimed in as she filched another fry. "There's just way too much aether floating around the city."

"That makes sense. I feel magic all the time now when I'm outside," Jaime said.

"You did not before?" I asked.

"Not like this. I needed to be on a ley line or near something magical. Now, it's like I'm constantly being bombarded," Jaime replied.

"Before what?" Gaetan asked around his burger.

"Before I became a vampire," Jaime said, staring hard at the mound of French fries.

Noticing her longing gaze, Gaetan motioned to his fries and said, "Help yourself. I got extra 'cause I knew that Nat would steal a bunch."

Nathalie made a face at him and asked, "Is you being a vampire a new thing then? I'd assumed you'd been one for a while."

"If, for a while, you mean a week, then, yeah, I've been fanged for a while." Turning her attention back to the fries, Jaime said sadly, "I don't think I can eat anymore."

"Have you tried?" I asked gently. "While I cannot eat solids, my sire could. There is a chance that you might as well." Guilt pricked at my conscience. I should have told her this earlier.

"I upchucked everything I ate for the first three days after the coup."

"That is normal. As your body transforms, it rejects everything but blood. Even those who eventually develop the ability to eat or drink human food cannot do so during that early stage. I am sorry, I should have explained all this to you. I have been a terrible sire," I said.

"Well, it isn't like there is a ton of other shit going on right now."

"I need to do better," I said, unwilling to give myself a pass on my responsibility even if there were many other things happening. "And that begins now. Let us see if you can eat."

"Just eat anything?" Jaime asked.

"It is probably best to start with something you enjoyed eating as a human," I suggested.

"That's pretty much potato anything or any way," Jaime said, pulling a thick fry from the stack. She regarded the golden exterior for a long moment before taking a bite. She savored the taste for a moment and then swallowed. When nothing bad happened, Jaime took a second bite and then a third. She grinned as she reached for a second fry. That was when it happened. Jaime turned green and fled from the table.

"Damn," I said and followed my childe to the bathroom.

I found Jaime retching over the toilet bowl. I gathered her long, deep red hair back and held her forehead as she expelled the contents of her stomach, including the vitae she had consumed after rising this evening. When she was done, she sat back on her heels.

"I guess eating is off the table." Her eyes glistened with blood-stained tears although I was unsure if the cause was vomiting or sadness. She closed her eyes and took a deep breath. "I was really hoping." Her voice quavered and tears escaped her closed lids.

I took her into my arms and rocked her as she cried. I did not hush her but just let the wracking sobs consume her, knowing this was the release she needed. Jaime kept a tight lid on her emotions and had not yet mourned her loss of humanity. All vampires, even those who welcomed the change, did so eventually. For me, it was the reality of never having sunlight on my face again, and it'd taken me several weeks to feel the loss. Then again, I had chosen my fate. It made sense that Jaime would take this harder.

We sat on the tile floor for a long time. Eventually, Jaime's sobs subsided, and she swiped angrily at her eyes, embarrassed for having broken down.

"There is no shame in mourning what you have lost," I said. "Especially since you did not choose this life. Why don't you wash your face and brush your teeth and join us in the kitchen when you are ready?"

I left Jaime to gather herself and returned to Nathalie and Gaetan. They had cleared the food away from the table and were talking quietly.

"How is she?" Nathalie asked.

I shrugged. "It is an adjustment."

"Tough break, not being able to eat," Gaetan said.

I agreed and changed the subject. "How attuned to magic are werewolves?" Not only did I need to gauge my childe's abilities, but I also needed to know what my guards were capable of.

Nathalie said, "It depends on the wolf. Most of us have some ability to detect it."

When she did not elaborate, I prompted, "And you?"

Nathalie looked distinctly uncomfortable. "Before, I would've said I was fairly attuned. Not quite like Uncle Josh, but I could generally pick up on magic items or magic users. Now, I can't always detect magic. I don't know if it's the wards, the amulet, or something else."

"What do you mean?" I asked.

"Well, you're a void. Something should be there but isn't. I know you're in the kitchen right now because I can see you, but I can't sense you. Not like I can sense Jaime and Gaetan."

"So you cannot tell that I'm a vampire?"

"No. Nothing. It's like you are not here at all."

"I get the same void from you if that helps," Gaetan said.

"Do I feel the same way to you?" I asked Jaime as she rejoined the group.

My childe shook her head. "No, I don't get an energy aura off of you or any magic, but I can definitely tell you are a vampire."

I frowned, confused. Why could Jaime sense me, but not the werewolves? Maybe something to do with my shielding? I decided to find out. Saying nothing, I dropped my shields.

"You are there now, but faintly. Kinda like a shadow," Nathalie said.

I reached up and unclasped the protective amulet around my neck causing both Nathalie and Gaetan to visibly flinch in their seats.

"Shit. I don't know what you did, but boy, I can sense you now. In a big way!" Gaetan said.

"Can you tell that I'm a vampire?"

"Loud and clear. Magic is radiating off of you, too," Nathalie said.

I raised my shields again. "How about now?"

Both werewolves regarded me for several seconds. After exchanging glances, Gaetan said, "Well, you're there now and registering as a vampire, but I'm not reading any magic at all. What about you, Nat?"

"The same," she confirmed.

I quickly re-clasped the necklace. The amulet worked by masking both my presence and my magic so the hex bag couldn't find me and siphon my power. Just shielding my power was ineffective since whoever had created the hex had likely included something personal of mine into it—probably some hair.

"Alright, so you cannot sense me at all when I am wearing the amulet and shielding, but when I am just shielding, you can," I said.

"Dammit, I owe Michael fifty bucks," Nathalie swore slapping the table.

Confused by the non sequitur, I asked, "What?"

Gaetan leaned back in his chair and laughed. "I told you not to take that bet."

Nathalie explained. "Michael came home from that meeting with you, Uncle Josh, and Marc Gautier talking about how overpowering you were, and I thought he was just full of shit. So he bet me fifty bucks."

I nodded, remembering the younger of Beau Roulet's two sons. I could easily see how Nathalie might interpret his version of my power as an exaggeration.

"So my magic detection hasn't gone wonky," Nathalie said.

"I don't think so." I said, "There is not any reason that the amulet I gave you should interfere with any of your abilities. If you think that it does, please let me know. I will remake it."

"Oh, okay," Nathalie said.

"That goes for you as well, Gaetan. If you think any of your senses have been hampered, let me know right away. I have not had time to make more protection amulets, but it is on my to-do list right after we find this hex bag that is causing me so many problems," I said.

"That amulet you made is wicked powerful. Can you teach me how to make them?" Jaime asked.

"I plan to." I smiled.

"Cool. What's next?"

"I think we should start our search. Perhaps with the carriage house? I hate to invade your privacy, so you can search your own rooms. You obviously don't need to go through the things you brought with you, but check under the beds, behind the furniture, under the drawers, that sort of thing. Jaime and I will concentrate on the common areas. Neither of you have sensed anything, have you?" I asked.

"I thought I felt something earlier this afternoon in the carriage house, but when I checked downstairs, I couldn't feel it anymore," Gaetan said.

"We will check the garage carefully then." I said.

Unfortunately, we did not get the chance. Before I had even taken a step in the direction of the carriage house, my phone buzzed. I looked at the number and winced. Detective Angelletti never called with good news.

"Detective Angelletti, what can I help you with this evening?" I asked.

"We have another murder scene, this time in the Faubourg. Can you come?"

I inwardly groaned. With everything else going on, I had hardly given the first set of murders a second thought. Now there was another. Resigned, I said, "Of course, just give me the address."

CHAPTER 10

I gave Nathalie the address, and we all squeezed into her tiny sports car.

"We're gonna need my Jeep sooner rather than later," Gaetan grumbled. "There's not enough room in this matchbox car."

"Have you got a four-door Jeep or something because otherwise I'm not seeing it being any bigger than this car," Jaime said as she squirmed to find a comfortable position in the back seat, elbowing me in the process.

"Yeah, it's a hardtop Sahara. It's got a lot more room than this," Gaetan said turning his head to look at us.

"Yes, but this is much easier to maneuver in the city. That's why we brought my car in the first place," Nathalie said as she deftly wove the car through the narrow French Quarter streets.

"I didn't think we'd be cramming four people in here though," Gaetan grumbled.

"Quit your bitchin'. You have plenty of room up here in the front," Nathalie told him. "How you guys back there?"

Jaime and I were very snugly ensconced in the back seat.

"Sardine like, but it's a short trip. No worries," Jaime said.

The address the detective had given me was a nondescript, white shotgun house. The front door opened before Nathalie even knocked, and I was mildly surprised when we were quickly ushered inside by Vinny Carlucci, the Salamand lieutenant.

"Glad to see you took my advice and got some guards," he said by way of greeting. "Werewolves. Bold choice," he added approvingly.

"Thank you, Monsieur Carlucci."

"Body is just up the stairs, first door on the left. Mistress St. Pierre and Detective Angelletti are already up there."

Nathalie nodded and led the way. I followed next, with Jaime behind me and Gaetan last. I felt a bit foolish about this entourage but reasoned it was easier than arguing with Josh and Marc all the time about my safety. And to be fair, with my magic fluctuating, it gave me some peace of mind.

Just before mounting the stairs, Nathalie asked in a low voice, "Mistress St. Pierre is the Undine Mistress, correct?" I nodded. Both she and Gaetan had been fully briefed by Josh about all the important New Orleans vampires, but it was a rapidly shifting field that even I had a hard time keeping track of.

"Why is she here?" Jaime asked and quickly puzzled it out for herself before I could reply. "Duh," she said smacking her forehead, "One of the victims was an Undine. Sorry, brain hiccup."

"No harm in that," I assured her. "I want you to ask questions if something isn't clear. That goes for all of you. We need to work together if we are going to catch this killer."

Nathalie paused just outside the door at the top of the steps next to one of Collette's guards, giving the interior of the room a sweeping glance, and then stepped aside to let me in. Mike Angelletti, Collette St. Pierre, and another man—probably one of her bodyguards—stood outside a blood pentagram containing another flayed body.

"Mistress St. Pierre," I said, entering the room. Again, the wave of malevolence I had felt at the first scene washed over me and goosebumps rose on my skin. Pushing the feelings back, I bowed slightly to the Undine mistress. We held the same rank as heads of covens, but there was still protocol to be observed.

"Mistress Grammont." Collette returned a slightly deeper bow which surprised me. She was a tall, pale woman made taller by four-inch stilettos. Her green eyes glistened with blood-tinged tears. The previous month had been difficult for Collette and the entire Undine coven. One member had been killed by a demon outside an art gallery, and several more had perished defending Marc Gautier against the Aether led coup several nights ago. The Undines were not a large coven to start with, and this new set of killings had further depleted not just the coven itself but also a prospective member.

I walked to Collette. "I am so sorry," I said, taking her hands in mine. "What can you tell me?"

"The human victim is Anthony Howell—Tony. He was dating one of my fledglings, Catherine Day. This is her house. I hadn't heard from Catherine in several days, and I was worried because she wasn't returning my calls, so I stopped by. Even after hearing about what happened to the Sylph fledgling and his lover, I did not expect to find this."

I nodded releasing her hands, "This looks very similar to the first murder scene."

Again, there were gutted candles set at cardinal points around the bed. A throw rug had been pushed to the side and bare hardwood exposed. The killer had drawn the pentagram in blood there but not nearly as elaborate and much messier.

"When I called Detective Angelletti, he told me that you thought a magic user controlled the Sylph vampire's mind and made him kill his lover and then himself. He suggested that we call you," Collette said.

"I am unsure of the protocol here," I confessed. The first set of murders, although it had claimed a vampire, had taken place in the human victim's home. This one had occurred in a vampire sanctuary. I was unsure how much the Undine mistress wanted me or would allow me to do.

"I don't think we have a protocol for this," Colette acknowledged. "I mean yes, we do have protocols if a vampire is killed in his sanctuary, with or without other victims. That is why Detective Angelletti is here, but those protocols assume the murder was committed by a

Hunter." Collette looked around the room. "This was not a Hunter, at least not a regular Hunter. Your expertise is both needed and wanted."

I nodded, "This does seem to be uncharted territory. Do you mind if one of my guards and my lieutenant join me while I examine the body and ash? Jaime knows what to do if I have problems pulling out of a vision, and Nathalie knows crime scene investigation."

"Of course. Whatever you need."

"The Master Gatekeeper, Nicholas Remy, also asked to be called if another murder occurred so he could examine the scene," I said.

"Why would the Master Gatekeeper care?" Collette's eyes narrowed suspiciously.

I explained quickly, "I think the murderer is using necromancy to control his victims, but I have never actually dealt with necromancy. I do not know what it feels like. Master Remy has and can confirm it," I explained.

"Necromancy?" Suspicion was replaced by alarm. "By all means, please call the Master Gatekeeper."

"I will be just a minute," I said and stepped back into the hallway where Nathalie, Gaetan, and Jaime waited with Collette's guard.

I issued orders quickly and succinctly. "Jaime, would you please call Master Remy and tell him we have another set of murders. See if he can come. Mistress St. Pierre has given permission for him to view the scene. Gaetan, if Master Remy can come, please let Monsieur Carlucci at the front door know to expect him. Nathalie, you come with me. Jaime, when you have finished your call, please join us."

"After I let Mr. Carlucci know, where do you want me?" Gaetan asked.

"Just wait outside the door here. The room will be too crowded otherwise," I said.

Gaetan nodded, and I returned to the bedroom with Nathalie in tow. Collette and Mike were in deep conversation by the body and did not seem to notice our entry. Her guard had taken a position along the room's periphery.

I did a quick magical sweep of the room, looking for traps or other hazards but did not find any. I found no magic at all. Again, all the magic that should have been teeming through the room had been sucked out.

Nathalie shivered next to me. "Are you alright? Do you feel something magic?" I asked her. Just because I could not sense it, did not mean Nathalie could not. Werewolves felt magic differently than mages did, and she might well perceive something that I could not.

Nathalie shook her head and shivered slightly before crossing her arms over her chest. "Not magic, just evil, and for a second, icy cold. The cold is gone now. The evil isn't."

I frowned, not knowing what to make of that. "Make sure to tell that to Nicholas—Master Remy—when he arrives," I instructed her.

"What do you need me to do now?" she asked.

"Just observe for the moment," I said.

By then the Undine mistress and the detective had finished their conversation and moved to join me.

"Do you wish us to leave the room while you examine it?" Collette asked.

"I have no issue with either of you remaining; however, if you wish to step out for whatever reason, that is fine as well. It can take several minutes for me to complete a reading, so there isn't much to see," I said.

Collette nodded. Before she could say anything else, Jaime hurried in from the hallway.

"Master Remy is on his way," she announced. I made note that later I would need to remind her not to interrupt conversations. Catching sight of the body on the floor, Jaime blurted out in sudden horror, "Good God, what happened to him?"

"Flayed. Just like the first human victim," I answered.

"Alive?" The revulsion evident in her voice.

"Probably. I will need to read the body and blood to make sure."

"Are you . . ." Jaime stopped the question as if suddenly realizing we were not alone. "Is that wise at this moment?" she said instead.

"I brought extra blood, just in case," I said. I had slid two bottles of blood into my purse on the way out of the house. I hoped I would not need them, but it was better to be safe than sorry.

"You are going to read the blood?" Collette's eyes widened. "Frederique always said it was too dangerous and refused to do it. She would touch objects, but never dead people or blood."

I responded, "It is dangerous, but we seem to have a serial killer ritually murdering people. The danger to our community outweighs any personal danger to me. Although that is why I want Jaime in the room while I read. If I become trapped in a memory, she can pull me out," I explained.

Jaime looked like she wanted to argue but wisely held her tongue. I thought about waiting until Nicholas Remy arrived; however, I did not want another discussion about the danger of what I was about to do. I walked to the blood circle and sat next to it. Before I started, I pulled one bottle of blood from my purse and sat it next to me.

"Now or never," I thought to myself before I ran my index finger through the blood and touched it to my tongue. Instantly, I was in Catherine Day's head, but I was not alone. The murderer, the Other, was there as well. I felt his cold presence here, the same as in Eddie Sykes' mind. However, the Other's control over Catherine was not as complete as it had been over the Sylph fledgling. This Undine was trained to resist mind control. The Other managed to get the vampire to slit her wrists but controlling her enough to draw the blood circle was difficult, making this blood circle was much sloppier than the first, and the Other had to go back and redo parts as Catherine would regain momentary control and jerk away.

The Other's patience had worn thin even before the circle was complete. He seethed with frustration. The battle going on for control in the vampire's head was fierce. Eventually though, the Other managed to complete the circle, and the vision faded. I sat with my eyes closed for a minute or two trying to regroup my thoughts.

"This set of murders did not go as planned," I told the group when I opened my eyes. I took a breath, "Catherine Day might have been a fledgling, but she was very strong willed. She nearly foiled the ritual."

"So she was being controlled by the magic-user?" Collette asked.

"Not very well, but yes. There was definitely the presence of another in Catherine's mind, but she knew it, and she nearly forced him out several times," I said.

"I am not surprised," said Collette. "Catherine was a CIA operative until six months ago. They trained her to withstand manipulation and mind control."

"How long had she been a vampire?" I asked.

"Less than a month. She was diagnosed with an aggressive form of cancer just before she left the CIA. In fact, that was why she quit. I had worked with her grandfather during World War II, and he asked if I could help—if I could turn her. Now I have to tell him she is dead." Collette added sadly, "She would have been a tremendous asset to the coven."

"Yes, I believe she would have been," I agreed.

"This circle looks like a two-year-old drew it. Wasn't the other one much neater?" Jaime noted.

"The previous circle was nearly perfect. The Sylph was not strong-willed at all. What happened here was quite different," I said.

I examined the circle more closely now, rather than giving it just the cursory glance I initially had. Jaime was correct. This circle was so poorly drawn that I was surprised it could be invoked. As much as I didn't wish to, I looked more closely at the body as well. The skin on the first victim had been peeled off in long, precise layers. Large gouges marred Tony's body especially near veins and arteries. These may have been deliberate, Catherine trying to slice deep to end Tony's pain. Deep sadness washed over me.

"Master Remy should be here soon. Maybe you should wait to do your next reading until he gets here," Jaime suggested gently.

I nodded, thankful for the break. The reading had drained me more than it should have, but not dangerously so. Spacing out the readings and feeding in between should help. I reached down and uncapped the bottle I had earlier sat beside me. I drank it cold. It was nasty and slightly congealed, but it did the trick, and I was feeling much better by the end of the bottle.

"Is Catherine's dust on the bed, Jaime?" I asked. The bed was where we had found the first vampire victim's remains.

"No. It doesn't look like the killer made it that far this time. The pile of dust is on the floor over here by the dresser," she dutifully reported. "I think she tried to write something on the top of the dresser," she said examining it closely.

I stood and joined Jaime by the large, white, distressed dresser. Scrawled on the top in red lipstick were the letters D and I. "Do you think Catherine or the killer left this?" Jaime asked.

"I would say Catherine. Does this mean anything to you?" I asked the Undine mistress. She shook her head.

"Are you sure the killer didn't leave it?" Jaime asked.

"I do not think so. The killer did not leave a message at the last scene. Why would he start now?" I answered.

"To taunt us?" Detective Angelletti offered. "Maybe there was supposed to be an E on the end of it?"

"Why not finish the message, then?" I countered.

"He was having trouble controlling the victim. Maybe halfway through the message she reasserted herself, and he couldn't finish," Jaime reasoned.

I did not think Jaime was correct, but she was thinking and reasoning, so I did not wish to discourage her. "I will see what the dust tells me once Master Remy arrives," I said.

I had expected to wait a while for the Master Gatekeeper to reach the crime scene, but within another five minutes, he arrived. Taking a two-minute phone call was one thing but dropping everything to head across town was quite another.

I stepped forward to meet Nicholas as he entered the room. His normally crisply pressed, black cassock was rumpled and unkempt, and his eyes had a dull sheen to them as if the events of the past week had aged him immeasurably. Perhaps they had. Mages had longer life spans than regular humans, and many extended that even further with magic. Master Remy could be the sixty years that he looked, or he could be three hundred sixty. I would put money on the latter figure.

"Master Remy, thank you for coming on such short notice," I said after making a slight bow.

"Of course. Anyway I can be of assistance," Master Remy assured me.

Jaime, Collette, and Mike had joined us, and I waived Nathalie over, quickly making the necessary introductions. Collette had met Nicholas in the aftermath of the coup attempt, but he did not know Mike Angelletti or Nathalie.

When the introductions were complete, Nicholas asked, "What do we know about what happened here?"

I laid out what we knew, "The set-up is similar to the first crime scene. The bed is set for sex magic, and then there is an area set for black magic. As with the first set of murders, it was a vampire/human couple, although the genders are reversed. This time the vampire, Catherine Day, was female and the human, Tony Howell, was male," I said.

"Same coven as before?"

I shook my head. "The first vampire was a Sylph; this one was an Undine."

Nicholas looked at Collette and bowed slightly. "My condolences on your loss, Mistress St. Pierre."

The Undine mistress nodded. "Thank you."

I continued, "The killer had a lot of trouble controlling this victim. Mistress St. Pierre said Catherine Day was a CIA operative and trained to resist mind-control," to which Nicholas nodded but added nothing more.

"I was about to read the body unless you want to do something first?" I said.

Nicholas raised an eyebrow at the mention of my reading the body, but he did not comment on it or try to dissuade me. "This is your crime scene. I am just an observer," he said.

I knelt next to the flayed body, careful not to touch the blood circle, and placed my left hand on Tony Howell's forehead. Opening my third eye, I saw events through his eyes. The panic I felt from him was tight and controlled, nothing like the unbridled terror that had coursed through Gina Breslin's body. The pain as Catherine but not Catherine flayed chunks of his skin was excruciating, but Tony remained clear headed trying to formulate an escape plan. He knew it was not Catherine doing this, that she was not in control of her own body, and Tony remained convinced until the last that Catherine would retake her body. Unlike with Gina, there were no whispers taunting him with what was going to happen next. Giving up on trying to inflict pain and terror the killer started chanting the phrase I only heard partly before. Like then, a wrenching pain threw me out of the scene.

My stomach threatened to expel the blood I had just ingested all over Tony Howell's body. Only through extreme willpower was I able avoid spoiling the crime scene and embarrassing myself. I sat completely still for several minutes to regain composure.

"Would you like some water? Or blood?" Jaime asked kneeling next to me.

"Just some blood, I think." My stomach was calm now, but I was tired again.

"Are you okay?" she asked quietly.

I drank the blood before answering. "It actually was not as bad as the last time. Was Tony a soldier?"

"Yes. How did you know?" Collette asked.

"His panic was contained. Tony knew that someone else was controlling Catherine. He was waiting for her to reassert herself."

"But she didn't," Collette said.

I shook my head, "There was something else very different in this set of murders. The last time he seemed to revel in the human victim's pain. He taunted her. Relished her terror. This time he was . . . frustrated. At first, I thought it was just because the killer could not properly control Catherine, but it was more than that. Tony did not panic. He was calm. Well, not exactly calm but not the fear the killer wanted."

Nicholas furrowed his brows for a moment and then asked, "Did the killer have Catherine chant anything?"

"Yes. At both scenes, just before I was pushed out of the vision by tremendous pain, he chanted a phrase I have never heard before. The first time it was only partial, but I think I heard it all this time," I said.

"Can you remember what that phrase was?" Nicholas prodded.

When I told him the phrase, "Pertinent te mihi in sepiternum," Nicholas paled.

"It is as you feared. We are dealing with a necromancer. That intense pain you experienced that forced you out of the vision—that was the soul being reaped by the necromancer. He was literally tearing the soul out of the body."

I shuddered. This explained so much.

Abruptly, Nicholas took a step back and bowed. "Thank you for allowing me to view the scene. I can be of no further assistance here, but there is some research I can do. I will be in touch." Without another word, he turned and left the room.

I sat on the floor, bewildered by the Master Gatekeeper's abrupt departure. The rest of the group looked equally confused.

"What just happened?" Collette asked me.

"I have no idea," I confessed. "Jaime, you have known Master Remy the longest. Do you have any idea?"

"None." Jaime slowly shook her head. "I've never seen him act like that."

An uneasy feeling settled in my stomach.

"Are we done here then?" Detective Angelletti asked.

I shook my head. "Not at all. There is still the message on the dresser and Catherine's dust to examine. I should read the lipstick tube she used next."

"It's over here on the floor," Nathalie said pointing with a purple gloved hand. "I brought latex gloves along but then thought maybe I shouldn't touch anything even with them on."

"It would have been alright. Just treat magic scenes as you would any crime scene and do not touch anything without gloves on," I said, once again thankful for Josh's nearly obsessive consumption of human popular culture. He loved crime shows.

I walked to near the dresser and picked up the lipstick tube. Suddenly, I was seeing through Catherine's eyes, and it was Catherine in charge, at least momentarily. She had thrown up mental barriers to keep the necromancer out, but he was hammering hard at them.

There was not much time, and she knew it, just as she knew what her fate would be. Despite this, she was determined to leave a message. She felt him breaking though her defenses as she pulled the cover off of the lipstick tube. *No time to write* Den of Iniquity. *Initials will have to do.*

The lipstick clattered to the floor as my vision ended. I steadied myself on the dresser as my knees weakened. "It was Catherine. She was trying to tell us Den of Iniquity," I said.

"Den of Iniquity? What's that?" Nathalie asked as she helped me sit down on the floor.

"It's a new club in the CBD," Collette said.

"I thought it did not open until Friday?" I asked.

"It had a soft opening about a week ago. Come to think of it, it may have been the same night as the first set of murders," Collette said.

"Soft opening?" Jaime asked.

"When you open a restaurant or club to a limited number of people before the official launch to make sure that everything runs smoothly. You get to work out any service or supply problems that might mar a grand opening," she explained, and I remembered that besides being the spy mistress for the vampire community, she also owned several successful restaurants and bars around New Orleans.

"Do you think that is where our killer is choosing his victims?" I asked. "I think Josh told me it was a Goth bar. Were Tony and Catherine into that scene?" I did not know much about Goth culture other than Jaime adhered to it. I would need to have her explain it more fully to me later.

"No. Tony and Catherine were certainly not Goth," Collette assured me.

"Why would they be at the club then?"

"Perhaps just to check it out? Catherine was an Undine, after all. Even though she had not been specifically tasked to do so, she might have taken the initiative to check out the new club in town. She was a go-getter."

That go-getting might have gotten her killed. I could not tell her sire that, however. Instead, I said, "Let me see what her ashes can tell me."

"You aren't going to do any more readings, are you? That can't be safe," Jaime said, kneeling down beside me, concern evident on her face.

"I will be alright. The readings have taken a bit out of me, but the vitae helped a great deal." I was depleting myself rapidly, but it was because of the readings, not because of the hex bag that we still had not located. I could feel the difference. The amulet was working well.

"But we're out of vitae. You already drank the two bottles that you brought, and I didn't think to grab any," Jaime protested. She obviously did not want me doing any further readings. "What if we sweep Catherine's ashes into a baggie or something, and you can read them later?"

"Mistress St. Pierre will wish to take the ashes for proper interment," I told Jaime.

"I can hold off on that if need be, Juliette. You shouldn't overtax yourself. I've never seen anyone read as much as you have in such a short amount of time. However, if you need vitae, this is a vampire sanctuary. There's probably some downstairs in the kitchen," Collette said and turned to her bodyguard who stood just inside the door. "Sean, would you go downstairs and see if Catherine has any blood in her refrigerator? Bring up whatever you find."

"Yes, ma'am," the guard answered before leaving the room.

Fine for the moment, I stretched out my hands towards the pile of vampire dust on the floor.

"Are you sure you want to do that now? Mistress St. Pierre said you could wait," Jaime said halting my hand.

I turned my head and looked directly into her eyes. "Thank you for your concern, but I will be fine." My tone firmly conveyed that I would tolerate no more questioning from her on this matter.

Jaime held up her hands in surrender. "Okay, but at least wait until he gets back with the blood. You might need it right away."

That was sound logic, so I settled back until the guard returned with four bottles of O negative.

Setting one of the bottles beside me, I steeled myself against the horrors to come and reached out my hand. I could clearly see myself as Catherine being borne up the stairs in Tony's arms and being rather unceremoniously tossed on the bed. Laughter. I could feel the Other with us, not controlling but offering suggestions Catherine would think were her own—the suggestion in our mind to light candles and place them around the bed. Only after she lit and placed the candles did she wonder where the strange urge to move the candles had come from. She shrugged off the idea as we fell back into Tony's arms. Suddenly, Catherine was no longer in control of her mind. While her focus was on Tony and what they were doing, the Other had asserted his dominance. Almost immediately, Catherine fought back. These were not the earnest but feeble attempts at reassertion and that I had felt during the Sylph ritual murder. Catherine nearly defeated the Other several times. She reasserted herself for several seconds, numerous times during the battle.

Tony recognized that something wasn't right. "Should I call someone?" A vicious chop to the throat silenced him as the Other took control, pushing both Catherine and me out.

I came back to myself and found every eye in the room on me. They all looked concerned. Jaime handed me a bottle of blood, fear on her face.

"What happened?" I asked. "How long was I gone?"

"Almost six minutes," Nathalie said, clearly shaken.

"Five minutes and 52 seconds," Jaime clarified. "I was about to bring you out—or at least try." She handed me a second bottle.

No wonder they look so worried. My visions rarely lasted even a full minute, and I was sure that none, even at the last murder scene, had ever lasted over three minutes. It was unusual for an Aether or any mage to become so consumed by what they saw that they could not break away, but it happened often enough to worry even the bravest among us. Jaime must have panicked, thinking I was trapped in the memory. Reading bodies and ashes were when these problems usually occurred. It was why most magic users refuse to read the dead—human or vampire.

"No, I'm fine" I insisted, "Really." And I was. Unlike my earlier reading, I had no urge to vomit. The panic and terror I had felt during the Sylph murder scene reading was absent. Catherine had been scared, but her fear had been under control.

"Did you find out anything important?" Collette asked.

"Yes and no," I said lifting myself up off the floor. "We need to go see the Grandmaster. I'll tell you all at once. Mike, can you call Sophie and tell her we're on our way?"

I quickly drank the last two bottles of blood while Mike made his call. We then filed downstairs and into the waiting cars to take us to Gautier House.

CHAPTER 11

$\mathcal{M}$ ike's call to Sophie provided the assurance that both Marc and Gabe would be available to meet with us immediately.

Sophie met us in the courtyard and led our entourage–Undine Mistress, Aether Mistress and lieutenant, Detective Angelletti, as well as various bodyguards–into the Grandmaster's office.

Marc rose from behind his desk and came around to greet us. Gabe stood up from his seat in front of the desk and took a security stance on the periphery.

"Sophie says that there has been another set of murders and that they struck the Undines this time. Please accept my sincere condolences on your loss, Collette," Marc said, ushering us to the comfortable seating area near the fireplace.

"Thank you, Marc," Collette said as she sat and smoothed the skirt of her smartly tailored suit.

Sophie had followed us in. "Do you need me to stay?" She politely inquired.

I look from her to Marc and said, "I think it would be a good idea."

Ever the consummate hostess, Sophie said, "Can I get anyone a drink then?"

Marc, Colette, and I all accepted glasses of wine while Gabe, Mike, Jaime, and the guards flanking the room abstained.

"Tell me what you have discovered," Marc said once everyone was settled.

I related to the group all that I had seen through my visions as well as Master Remy's confirmation that this was necromancy. Marc, Colette, Mike, and Sophie sat quietly for several minutes, digesting all the new information.

Finally, Marc broke the silence. "Remind me, Juliette, during the first set of murders–the Sylph murders–the necromancer was in control even before the couple got to the bedroom."

"Yes," I confirmed.

Marc asked, "Why the difference? This time he waited until they were having sex to take over, right?"

"I think because the Sylph, Eddie Sykes, was mentally weaker or lacked the training and that made him an easier target. Colette told me that the Undine victim was a former CIA agent and trained to fight mind control and manipulation. Our necromancer is quite cunning and waited until a moment of passion, when her guard would be down, to take over. He actually seemed to have slipped in during her orgasm although Catherine fought back almost immediately," I explained.

"How would the necromancer have known she was trained? Is he stalking particular victims?" the Grandmaster asked.

"I am not sure if he is stalking these victims or if they are random, but a simple magical probe of her mind would tell him if barriers were up or not. Finding them up, he simply waited for a time when they fell or were weakened," I answered.

Marc steepled his fingers and thought for a moment. "This message the fledgling left—was she trying to tell us this was where they met the killer, or was it simply the last place she and her lover were? Did you get a sense either way, Juliette?"

I shook my head. "No, only that it was very urgent to leave the message."

"Collette, she was your progeny. What is your sense?" Marc asked.

"I think if they had found something concrete at the club, she would have reported it immediately, not gone home to have sex. I think it was the last place they had been."

I thought for a moment and then said, "It may be that something that seemed inconsequential at the time happened at the club, but later, when the necromancer took over, it took on new meaning."

Collette nodded. "That is quite possible."

"Either way, Den of Iniquity is a place to start," Marc said.

"Josh mentioned going to the Grand Opening on Saturday although when he proposed it, it was just going to be a fun night out," I said.

"I'll be there as well," Collette said. "I was given a VIP invitation."

My eyebrows shot up and Marc asked, "Is that unusual?"

"Not at all. Josh, as owner of The Cowboy and Chintz, probably received one also. It is common to issue VIP invitations to other club owners. It fosters a sense of community, and it's a way to show off," Collette clarified.

"What do you know about Den of Iniquity and the owner?" Marc still seemed concerned about the VIP invitations. They worried me as well.

Collette thought for a moment and then said, "Off the top of my head, it is a sole proprietorship owned by Rob Winters. He's a businessman from New York. I met him once, shortly after renovations on his building began. He was a bit arrogant, but nothing unusual. He was sure that his club would be the hottest thing to hit New Orleans since forever."

"When was that meeting?" Marc asked.

Collette paused, mentally calculating. "Four months ago, I think. I'll check. I'll also see what else I have on him in the files and call New York. He may have shown up on the Undine radar up there."

"Alright. I want to call Master Remy and see what his research has turned up," Marc said. "Is there anything else?"

The others murmured no, but I said, "If I could have a moment after everyone else leaves?"

"Of course, Juliette. I'll see the rest of you later," Marc said as he dismissed us.

Jaime looked at me and mouthed, "Should I stay?"

"You do not need to," I told her, and she hurried for the door. Gabe, even though dismissed, lingered by the door. He seemed unwilling to leave the Grandmaster alone with my werewolf bodyguards and me. And considering werewolf and vampire history, I couldn't blame him.

"Gabe, would you join us?" I asked, and he walked back to the sitting area taking up a position behind his brother's chair.

"I know bodyguards are not generally introduced, but this is . . . an unusual situation, so I thought it best to make them known to you," I explained to the grandmaster and his lieutenant as I beckoned Nathalie and Gaetan over. Once they had moved from their unobtrusive positions at the wall, I made formal introductions. Both Gabe and Marc were neutrally guarded in their reactions to the werewolves, and Nathalie and Gaetan were properly but not overly deferential to the vampires.

Marc took a long moment to assess Nathalie. "You are Beau's eldest and heir, correct?"

"Yes, sir," she said.

Marc nodded looking at her intently before he nodded. "You have quite a bit of power. Beau made a wise decision choosing you to succeed him. I think Juliette has also made a wise decision. Do your best to keep her safe. She is our best hope for survival," he said solemnly.

Nathalie seems confused by the last pronouncement but didn't question it. She simply said, "Thank you, sir, I will."

"Please tell your father that I am looking forward to seeing him again soon."

"Of course, sir," she replied.

"Good. Did you need anything else, Juliette?" Marc asked.

"No sir, that was all."

"Then I will see you later," he said by way of dismissal.

~

ONCE WE WERE TUCKED into Nathalie's backseat, she asked me, "What did Grandmaster Gautier mean when he said that you are our best hope for survival?"

"You know about the prophecy, right?" I asked Nathalie.

"Something about some moron opening the Gates of Hell on the second full moon of December," Nathalie said dismissively as she shrugged her shoulders.

"The prophecy states that, 'on the night of the cold blue moon, one with magic in blood and bone can open Gates of Hell. Only another with magic in blood and bone can stop it.'" Jaime recited.

"And what, Juliette, you have magic in blood and bone? Don't all magic users?" Nathalie scoffed.

"Not all magic users are magical," I explained shaking my head.

"Huh?"

"All magic users–mages–can draw magic–aether–from nature and the elements, but only three special types of magic users have magic in them," I explained.

"So anyone can learn to be a mage since they draw in magic?" Nathalie asked.

"Not really. Even though most mages do not have magic in them, they are born with a special ability that allows them to draw aether to them and use it. Normal humans cannot do that unless they possess some sort of magical item."

"Okay, some people are born with the ability to use magic, and others are magic?"

"Yes. There are three types of mages who themselves are magical: necromancers, thaumaturges, and seers." I ticked them off on my fingers.

"And you are?"

"A thaumaturge. My specialty is healing. My thaumaturgy has been a closely guarded secret for most of my existence, or at least I thought it was a closely guarded secret. Apparently, it was far more widely known than I realized," I said wryly.

"So everybody knows now?" Nathalie asked.

"It is more like an open secret. Far too many people, including some very dangerous people, now know," I said.

"If you are magical, don't a lot of people want you? You're kinda like a human magical object," Gaetan said.

"She's a friggin' unicorn," Jaime proclaimed practically jumping up and down in her seat.

Ignoring my childe, I said, "Yes, to both your points, Gaetan. I am a human or rather vampire magical object or unicorn, and many people would like to either control me or drain my magic from me for their own use."

"Have you got any more bombshells like this you'd like to let your security in on, Juliette?" Nathalie asked.

"Maybe I just need to tell you and Gaetan the entire story from the beginning. I am not trying to keep you in the dark. It is just so much has happened in such a short amount of time, some things fall through the cracks," I said as Nathalie swung the car into the gated courtyard and cut the engine. "Let us wait until we get inside, and I will tell you everything."

"Do you want me there for this discussion?" Jaime asked.

"Actually, yes. You may remember things I do not or just do not think are important enough to include," I told her.

"No problem."

I waited to start my story until we were all comfortably seated in the vast living room upstairs. "I was born in the French colony of St. Domingue in 1765. My father was the fourth son of the Chatelain de Chătillion, so he immigrated to the colony and set up a prosperous rice plantation."

"When you said you were going to start at the beginning, I didn't realize you meant your birth and lineage," Gaetan interrupted.

"It is important actually and has great bearing on later events in my life," I explained.

"Shut up and let her tell her story" Nathalie snapped at Gaetan. She leaned forward, eager for more. "So, you're an aristocrat."

I fluttered my hand. "That is not what is important. The fact my paternal grandmother was a mage is. My aunt Marguerite—my father's sister—was a seer," I explained.

"Is this where you get your thaumaturgy?" Nathalie asked.

"No, actually, my thaumaturgy comes from my maternal line. My mother's mother was a thaumaturge."

"So you have magic from both parents? Wow. No wonder you're so powerful," Gaetan remarked.

"Yes. My mother was one quarter African and the illegitimate daughter of a rice planter on the island; however, my father did not care about her legitimacy or her racial components. He married her anyway. As the fourth son, he stood little chance to inherit, so he had gone to St. Domingue to make his fortune. He met my mother, fell in love, and married her."

"Was your mother a thaumaturge?" Nathalie asked.

I shook my head. "Thaumaturgy tends to skip a generation in families. My mother was a powerful mage–a water elemental."

"Did your father know about her magic when he married her?" Jaime asked, as fascinated by my lineage as Nathalie was. Gaetan seemed slightly bored.

"Oh, yes. He was magically sensitive, much like Josh is. He could not cast, but he knew all about magic. It was the family secret. Anyway, I came along in due course, and I showed early aptitude as a fire elemental. Apparently when I became afraid of the dark, I would magically light the candles in my room."

"Wasn't that dangerous? With threat of fire and all?" Nathalie asked.

"Quite. They tasked slaves to sit in my room to make sure that lit candles did not catch anything on fire. I was not much more than a year old or so when that happened. By then, my mother had told my father about her mother being a thaumaturge. They waited and watched. I think they both hoped I would not be one."

"Wait a minute. If you were lighting candles, how did they not know you were a thaumaturge?" Gaetan asked.

"They assumed I was calling aether to me and using it. Some

elementals come into their powers quite early, others not until later in life."

"Ok, but why were your parents hoping you weren't a thaumaturge?" he was much more interested now.

"It was dangerous. Having the ability to cast magic was perilous enough. They were still burning supposed witches at the stake. To be a thaumaturge meant everyone wanted you dead. Humans wanted to safeguard themselves from the supposed powers of Satan, and mages wanted that power."

"But you turned out to be," Gaetan said.

"My thaumaturgic powers manifested around the time I was four. One of the old slaves had broken his leg. Badly. The bone was sticking out. My mother, as plantation mistress, went to tend him, and I went along. She told me to sit quietly while she saw to Old Célestin. Mother was busy pulling things out of her medical bag while he just lay on the cot moaning. I just meant to hold his hand–to comfort him. However, as soon as I took his big hand in mine, I could see in my mind what was wrong and how to fix it. So, I did. With my magic."

"That must've caused quite a stir," Jaime said.

"I do not know how, but my parents managed to keep the incident quiet. My mother began training me how to shield my power so that others would not know what I was. She also taught me how to heal just enough to save a life or in small increments over time."

"So that it looks more like natural healing. To keep you from being burned," Gaetan said.

"Exactly. It is one thing for me to heal someone in a room full of supernatural creatures–they all know about magic–but I would not do so in a room full of humans," I said.

"But you healed Master Remy from demon fever," Jaime pointed out.

"Gatekeepers know about magic. While technically, yes, they are human, they are all mages, so I do not count them. Plus, you already knew about me being a thaumaturge."

"Wait, Gatekeepers? Like our childhood bedtime stories?" Nathalie asked sitting forward in her seat. "You introduced Master Remy as one earlier, and I wanted to ask, but it wasn't the time. Then I kinda forgot."

"Yes, but I am not quite to that part of the story yet. They are real, and I will explain all about them when I get there. Or maybe Jaime will. She knows more, having once been one."

"You're going to make me tell them how I got kicked out of the Order. That's so embarrassing," Jaime said rolling her eyes.

"Think of it less as being kicked out and more as a transfer from the Gatekeeper Order to the Aether coven. And you got a nice promotion," I told my childe. "Back to my story. My mother taught me non-magical healing as well as elemental magic. My father brought in tutors and gave me an Enlightenment education," I continued.

"Wasn't that unusual for a girl?" Nathalie asked.

"My sisters were a great deal younger than I, and there was no male heir. For a long time it seemed that I would be the only child, so he gave me the education generally reserved for boys. Since I was a considerable heiress, when I was 16, my father took me to France. The stated reason was to find me an aristocratic husband, but it was really so that I could study magic with my grandmother. Sadly, my stay was cut short when my Aunt Marguerite had a vision that if I stayed any longer in France that I would die at the guillotine. Father broke off the marriage negotiations, and we went back to St. Domingue."

"She saw the French Revolution?" Gaetan asked. "Kinda cool. You didn't die, so this means that seer's visions aren't always correct?"

"Seers see a possible future. Generally, things can be done to change it, although my aunt felt that there were fixed points—the things that would always happen."

"How did you get to New Orleans?" Nathalie asked, turning us back to my narrative.

"That was a different but related revolution. We returned to the colony, and my father arranged a socially advantageous marriage to a gens de colours coffee planter named Etienne de Grammont. I was pregnant with our first child when the slaves revolted, and the Haitian Revolution began. My husband put me on the next departing ship and sent me to safety here in New Orleans. My parents and sisters died in the initial uprising. Etienne stayed behind to salvage what he could, but he stayed too long and was killed."

"So you were alone in New Orleans with the baby?" Nathalie asked.

"No, it was not quite like that. Many fled the colony and came here to New Orleans. One of my best friends and her family made it out and settled here, and I had also traveled with slaves."

"You owned slaves?" Jaime asked.

I pursed my lips. This was not something I was proud of. "Both my father and husband owned slaves. When they died and the slaves' ownership passed to me, I freed them. I had been taught the Enlightenment ideals, including all men were created equal. Unfortunately, that idea clashed with prevailing economic policies at the time."

Jaime gave me a dark look, but Nathalie asked, "What happened to your child?"

"She came early and was stillborn. I fell ill with childbed fever. That was how I met Frederique Deroche, the Aether coven mistress."

"She's not your sire though," Jaime said.

"No, I was very ill, and my housekeeper brought in a voodoo priestess. Since voodoo was an outlawed religion, it did not seem strange that she would only visit under the cover of darkness. Frederique sensed my magic right away–I was far too weak and ill to shield it. She helped nurse me back to health, and we became friends. We did not speak of her nature for a long time although I knew she was a vampire as soon as I recovered from my fever. In those days, many of the Aether coven members were also leaders of the voodoo community, serving as priests and priestesses. Having been a mambo on St. Domingue before the revolution, I was quickly welcomed into the fold. The fact that I was still human, and a healer assured my place. I made friends with many of the coven members and at least one enemy–Honore Rochon."

"Why does she hate you so much?" Jaime asked.

"I was everything she was not socially. Even though we were both 1/8 African, I had been born legitimate while she was the product of a white master raping his slave. I was loved and cherished, but she was beaten and whipped. She thought that I had been handed everything on a silver platter, and she was not wrong, but she resented and hated me for it. Taking Andre de la Croix as my lover only added fuel to her hatred."

"Who was this Andre guy?" Gaetan asked.

"He was the Aether lieutenant and later my sire. Andre told me he had never been romantically involved with Honore, and I believed him. I asked Frederique if she knew of any liaison between Honore and Andre, and she told me no. As far as I know, Honore chased, but never caught Andre—at least until after I was staked. They were apparently quite the couple after that."

"Why did you become a vampire?" Nathalie asked.

"I wanted to be part of a family again, and that was how I saw the coven."

"Why not just get married again?" Gaetan asked.

"Marriage in the 1790s was far different than it is today. Legally, everything I owned became my husband's upon marriage. He could have beaten me or raped me whenever he wished. He could have squandered my fortune. I did not wish to lose my freedom and autonomy. My first marriage, even though he did not beat me, was deeply unhappy. I saw no reason to do that to myself again, and after the complications of Camille's birth, there was no chance I would ever carry a child to term. And quite honestly, immortality sounded very good to me."

"How has that turned out for you?" Jaime asked wryly.

"Not as I had planned. Being staked for two hundred and some odd years, how do you say, sucked."

"How long were you a vampire before you were staked, and why were you staked?" Gaetan asked.

"I had only been a vampire for about three years when I was staked. As for why, that is where the Gatekeepers come into my story. Jaime, why don't you explain?"

Jaime squirmed uncomfortably in her seat. "Really?"

"Really," I said.

Jaime furrowed her brows, probably considering what to say. "Since you both said you'd heard childhood stories about the Gatekeepers, I guess we should start there. Our history claims that originally the Gatekeepers had just one charge: Guard the Gates to the other worlds. Eventually, that job expanded to keep the supernatural world secret from the human world. The Gatekeepers were pretty powerful and had amassed a huge amount of knowledge of supernatural beings by the 14th century or so. About that time the Catholic Church decided to get rid of us all–mages, vampires, werewolves–the whole lot of us. By the way, all Gatekeepers are mages. The Church wanted to use Gatekeeper knowledge about everybody to get rid of us. They started the Inquisition to do this. They succeeded in killing a lot of Gatekeepers, regular mages, vampires, werewolves, and a not insignificant number of regular humans. Mages, vampires, and werewolves melted further into the shadows, but the Gatekeepers went underground. We let the Inquisition–and everyone else–think the Church had wiped us out. We watched and recorded. Gatekeepers only stepped in when events threatened to reveal the supernatural world to the humans."

"You were a Gatekeeper?" Gaetan clarified.

"Yeah, until I became a vampire. The Order is humans only, but I'm acting as liaison to them. I'll tell you my story later. Right now, we need to get back to Juliette." Jaime said and resumed her story. "Gatekeepers act kinda like the supernatural police. We are equal opportunity–we take out humans, vampires, and werewolves who threaten to breach security. The Gatekeepers also watch anyone with the ability to open Gates. They assign every thaumaturge or necromancer a guardian. In the mid-1790s, the New Orleans Gatekeepers heard a rumor that the Aether coven here wanted to open the Gate at the time of the prophecy. The Gatekeepers decided that since Juliette was a thaumaturge and an Aether clan member, that she would be the one to do it."

"You wouldn't do that, would you?" Nathalie asked.

"Good God, no!" I said emphatically. "I cannot think of anything worse. Regardless, I was never approached about it."

"To be fair, a lot of Gatekeepers weren't sure she'd do it either. I read the trial transcript. It could've gone either way," Jaime said.

"They put me on trial?" I asked. I did not remember this from my torpor state.

"In absentia, before you were even staked," Jaime said a little sheepishly. "Actually, the staking was a compromise. Your guardian was sure you would not open the Gates even if Andre asked you to. He persuaded the other Gatekeepers to stake you rather than outright kill you."

"I'm not sure that's a comfort, Jaime," I said dryly.

"Anyway," Jaime continued. "Juliette and her sire, Andre, were staked by Gatekeepers who staged it to look like Hunters had taken them. They didn't have any interest in Andre, so they stashed him in an abandoned sugar warehouse where he was eventually found. The Gatekeepers moved Juliette around every few years–crypt to crypt." She grimaced, "We almost lost her during Katrina. Master Remy made sure she remained safe and finally moved her out to a crypt in Metairie."

"I don't understand. If the Gatekeepers thought Juliette was a threat, why not just kill her?" Gaetan asked.

Jaime looked at him steadily, "Gatekeepers don't kill innocent beings. She had done nothing wrong. There was just the thought she might. Gatekeepers aren't interested in killing every supernatural creature on sight like Hunters are. We only, or rather, they only, kill those who have done something that risks exposing the supernatural community to the wider human world."

Gaetan seemed satisfied with that answer. I, however, had questions of my own.

"Why did they keep moving me?"

Jaime shrugged. "Above my paygrade, but I'd guess that it had to do with the fear that humans might open whatever crypt they had you stashed in," Jaime hypothesized.

"How exactly did Andre find me? Or was I 'allowed' to be found?" I asked.

"Honestly, I'm not sure. If Andre and Honore hadn't worked

Rebecca over so hard to get your location, I would say yes, that someone above my paygrade decided to let you be found." Jaime said.

"Rebecca is one of the Gatekeepers?" I asked.

"The one who hates you so much. You met her when you healed Master Remy of Demon Fever."

That at least explained the young woman's hostility to me.

"Rebecca said she had to do some serious magical jujitsu to get away from those two," Jaime continued.

"She would have needed to. Honore is good, and while Andre was lazy, he was also powerful," I said.

Jaime nodded. "Do you want to take the story back over here?"

"Thank you." I said. "As Jaime said, Andre found me in a crypt in Metairie Cemetery. He un-staked me and took me to Gautier House where a formal introduction to the Grandmaster was made. As we were leaving, Josh stumbled in carrying Chris Gautier, the grandmaster's nephew. He had been attacked by a werewolf," I continued.

"Daddy was so mad, thinking that one of the packs had broken the peace like that and then wouldn't fess up. I don't think I've ever seen him rant like that," Nathalie said shaking her head.

"Well, it wasn't a pack werewolf who did it, so they really couldn't confess, and we did quickly clear that up. I healed Chris and found that a Stray was menacing the city. Soon, we realize it wasn't one Stray but an entire pack—a man-eating pack—that had invaded the city and was causing havoc. About that time, several summoned demons showed up in the city," I said.

"Actually, the demon activity picked up a bit later–after the fire, remember?" Jaime prompted.

"Ah, yes. On the night of the September full moon, I was performing the ritual to keep Chris Gautier from becoming a werewolf and missed the monthly Aether coven meeting. There was a fire, and it appeared that everyone there had died."

"But some did escape," Gaetan noted.

"Yes, and now it seems that there was an inner-coven coup attempt by Honore to get rid of Frederique Deroche. Something went wrong, and Honore and her compatriots were severely injured. They went into torpor to heal. Nobody could find any of them, so I became Aether Regent, just a placeholder until a new master or mistress could be found. I was not interested in leading the coven. The Stray attacks continued, and Jaime introduced herself to me. I had never heard of the Gatekeepers or the prophecy. I wasn't terribly gracious to Jaime initially, I'm afraid."

"You took all of it way better than I thought you would," Jaime assured me, and I smiled back.

"Meanwhile, I was warding the city to keep the werewolves out and getting a crash course in 21st century life from Josh," I said.

"Yeah, how exactly did you and Uncle Josh hook up? You're not his usual type," Nathalie asked.

"My sire was killed in the fire, and I was a little . . . lost. Josh stepped in and took me under his wing."

"That's not all he took you under," Jaime mumbled, and Nathalie snorted with laughter.

"Don't get me wrong," she said. "You're good for him. I've never seen him so happy, but you're way more refined than he is. You're a bottle of Cristal to his Dixie beer."

"There is a lot more under that rough exterior than most people realize," I protested before I went on. "Josh appointed himself as my bodyguard while I warded the city. The fire had occurred by this point, and it was not safe for me to be out casting that much magic without someone to watch over me."

"Why not just have Jaime look after you? She was your guardian after all," Nathalie asked.

Jaime jumped in, "I'd pretty much been re-tasked to hunt down the influx of demons being summoned into the city. I have a talent for banishing them. We kept a rotating watch on Juliette, but Josh was the best solution."

"Who was summoning the demons?" Gaetan asked.

"Honore and the other members of the Aether coven who survived the fire. They had recovered, come out of torpor, and resurfaced. Honore had the coven signet ring and claimed leadership. I, of course, had no idea initially that she had killed Frederique, or that she was summoning demons to destabilize Marc's rule. She made a deal with the Stray werewolf pack to cause problems as well. Honore is devious. She had invited numerous foreign Aether into the city to help her. On the last full moon—the blood moon—they attempted the coup. Jaime was the one who realized what was happening and warned me," I said proudly.

"It took all of us to put down the attempt too," Jaime said. "Loyal vampires and Gatekeepers. The Rogue Aether had summoned a bunch of demons. It was a bitch to cover up afterword. Lots of magic was cast to remove all traces from people's memories. Luckily, it was so late that most the people who saw anything were drunk, and no one had the wherewithal to upload anything to YouTube."

"That was a miracle," Gaetan said.

"Tell me about it," Jaime replied.

"I think you know the rest. Did I leave anything out?" I asked.

"The incubus attack on you, my turning, and the hex bags," Jaime reminded me.

"I do not know how I forgot about the incubus. A few days before the coup attempt, an incubus in the form of my dead sire appeared and tried to drain me of my magic. I was able to banish him, but he greatly weakened me. Jaime found me and called Josh. He nursed me. I am sure the Rogue Aether engineered the attack to remove me before the coup."

"You aren't just with Uncle Josh out of gratitude, are you?" Nathalie demanded.

I smiled. "Not at all. While I am grateful for what he did, my feelings for him have nothing to do with gratitude."

Nathalie seemed mollified.

I continued the rest of the story, "During the coup attempt, Jaime was gravely, actually mortally wounded, although I did not realize it at the time. I used all my inborn magic during the earlier fights and could not use my thaumaturgy to heal her. I gave her my blood instead, and she became a vampire. As you already know, during the coup or shortly after, a hex bag was left to drain my power," I finished.

"The Grandmaster . . ." Jaime began.

I cut her off. Marc did not want it widely known that he'd been hexed. I frowned and gave a little shake of my head, hoping Jaime got the message. "The Grandmaster also called out a Hunt on the Rogue Aether, but you already knew that."

"I think I'm gonna be glad when those extra werewolves get here. You are a much bigger target than I thought," Gaetan said.

Nathalie shot him a look. "She warned us, so don't go pulling that 'this is bigger than I thought' crap, Gaetan. Just because you didn't take the threats to her seriously before, doesn't mean that *I* didn't," she snapped.

"I didn't mean it like that," Gaetan said. "I just think that we both need to be with Juliette every time she leaves the house unless Josh or Jaime is also with her. If she's attacked, it will not be by a single attacker, they'll come in force. One of us might be able to save her but would probably die in the process."

"Do you think the threat is that high?" I asked, suddenly a lot more worried than I had been.

"I would rather be safe than sorry. It is better to overestimate your opponent in this case than underestimate them," Gaetan said standing up. "I want to walk the perimeter with one of the house guards to look for any gaps in security that need to be fixed."

"I can take you around. I noticed a few things that might need to be changed," Jaime offered.

"I should go downstairs and start on the rest of the amulets," I said, even though I was still tired from my earlier readings despite drinking several bottles of blood.

"No." Jaime said with finality. "You've done too much magic already tonight. You cannot drain yourself back to nothing. What if your amulet stops working because you're too weak? Wait until tomorrow night when you're fresh and I can help you. I know I can't charge the werewolf amulets, but I can help you with the initial steps. Let's get the security concerns out of the way first—we'll look for the hex bag outside while we're at it. Just rest."

"I do not need to be managed," I retorted.

Jaime stood with her hands on her hips and said apologetically but firmly, "I'm sorry, Juliette, but in this case you do. If you attempt more magic tonight, it will probably fail, and if you were thinking clearly, you'd recognize that." Stepping close she implored, "Please, you are the head of my coven and my sire, and I need you. What am I going to do if you hurt or exhaust yourself?"

Those last few words broke through my anger and stubbornness. She was right. I was too tired to do magic properly, and I might well hurt myself.

"You are as bad as Josh," I grumbled. "I hate being managed."

"We do it because we love you," Jaime said sweetly.

"Go, do your security thing. I promise I will not do any magic," I said.

Jaime stood. "Thanks, Mom," she said before she quickly dropped a kiss on my cheek and hurried from the room.

I sat in stunned silence and watched her go.

CHAPTER 12

ears gathered in my eyes when I heard the downstairs courtyard door close.

"Are you alright, Juliette?" Nathalie asked gently.

Hastily wiping the tears away, I put on a bright smile and said, "Of course. Jaime's gesture was just . . . unexpected."

"You expected her to hate you." Nathalie was a keen observer.

"Would you not?" I said emphatically. "I changed her without her consent, and it cost Jaime her family," I answered.

Natalie shrugged, "It doesn't sound like you had a lot of choice. You could either try to heal her with your blood or let her die. She's a smart kid, if tragically dressed," she added with a smile. "I'm sure she weighed the options and realized that immortality is a lot better than death. Besides, it looks like she sees you as her mom now," Nathalie reasoned.

"There is a certain symmetry to that," I said after a moment.

"How so?"

"The first time I met Jaime–that she made herself known to me–was in St. Louis Number One. I was visiting my daughter's crypt."

"You still go there?"

"Not as often as I should," I confessed. "Since my return, it has been one crisis after another. Now that I am coven mistress, even if there are just two members, there are even more demands on my time."

"On your magic, too," Nathalie noted. "How dangerous is this hex bag that were looking for?"

"To you? Not at all. It should affect none of you. It is aimed solely at me. I have an amulet," I gestured to my necklace, "that keeps the worst of it at bay."

"We need to find that bag and destroy it sooner rather than later, though," Nathalie observed.

"Yes," I agreed. "I will not be at full strength until we do."

"I've got to say, you're pretty powerful even under the hex."

"Nonetheless, I am going to need all of my power to fight what is coming."

"Should I go outside and help them look? Will you be all right in here alone?"

"I will be fine. I do not need a babysitter. I promise. I will work in my ritual room preparing for tomorrow night, but I will cast nothing. Besides, I think Josh said he would be home soon," I said.

"Mission accepted: find and destroy one nasty hex bag," Nathalie said as she stood. "Juliette, I hope you didn't take offense earlier when I asked about you and Josh. It's just he's kinda like family, you know? Even though he's a vampire, I consider him just as much my uncle as Gaetan's dad."

" No, I did not take offense earlier. Family is more than blood. I understand that better than anyone does. I think it is sweet that you worry about him."

"Good." Nathalie said and went to join the others outside.

Why is it that now that I had finally found the love and acceptance that I had always craved, I was probably going to lose it? I shook my head to rid myself of the maudlin thoughts and went downstairs to my ritual room. Although I kept my promise of not casting, I made the most of the next few hours by carefully searching through my many boxes of trinkets to find the perfect crystals or other tokens to make the were- wolf amulets out of. Luckily, most already had holes bored through them, so attaching the long leather cords that would act as necklaces was easy. For the two wooden tokens that did not, I carefully used my athame to create the opening needed. I lined everything up neatly on my workbench, ready for the next evening. Then I saw the small, black, velvet bag I had left on the shelf a few nights after the coup. Guilt flooded me as I realize that I still had not magiked the Gautier jewelry to protect the family from further hexes. Jaime and Josh would need protection as well.

I sighed. What had looked like a large, but manageable project for the next night had grown exponentially. At full strength, I could not make and charge all of these amulets in one night. Even with Jaime's help, I would be lucky to get half of them done.

I shook the contents of the jewelry bag out onto the table and carefully set the three Gautier signet rings–one each for Gabe, Marc, and Sophie–and the St. Christopher's necklace for Chris next to the makings for the other amulets.

I needed to prioritize. I would magic the Grandmaster's signet ring first thing tomorrow night. Luckily, this was his personal signet, not his ring of office since I'd had it for several days.

I then paced out and decided that there was space for a second protective circle in the room. I would have Jaime draw hers and create the amulet shells for the other werewolves.

Pleased with my evenings work, even if I hadn't been able to cast, I turned off the light and went upstairs to wait for Josh.

I WENT to my ritual room shortly after rising the next evening. I should have been at Anne Stokes' art opening with Josh, but I sent him alone with my regrets. There was too much to do here. I hoped Toussaint and his protégé would not take my absence as a slight. It certainly was not meant to be. As coven leader, I was expected to attend such affairs and normally delighted in them. I had been looking forward to this opening, but it wasn't to be.

I found Jaime rocking back and forth on her heels in front of the door.

"You are going to let me help you, aren't you?" She asked.

I nodded and smiled. It was nice to have an eager apprentice.

"I have a mage lock on the door, but it is keyed so that either of us can open it," I explained. I showed her how to unlock the door and then relocked it. Jaime was a quick study; nonetheless, I made her lock and unlock the mage lock several times to make sure she could do it easily. With all that was going on, there was no telling when she might need the safety of this room quickly.

"On another night I will show you how to craft a mage lock that is unique to you," I said, finally opening the door and ushering her inside.

"One that you can't break?" Jaime asked.

"Any mage lock can be broken with enough time and magic, but I will teach you to craft one that is very difficult to break," I explained.

"Cool," she said. "You said you needed to make the werewolf amulets?"

"You are going to craft the outer shell of the amulets. I need to put protection spells on the Grandmaster's ring to keep him safe. I should have done this several nights ago," I said.

"Divide and conquer. Sounds like a plan."

"I paced it out last night and there should be plenty of room for you to draw your own circle over there." I indicated a spot near mine.

"I'm on it!" Jaime said as she sketched a protective circle in chalk on the floor.

I took the Grandmaster's ring and stepped into my circle. Taking my athame out, I nicked my wrist to invoke the circle. I then sat down and worked. The protection spell itself was already long and complicated, but it took even more time since I was I adding further layers of protection. Despite the magic I had poured into the complex matrix, I felt fine and only a little drained. Unfortunately, it had taken a lot of time. It was nearly midnight when I was finally satisfied with the spells.

CHAPTER 13

*A*fter finishing the Grandmaster's ring, I decided that both Jaime and I needed a break. She had industriously been working on the shells for the werewolf amulets and had made great progress. When we went upstairs, we found a thoroughly dejected Nathalie sitting at the kitchen table, staring blankly into a mug of chicory coffee.

"What is wrong?"

Nathalie sighed, "Even though we searched the courtyard and carriage house last night for the hex bag and found nothing, I went over the area again. But I swear I felt something down in the garage earlier."

"Didn't Gaetan say the same thing last night?" Jaime asked.

"Yeah. We both looked but couldn't find anything. I'm almost wondering if I shouldn't shift into wolf form and see if that makes a difference," she said and took a sip of her coffee.

"I doubt it would hurt," I said, pulling a mug of my own from the cupboard. Coffee sounded good right about now.

"Could you stay with me while I look? I might need human hands," Nathalie asked.

As much as I wanted to get back to work on the amulets and

protection, finding the hex bag was as important if not more, and I probably should not overtax myself magically. "Of course," I said. "Let me make a cup of coffee, and I'll meet you downstairs."

Nathalie had already shifted by the time Jaime and I entered the courtyard. I opened the door to the carriage house, and Nathalie trotted up the stairs to the upper rooms where she took her time sniffing around the furniture, under the beds, and in the closets. Then, she went downstairs and made a thorough search of the garage but found nothing. Nathalie's head hung low, and she reminded me of a whipped dog. We had just moved back into the courtyard when Josh arrived home. Her ears went flat to her head as Josh pulled to a stop near me, and I heard her growl as she made a beeline for the rear of the Mustang.

"Sorry I'm so late. Anne's opening was great—a lot of people and she sold out—but then we had another problem at Chintz," Josh said as he turned off the engine and he got out of the car.

"Now what?" I asked.

"Damn liquor license," he said before spotting the wolf crouched behind his car. "What's going on with Nat?" he asked, watching Nathalie's wolf form.

"I'm not sure," I said following her around the car. By the time I got there, Nathalie was on her belly, wedged under the license plate. While not huge in werewolf form, she was the size of a small St. Bernard. I had no idea how she contorted herself to get under the Mustang's low clearance, but she managed. I heard her growl, yelp, and then growl again before she backed from under the car with something in her jaws. She spit the object at my feet and then swiped at her muzzle with her paw several times.

I bent to pick up the bag and stopped, feeling malevolence wafting off it. "Well, if this is not the hex bag against me, it is against one of us. Let us take this inside so I can examine and neutralize it. Jaime, do you feel anything off the bag?"

When she shook her head no, I asked her to carry it into the house for me.

Nathalie disappeared back into the carriage house to shift, and the others followed me into the main house.

"Should either of you be handling that?" Josh asked worriedly.

"Since Jaime is not feeling the malice, the magic is not directed at her. She will need to break the hex since I am fairly certain that is what is siphoning my power. I do not wish to have any direct contact with it," I explained.

"How does she break the hex?" Josh asked as we walked into the kitchen.

"The same way I broke Marc's hex—salt water. Do we have salt somewhere around here?" I deposited my now empty coffee mug on the counter.

Josh walked to a cupboard and pulled out a recognizable blue, cylindrical container. "Why do I think we should keep a large supply of this on hand?"

"Because you are a smart man," I said as I put the stopper in the sink and turned on the faucet. Taking the salt from him, I dumped the entire container into the filling sink and swished it around with my hand.

I swayed slightly growing light-headed. Even with my amulet on, being so close to the hex bag was having a detrimental effect.

"Whoa there, Juliette," Josh said as he caught me around the waist. "Jaime, I think you'd better break that hex now."

Her eyes wide, Jaime did as she was told. She plunged the bag into the salt infused water, forcing it to the bottom of the sink and holding it there.

The spell broke with an audible pop, and a pressure lifted that I had not realized was there. I sagged against Josh in relief.

"Juliette!" Josh mistook my relief for something more serious.

"I am fine," I assured him as I straightened up. "Just very glad that is over."

Now that the hex had been neutralized, it was safe for me to handle whatever was in the bag. I would not be able to read it—the salt water destroyed that residue—but all voodoo practitioners had a style signature. I might recognize who made the bag.

I pulled the burlap bag out of the sink and placed it on the counter. Untying the leather cord that bound it, I dumped the contents out. As I expected, a poppet tumbled forth. It was a crude representation of me–a brown rag doll with stitched x's for eyes and a vivid slash of red for a mouth clothed in a facsimile of my gala dress, and I would bet the fabric was from the hem. A hank of my own black hair was glued to the head, and around its neck was a large crystal pendant, which I suspected held my drained power. The crystal was almost the length of the doll's body. It was Honore's handiwork. I recognized the style.

Carefully, I removed the pendant and held it out to Josh. His fingers wrapped around mine as he took the pendant from me.

"Is this it? Is this what's been causin' all your problems?"

I beamed with the feeling of overwhelming relief. "It is."

"What do we need to do with it?"

"Crush it," I said.

In the next instant, Josh dropped the crystal to the floor and brought the heel of his cowboy boot down heavily onto it. The crystal splintered, and all the magic that had been sapped from me returned in a rush. I felt as if a giant wave had hit me, and I staggered under its force. Josh reached to steady me, and magic cracked between us when we made contact. To his credit, he didn't let go, but instead held on until I gained my equilibrium.

"Are you gonna be okay?" He asked concerned.

I nodded, trying to bring all the excess power and energy under control. Magic swirled around me like a hurricane. "I had better go downstairs and bleed off some of this excess."

"You're lit up like a magical Christmas tree," Josh said. "How're you gonna use up that much energy?"

"Jaime and I are going to create a Focus. That is, if Jaime you would like to help?" I said.

"Hells, yeah!" She said and bounded out of the kitchen towards the back stairs.

"This will take the rest of the evening. After I bleed off the excess into the Focus, I need to create the rest of the werewolf amulets and protection charms," I warned Josh.

"Why not just make the amulets and charms right off?" He asked.

"There is too much magic for delicate spell work. I cannot properly control it."

"You'll be careful, right? Granny said havin' too much magic was just as bad as not havin' enough," Josh said.

"I promise," I said, but refrained from kissing him before leaving the kitchen to join Jaime. I was afraid of what opening the magical conduit between us might do to him when I was in this state.

Jaime had unlocked the ritual room and was anxiously waiting when I arrived. "Do you want me to keep making the amulet shells while you get your magic under control?"

"While that would be the most effective use of time, no. I'm going to teach you how to make a Focus unless you already know how," I said.

"I've seen them used, but I don't know how to make one. I'd love to learn," Jaime said.

"I think the Focus will be the best way to store this excess energy," I said and pulled my trinket box from a shelf dumping the contents onto the worktable being careful not to mix these items with those already laid out. I searched through the crystals and semiprecious stones to find something that could properly hold my power. Finding nothing, I turned to Jaime and said, "Would you run upstairs to my bedroom and bring down my jewelry box? It is the wooden casket on the mirrored dresser."

While nothing in here was suitable as a Focus, there were several bits of amethyst that could be made into protection amulets. It might be good to have extras handy. Not sure when I would find the time to make them, I set the amethysts aside and put the rest of the crystals and gems back into the box and returned it to the shelf.

Jaime returned in a few minutes with my jewelry box.

"Thank you," I said, taking the box and placing it on the worktable. I unlocked it with a word and a drop of my blood.

"You blood lock your jewelry case? What have you got in there?" Jaime asked. A blood lock was a sophisticated form of mage lock that required blood and was extremely difficult to break. The box contained not only expensive heirlooms and magic pieces but was also itself magic.

"There are very important things in this case," I said as I pulled out trays and smaller jeweler's boxes. As I continued to take out items, Jaime's eyes grew wide.

"Oh. My. God! You have a box of holding. How much stuff do you have in there?" Jaime squealed.

"A lot," I said, closing the lid. I sorted through the smaller boxes until I found the one I wanted. I opened the black velvet case to reveal an ornate silver necklace with a large diamond pendant. My paternal grandfather had presented the piece to my grandmother on the birth of her fourth and youngest son, my father. Grandmere had given it to me when I was presented to the court of Louis XV. I didn't mention to Jaime that there was a matching tiara commissioned some years later. I would save that surprise for later.

"That diamond's as big as my fist!" Jaime exclaimed. While the stone was good sized, about as large as a dove's egg, it was nowhere near as large as she claimed. "Is it real?"

"Yes, it is real." I laughed and briefly toyed with the idea of removing the pendant and affixing it to something less ostentatious but decided against it. The thick rope chain that held the diamond was long enough to tuck discreetly beneath my blouse, and anyone who saw it would think it was paste, anyway.

Jaime asked, "What should I be doing?"

Indicating a box of chalk on the worktable, I said, "Would you please draw a protective circle? Do not invoke it yet, though."

Jaime moved quickly to do my bidding. The faint outline of my last circle was still on the floor. Looking at it she asked, "What size do you want? Same as your last?"

"Um . . . No, it should be larger. There needs to be room for both of us in it," I said as I scanned the bookshelf.

"You want me in the circle with you?" Jaime asked excitedly.

"Of course. How else would I teach you?"

"Master Remy just had me watch from the outside," she said.

"I want you to feel what I do to the magic and how it responds. I think you will learn faster that way," I explained. Master Remy's technique was the normal method for magical instruction and how my mother had taught me. However, she'd had years to impart her wisdom; I would have a few months at best, if we could not stop the prophecy, to prepare Jaime. My paternal grandmother had had the same experience with me when I was sixteen. Grandmere was a powerful mage with a very different style of magic than my mother, and because Papa planned an aristocratic marriage for me, she knew she would only have a few months before I married, so Grandmere had taken a more direct teaching approach and invited me into her protective circle. I hoped I would be as successful with Jaime as Grandmere had been with me.

I banished the memory and got to work. While Jaime prepared the circle, I wanted to familiarize myself with the process of making the Focus.

I pulled my grimoire off the shelf and flipped through it. Both my mother and grandmother had showed me the process, but I had never made one myself. Since my magic came from inside me, there had never seemed to be a need for one. The events of the past few weeks had given me several sound reasons to rethink that.

I remembered seeing the instructions when I looked for protection spells a few days earlier so soon found it again. I skimmed the directions to make sure that I had forgotten nothing and then closed the book.

"I'm done," Jaime announced.

Even though I was sure her protection circle was more than adequate, I checked her work anyway, thinking to offer tips or suggestions. However, I had none. It was a near perfect piece of work, and I praised her for it. Jaime bloomed under my kind words.

I gestured her into the circle and invoked it with a drop of my blood.

"Go ahead and sit," I said, making myself comfortable on the worn wooden floor. Jaime sat facing me, and I placed the diamond necklace on the floor between us.

"Have you ever seen a Focus made before?" I asked.

Jaime shook her head. "Master Remy has one, but he made it a long time ago."

"It is generally a long process," I explained. "It can take weeks or even months depending on the caster's skill, power, and stamina. I am unsure because of my excess power levels how long this will take. I will create mine, and then, you can create one of your own."

"I don't have a gem or anything like that to use," she said sadly.

"Do not worry. I have plenty. We will find you something appropriate," I said.

"You'd just give me something like that?" Her eyes grew large and round again.

"Of course. You're my childe, my apprentice. It is my duty not only to teach you but also to make sure that you have the materials you need."

"Oh. The Gatekeepers didn't quite see it like that. I mean, they made sure we had enough to eat and a roof over our heads, and they trained us, but we needed to scrounge spell components for ourselves," Jaime explained.

"Whatever you need and I have here is yours to use. I only asked that you let me know if you use something unique, like one of the gemstones, so that I can replace it. Also let me know if the supply of herbs runs low."

"Yeah, sure. I'll do that," she agreed, although the look on her face told me she wasn't quite sure if I was serious or not.

"Truly," I emphasized, "whatever you need is yours. I will set up a bank account for you in the next few days with a monthly allowance. In the meantime, if you want money, just let me know. I wanted to do it sooner, but dealing with my power drain seemed more pressing," I explained.

"Why? Why are you being so nice and generous? What's in it for you?" Jaime demanded suspiciously.

"As I said, you're my childe and my apprentice, but you are also the Aether lieutenant. Coven takes care of coven." While this is not always the case, that was how it would be under my leadership. "What do I get out of it? A second-in-command who has the tools she needs to fight what is coming. Money will not matter if they manage to open the Gates of Hell."

That seemed to satisfy Jaime, and the tautness and tension in her body eased. The angry energy that had been drawn to her during our conversation dissipated, and I quickly changed the subject. It was obvious that Jaime had deep-seated trust issues, but I did not have the time to deal with them now. Focus magic required calm, clear thought. I could work on Jaime's insecurities later.

"All right," I said. "To create a Focus, you are going to meld your magic into the stone."

"How do you do that?" She asked, leaning in to inspect the stone.

"There are tiny fissures in the gem, too small for the eye to see, and you let your magic soak into them."

"So there's only so much power each gem can hold?"

"Exactly," I said, pleased that Jamie grasped this. The fact that she was very intelligent would make teaching her much easier although I anticipated she would have many questions for which I didn't have straightforward answers.

"How do you know when the gem is full?"

"It will tell you."

"Tell me? Like the gem talks?"

I chuckled. "Not exactly. You will feel a gentle push back of your magic from the stone."

"So when it is full, it pukes magic back at you?" Jaime asked.

I considered that for a moment and nodded agreement that that was an apt description for what took place. "What happens if you force the Focus to take too much magic?" She asked.

"Bad things. The gem will shatter and unleash all of its stored power. That power will flood back to its owner."

"Like when Josh broke the crystal earlier?"

"Far more magnified. That crystal was a baby focus. This gem will hold far more power when it is fully charged."

"So a AAA battery versus car battery?" Jaime asked. I was coming to appreciate the novel ways she illustrated magic concepts so she could understand them. I had a feeling that I would learn as much from her in the next few months as she would from me.

"Yes," I answered.

"Why did you let Josh crush the crystal or was he not supposed to? Couldn't you just use that baby focus?" Jaime said.

"I could not use that focus even though it contained my magic. Another caster created the matrix to work for him or her. I mean, I suppose that I could have used magic to break the matrix and re-key it to me, but it would have taken a lot of time and magic. Crushing it was an expeditious move and exactly what I wanted him to do," I explained.

Jaime nodded, and I picked up the gem. Cupping it in my palm, I opened my third eye and spooled my magic. The hurricane of power around me concentrated and became more focused, almost like a waterspout or tornado. From the base, I took a single strand of power and fed it slowly into the gem. I sat like this for hours, carefully filling the various fissures and crevices of the diamond revealed by the spirit plane. I felt dawn approaching and stopped. Much of my excess magic and power now resided in the necklace, but it was nowhere near full, and I still had more to export. After sundown, I would need to return and finish the process. I calculated that sometime the next night all of my excess magic and power would be in the Focus. I could then safely create the protection charms and charge the werewolf amulets. There would still be room in the focus for more magic, and over the next few weeks, I could add a little more each night. Tomorrow night I would start Jaime on her Focus. My apprentice would not have the power or stamina to feed the Focus for hours on end as I had done. The creation of her Focus would take an hour or two a night for at least the next month or possibly longer depending on the gem I chose for her.

Jaime blinked sleepily as I took down the magic circle. "That was . . . Wow. I can't believe you could do that for so long."

"I normally would not be able to. It was because of the excess magic and power that the baby Focus gave back to me," I explained.

She nodded and said, "Thanks for trusting me to be in the circle with you. I really learned a lot."

I smiled. "I am glad. Now off to bed with you. I do not need you falling into daytime torpor down here. I have no interest in lugging you up the stairs."

"Okay. I'll see you after sunset," Jaime said and trudged up the back stairs.

I mage locked the room and wondered at the chances of Josh still being awake.

CHAPTER 14

My lips curled into a smile as the delicious aroma of chicory teased me awake. My eyes fluttered open and rested on the steaming mug of coffee on the bedside table next to a bud vase containing a single red rose. I heard the drone of the shower and Josh singing an old Willie Nelson song. This was how I wanted to wake up every day for the rest of my existence.

All too soon, I remembered my days were probably dwindling rapidly. It was already October, and the prophecy spoke of the cold, blue moon. There was one on December 31 this year. If the necromancer succeeded in opening the Gates of Hell, I would need to sacrifice myself to close them. Frowning, I banished my dark thoughts. I could dwell on them later, but for now, there was work to do. I sat up and reached for my coffee. The first task was to bleed off the rest of this excess energy and power. While I did that, Jaime could create the last of the werewolf amulet shells. Then I could charge those amulets and get to work on the protection charms. There was so much to do, but there were only so many hours in a night.

The shower turned off and Josh changed songs to a sappy love ballad. He walked into the bedroom a moment later, drying his hair with a towel.

"Morning darlin'," Josh said when he saw I was awake. He padded over and placed a damp kiss on my lips.

"Good morning," I replied, smiling up at him.

"How'd it go last night? I tried to stay up, but just couldn't. I was almost wondering if you and Jaime were gonna bed down in the ritual room there."

"I pushed for as long as I could. I should have stopped sooner. Jaime almost fell into daytime torpor downstairs. Do not worry; she made it to her bedroom. I personally have slept on enough uncomfortable surfaces and will always find a soft bed with you if I can," I said.

Josh laughed. "But how did it go? You're still lit up like a magical neon sign."

"I bled off a lot of magic, but obviously there is still more that needs to go into the Focus."

"So you and Jaime will be in the ritual room for most of the night?" He asked.

"I am sorry," I apologized.

"Don't worry. While I'd love to spend time with you, we both have duties, and I should probably show my face at The Cowboy before someone starts thinking I sold the place."

"Why would anyone think that?" I asked.

"Because my manager, as competent as he is, is a damn drama queen. Every time he finds out that I've invested in a new club or started a new venture, he's convinced that I'll lose interest in The Cowboy and sell," Josh explained.

"You would not, would you?"

"Naw. I love that tacky bar. It speaks to my soul. Plus, it's a safe place for the LGBT crowd. The world's become a lot more accepting of them, but they still need a safe place to go."

"Then I expect you need to go and put everyone's mind at ease," I said, sliding out of bed.

∼

Jaime and I spent most of the night ensconced in the downstairs ritual room. I carefully threaded my excess magic into the diamond pendant while Jaime watched. I had had second thoughts about her creating the amulet shells while I created the Focus. I thought it might be too much magic in a confined space, even with our protection circles. Also, keeping Jaime with me, even though it was boring, would teach her patience, and she would need a lot of it to become a great mage. To her credit, Jaime never once complained and didn't even fidget.

Just before 3 AM, I spooled the last of my excess energy into the gem. The diamond was not yet full, and I still had my own magic that could have been put in it, but I stopped. I needed a break and was sure that Jaime did too.

I opened my eyes, let out a breath, and put the pendant on the floor. I smiled at Jaime.

"Are you done?" She asked tentatively. "I didn't feel any magic regurgitation."

"I am finished for now. You are right, the Focus is not full yet, but I have channeled all the excess energy into it. I, for one, would like to get out of this room for a few hours. We can start fresh on the charms and amulets at sundown."

"Aren't you and Josh supposed to go to that club opening tonight?" Jaime asked. "Or is Josh going without you?"

I'd forgotten that the Den of Iniquity's grand opening would be tonight. I needed to see if I could find why Catherine Day was so desperate to leave the club's name as a clue. I pursed my lips, thinking.

"Josh will not want to arrive too early, so I should have time to magik one of the Gautier's rings before I go. Depending on how long we stay, I may be able to cast another when we get home," I said.

"I know you want me to make the rest of the amulet shells, but I was really kinda hoping to go to the grand opening too. It is kinda my scene after all," Jaime said, gesturing to her black clothing, combat boots, and heavy eyeliner. "I'll understand if you say no, but . . ." She let the last hang there expectantly.

I did not answer her right away as I parsed through the options. "You can go; just please be careful. I do not want you to be among his next set of victims," I said finally. "I prefer if you did not go alone though. See if one of the guards can go with you."

"I don't need a babysitter," Jaime said sullenly.

"I am not really suggesting a babysitter, just a friend to go with and watch out for any weird signs. Take one of your Gatekeeper friends. Clubbing has got to be more fun with a friend," I said.

"You realize that is basically a babysitter, right?" she asked.

"Or you could ask Gaetan."

"I . . . I," she stammered, looking down at her hands.

I smiled. "He is very good looking, but maybe a little old for you. Chris Gautier would be in a more appropriate choice. On second thought, do not ask Chris."

"Why not? What's wrong with Chris?" Jaime demanded.

"Absolutely nothing is wrong with him. It is just that I have already saved him from becoming a werewolf, and I do not want to have to tell Marc how a necromancer got his claws into his heir."

Jaime wrinkled her nose. "That's fair. Maybe I'll see if Nathalie wants to make a girl's night." She stopped, "Wait, won't you need the guards?"

"I'll have Josh, and a bodyguard trailing after me to a club opening might be awkward."

I took down the circle, and my apprentice stretched languidly.

"I may need to go spar with Nat to work out some of these kinks," she said.

"That is not a bad idea. Before you go, what is your element?" I asked. All mages had an affinity for one of the five elements, and that would help me find the proper gemstone for Jaime's Focus.

"Fire, mostly although I have good control over earth most days," she said.

I nodded. I had suspected she was a fire elemental when we warded Gautier House since our magics had blended so well. I was a spirit elemental with a strong secondary ability in fire. In fact, most people thought I was a fire elemental, because admitting to being a spirit elemental was dangerous. Only three types of mages had spirit magic—thaumaturges, necromancers, and seers—and all were rare and exceedingly prized for their powers.

"I will see what I have that is appropriate," I said. There was a ruby brooch in my jewelry casket that should work well. It was a beautiful piece with delicate silver filigree encasing the large stone. Even so, I never wore it. The broach had been a gift from my husband, Etienne when, after eight years of marriage, I'd finally become pregnant. Sadly, my daughter had not lived to draw a breath, and I found the reminder of Etienne disconcerting. It was appropriate that I bestow the brooch upon Jaime, my new childe.

Josh greeted me at the top of the stairs with a glass of wine.

"I figured it was even money whether you'd want wine or vitae, so I chose wine," he said.

Taking the glass in my right hand, I curved my left behind his head. I kissed him deeply. "You spoil me," I sighed as I broke the kiss.

"Darlin', that's the idea. Are you done for the night?"

I smiled. "I have no plans to cast anymore this evening. What do you have in mind?" I asked suggestively.

"Since we haven't had much time together these past few nights, I was thinking we might turn in early and get reacquainted."

I thought that was a fine idea and led the way to our bedroom.

CHAPTER 15

"*I* have a bad feeling about this, Josh," I said sliding my feet into strappy black heels.

"Do you want to not go? Just say the word, and we stay home, darlin'," Josh said as he pulled on one of his black cowboy boots.

I sighed, "No. We need to go. I need to see what Catherine Day saw."

"It'll be fine," Josh assured me.

"Still, I want you to wear this," I said, taking a small, slender box off of my dresser and handing it to Josh.

Josh grinned as he took the gift from me. "What's this?"

"Just a little something that I magiked up for you," I said. "It is a protection amulet." I had created it earlier that evening instead of working on the Gautier protection charms. I felt slightly guilty about that but reasoned that Josh was going to the Den of Iniquity tonight, and he had a more pressing need. I only wish that I'd had enough time to create a charm for Jaime too. I had to console myself with the fact that my childe would be with both of my werewolf bodyguards who would be on the lookout for any weird behavior from her or strange magic in general. With that thought, I took my phone off the bedside table, switched the ringer to vibrate, and slid it into the pocket that I had discreetly sewn into my dress. I had sewn pockets into all of my ready-to-wear dresses, greatly saddened that even after 200 years they still were not standard.

Josh drew out the pendant—a small, wooden tree of life bound in silver and attached to a leather thong—and fastened it around his neck. He then leaned over and kissed me deeply. "Thank you," he said. "By the way, you look amazin' tonight."

"Is it appropriate?" I had mostly mastered the intricacies of modern fashion, but there were still times that I needed advice. Tonight, I had chosen a simple knee-length, black dress with a modest v-neckline paired with a pair of black stiletto sandals and a black velvet choker. I had also applied far more make-up than I normally wore.

"Yeah, I think so. This might be a better question for Jaime. She seems into all this Goth stuff," he said, rolling up his sleeves. His version of Goth was black cowboy boots, black jeans, and a black shirt. "Since this is openin' night, there will be a lot of looky-loos there, so we shouldn't be too out of place."

"Looky-loos?" I asked.

"People just stoppin' in for a look-see. It ain't their normal scene, but it's new, so they stop by and look around. Winters also sent out special VIP invites to the other club owners, and we are an eclectic bunch," Josh explained.

THE CLUB WAS PACKED when we arrived; however, thanks to Josh's uncanny ability, we found a close parking spot. When Josh produced the special VIP invitation, we were immediately let through the red velvet ropes and into the club ahead of the mass of people crowded on the sidewalk. Inside there was a crush of people. The music was so loud that the walls hummed, and flashes of strobe light intermittently illuminated the dark interior allowing me to make out stone arches and stained-glass windows giving the place a gothic cathedral feeling. The dance floor was a mass of writhing and sweating bodies. Josh pushed a path through the crowd and led me to one of the several bars dotted along the club's walls. Despite the warning that this might be the hunting grounds for the ritual murderer, a quick scan detected at least a dozen vampire auras in the crowd. I also felt Nathalie and Gaetan somewhere in the mob. There was also something dark and deeply sinister in the air. It was similar to the oily feeling I'd had at the crime scenes but somehow different.

Without asking, Josh pressed a glass of champagne into my hand. Leaning close to my ear, he yelled, "Let's find Winters and pay our respects. I think the VIP room is over there."

The VIP section was indeed where Josh indicated but getting there was no simple task. Josh seemed to know everyone in New Orleans, and every few feet we were stopped as people pantomimed introductions. The longer it took, the more agitated I became. My skin was crawling from the sinister feeling in the air by the time we reached the bouncer who waved us through indicating the stairs that led to the second floor.

It was quieter here on the stairs, and Josh leaned in asking, "Are you sure you want to do this?"

"We should be alright," I said, the creepy-crawly feeling having subsided. Josh led me up the rest of the stairs to the second-floor gallery. The music was again painfully loud, but there were fewer people here. Any sort of meaningful conversation was impossible, and I wondered if this was the VIP area. If it was, I was underwhelmed. Josh took my hand and led me to a set of the heavy wooden doors. Once we stepped inside, the noise receded behind us. For a moment, I thought the room was magiked, but no, it was just good old-fashioned soundproofing. Here, I could see why Josh referred to this as a club for wannabe vamps. It was everything that popular culture decreed vampires liked. Heavy red and gold brocade curtains set off sumptuous wallpaper of the same colors. Black damask covered chairs and settees were grouped in intimate seating groups. A large mahogany bar dominated one wall. Faux candlelight illuminated the room from crystal chandeliers.

A tall, cadaverously thin man broke away from the group he was talking to and approached us. "Josh Bouchard, isn't it? You own The Cowboy and Chintz, right?" He said holding out his hand. "I am Robert Winters. Rob. Welcome to Den of Iniquity."

Josh took it and gave the man his best 'awe-shucks' smile. "I see my reputation precedes me."

"And your lovely companion. Juliette de Grammont?" Magic cracked between us when he shook my hand despite both of us shielding. A million icy needles felt like they were piercing my skin where our hands met and that oily magic feeling from the crime scenes began to move up my arm. *Oh shit. This is our necromancer! How can I warn Josh?*

"You have me at a disadvantage, Mr. Winters," I said with a coolness that I did not feel. *How had we not known this was our necromancer?* No one's background checks had discovered anything out of the ordinary about the man. Anger was quickly replacing my fear.

The necromancer and I regarded one another. My new nemesis was several inches over six feet tall, with long, black hair, a mustache, and goatee. Cold, dark eyes gave him a menacing demeanor despite his oozing fake charm. He'd known exactly who and what I was before I had ever stepped into the room. It was *his* magic on the baby Focus. He knew me inside and out, while I knew next to nothing about him. It was time to shift that dynamic.

I opened my third eye to read his aura but learned little. He was clearly shielding as much as I was. I read ambition and lust, but no magic. I was unsurprised. When my shields were fully up, nothing less than physical contact by another mage, which I'd already made, would reveal my magic.

"Are you to enjoying your evening?" He asked with fake sincerity.

"It's great," Josh drawled. "You've got a helluva crowd out there."

"It is going rather well," Winters preened.

I said nothing but nodded my head in fake agreement.

There was no way to tell Josh what I had just discovered with Winters right there, so I contented myself with discovering as much about the club and how he snared his victims as I could. As the two club owners engaged in inane chitchat, I carefully but discreetly scanned the room. There were no overt or even subtle occult symbols anywhere. I thought this would be where he chose his victims, but it was possible I was wrong. There was nothing obviously out of the ordinary here except perhaps bad decor.

Another group of club owners entered the VIP area and joined us. Josh made introductions, and after a few more minutes of pleasantries, Josh and I made our escape.

We found Gaetan, Nathalie, and Jaime close to the bottom of the stairs trying to look casual. It was heartwarming to think that if we encountered any trouble, the trio was poised to come to our aid. My childe was clearly in her element, the other two less so, standing stiffly and far too alert for the club atmosphere. At least they looked the part. I wondered absently if Jaime had done their make-up and how she had convinced Gaetan to wear guyliner.

"You don't want to stick around, do you?" Josh asked, practically shouting in my ear to be heard over the music.

I shook my head vehemently and nodded towards the front door. I hadn't expected Nathalie, Jaime, and Gaetan to follow us, but to my relief they did. As much as I wanted to tell everyone that Winters was a necromancer, this was not the time or the place.

Outside, the queue to get into the club stretched around the block. Most were twenty-somethings dressed in black leather and lace. Several were decked out in frock coats and corsets.

"Now what?" Josh asked me once we were finally clear of the crush.

"Robert Winters is our necromancer," I said quietly as I furtively scanned the area. I did not want to be discussing this out here in the open, but they all needed to know before we all split up again.

"Alright, we need to get the hell outta here then. We'll meet back at the house. Juliette, when we get to the car, call Sophie, and let her know so she can tell Marc," Josh said. I was already pulling my phone out to do just that.

"I'll call Master Remy and let him know," Jaime said.

~

JOSH and I sat pensively on the couch, two untouched glasses of scotch before us when the three youngsters joined us. I had called Sophie and was put straight through to the Grandmaster. After I told him what I had discovered, he thanked me and asked that I be available for a meeting the next evening. The phone call had left me almost as unsettled as my encounter with Robert Winters. Marc Gautier had taken the news far too calmly, almost as if he was uninterested. Josh had unsuccessfully tried to calm my agitation.

Jaime looked at me as she sank into one of the nearby club chairs. "That was unexpected, right? Rob Winters being the necromancer, I mean, or did I just completely miss something in the last couple of days?"

"That was unexpected," I said, sitting forward and picking up my drink. "There was nothing out of the ordinary in Collette St. Pierre's files. She was waiting to hear back from New York when I talked to her two days ago, but she had not discovered anything unusual. What did Master Remy say?"

"He was way weird. He thanked me for the information, said he had to go, and hung up on me." Jaime looked as unsettled as me. "I don't understand how Master Remy didn't know about this guy. The Gatekeepers are tasked with keeping tabs on thaumaturges, necromancers, and seers."

"He might be embarrassed that he didn't know who this guy was," Gaetan said. "I mean, it's his job to know this stuff, and by all accounts, Winters hasn't been hiding since he got to New Orleans. It seems that someone should have known he was a necromancer by now."

"Not necessarily," I said. "Winters was shielding heavily. I only knew because when he shook my hand, our magics connected. I do not think I would have known otherwise. I *do* think you are correct about the embarrassment part, however. Master Remy should have known about a new necromancer in town unless there was some sort of communications break down. Although the Grandmaster had the same blasé attitude when I told him."

"Do you think they knew and didn't tell us? That big of a communications break down is pretty unusual in this day and age. Between phones and the internet, things are well covered. It isn't the days of letters and couriers." Jaime said.

"Ain't no point in debating what the higher ups knew." Josh deftly turned the conversation by asking, "Juliette, did you get anything else off this guy?"

"He is the mage that created the baby Focus directed at me. Since the poppet was Honore's work and the Focus was his, we now know for certain that they are working together."

"Is he our killer?" Josh asked, taking a swig of beer. "I mean, I know he's a necromancer and we're lookin' for one, but is he the right one?"

"I think so, but I am not sure. When I read the bodies, it has been so traumatic that I have had trouble with the subtleties."

"How so?" Nathalie asked.

I clarified, "I could tell from my readings it was a male necromancer—who was strong—but the rest is hazy. It is almost like I can see part of the picture, but everything else is blurry. I also only had the briefest glimpse of Winters' magic tonight. He was heavily shielding."

Josh nodded, "Yeah, I couldn't have told you he was a mage at all. I didn't feel any magic from him. It was just like with you, Juliette. Normally, I don't get a magical aura off of you at all. I did get a seriously oily and icky feeling from the club though. Not quite like the first crime scene, but close."

"The trip was kind of a bust for me," Jaime admitted. "There were way too many people in there. I saw a bunch of Gatekeepers and vamps, but my magic couldn't differentiate between the mages' magic or something active in the room. I had that oily feeling too, but it isn't magic. I don't know what it is. I might have better luck if we went on a night when there were fewer people."

"I pretty much had the same problem," Nathalie sighed. "I think all the magic was coming from the mages, but I can't say for sure. I did get cold though, like at the crime scene the other night."

Gaetan shook his head in exasperation. "I'm no help. There was a shit ton of magic in that room, but whether it was coming from the people themselves or somewhere else, your guess is as good as mine."

"All the magic I felt downstairs was from mages, but we were not there for very long." I turned to Jaime, "I like Jaime's idea of going back on a night when it is less crowded."

"I don't think you or me showing back up there is a good idea, darlin'," Josh said gently.

"No, you are right," I agreed. "You and I cannot go back, but Jaime, Nathalie, and Gaetan should be able to go and not attract too much unwanted attention. Wait a few days for the crowds to die down and then go back?"

Jaime nodded. "I'm down with that."

"Did any of you see Winters?" Josh asked.

"We weren't among the 'pretty people' allowed upstairs," Nathalie commented dryly.

"The VIP room, at least the one we were in, didn't have any magic to it. I didn't see anything even passive in there." I noted.

"Passive?" Gaetan asked curiously.

"Some magic—symbols, runes, and some magic items—are passive until something triggers them," I explained.

"Wouldn't you searching magically for them activate them?"

"Not necessarily. Many are set up for specific triggers."

"Great," Gaetan mumbled.

"It is not as bad as it sounds. They are generally small and only cover a certain distance," I said.

"So he can't cover the entire building?" Gaetan asked.

"Not without hundreds of them," I promised.

"I looked for symbols downstairs, but it was just too crowded," Jaime said.

"When you go back, check the ceiling. I doubt he put them some-where that a casual observer might look."

Jaime nodded wearily.

"Jaime, are you up for more casting or are you wrung out?" I asked.

Jaime popped her head up, but then slumped back against her seat. "I'm sorry. I want to, but I'm kinda wiped. I might do more harm than good."

"It is no problem. You have been an absolute trooper these last few nights," I said sincerely. I would have been more surprised if she had had the energy. As it was, as much as I did not want to, I thought that I had enough energy to charm one piece of Gautier jewelry. My encounter with the necromancer had put me on edge, but these protection amulets needed to be done. If Rob Winters knew enough about me to siphon my energy, I worried what he might do against the Gautiers. I extricated myself from Josh's arms and stood up.

"You gonna go back to work?" He asked with a note of disappointment in his voice.

"I am sorry. I promise I will not work too late," I told him.

"Well, if you're gonna work, I might as well head into Chintz and check on things. Hopefully, nuthin' else has gone wrong. You aren't overworking yourself and overextending yourself, are you?" Josh asked looking at me intently.

"I am being very careful," I promised and went downstairs.

The protection matrix that I placed on Gabe Gautier's ring was every bit as complex and powerful as the one I put on his brother's. Luckily, it did not take quite as long to complete. Since I had done Marc's just the day before, I knew how to counter some of the difficulties in constructing this many layers and what shortcuts I could safely take. I was nearly finished when the ritual room door opened, and Jaime stepped inside. Annoyed at the interruption, I looked up from my work. Her wide-eyed look and shaking hands drained my anger and replaced it with fear.

I nodded to her, letting her know I had seen her, and quickly finished the last of the spell. As soon as it was done, I asked, "What is wrong?"

"It's Gabe Gautier. He's upstairs. The necromancer attacked him. Come quick!"

I did not need to be told twice. I dropped my circle and ran up the stairs behind Jaime.

The stench of sulfur hit me as soon as I entered the living room. Gabe lay sprawled on one sofa in an uninvoked protective circle. Mike Angelletti sat in a nearby armchair. The circle surrounding him was active.

"I wasn't sure what to do, and I wasn't sure how long you would be, so I put them both in protective circles. Detective Angelletti's invoked, but I couldn't get the one around Mr. Gautier to," Jaime explained. "Sorry."

"There is nothing to be sorry about. You did the right thing," I told Jaime, lightly touching her shoulder before going to Gabe's prone form. I examined him quickly. There were no obvious cuts or abrasions on the city's lieutenant, but blood seeped from his eyes, nose, ears, and mouth.

"Was he hit in the head?" I asked Detective Angelletti. A brain injury could cause that sort of bleeding.

"Magic, I think," he answered. That explained why Jaime couldn't invoke the circle. It was likely that Winters still had a hold of him.

I knelt next to Gabe and put my hand on his forehead. I closed my eyes and opened my magical third eye to enter the spirit realm. I was dismayed by what I saw. Thick black bands of magic bound Gabe tightly boring into his eyes, ears, nose, and mouth, slowly leaching the life force from the city's lieutenant. A stout magic cable, which I was sure led back to Winters, trailed from Gabe out the door. I needed to break that cable quickly. The longer Gabe was attached to Winters, the more of his soul would be lost.

My first thought was to sever the cord. However, Jaime's protection circle had not severed it when she tried to invoke it, so my invocation would meet the same fate. I had brought no weapons with me into the spirit realm, and there was not time to leave and come back. All I had was my magic. I had a wild and desperate thought that I did not know would work or not. Not long ago, I had been discussing magic with Gabe's nephew, Chris. He asked me if I could "fry" someone—use my elemental fire magic to burn someone from the inside by touching them. *Nothing ventured, nothing gained.*

Praying my magic would hurt Winters but not Gabe, I grabbed the thick cable with both hands and poured my fire magic into it. Gabe screamed, but so did the necromancer. I felt it through the cable as the tentacles briefly released Gabe and then latched back on. My jolt of fire magic had surprised the necromancer enough for him to momentarily let go, but Winters was unwilling to give up his prize so easily. I redoubled my magical efforts, pouring even more fire magic into the cable. Winters howled again, and Gabe screamed piteously. Another jolt of magic and more screaming. Now I was seriously afraid that my fire magic might kill Gabe before Winters gave up. Reasoning that Gabe would be dead either way and that if *I* killed him, he would at least retain part of his soul, I spooled more magic and pushed it again. Finally after what seemed like hours, Winters disengaged. The tentacles released Gabe, jerked from my hands, and retracted from my sight.

My spirit-self slumped, trying to regain my strength. From where I lay, I could tell that the detective did not have any cords or other magic attached to him. That, at least, was a relief and one less thing for me to worry about. When I gained my second wind, I stepped out of the spirit realm and back into my living room.

Gabe moaned softly next to me. I was not sure what sort of damage the necromancer had done to him or what harm my own fire magic might have caused, but I needed to see if I could repair it. Taking a deep breath, I placed one hand over Gabe's heart and the other on his forehead. I called the remainder of my power to my core. There was not much left, and I hoped it would heal the worst of the damage.

Taking a deep breath, I poured my healing magic into Gabe. It took quite a while for my magic to stitch up the large hole I found in Gabe's soul. I was meticulous and refused to hurry. Once done, I let my magic explore and repair the physical damage. I was unable to fix it all. I was just too drained.

I finally broke contact and sat back. Jaime handed me a mug of lukewarm blood that tasted as if it had been repeatedly reheated. Despite the less than optimal taste, I gulped it greedily. As soon as I finished, she handed me another. I saw Nathalie was feeding vitae to Gabe in the same efficient manner, and Gaetan was bringing a constant supply from the kitchen.

After I finished my third mug, I said, "Mike is fine. You can release him from the circle."

Jaime took down her circle, and Mike immediately went to Gabe's side. She looked chastened and mumbled, "Sorry."

"Don't you dare apologize," I told her firmly. "You did the right thing. You were confronted in our house by an unknown magical threat. You took steps to neutralize it. Even though Mike had not been affected, you did not know that."

"I guess I should not have brought him here," Mike grumbled.

I sighed in exasperation. "No, Mike, I did not mean that. You did the right thing as well by bringing Gabe here. I am the one best able to deal with this sort of danger. What I am saying is that you both did exactly what you should have done."

"Oh, okay," Mike seemed mollified. *Damn men and their fragile egos.* I thought to myself in irritation.

"How long was I gone?" I asked. Time moves differently on the spirit plane. What seemed like minutes could actually be hours or even days here in the physical world.

"About 20 minutes," Nathalie said. "I called Josh, he should be back soon, and Jaime called the city's Steward. They are sending someone."

I nodded. "Can you help me to the chair?" I asked. Nathalie obliged. "How do you feel, Gabe?"

"Like I went 15 rounds with Mike Tyson, Evander Holyfield, and George Foreman all at once. I think I lost," he groaned, still grey and hollow looking from blood loss.

Nathalie's keen ears picked up something, and she said, "I think the Grandmaster and the Steward are here. I'll go down and get them."

She returned trailing Marc Gautier, Sophie LeTellier, and four bodyguards. I was momentarily surprised that the Grandmaster and Steward had come themselves and then realized that of course they would; Gabe was their brother.

I started to stand, but Marc held up his hand. "Sit, I'm sure you need the rest," he instructed me.

Sophie sat down next to Gabe and took his hand. "You gave us quite a scare, little brother," she said softly. "Are you all right?"

"I've been better," Gabe grumbled.

"What exactly happened?" Marc asked. "My instructions were to watch Winters."

"I swear, Marc, that was all we were doing. We waited for him outside his club and followed him—at a distance—to a house in the Garden District. He went inside, and we moved in for a better look, and honestly, I don't know what happened after that," Gabe said.

"It had to be some sort of trap," Mike said. "Gabe was ahead of me and as soon as he stepped onto the curb, he collapsed. I wasn't sure if it was magical or not, but I figured even if it wasn't, this was the best place to bring him."

I nodded. "It sounds like Gabe tripped a ward, and Winters attacked."

Marc sighed. "There goes our element of surprise."

"I doubt we ever had it," I said. "I am sure that he was well warned by Honore to expect you."

"I suppose you are right," Marc said. "What about the murders? He is our murderer, correct?"

I grimaced. "I am not as sure of that. I get impressions when I read the bodies and ashes, but not everything. I am pretty sure, but not completely."

Marc nodded.

I heard the front door open and Josh's boots clomping up the stairs.

"I came as soon as I heard," he said when he entered the living room. In a breach of etiquette, Josh ignored the Grandmaster and crossed directly to me. "Are you all right, darlin'?"

I stood and put my hand on his cheek. "I am fine," I said, touched, but confused by his concern. "Gabe was the one injured."

"When Nat called," he said searching my face, "all she said was that you'd gone into some kind of trance and weren't responding."

"I was on the spirit plane," I explained, and wondered why Jaime hadn't told Nathalie. Then I remembered Jaime had called Sophie and was probably on the phone at the same time. I was going to have to give my bodyguards a brief lesson in magic. There was too much they did not know or understand in order to guard me properly. I now understood why bodyguards were typically drawn from one's own coven. It was not just the loyalty factor; it was also because they understood each coven's special abilities.

"I was never in any danger." This was not technically true, but Winters was too focused on Gabe to anticipate my attack. Also I did not want to worry Josh. Winters would not be caught off guard again, I was sure.

Josh turned to Gabe. "Are you okay?"

"Relatively speaking. I feel like shit, but I think I'll recover," Gabe said and looked at me.

"Winters had a good hold on you, but it was not for very long. I healed the tear in your soul, but he got a piece of it. You will always be more vulnerable to him than the rest of us are," I said.

"So he can control me?" Gabe straightening in alarm.

"No, not the way he has his victims, but he will have an easier time draining your soul if he gets ahold of you again like he did this time—unaware and vulnerable." I drew out his signet ring from my pocket. "I just finished casting the protection charms on this before I came upstairs. In light of what has happened, I would like to keep it a little longer and place one more layer of protection on here—specifically to protect your soul. I can have it to you by midnight."

"Yeah, thanks," Gabe said.

"Marc, your ring is finished and locked in my ritual room. I will go get it," I said.

"You don't need more time with it?" the Grandmaster asked.

"No. Yours and Gabe's already have soul protection on them. But since Winters now has a piece of Gabe's soul, I need to make sure that he cannot use that piece to defeat my protection spells."

"He can use Gabe's own soul against him?" Marc asked.

I nodded. "In essence, it is a backdoor. I will be barring it."

"Good," Marc said. I hurried downstairs to the ritual room and retrieved the Grandmaster's signet ring. When I returned, Marc was questioning Gabe. "The house in the Garden District, was it his residence or a kill site? Do we need to get a cleanup team over there?"

Gabe shook his head. "It's Winters' primary residence. We know from the Undine that he also has a loft apartment close to the club that he often stays at, but his name is on the deed to the Garden District property."

"Out of curiosity, how close to the house did you get before you tripped the wards?" I asked.

"I had just stepped from the street onto the damn sidewalk," Gabe said.

I raised an eyebrow. "Anyone and everyone you have watching him needs to be warned."

Marc frowned. "I think all vampires need to be warned. Sophie, if you could call the coven leaders when we get home and have them warn their members to avoid the house."

"Of course," Sophie said and noted the address Gabe gave her.

"Are humans susceptible to this?" Marc asked me.

I paused and reviewed what I knew about necromancy.

"Not by just stepping onto the sidewalk," I said finally. "As I understand it, there are two ways that necromancers steal souls for their magic. The first is that they create a thrall—someone to draw soul power from. Every time necromantic magic is used, the thrall loses a little bit of his or her soul. The thrall becomes weaker and weaker until he finally loses his entire soul and dies. The second way is to rip an entire soul from a person at the moment of their death—as was done to the murder victims. That soul is stored in a Focus and used like a battery," I explained.

"How are thralls made?" Marc asked.

I grimaced again. "I am not really sure. There are some references to necromancers and their activities in one of my grimoires, but I am unsure how accurate they are. There is a passage about thralls. Some bargain between the necromancer and thrall is made, and it must be consensual."

"Who'd be dumb enough to give consent for something like that?" Mike asked.

"It is not a matter of being dumb. From my reading, it was usually a matter of being desperate. Necromancers used to reward thralls monetarily. Many a starving peasant would gladly give up a piece of his soul to keep his family in food," I said. "I expect they could make the same sort of deal even today."

Mike nodded. "Well, the Stray werewolves took out a lot of our homeless population, but there are enough other desperate people who'd take a buck to get their next fix. Most people nowadays don't believe in souls, anyway."

"Exactly. Most will think they are getting something for nothing," I said.

"So humans can't fall prey to him by just walking through the sidewalk wards, but we can," Gabe said.

"Yes, because we are technically dead," I said. "Even with that, he could not take your entire soul at once."

"What stops him from creating wards like this all around the city?" Marc asked.

I had not even considered that. I put my head in my hands. "Not a damn thing."

"Fuck," Gabe muttered none too quietly.

My apprentice spoke up. "I think there's a way to keep us safe."

I looked at her, intrigued. "What are you thinking?"

"Even if he has the magic to do this, it's gonna take time. Juliette warded the entire city against werewolves, and it took her weeks to do it," Jaime reminded everyone. I saw where she was going with her idea.

"I could go back, tap to my existing matrix and tweak it to stop the vampire soul stealing," I said.

Jaime nodded enthusiastically.

"How long will that take you?" Marc asked.

"I do not know. I've never done such a thing. In theory it can be done, but I need to figure out the anti-soul stealing spell I'd need to layer in," I admitted.

"Can't you just use the same spell that you used in the rings to protect us?" Marc asked.

I shook my head. "No, I keyed those to you personally, and I could do it because part of your essence was already in the object. This would need to be a much broader spell, and it will take me some time to research it."

"But it can be done?" Marc asked.

"Yes," I assured him. "I just need time."

"Shouldn't the spells be separate? So if you take down the anti-werewolf wards, the anti-necromancy wards stay up?" Josh asked.

"If we had the time, yes, but I would take another month for me to set up completely separate wards for necromancy. Doing it this way, I can protect the entire city at once," I said.

"I have ordered Winters be constantly watched. We will know if he goes anywhere other than his club or his residences," Marc told me.

"It seems that I have a small window then," I said.

"We will leave you to it," Marc said and rose. He and his entourage left, leaving me to deal with yet another magical conundrum.

CHAPTER 16

*J*aime worked a miracle and arranged a meeting with
Master Remy for early the next evening. She offered to
accompany me, but I declined. I needed her to finish the
werewolf amulets so I could invoke them, and at least some things I
needed to discuss with Nicholas were not for her ears yet.

Nathalie drove me in her cute red sports car to the church that
served as the Gatekeeper headquarters here in New Orleans.

"Kinda cliché, isn't it?" My bodyguard commented dryly in reference to the building as she parked the car.

I laughed. "Josh said the same thing. At least we will be on holy
ground."

"No demons to worry about then. Do necromancers have power
on holy ground?"

"I believe it is much more difficult for them to operate on holy
ground, but not impossible. That is something I should ask Master
Remy," I acknowledged.

We were met at the door by Rebecca—the dour Gatekeeper my
sire had tortured to locate me—and led to the rectory. I was glad
that I had convinced Gaetan to stay at the house. The waves of
hostility rolling off the young Gatekeeper were bad enough with just

Nathalie and me. There might have been open confrontation had I brought the second werewolf. Nathalie, hyper-attuned to body language and attitude, took up a defensive stance between Rebecca and me.

"Take the hostility down a notch, ladies," I warned. I did not need this to turn into a brawl.

The Gatekeeper shot me a dirty look. "I don't see why you had to come here."

"I am here at Master Remy's invitation and for his convenience," I patiently explained to the young woman. I knew from things Jaime said that many of the Gatekeepers were unhappy with the alliance between themselves and the New Orleans vampire and werewolf communities. For centuries, they had kept their distance, watching and surreptitiously intervening in supernatural affairs only when our presence was at risk of discovery by humans. Circumstances were forcing us to work together, but everyone was on edge, and I did not wish to add to the antagonism. Rebecca had further reason to hate vampires since she had been tortured into revealing where my staked body was hidden.

The young woman grunted ungraciously but said no more as she let us down the long, barren hallway and knocked on the heavy oak door. A muffled voice granted entry and Rebecca opened the door for Nathalie and me.

Nicholas Remy rose at our entrance. "That will be all, Rebecca," the Master Gatekeeper said dismissing the girl when she followed us into the room.

"But Master . . ." she began.

"Please close the door behind you," Nicholas said firmly.

The girl ceased protesting and withdrew. Only when the door shut soundly behind her did the Master Gatekeeper address me again. "Thank you for coming to me, Juliette. Things are complicated, and I can't leave at the moment."

"Thank you for making time for me on such short notice," I replied. "May I introduce my bodyguard, Nathalie Roulet? You met briefly at the last crime scene. She's the Alpha werewolf's daughter."

Even though bodyguards were generally ignored, I thought this was an important introduction to make.

Nicholas nodded. "It is a pleasure to see you again, Ms. Roulet. It is good to see Juliette in such capable hands. Guard her well; she is precious."

I winced and the reminder of my fate—as if it was not always on my mind anyway.

"Yes, sir." Nathalie had the same look on her face as she had when Marc Gautier had said something similar. I knew there would be questions later. She quietly withdrew to the periphery of the room.

Nicholas came out from behind his desk and gestured to a pair of club chairs near the disused fireplace. "Shall we sit?"

I nodded and sat in one of the chairs. Nicholas folded himself gracefully into the other.

Without preamble he said, "Jaime told me a necromancer attacked the city's lieutenant last night."

"Yes. Gabe and another vampire were following Robert Winters when they inadvertently tripped a ward."

"Carelessness?" Nicholas asked with a frown.

I shook my head. "The ward extended to the public sidewalk. Any vampire could have tripped it."

"That is problematic," Nicholas said.

"We have notified vampires to stay away from his house."

"A wise course of action. Are you worried he might ward other places in the same way?"

"Yes. I plan to add an anti-soul stealing spell to the existing anti-werewolf ward. I have a few ideas on how to construct the spell, but it is not my specialty. I hoped you might know or at least have a resource."

Nicholas nodded and stood. "When I heard about the attack, I pulled the references I had on necromancy. I have a passing acquaintance with it, but probably not enough to truly help." He walked back to his desk and took a slim, blue-bound volume off the top. "I believe you will find this grimoire useful. There are several spells and wards in here," the Master Gatekeeper said, handing me the book.

I sighed in relief. "Thank you. At least we know who will try to open the gate and where now."

"Juliette, are you prepared to do what is necessary to close and seal the gate, should he succeed in opening it?"

I grimaced. "I am very much hoping that it will not come to that, but yes, I will sacrifice my life to close the gate."

"My dear, you understand that closing the gate and sealing it are two different things, don't you?" Master Remy asked.

"No," I said, drawing the word out into far more syllables than it actually contained.

Master Remy leaned forward intently, "It is of the utmost importance that we do not allow him to become any more powerful."

"Do you think he plans to use the souls to help him break the seal on the gate?"

"Not to break the seal," he shook his head. "That will be the easy part. He'll need the extra power to open the gate."

I frowned. "It is not a one-step process?"

"No."

"How exactly does he open the gate, and if he succeeds, how do I get it closed again?"

"According to my research, the mage who wishes to open the gate sets up an altar just outside the gate and sacrifices himself on it. This will break the seal. He is now in spirit form and must be strong enough to pull the gate open. I assume this is where he will use the souls. The stronger he is, the further he can open the gate and the more demons can escape onto this plane."

I took a minute to digest this. "So if he breaks the seal, there is still time to stop the gate from opening. If I'm strong enough to kill him on the spirit plane before it gets it open, does that end it?"

Nicholas shook his head sadly, "The gate must still be resealed or anyone with enough magic can open it."

"Well, you can't blame me for hoping," I said. "So, I either must defeat the mage before he breaks the seal and opens the gate or defeat him, close the gate he opened, and then kill myself to seal it."

"Yes."

I put my head in my hands. "What if I am not strong enough?" I asked.

"I pray you are. If not, there will be Hell on earth," Master Remy said bluntly.

"And my sacrifice will be for nothing," I said bitterly.

"No. Even if all you manage is a temporary seal, it will give us valuable time to close the Gate before anything else escapes."

"But the other side will try to open it back up. Trying to break an imperfect seal," I said.

"Yes."

"So I must be strong enough." I needed a drink. Badly. "I must close the gate before I commit suicide. I am correct in assuming that it will take all of my blood to seal the gate?"

"Yes, all of it. I am sorry this has fallen to you, my dear," Nicholas Remy said reaching forward and placing his hand on my shoulder. That act of kindness broke me and the list of questions I had for him fled my mind. His touch was warm and comforting, and I cried.

Nathalie said nothing to me on the drive home. She was in the same room when Remy and I discussed the Hellmouth, a silent sentinel to my fate. I knew she had her own thoughts on the matter, and I was betting that eventually she would let me know them. I had felt her hackles rise when I talked about my sacrifice, and she was still bristling.

I did not have to wait long for Nathalie to let me know what she was thinking. When we arrived back at the house, she made a quick circuit of the interior to make sure that there were no intruders. Even though we had several outside guards, both Nathalie and Gaetan insisted on inspecting inside every time we returned from an outing. I thought it was a bit excessive, but I was not the expert.

I was settling into a comfortable chair in the living room with the Gatekeeper's grimoire when Nathalie slammed two rocks glasses and a bottle of Jack Daniels down on the coffee table in front of me.

I looked up from the book and remarked dryly, "Try not to break the bottle before we have drunk it, will you? It would be a terrible waste of alcohol."

My bodyguard growled at me, actually growled at me.

Unfazed, I said, "Please, sit."

It had become obvious to me since my return that the younger generation did not hold to the same boundaries that I did and that if they wish to say something, they would say it whether or not it was their place to.

Nathalie sat and pulled the bottle towards her to open it. "You lied to me and Gaetan," she accused as she poured liberal amounts into each class. She then pushed one glass towards me.

"I most certainly did not," I snapped indignantly and snatched the glass.

"We asked you if there were more things we needed to know. You neglected to mention that you were going to commit suicide," she retorted.

"I told you about the prophecy," I protested.

"And left out the part about dying! Why did you hire us if you plan on dying, anyway?"

I carefully weighed my words as I sipped my whiskey. Finally, I said, "I hired you and Gaetan to keep me alive so that I could die at the right time."

"What sort of bullshit is this?" Nathalie demanded.

I really liked this woman. She was blunt and to the point. In another time, in another place, we could have been friends. Sadly, this was neither.

I sighed heavily. "It is not exactly what I want either."

"Does Uncle Josh know? The part about dying, I mean?" Nathalie asked.

I nodded.

"And Uncle Josh is okay with this? With you sacrificing yourself?" Nathalie prodded.

I paused, wondering how much to reveal. It would be nice to have a female confidant. Sophie was my friend, but she was also Steward of the City, and its safety, as well as the Grandmaster's, was paramount. Plus, our respective duties kept us too bit busy to share confidences very often. Jaime was too new in her life as a vampire and position as my lieutenant to bear the responsibility of knowing my fears as well. I felt guilty enough that she would inherit this mess after I died. Besides, I was trusting this woman with my life, why not my feelings as well? I took a sip of whiskey and decided for candor.

"Okay is not the word that I would use for it. Denial, I think, is closer to it."

"Denial?"

"He does not think it will come to me needing to sacrifice myself. Josh is sure we will stop the necromancer before he can break the seal and open the gates," I explained.

"But you don't think so." It was a statement, not a question.

I smiled. "Josh is an optimist, and it is one of the things that I love most about him. I, however, am a realist. I think it is even money that we can stop Winters before he gets that far. I hope we can stop him, but there is a very real chance that this will not happen. You saw what happened to Gabe."

Nathalie shuddered and refilled her glass. "Are you okay with this? Sacrificing yourself?" she asked, passing the bottle to me.

"I do not really have a choice," I sighed.

"There's always a choice," Nathalie declared with the naivete of youth.

I sighed, "The other option is for me to allow Hell to reign on earth. That is not much of a choice, in my opinion. Understand, I do not want to be a martyr, but if that is the only thing that will save my friends and the city, I will do it."

"Does everyone else know you need to die at the end?"

I shook my head. "Most assume, as you did, a smear of my blood will seal the gate. As far as I know, only you, Josh, Master Remy, and I realized I must die."

"Grandmaster Gautier doesn't know?"

"No, and I do not want him to. It will conflict him, and we do not want that. Likewise, Jaime does not realize it either."

"I'm not sure she can handle something like that yet," Nathalie said.

"Neither am I."

"You realize how fucked up all of this is, don't you?"

"Far more than you," I said.

"Then I guess I'd best keep you alive so you can do it."

We drank to that idea.

CHAPTER 17

$\mathcal{I}$ found Sophie in the old butler's pantry off the kitchen. She had long ago converted it into her office, and she ran much of the city's and Marc's affairs from here. While large for its original purpose, I had thought the space cramped for its current use. When I asked Sophie about it, she'd smiled, winked, and said, "I know."

"I do not understand," I had said.

"No one likes the confined space, so no one stays for very long. They state their business and leave. It is very conducive to getting work done. If I want to visit with someone, we go and have a cup of coffee or a glass of wine in either the library or the kitchen."

I could see the wisdom of this. Many times, well-meaning friends stopped by for visits while I had been doing the plantation's books and made themselves quite comfortable in the study's oversized chairs. They would chat away while I sat with ledgers spread before me on an enormous mahogany desk, desperate to get back to work.

As soon as Sophie saw me, she jumped up. "Do you have time for a glass of wine?" She asked. Whatever she was working on must not be too pressing.

I shook my head. "I am sorry, but I need to get home. I just wanted to stop by and give you this back." I took a small ring box out of my purse. "It is now fully charmed with a wide array of protection spells. I just gave Gabe his."

Sophie took the box from me and opened it to reveal a delicate signet ring. She took it out and slid it on. "It feels . . . heavier? Or is it just because I've not been wearing it for a few days?" she asked.

"It is a little heavier. The magic makes it so. Is it uncomfortable?" I asked.

"No. No. It is fine. I was just wondering," she said and grimaced as her phone rang. "I'm sorry, I need to take this."

I stepped back as she answered the phone, unsure if I should leave or not.

"Dammit," she swore. "Actually, Juliette is here with me now. Let me put you on speakerphone." The steward motioned me back into the room, and I pulled the door closed behind me. I sat in the uncomfortable chair in front of Sophie's monstrous desk.

Sophie tapped the phone, and Detective Mike Angelletti's voice filled the small room. "I'm sorry to be the bearer of bad news, but there's been another ritual murder," he said.

I sighed wearily. "Where did it happen this time?"

"Here in the French Quarter."

"I can be there in less than 10 minutes," I said, rising from my chair.

"Well, there's a problem. The human authorities are involved."

I groaned. I knew from the werewolf attacks that covering up the supernatural once the humans got involved was much more difficult. "What do you need me to do?" I had once magically altered a body to make a werewolf attack look like a knifing, but I was not sure what I could do with a flayed body.

"I'm on my way to the crime scene now. I'll swing by Gautier House and pick you up."

Sophie ended the call. "I'd better go tell Marc."

We walked down the corridor together, neither speaking. Nathalie stood up from the chair she was sitting in just outside the grandmaster's office. "What's wrong? You both have matching grim expressions."

Sophie knocked lightly on Marc's door and let herself in while I quickly explained the situation to Nathalie.

Sophie had not emerged from the Grandmaster's office by the time Mike Angelletti arrived. He looked at Nathalie and me and said apologetically, "I can't get you both into the crime scene. There are too many officers there that would ask too many questions. The only reason I can get Mrs. Grammont in is because she's listed as an official consultant for the department." Soon after my return to New Orleans, I was approached to help the detective unofficially. The police commissioner, who conveniently was also the head of the Salamand coven, had made that position official last week.

Nathalie started to protest, but I interrupted, "I will be perfectly safe with Detective Angelletti. Besides, the necromancer can hardly attack me in front of half of the New Orleans police force. I will meet you at home."

Nathalie grumbled but let me go with Mike.

"I am sorry," I apologized as I slid into the front seat of the unmarked police car.

Mike shrugged. "She's just doing her job."

"How did the human authorities become involved in this one?" I asked.

"Someone called 911 about 30 minutes ago. They sent a uniform—someone not on our payroll—and he discovered the scene," Mike explained. Many of the NOLA police officers were vampires, servants, or paid to look the other way. It made keeping the supernatural community a secret easier.

"Who were the victims?" I asked not sure if I wanted to know.

"The human is Aiden Hempstead. He was being groomed by the Gnome. The female victim was Tessa Mickelson. Of course the police don't know about her. At this point they just think she's missing and is the chief suspect."

I nodded. "She is a Gnome, correct?"

"Yes, a fledgling. I think she's been a vampire for less than a year."

"Can you get me into the room alone? Without humans, I mean. You can be there."

Mike pursed his lips. "That might be hard. What do you need to do?"

"I would like to read the scene as I did before. Maybe do a bit of blood working."

"I'll do my best. Can you do it and just wipe the memories of anyone who sees you?"

"Maybe?" I said uncertainly. "The readings took a lot out of me the last time. They were intense. I may not have the power to do a thorough job."

Mike nodded his face grim, "Let me see who is on scene. That will be the determining factor."

We pulled up to a well-kept house in the French Quarter and parked behind several police cruisers and the coroner's van.

"Shit. The ME is already here," Mike said in frustration.

"What does that mean?"

"The body has probably been moved, and it's going to be very difficult to clear the scene."

"I will work with what we have then," I said.

Mike flashed his badge and the uniformed officer let us past the yellow crime scene tape. A half-dozen people milled around the courtyard. Mike gave them a brief nod as he led me into the house.

"The scene is upstairs in the bedroom," he said, leading the way. We encountered a few people, each greeting Mike, but not hindering our progress or inquiring as to who I was—at least, that is, until we reached the master bedroom door. There was another uniformed officer standing sentry, but it was the two men in suits blocking the door that arrested our progress.

The taller of the two men, Paul Barthelmy, hailed us. "Detective, I see you were able to persuade Mrs. Grammont to come and look," he said affably.

"Yes, Mrs. Grammont graciously agreed to view the scene and give her opinions," Mike said.

"Commissioner, it is good to see you again," I said, nodding to him. Not only was Paul the New Orleans police Commissioner, but he was also the Salamand Coven Master. He, along with key members of the police department, was responsible for keeping criminal activity of the paranormal variety hidden from humans. I did not envy him his job.

"Mrs. Grammont—Juliette, thank you for coming. This is Detective Chuck Spencer. Chuck is our in-house occult expert," Paul said.

The second man, a good-looking blonde in his mid-30s, was decidedly put out. "I don't see why an outside consultant needs to be brought in. I am every bit as qualified to read occult symbols," he said.

Choosing to ignore the young man's pique, I said, "It is a pleasure to meet you, detective. Are you a practitioner or is your interest solely academic?" I asked, extending my hand.

I felt the faintest tingle of magic as our hands touched although his reaction was much stronger. He jumped back as if I had shocked him.

"I'm so sorry," he hastily apologized. "It must be static electricity."

I smiled and nodded.

This man was a mage, although untrained. I doubted that he even knew he had the ability, but I knew raw power when I felt it. His reaction to me was most telling. A trained mage would not have jumped as he did. Very interesting.

"Chuck, this is Juliette de Grammont; she is taking over Frederique DeRoche's store over on Royal," Paul explained.

Chuck's eyes swept over me, and he blurted out, "But you're not . . ." before he could stop himself.

I laughed, knowing what he was going to say. Dressed in a short, gray, pencil skirt and a black, short sleeve blouse with modest heels, I was not what one would expect from a voodoo priestess. I did not have the heart to tell him that Frederique's long flowing skirts and wild hair had all been for show. "No, I do not look like the stereotypical mambo. But rest assured that I know my craft, and I am well-versed in several other magical styles."

Chuck blushed and hastily tried to cover his faux pas. "I was very sorry to hear about Mrs. DeRoche's death."

"It was quite a blow," I said.

He cleared his throat and said, "Shall we go take a look?"

"Would it be possible to view the scene with no one else in there?" I asked. "I mean without the crime scene techs and other officers."

Paul nodded. "I always cleared the room for Frederique too."

True to his word, the police Commissioner cleared the room of personnel, leaving only Mike, Chuck, Paul, and me. As soon as I entered the room, the hair on my arms raised. I saw Chuck visibly shudder. Neither Paul nor Mike seemed affected.

I took only a few short steps into the room before I stopped to observe the scene as a whole. It was like the other two scenes, at least at first glance. The longer I studied it, the more "off" it became. There were odd voids in the evidence patterns. The body and the magic circle were just as they had been at the earlier murderers, but from there subtle differences appeared. The candles for the sex magic were in the right position, but the bed itself was splattered with blood, indicating the attack on Aidan Hempstead had begun there.

A wide blood smear leading from the bed to the magic circle showed where Aidan had been dragged. However, there was a second smear bisecting it as if someone had carelessly walked through it.

One of the crime scene techs? No, they would not have been so careless. First responders? Possibly? Make sure to ask Mike or Paul.

I was carefully walking the periphery of the room when Chuck stumbled and nearly fell onto Aiden Hempstead's corpse. "Watch out!" Mike said as he seized the swaying man by the arm and pulled him away from the central crime scene.

"I . . . I'm sorry. Suddenly, I just got lightheaded," the young detective said, almost slurring his words.

Paul Barthelmy quirked an eyebrow. "Weak stomach, detective?"

"No, Sir. I'm not queasy, I promise." Chuck shook his head as if to clear it.

From my position, the odd voids and blood smears suddenly made sense, and I looked up. On the ceiling, someone had carefully constructed a magical trap. Anyone with magical abilities who walked into the circle would find their magic being siphoned off. It was probably a trap set for me, but Chuck had triggered it. I wondered how hard it was going to be to wipe the mage's mind once I finished saving his skin.

I caught Paul's eye and mouthed, "Magic."

His countenance became worried as he nodded.

I opened my third eye and entered the spirit plane. I saw the dark magic immediately. Hundreds of delicate black tendrils encased Chuck. From where I stood, I could not see a central origin point for all the tendrils and cringed. There was no way I could remove these in time one at a time. I carefully walked around Chuck, looking for something of substance to attack, and I found it on his back where the tentacles all merged into a single strand about the diameter of my arm. This was definitely Winters' work.

Hoping to catch the necromancer off guard again, I seized the rope-like strand and pushed my fire magic into it. I could hardly believe that it worked a second time. I felt Winters scream and retract his magic tentacles. I stepped back onto the material plane and watched Chuck sag heavily against Mike. Both Paul and Mike looked stricken.

"Lay him over by the wall," I instructed and pulled a small chair from the vanity towards the circle. Careful not to enter the circle myself, I slid off my shoes and climbed onto the makeshift stool. I was still almost a foot from the ceiling but hoped that I was close enough. Fumbling in my shoulder bag, I drew out a large, gold atomizer.

Paul walked over to see what I was doing and asked, "You're going to spray perfume, Juliette?"

"It is holy water," I explained, and sprayed the contents of the bottle onto the chalked circle. It hissed and sputtered when the water hit. With an audible pop, the circle broke.

I hopped down to examine Chuck, who was trying to stand.

"You tampered with a crime scene," he accused, struggling to rise, but Mike gripped him by the shoulders. "Let me up, God dammit!"

I put a cool hand on his forehead and whispered, "Quiet."

Chuck's struggle ceased, and I went to work altering his memory magically. I needed to put quite a bit of my own magic behind it, because the young detective had a great deal of willpower and resisted my initial attempts at manipulation.

Finally, he blinked rapidly and said, "What, what just happened?"

"You became lightheaded. Have you eaten yet today?" I asked calmly.

"Um, I . . . No. I don't think so," the man admitted.

"You need to eat. Your blood sugar is low," I said coldly, lacing my words with power so he believed them. "Mike, could you take the detective to get a burger, and I will finish up here with the Commissioner?"

Mike helped the clearly confused and embarrassed Chuck to his feet and said, "I wouldn't mind a bite myself. I haven't had dinner yet. There's a great diner down the street."

"Um, sure," Chuck mumbled and hung his head. "I'm sorry, sir," he said to Paul.

"It happens to the best of us, burning the candle at both ends. You need to take care of yourself. Go get yourself some dinner, then get back here, and canvas the neighborhood. See if the neighbors saw anything," Paul said.

After the two detectives left, Paul rounded on me. "What the hell just happened, Juliette?"

I pointed to the ceiling and the broken circle. "Robert Winters laid a magic trap, and it snared your detective," I explained.

Paul gave me a dark look. "Obviously. But why him? Mike was right next to him, and he wasn't affected."

"Chuck is a mage, and Mike is not," I said.

"What?" he exclaimed in disbelief. "Chuck's a mage?"

I nodded. "I am pretty sure he is untrained and does not even know he has powers. How did Frederique not identify him?"

"I don't think she ever even met him. Chuck started as a beat cop, but a couple of years ago he left to go to college. He came back and made detective a few months ago. This is the first case that has touched on the occult that the police have caught in a while."

"He is from New Orleans?" I asked.

"Yeah. He grew up in the foster care system. His parents are dead—

no other living relatives. It's amazing that he turned out as well as he has," Paul remarked.

"He is amazingly resilient," I said.

"Is that going to be a problem?"

"I am not sure. Mages, even untrained ones, are notoriously difficult to manipulate. I have altered his memories, but his mind is strong. The actual events may resurface."

"Would he be a candidate for cultivation and training?" Paul asked.

I shrugged. "I am surprised that no one from the local magic community has not tried to apprentice him."

"He doesn't believe in the supernatural. He is fascinated by the occult but doesn't think it is real. Everything he knows is from books. That's what we were discussing when you arrived. He took a bunch of courses in college and wants to be our in-house occult expert."

"Is he being groomed by the Salamand?" I asked. I knew the Salamands regularly recruited new coven members from the police department. It was one of the ways they hid the presence of the supernatural community. I did not wish to poach another coven's possible recruit.

Paul shook his head. "Not at this point, and it seems like he would be a better fit for your coven. Y'all do seem to be down a few members," he added.

I chuckled humorlessly. "Just a few. I will talk to Marc about it. We certainly do not need an uninformed officer stumbling onto our existence."

"And I'd hate to have to kill him," Paul deadpanned. "Chuck is a good cop. The city needs more like him. Anyway, is the scene safe now?"

I nodded. "Yes. I have dismantled the circle, but everyone is going need to be extra careful when dealing with these murders."

"Are you going to read anything in here?"

I looked around. I was not sure if there was anything that the crime scene techs had not handled and thus contaminated for my purposes. I shrugged. "I will at least try to read the bed, but I may only get impressions left by police personnel."

I walked to the bed and saw the fine powder of vampire dust on the pillow. I closed my eyes and placed my palms on it.

Suddenly, I was kneeling over Aidan Hempstead with a black silk scarf in my hand. "Can I tie you up?" Tessa but not Tessa asked him.

"You can do anything you want to me, baby," Aiden said, and then the scene vanished.

"That was not helpful," I sighed and opened my eyes.

I turned from the bed and walked to Aiden's body. He too was flayed alive. As much as I did not want to, I knew that I at least needed to attempt reading the body. I knelt next to Aiden's head. The killer had stopped stripping the skin off before reaching the poor man's face, so I place my palm on Aidan's forehead and once again opened my senses.

Pain flooded my body as I saw Tessa Mickelson leaning over me. She had a sickly, predatory smile on her face. "Your sacrifice is for the greater good," she said maliciously.

The pain became too much, and I broke contact.

"Anything?" Paul asked.

I shook my head. "Not really. It was the same necromancer riding Tessa. I assume that since Winters laid the magic trap that he is also our killer. One thing was unique, however. She did not seem to be fighting for control." I frowned. "She was there, but not."

"What do you mean?" Paul asked.

"Her being was still there, but asleep? Maybe Winters forced her consciousness into torpor?" I reasoned.

"He can do that?"

"I really do not know," I said dismayed.

Paul frowned. "Do you need to read anything else?" He asked.

A wave of exhaustion rolled over me. "No, I am afraid that reordering the detective's brain drained me."

"Well, let's go then. I'll let the techs back in to finish their jobs and take you home," Paul said.

"Yes, I need a ride. I seem to have lost mine," I said remembering that Mike had left with Chuck.

"Do you need to eat?" Paul asked as he led me downstairs. "We can detour down Bourbon Street if you need."

"I will be fine until I get home," I assured him. I really did not want to drink a drunk person right now. Another officer fell in behind us, and I recognized him from meetings at Gautier House. He was the Salamand Master's bodyguard.

"Do you need me to drive you somewhere, sir?" The younger vampire asked.

Paul nodded. "We need to take Madame Grammont home and then stop by Gautier House."

"Of course," the man said and led us to a dark sedan.

As we settled into the back seat, Paul asked me, "Where is your bodyguard?"

"I left her at Gautier House when Mike came to get me. He said it would be too difficult to get both of us into the crime scene. I assume she has driven herself home by now."

"You really shouldn't be alone," Paul warned.

"I expected to be with Mike the entire time. He is an excellent substitute for Nathalie. Now, I am with you. I expect am still in excellent hands."

"The wolf is working out then?"

"Amazingly well," I assured him.

Paul grunted. "How do we deal with our new threat?"

"The necromancer?" I asked, surprised by the abrupt change of topic.

"Yeah. Is he going to keep killing?"

"I expect so. He is harvesting magic and souls. So far he has taken a vampire from a different coven each time."

"Is that just a random coincidence?" Paul asked.

"At first I thought so, but now I am wondering. If he could capture souls from each coven, that would significantly magnify his magic since vampire souls are powerful, and each coven has its own special abilities."

"What is he going to use this for?"

"I assume to open the Gate in December."

"It's only October. Isn't it a bit early for that? I mean, it completely tipped his hand."

I sat back and pondered that for a moment. "Maybe the killings have been easier than he expected."

Paul asked, "Can we just kill this bastard?"

"Getting past his magic is going to be a problem. You know he attacked Gabe last night."

"Yeah, I heard. Can you do anything?"

"I am working on it," I promised.

CHAPTER 18

athalie and Jaime were sparring in the courtyard when we pulled in. The two women broke off and jogged over to the car as I got out.

"Where's Detective Angelletti?" Nathalie asked, peering into the back seat.

"He had other business to attend to," I replied vaguely.

I turned back to the car. "Paul, thank you for the ride. I will let you know what Marc and I decide about Detective Spencer." He nodded as I shut the door firmly and the black sedan backed out of the courtyard.

"He was supposed to stay with you the entire time! That's the only reason I let you go without me," Nathalie huffed.

"It was unavoidable," I assured her, "but I was in good hands with the Salamand Master and his bodyguard," I assured her.

She shot me a hard look. "If you die on my watch, Dad will never forgive me. Neither will Uncle Josh."

"How was it?" Jaime interrupted.

"Horrible—but enlightening," I said. "See me when you are done and we can talk."

A very sweaty Nathalie said, "We're done. I need to shower."

"Rematch tomorrow?" Jaime asked.

"Sure. You keep me on my game," Nathalie said and loped off to the carriage house.

Jaime followed me into the house. "Winters laid a trap for me," I said.

"It obviously didn't work," Jaime observed.

"I was lucky. The trap sprang on a previously unknown mage."

"Oh, that's interesting." Jaime raised an eyebrow.

"We may have a new recruit sooner than I anticipated." I deposited my purse on an occasional table situated by the top of the stairs.

"Who is this person?"

"A New Orleans police detective by the name of Chuck Spencer."

"I've never heard of him." Jaime draped herself bonelessly across one of the club chairs.

"He is clearly untrained. Master Barthelmy said that Spencer had been away from the city until recently," I said taking a seat on the couch.

"Do you want me to check him out?"

"Would you?" I asked.

"Yeah. I'll see if any of the Gatekeepers know anything, and I've still got my street contacts."

"That would be wonderful," I said.

"Did you learn anything new about the murders?"

I shrugged. "Not really. I am fairly certain that Winters is our killer or working with him."

"Two necromancers?" Horror laced her voice.

"I think it unlikely, but it is a possibility. The trap was set by Winters. That I am sure of. Beyond that . . ." I shrugged again. "Another thing: the vampire was not fighting the necromancer this time."

"Really? I know you said the other victims were desperately trying to regain control. Why didn't this one?" Concern was evident in her voice.

"I think she was unconscious or in torpor," I said.

"Shit."

"Exactly."

"How did he manage that?" Jaime pulled herself up straight and leaned forward intently.

"I have no idea. Perhaps a powerful blow to the head?"

"It takes a lot to render a vampire unconscious. The easiest way would be to stake her."

"I will need to keep thinking about this," I said.

"I'll hit the streets and see if I can find out anything about this Detective Spencer," Jaime said as she stood.

I sat for a longtime considering the events of the evening after Jaime left but came to no firm conclusions.

JAIME MET me in the kitchen early the next evening as I was pouring myself cup of coffee.

"I found out some stuff," she said bouncing on her toes.

"About Spencer?" I asked.

She nodded. "That too. I've got some feelers out for more information, but this is about something else."

"Okay. Do you want to tell me what?" I asked.

She looked around anxiously. "Could we go down to the ritual room?"

"Of course." I wondered why Jaime was acting so strangely. I did not think Nathalie had told her I needed to sacrifice myself to seal the Gate. She was not acting as if she knew that. I took my coffee mug and followed Jaime downstairs.

"What is this all about?" I asked once we were securely behind closed doors.

"It's about what happened between you and Josh—the power and energy transfer," Jaime said.

"You found something that explains how that happened?" I asked.

"I think you two were soul-bonded."

I stopped short. "Soul-bonded?" I had heard legends about the phenomenon but had given them little credence. As far as I knew, stories about two mages being mystically linked were tales told to children.

"It is the only thing that explains the transfer without casting," Jaime said.

"Soul-bonded?" I asked again stupidly.

"I think so," Jaime said.

I sat heavily on the floor. "That cannot be. He is not a mage."

"He has family magic. His grandmother on his father's side was a thaumaturge. But you already knew that didn't you?" she accused, leaning against the worktable.

"It was not my secret to tell," I said.

Jaime shrugged. "I really had to dig and cross reference to find it."

I should have known that my childe would be like a terrier with a bone. "I would appreciate you not saying anything about this to anyone."

Jaime nodded. "My lips are sealed—both about Josh's ancestry and your soul-bonding."

"Thank you. My knowledge of soul bonding is scant. I know the legends say it is momentous and life altering for those involved, but beyond that I know very little," I confessed.

"Normally it occurs between two mages, and they become linked," Jaime explained "You can draw on his strength to augment your own, and he can do the same."

"It is kind of like being mated, it isn't?"

"Usually, but not always. There have been instances of two mages of the same gender who were not homosexual being bonded. There have also been a few instances of family members being bound. Generally though, yeah, it's a mating. You can sense the other person's emotions and tell if they are in trouble."

"Oh. Okay. What else can you tell me? What about pain? If one is hurt, does the other feel it?" I asked.

Jaime grimaced. "Yeah. That seems to be the serious downside to this arrangement."

"Is there any way to break the bond?"

"Other than death? I don't think so," Jaime answered.

I had a moment of panic. "Does the death of one cause the death of the other?"

"No. Human mages have survived decades after their mate dies."

"What about a vampire's final death?"

Jaime shrugged. "All the recorded accounts of soul-bonding that I found have been between two human mages."

The only legends that I had heard were between human mages as well. "Are you sure this is what has happened?"

"It is my best guess, but it is only a guess. Master Remy might know more," Jaime suggested.

I pursed my lips. "I will take that into consideration. Thank you."

"I'm sorry that I'm not more help."

"No, really. I appreciate you looking into this for me." I stood pondering my apprentice's words for several long moments.

Jaime shifted nervously and then said, "I know this is a lot to take in, but I also dug up some stuff about your police detective."

That snapped me out of my deliberation. "Chuck Spencer?" I asked.

"Yep."

"That was fast," I said, pleased with her diligence.

Jaime said as though reciting, "Chuck Spencer: born Charles Xavier Spencer to Henry and Margaret Spencer on April 19, 1975 in New Orleans, Louisiana. His father, Henry, was an up-and-coming chef and his wife, Peg, ran the business side of the restaurant. Things seem to go very well for the couple until both were killed in a botched robbery attempt at the restaurant in December 1980. Chuck witnessed the murders. He had no living relatives and entered the foster care system. Chuck often acted out, fighting with other children in the families they placed him with. Even when he was the only child in the home, he was disruptive. He bounced from home to home and had quite a rap sheet by the time he was 14. Mostly B&E and petty theft. Then he boosted a car and ended up in juvie," Jaime said.

"Can you translate that last bit for me? Juvie, boosting a car, and B&E?" I asked. There were still so many things I needed help with.

"Oh, right. Sorry," Jaime said sheepishly. "Juvie is juvenile detention. It's jail for kids. B&E is breaking and entering. Boosting a car means he stole it."

"Thank you."

Jaime continued, "Apparently his stint in juvie helped scare him straight. When he got out, he joined a mentoring program."

"He became a mentor?"

"No, he got one. A cop by the name of Sean O'Malley. O'Malley and his wife took Chuck in, and he's been on the straight and narrow ever since. After Chuck graduated high school, O'Malley pulled a few strings and got him into the police academy. Actually graduated third in his class."

"So bad boy gone good? Or at least scared straight?"

"Looks like it. He joined the PD as a foot patrol officer. Six years ago, he left the city to attend LSU full-time. He came back after graduation, took the detective's test, and earned his shield."

"Did anyone you talk to know anything about his magical abilities?" I asked.

"No. Even though Chuck was born here in New Orleans, his parents weren't from here. Since they were both only children of deceased parents, there wasn't anyone to nurture his magic. My guess is that his dad didn't contact any of the local mages or someone would've looked out for the kid."

"The O'Malley's do not have magic?" I asked.

Jaime shook her head. "No. I wondered that too, but they don't show up in any Gatekeeper records."

"Could the records be wrong? I mean, they missed Chuck Spencer altogether. They also seem to have missed Robert Winters." I had been so thrown during my last meeting with Nicholas Remy that I had forgotten to ask how Winters had slipped by the Gatekeepers.

Jaime shrugged. "I don't know about Winters, but both O'Malley's were lifetime residents of the city with long family ties. If there were something, it would've been picked up. The reason Spencer flew under the radar for so long is that his parents weren't from here and made no contact with the local mage community."

"Master Barthelmy says that the occult fascinates Detective

Spencer but doesn't believe in it. To him it is purely an academic pursuit," I told Jaime.

"It sounds like he's in deep denial about what he is. Chances are he started looking into the occult when his powers manifested and has explained them away somehow," Jaime mused. "I was pretty freaked when mine showed up."

"How old were you?"

"Fourteen. It was right after I started living on the streets. My powers were actually the reason I was willing to listen to what Sarah said about the Gatekeepers. She told me they could teach me how to use them."

"I wonder how many children with magical abilities go untrained," I said.

"Detective Spencer really is an outlier," Jaime said. "The Gatekeepers had been keeping tabs on me when I was in the system, waiting for my powers to manifest. They lost track of me when I ran away but were actively looking for me."

"Do the Gatekeepers track all supernatural creatures?" I asked.

"They try. The archives on mages, vampires, and werewolves are really quite extraordinary."

"I bet they are," I said dryly. "Is there anything else I need to know?"

"No, that was all I could find out last night."

"Then, are you ready to learn how to make magic jewelry on your own?" I asked, standing up.

"Sure! Where do we start?"

"With you. Specifically, a piece for you."

"Great!"

"Do you have a piece of jewelry that you like and often wear?" I asked. "Maybe one of your bracelets?"

Jaime wore several bracelets on each wrist. Most were leather, but some were made of metal.

"There is this one. I almost never take it off, even in the shower." She held out her arm and showed me an exquisite, delicate, silver bracelet. Two Celtic knots bracketed a dark green stone. The bracelet was an odd contrast to both her other jewelry and to herself.

"What is the stone? It is not an emerald, but I'm not sure what it is."

"My mom said it was green amber and would bring me luck."

I nodded. "Green amber also signifies immortality."

Jaime twisted the bracelet and looked wistful. "Well, it didn't help her, but I got the immortality."

"What happened to your mother?" I asked gently.

"She died in a car crash, along with my dad. I was six."

"I am so sorry."

She shrugged. "I was staying with my Gran up in Port Allen while my parents celebrated some big promotion that Dad got. I-10 iced up and a semi hit them."

"Your grandmother raised you then?" I asked.

"For a while. I was about ten when she died and got stuck in the system."

"System?"

"The foster care system. It. Sucked. Ass," she said emphatically.

I remembered Paul Barthelmy saying Chuck Spencer had been in foster care and that it was amazing that he turned out as well as he had. I nodded.

"Nobody wanted to adopt a 10-year-old, so I bounced around for a couple of years until one of my foster dads decided to have a go at me. I ran away and lived on the streets after that," she said, looking at her feet.

"Had a go at you? Do you mean that he raped you?" I did not know why this shocked me, but it did.

"He tried to. I screamed bloody murder and his wife came in. He tried to pretend that it wasn't what it looked like. I didn't stick around to see if she bought his bullshit or not."

"How old were you?" I asked, still stunned by her revelations.

"I'd just turned fourteen. I spent about six months on the streets, and then the Gatekeepers found me."

"I am surprised you trusted them," I said.

"I didn't, not really, but I was hungry and tired of sleeping on concrete, and I had these crazy powers that were manifesting. It was one of the female gatekeepers, Sarah, who found me. I doubt I'd have gone with one of the guys."

"How long were you with them?" I asked.

"Going on five years. The first year was the hardest. I was sure that Master Remy was some sort of perv or something, but he's not. Eventually, I decided that I could trust him, and he took me under his wing. Like I said, I had just started coming into my powers when Sarah found me, so the Gatekeepers helped me figure what that was all about."

"Your family did not have magic?" I asked. That was unusual. Magic generally passed from mother to daughter or father to son. It might skip a generation, but it was highly unusual for a mage to appear in a completely un-magical family.

"Now that I think about it, Mom did. She did little things around the house like turn on lights without touching the switch. She might've been able to do more, but I was too young to understand. After she and dad died, I was living with dad's mom, and she definitely didn't have magic. It really freaked me out when my power showed up. Luckily, Sarah, and later Master Remy trained me."

"I am so sorry that I messed that up for you," I said and meant it. I really liked Jaime and I knew she would be an asset to the coven, but I wished that her turning had been her choice.

"You saved my life that night. I mean, yeah, initially I was really pissed, but both Master Remy and Grandmaster Gautier talked to me about how it happened. It's pretty obvious that you hadn't been trying to turn me when I look at all the facts. Plus, I'm liking the perks," Jaime explained with a grin.

"Perks?"

"I went twelve rounds with a werewolf last night and held my own. Before? She would have cleaned my clock. I didn't even break a sweat," she said smugly.

"Nice to know that your vampire skills are being put to good use," I laughed.

"Seriously, Juliette, I'm good with how things turned out. I don't regret it, and I hope you don't either," Jaime said and turned to look at me.

"The only thing I regret is not having your prior consent. I am proud to have you as my childe and my lieutenant," I said and touched her arm.

"Good. I think that's enough girl sharing for one day. Let's do some magic shit!"

I laughed again.

It was a productive night. Jaime successfully charmed her bracelet, and I charged the remaining werewolf amulets. Josh would be relieved that we could finally bring in the rest of the werewolves and have our full house guard contingent.

When we finished just before dawn, I said to Jaime, "I hoped that we could start on your focus tonight, but it will have to wait."

She looked disappointed. "Oh."

"The anti-soul stealing wards needs to be added to the existing magical matrix around the city, and I really need your help to do it," I explained.

Jaime brightened. "Oh, I totally understand. The anti-soul stealing thing is really important. You want my help?"

"Yes. We can work in tandem, and it should cut the time needed to complete the spells almost in half. I promise that as soon as we get the city warded against the threat, we will start on your focus. I just do not want what happened to Gabe to happen to any other vampire."

Jaime visibly shuddered at the memory. "No, neither do I if we can help it. That was horrible."

WHEN I CAME UPSTAIRS, Josh handed me a glass of dark, red wine and asked, "Do you want to tell me what's troubling you?"

I smiled wanly. "I think the better question might be what is not troubling me."

He led me to the couch and pulled me gently into his arms, careful not to spill our drinks. "I know you have a lot on your mind, but something has changed. You're more pensive than normal."

He was right. For hours, I had been mulling over what Jaime had told me. The implications of Josh and me being soul-bonded were enormous and more than anything, I was scared for him. I knew what my fate probably was. I was not especially happy about it, but I had more or less accepted it. Being joined with Josh was a huge . . . complication. What would happen to him when I sacrificed myself to seal the Gate? Could he survive it? Would he even want to?

I reached up and stroked his cheek with my free hand. "Jaime has done some research about what happened between us," I finally said.

"You mean the power transfer?" He asked.

"Yes," I said solemnly.

"That ain't a happy face, Juliette. What did she find out?"

"Do you know anything about soul-bonding?" I asked.

He shrugged. "Some. My aunt and her husband are bonded. It really helped them when my cousin was killed. They drew on each other to get through the grief. Why? Wait," he sat up straight, "is that what Jaime thinks happened to us?"

"She says it's the only thing that makes sense."

"I thought only mages could be soul-bonded," he said.

"Honestly, this is a huge hole in my magical knowledge. I just thought soul-bonding happened in legends. In the stories I heard, it was always two human mages. However, your grandmother was a thaumaturge. Your aunt and uncle are mages. You have magic in your family and are sensitive to it. You cannot cast, but the line might be strong enough in you," I explained.

"Well, this is a good thing then!" He exclaimed and then suddenly became quiet and looked hurt. "Unless you don't feel that way." Josh began to shift away from me.

I grabbed for him, heedless of my spilling wine. "That is not what is troubling me. I do love you."

"Then what's the problem?"

"I am very worried about what this might mean for you."

"I don't understand."

"As I understand it, this bond is normally between two human mages. I am a Vampiric mage, and you are a vampire with magical sensitivity," I explained.

"You think the soul-bonding might not work the same way with us?"

"I have no idea, and that scares me," I confessed.

With maddening calmness he said, "Then we'll ask. I'll call my aunt after we get up tonight and see if she or Uncle Owen knows anything."

"They are still alive?" I asked. Mages lived a long time, longer than humans, but Josh was almost two hundred. They must use magic to extend their lives.

"Yeah. They're really gettin' up there now, but their magic has greatly extended their lives."

"How do they feel about you and Emma being vampires?"

"We don't talk much about it. It's kinda like politics and religion—the less said the better."

"Is anyone else in your family still alive?" I asked.

Josh shook his head. "Naw. My cousin and Gram were killed during the war. Mom and Dad were human and died at the end of their natural lifespans."

"What happened your grandmother and cousin?" I asked.

"They were workin' with other Allied Thaumaturges to bring down Hitler and his Nazi's on D-Day. Nazi necromancers killed them."

"I am so sorry. Hitler was not . . .?"

"Naw. He and his henchmen were just deep into the occult. He managed to find a couple of necromancers to work for him but nothin' more."

I nodded. "Do you think I should speak to Master Remy about the soul-bonding?"

Josh blew out a breath. "Yeah, I think so. We don't want too many people to know, but he'll probably have some answers. Jaime hasn't already talked to him?"

"No. I asked her not to. She used the Gatekeeper archives to trace your lineage, so she knows about your grandmother being a thaumaturge, but she said she did not and would not talk to anyone about it."

"You know that Jaime might be wrong about the soul-bonding thing. It could be something completely different. Let's talk to Aunt Delia, Uncle Owen, and Master Remy before you start worrying about what might happen to me."

"I..."

"No more invitin' trouble tonight," Josh insisted. "Come on, let's get some club soda on this wine before it stains."

CHAPTER 19

My plans to add the anti-soul stealing spell to the city's existing ward matrix with Jaime hit a snag. Nathalie staunchly refused to let us leave the house to cast in the open without both her and Gaetan present to guard us. Since Josh and Gaetan had left for the swamps before I had even awoken, I had to settle for Jaime and Nathalie standing guard while I worked on the matrix alone. I understood the need for both guards, but my progress was maddeningly slow. I also understood the need for both Josh and Gaetan to go to the swamp. Josh needed to deliver the werewolf amulets, pick up our remaining house guards, and meet with Beau. Gaetan had a few personal details to tie up and the rest of his and Nathalie's belongings to retrieve.

I was just out of sorts which caused me to have trouble concentrating. The anti-soul stealing spell in the Gatekeeper's grimoire was complicated, and as my mind wandered to my myriad problems, I found that I often needed to redo sections I had just completed because they were incorrect. My lack of focus disgusted me.

Eventually, Jaime suggested that I take a break. She sat beside me on one of the many benches along the River Walk looking at the water

"What's wrong, Juliette? I've never known you to be this preoccupied," she asked.

I sighed deeply. "I keep thinking about what you told me yesterday—about the soul-bonding."

"I thought you liked Josh?" She asked misunderstanding my meaning much as Josh had.

"I do like him. I love him. That is why I am concerned."

"I don't get it," she said.

"What are the implications of a non-mage being bonded to a mage—if we are really bonded?"

"Nothing bad has happened so far," she pointed out.

"I have not been in magical combat yet."

"Yes, you have. You've fought Winters—twice," my apprentice pointed out.

I shook my head. "Not really. I caught him by surprise both times, and he retreated without a fight."

"I don't know enough about this to offer advice. The only person I know who might is Master Remy."

"Could you set up a meeting for me with him? There are actually several things that I need to speak with him about."

"When do you want to meet?"

"As soon as possible. Tonight, if that is convenient for him."

"Sure. Let me call him."

Luckily, the Master Gatekeeper could meet with me. Neither Jaime nor Nathalie was happy about being barred from the meeting room, but I could not deal with their reactions to any of the possible revelations. I was having enough problems dealing with my own reactions. While the meeting did not give me all the answers I wanted, it left me substantially more informed than I had been. I also had Nicholas Remy's promise to make discreet inquiries into the remaining issues.

Using his second sight, Master Remy confirmed that Josh and I were indeed soul bonded. I had not known it was even possible to see the bond let alone what it might look like in an aura. He explained that when a couple is soul-bonded, a faint outline of one partner's aura can be seen around the other. I could not decide whether I was dismayed or elated. Soul-bonding was a rare gift, Master Remy stressed. While he had heard of at least one mage/non-mage pairing, he did not have any details and could not put to bed my fears about Josh's safety. He promised to look into that matter as well as the issue of two vampires being bonded. But he could offer no concrete answers about what would happen to Josh if I was forced to sacrifice myself to seal the Gate.

"To that my dear, I have no clear answer," he said. "We've never had to seal a Gate before. We have had plenty of mages die before their bonded partners, however. Death breaks the soul-bond. The survivor goes into a period of extreme mourning, and a few—a very few—have died from that grief. Usually the surviving partner recovers and lives out his or her life. I shouldn't think you have that to worry about that with Josh."

In frustration I said, "I swear, I thought this was already settled in my mind. If Winters, or whoever wanted to open the Gate, kidnapped someone and wanted to trade their life for mine, I would not do it. That person would just have to die. Somehow this is different, and I do not understand why."

Master Remy thought for a moment. "Perhaps because you fear it will be by your hand. If Winters kidnapped and killed Josh—even if you refused the deal—that death would be by Winters. If, however, when you slit your own throat, you slit his as well, I could see where you might feel it was different."

"I must make the sacrifice," I said, leaning forward. "I know that. It was just easier when I did not know that I might harm him as well."

"Juliette, nothing about what is being asked of you is easy. For that, I am eternally sorry. Our greatest hope is that we can stop Winters before he opens the gate," he said sympathetically.

"He grows more powerful with every soul he harvests. The last vampire did not even struggle," I said despondently.

"What?" Remy said in surprise.

"I am sorry. I thought you knew. I repeat my story and findings to so many people I forget who I have spoken to and who I have not."

Remy waved away my apology. "It isn't as if it happened weeks ago, and I'm just now hearing about it. Explain to me what you mean—the vampire didn't struggle."

I related to the Master Gatekeeper what I had read in the last vampire's dust. Remy looked pensive and took several minutes to digest this new revelation.

"This is disturbing. Deeply disturbing. I can think of very little, outside of staking, that will render a vampire unconscious for any length of time at all," Remy confessed.

"Could it be some sort of new drug? Josh is complaining that the clubs are full of them," I asked.

"To my knowledge, even the most potent drugs aren't effective on vampires for more than a few minutes, but with all the new synthetic drugs I suppose it is possible that something could be concocted."

"This could be disastrous if someone has developed something like that. Winters could take over any vampire with that."

"Let's not panic yet. There may be another explanation. There wasn't a stake found at the crime scene, was there?"

"Not that I know of, but the crime scene techs had been in there before I saw the entire scene. They may have found something. I will ask Master Barthelmy."

"Was there sex magic at this scene?"

"Yes, just like the others."

"He couldn't have used a stake then. The partner would have noticed," Remy mused. "Your drug idea seems a bit more plausible. I will have the Gatekeepers keep an eye and ear out for any new designer drugs that are out there. I will let both you and Grandmaster Gautier know what I find."

Changing the subject, I asked, "You wouldn't happen to know anything about a New Orleans police detective by the name of Chuck Spencer, would you?"

"The one that Jaime was here researching?"

"Yes."

"Not a whole lot, yet. I have opened a file on him. His parents were from Atlanta, and I have a call into the Sentry in that city for any information he has on them. Not all the Sentries have managed to put their archives online yet. It is a terribly slow process."

"Do mages often fall through the cracks like that?" I asked pointedly. "This is the second one."

Nicholas winced. "It happens more than we like to admit—although the Internet is making things so much easier. It used to be that when a mage or vampire relocated, the Sentry or Gatekeeper in his or her hometown would send a copy of the file to wherever the supernatural creature moved to. Sometimes the Gatekeepers and Sentries in the new cities would need to request files. Certainly, not everyone left forwarding addresses."

"That sounds terribly cumbersome and not very efficient," I said.

Nicholas winced again. "It wasn't. It was a reaction to the Inquisition. The Gatekeepers were too worried about detection to do much spell work, so we sent the physical files written in code via courier."

"I wondered why there wasn't some sort of magical archive," I said.

"There used to be—centuries ago—but the Church gained access to it, and we had to destroy it. Luckily, they did not get much information before we did. They retrieved a handful of Gatekeeper names however, and that was enough to kick off the Inquisition and subsequent witch hunts."

I nodded. "I can understand your caution."

"We spent centuries re-creating the archives we lost and tracking known supernatural creatures. Werewolves have been the easiest. They live in packs and rarely leave their home territory. Even vampires aren't that difficult. Since every vampire must introduce himself to the city's Master, we just watch who shows up. Mages are much more difficult. Sometimes they form covens, but not always. One advantage is that there are only 35 magical family lines left. With birth and death records now online, finding new mages is much simpler. One of our biggest problems is one of human resources right now. There are simply too few Gatekeepers and Sentries to do all of the tasks. And we must safeguard our data bases against hacking. We cannot allow what happened during the Inquisition to occur again."

"Perhaps now that the Gatekeepers are out of the closet, so to speak, recruitment will be easier," I said.

"I have had a mage or two show up at the church doorstep—not necessarily wanting to join but offering to help if needed. That certainly has never happened to me before," Master Remy admitted.

"I can't think that the mages would want the Gates opened any more than the rest of us do."

"No, although not all are aware of the prophecy or how close to coming to fruition it is."

"Maybe it is time to let them know."

The Master Gatekeeper nodded. "I think you are correct, Juliette. I will speak to the Head of the Gatekeeper Order about it. We need as many soldiers in this fight as we can muster."

I added, "Perhaps with a bit more magical help, I can even take out Winters and eliminate that threat. I should have followed the black magic cord back to Winters last night and tried to kill him then. He probably thought he had me trapped, and I could have caught him completely unaware."

"Why didn't you?" The mage asked.

"My first impulse is always to save whoever is being attacked. Chuck Spencer would be dead if I had done that," I said.

"The life of one for the lives of many," Master Remy pointed out.

"I know," I said, trying not to berate myself for the choice that I had made. "It was a snap decision, and I cannot go back and do it again."

"You did what you thought was right in the moment."

I nodded. "We need to come up with a plan to eliminate Winters before the cold blue moon."

"Yes. I know the city's lieutenant is pushing for assassination," Nicholas said dismissively. "I spoke to Marc Gautier earlier this evening."

"You do not think it will work?"

"We will need to get through his magical defenses first, and he seems to be several steps ahead of us on that."

"I know. I was wondering if the Gatekeepers along with Jaime and me could muster the power to break the wards on his house."

"I'm sure we could, but then he would know we were coming, and chances are we wouldn't have enough power to defeat him in magical combat after that expenditure."

"A bullet would not do it?" I asked.

"I highly doubt it. A mage of his power could easily conjure shields with warning," Remy said.

"And he would have plenty of warning since we need to take down those wards," I said.

"Exactly."

"Ugh, I cannot believe I missed my chance to kill him—twice!"

"Perhaps next time."

"I truly doubt I will get a next time. In any case, I would have to stop thinking about saving the victim in front of me and concentrate on the perpetrator," I sighed.

"Juliette, do not berate your humanity," Remy said soothingly. "You are a trained healer and thaumaturge. It goes against your nature not to help the injured. There is time. We know who the necromancer is for certain. We know where he is. In a way, these murders are a good thing. They revealed our enemy early, and that gives us an advantage."

"The Salamand Master commented on that at the last crime scene. The cold blue moon is not for several months yet. Why did Winters start culling souls so early and in such an obvious way? It's almost as if he wanted us to know."

"Maybe he did," Remy said.

"To what end?" I asked.

"*That* is what we need to figure out."

"I do not mean to be impertinent, but how exactly did the Gatekeepers lose track of Winters?" I asked.

Master Remy sighed. "We didn't so much lose him as we thought he was dead."

"Pardon?"

"He faked his own death about ten years ago. Robert Winters isn't his real name. He was born Robert Snowdon."

I was curious, "How do you know this is the same man?"

"His former guardian recognized him from a photo I sent to the other Chapter Houses. One of the other Gatekeepers did some research and discovered that about six weeks after Robert Snowdon died a fiery death on a highway in Seattle, Robert Winters appeared in New York City."

I nodded, not completely satisfied, but I doubted that the Gate-keepers were either. I thanked the Master Gatekeeper for his time and stood to leave.

"Juliette, be careful. Whether he goes by Snowdon or Winters, this necromancer is dangerous," the mage cautioned me.

I nodded and left the office.

I was still disquieted after my meeting with Master Remy, but I was able to return to the matrix and resume warding with full concentration, at least some of my questions answered.

Sometime after 2 AM, Gaetan returned from the swamp and joined us in the Quarter. Jaime helped me alter the matrix, and together, we accomplished substantially more than I had alone.

When we returned to the house shortly before dawn, Josh was waiting for me with a goblet of warmed blood which I took gratefully.

"How'd it go?" He asked, drawing me close.

"It was a slow start," I admitted, snuggling in. He made me feel safe.

"Too much on your mind?" he asked.

"Is this a side effect of the bond—you knowing what is going on in my head?" I asked, drawing back to look at him.

He laughed and pulled me close again. "I didn't need a bond to tell me you were out of sorts. I was feeling the same way at the beginning of the night."

I gave him an edited account of my discussion with Remy. I left out my fears about what would happen to him after my sacrifice. While he knew I might have to kill myself, it was not sitting foremost in his mind, and I did not want to place it there.

"So it's official—we're bonded?" He asked.

"Master Remy confirmed it. We are quite possibly the first vampire-mage/vampire-non-mage bonding in history."

"Ain't that the shit!" he crowed. "I wasn't able to get a hold of Aunt Delia or Uncle Owen, but I left a message. I expect that they'll call back tonight after sundown."

"When you talk to them, ask if they have heard about other mage/non-mage bondings. Master Remy said it was unusual, but not unprecedented. He is going to research earlier reports as well."

"I will ask them anything and everything you want me to, darlin'," Josh said before kissing me deeply.

THE REST of the week passed in a blur of casting as Jaime and I worked to get the anti-soul stealing spell woven into the existing matrix before Winters noticed it was there and tried to counteract it. After that first night, we wove the spell but did not immediately charge it.

"Are you going to charge the entire matrix all at once? Is that safe?" Jaime asked.

"I am going to use the Focus. That should give me more than enough power to do it all at once. Even though the area is vast, it is a single spell woven into an existing matrix," I reasoned.

"You'll deplete your Focus," Jaime argued.

"There is plenty of time to renew it," I reasoned. "We need to get this done while his attention is elsewhere."

"Speaking of that—where is his attention?"

I grimaced. "That I am not sure of. I would guess he is trying to find his next set of victims."

"Well, he isn't having much luck with that. The Gatekeepers watching the club report that vampire attendance at the Den of Iniquity has been nil since the report of the last set of murders."

"All the more reason to get the spell finished. He will need to start hunting outside of his club soon. We need to make this as difficult for him as possible."

There was another reason to finish the casting. Josh's new club, Chintz, was opening this weekend, and I wanted to enjoy myself—not worry about this damned matrix. There had been several more problems getting the club ready, but Josh was confident they would still open on Saturday.

"You know I only bug on you because I worry," Jaime said. "I'm really not trying to second-guess you."

I laughed, "Yes, you are, but I know it is coming from a good place, and you often have valid concerns. If you do not ask questions, you cannot learn."

"Did you ask a lot of questions while you were training?" she asked.

I considered that for a moment. "Not nearly enough and usually not the correct ones. I have a great deal of knowledge about herbs and healing, but I am weak on mage lore. My shields and wards are excellent, if I do say so myself, but I have almost no offensive magic."

"I might actually be able to help you there," Jaime said eagerly. "Every Gatekeeper trains as a Battle Mage. Even though I only had a few years with Master Remy, he said I was a fast learner."

"I may need to take you up on that offer. My grandmere's grimoire has several offensive spells, but I think most will require significant modification."

"We can do that circle thing again, but this time I'll cast, and you feel the magic," Jaime suggested.

"I would like that."

We worked hard on the matrix returning home nearly exhausted at the end of each night, but finally in the wee hours of Saturday morning the complex spell network was ready to charge. I chose Josh's new club, Chintz, as the place to invoke the entire nexus. It sat on the Bourbon Street ley line to boost my power, and I could cast in relative secrecy and security.

Josh had sent everyone home to get some rest before the evening's Grand Opening. There would be no soft opening for this club.

In preparation for my ritual, I sanctified the space. That was when I found another hex bag—this one directed at Josh and the club. It explained all the problems that had befallen the enterprise in the past few weeks.

"I was starting to wonder if this place was cursed or something," Josh said when I showed him the bag. "I've never had this much trouble with an opening. Was it Honore?"

I nodded confirmation and quickly destroyed the bag, breaking the hex. Then I smudged the entire area for good measure. Finally, I knelt in the middle of the dance floor and offered a silent prayer for strength and focus. When I was ready, I cut my forearm, allowing my blood to flow over the Focus as I brought it down hard on the floor. Power flowed from me through the Focus and directly into the ley line. From there it spiderwebbed out to all corners of the city, invoking the spell. I continued pouring power until I was sure that I fully charged all parts of the matrix. When I ceased, I thought I heard a howl of indignation from Winters.

I smiled and sat heavily on the floor. Josh was next to me in a moment.

"Darlin', are you all right?" He asked, pulling me against him. I felt his power flow into me, refilling the reservoir I had emptied.

"I will be fine," I said and licked my wound shut.

Jaime handed me a bottle of blood and asked, "It worked, didn't it? I felt a hell of a jolt."

"Yes, it worked. A bit better than I thought it would."

"So you have neutralized Winters' power?" Josh asked.

I shook my head. "No. I am not that powerful. He can still cast directly. My wards are not strong enough to prevent that, but he cannot again snare anyone like he did Gabe. I also put extra protections on all the cemeteries and hospitals so he will need to expend a lot more power to raise the dead there. This matrix should protect all but the weakest sentient dead."

"So no more murders?" Jaime asked.

"I hope not," I said.

"I'll call Sophie and Master Remy to let them know it is done," Jaime said.

"How are you?" I asked Josh. "Did you feel it when I invoked the spell?"

He chuckled. "Oh yeah. It was a hell of a rush."

"How is your arm?" I asked.

He showed me his left arm.

A thin line followed the same path that I had cut on my own inner forearm.

"Did it hurt?" I asked.

"Not really. More pressure and a kind of itching," he said.

"Did it bleed?"

"Nope. And before you ask, my power levels are fine. I didn't feel you pull or anything while you were casting. When I took you in my arms, I felt some power transfer to you, but I got it right back again. Aunt Delia said that sort of thing is normal."

"I know. I just wondered if it would be different since you are not a mage."

"The sensations are pretty much spot on what she and Owen described to me. You can ask them for yourself when they get here next week." Josh had related their conversation in detail to me, but I still had reservations.

"I know you think I am being silly," I said.

"Not silly. Cautious, yes, which ain't a bad thing."

When Josh had finally spoken to his aunt and uncle after a series of missed voicemails and explained what had happened, the pair had insisted on coming to New Orleans.

"We're due for a visit," Delia said. "It has easily been 25 years since we've been to the city and probably 10 since you've been back to the ranch."

"I'd love to see y'all again, but it ain't safe in the city right now," Josh had told them.

"Which is exactly why you need us," they had countered. "This will need to be an all -hands-on deck affair to prevent the prophecy. Owen and I might be getting up there in years, but we aren't ready to be put out to pasture yet. Can you find us a house to rent?"

Josh put his foot down at that. "If y'all are coming for a visit, you need to stay with us. There's plenty of room, but more important, we have 24-hour security."

They argued for several minutes over that point, but eventually Josh won. I was a bit nervous about the arrangement. How would his family view me? I would just hope for the best.

CHAPTER 20

I could not have envisioned two more different club openings. It wasn't the crowd size that differed—there was a line down the block outside of Chintz—but the energy and ambience.

There was a darkness—a menace—to the Den of Iniquity that was completely absent in Chintz. The people at the Den had seethed with lust and an even darker, more bestial hunger. The crowd at Chintz was frivolous and fun loving. That wasn't to say that there were not any number of impassioned people in the crowd—there certainly were—but the overriding emotion was joy.

"So, whaddya think, darlin'?" Josh asked in my ear as we reclined in the red pleather round booth near the stage.

I regarded the room for a long moment before answering, taking in the happy, laughing faces of not just the patrons, but of the servers as well. A rowdy, bachelorette party whooped and hollered as yet another brave soul got up to sing karaoke in the yellow pleather round booth opposite us.

"I think it is a smashing success," I said, smiling up at him.

"I gotta say, there are a lot more people here than I reckoned. Actually, a lot more locals," he said pointing his beer bottle to the crowd.

I raised an eyebrow. "A lot more vampires, you mean?"

"Yeah. This ain't their normal shtick," he said, gesturing to the decor. It was, in a word, tacky. Every horrible trend from the last 70 years or so vied for prominence in the room. Numerous disco balls twirled over the dance floor, and neon frames set off the dozen or more velvet Elvis paintings. Diner booths in every imaginable color and style seemed haphazardly strewn through the space, and there was not a single dark corner to skulk in.

I shrugged. "They know it is safe here. No chance for Winters to catch them unaware. I think some of them are actually having fun." I turned my head to watch a Sylph Initiate mount the Flying Unicorn—a mechanical bull painted white and bedazzled to resemble the mythical creature. The vampire let out a shriek of pure delight as the "unicorn" tried to throw her.

"They'll really get into it when we start the themed decade nights. It'll give some of them a chance to raid their closets and relive the nostalgia of when they were turned," Josh said.

"Why didn't you start with one of those?" I asked.

"I thought about it, but I just couldn't decide, so I put all the theme choices in a bowl and randomly chose one. I have to admit I am partial to the tacky Tiki bar choice. It is one of my favorites," Josh confessed.

"I can't imagine you at a Tiki bar," I laughed.

"Oh yeah, it's like relivin' the late 70s and 80s all over again. This is one of my favorite shirts," he said proudly, pointing to the well-worn but still gaudy green linen shirt with bright pink flamingos prominently dotted along the fabric. Josh had even foregone his habitual cowboy boots for a pair of leather sandals. I had not known he owned anything but cowboy boots. He had even worn boots to the black-tie Museum Gala last month. Granted, they were designer and probably cost as much as my gown had, but they were still cowboy boots.

As much as I wanted to just enjoy tonight and Josh's triumph, my mind refused to let the murders rest. I was becoming obsessed with figuring out how Robert Winters had subdued his last victim. Paul Barthelmy had gone through the crime scene evidence and assured me that nothing even resembling a stake was found at the scene. The Gatekeepers had likewise discovered no new club drugs that could render a vampire inert. I had one last avenue to explore. Perhaps Olivia Dupont, the dead fledgling's sire, could shed some light on what had happened.

A hand waved in front of my face. "Earth to Juliette," Josh said, breaking through my musings.

"I am sorry," I apologized sincerely. He had worked so hard on this club despite Honore's hex on it, and he should be able to savor his success.

"No apologies needed. You've got the weight of the world on your shoulders right now. I wish I could do more to help."

"You help in more ways than you know," I told him and meant it. He was an anchoring presence. Josh's calm demeanor kept me on an even keel, and I drew on his strength.

"We'll figure this out," Josh promised.

Chuck Spencer interrupted us just then. "Mrs. Grammont?"

"Detective Spencer! What a pleasant surprise. I did not expect to see you here," I said. Clearly, he was not working tonight because he wore a loud blue Hawaiian shirt dotted with palm trees. He had a pink lei around his neck and held one of the bar's signature drinks in a hollowed-out coconut. "Come, join us. This is my partner, Josh Bouchard."

Chuck hesitated a moment and then slid into the booth beside me.

"You're about the last person I expected to see here," Chuck confessed to me, "but then again, I would not have pegged you as a Voodoo Queen either."

"Juliette here is full of surprises," Josh drawled as he looked at me questioningly. I gave his hand a quick squeeze under the table. I should have warned him that Chuck Spencer was likely to seek me out. The detective's magic was drawn to mine—it was searching for a teacher—so even though Chuck would not realize it, his magic compelled him to interact with me.

"I am not sure that I would have thought you the club type either," I said.

"I try to get out every once in a while. All work and no play makes Jack a dull boy—Chuck a dull boy. I like to check out the new places that open up," Chuck said shrugging.

"You must be rather busy then. I swear something new opens up every week," Josh said.

"Honestly, it's a little advance work. I like to check out the new place to see if they are likely to be trouble spots."

Josh caught my eye and smiled. Chuck Spencer didn't know that Josh owned Chintz. He leaned forward towards the detective and said conspiratorially, "So, detective, what about this place? Are we safe?"

"Other than the odd bar fight, which those burly bouncers seem more than capable of taking care of, I'd say yes. This place is far too well-lit for illicit drug trade, and there's no back room for illegal gambling. There are a lot of upscale locals here, so I doubt prostitution would flourish either," Chuck said.

"I thought Juliette told me you were a homicide detective?" Josh asked.

"I am."

"You gave quite a rundown of things other than homicide that might happen here."

"All things that lead to murder though," Chuck said.

"Fair enough," Josh said and took a sip of his Dixie beer. "Other than not being a hotspot for crime, what you think of the place?"

"I think I kinda love it. It is tacky as hell and speaks to my soul," Chuck confessed, and we all laughed. We were interrupted again, this time by one of the bartenders leaning across the back of the booth speak to Josh.

"Sorry, darlin', but duty calls," Josh said after the bartender left.

"Is everything all right?" I asked, frowning. I had destroyed Honore's hex bag this morning, but she might have cast something else.

"Not a hex. Seems the owner underestimated how popular those fruity concoctions would be and didn't order enough Bacardi. We're down to our last box. I gotta run to The Cowboy for some more." He said and kissed me. "I'll be back soon. Keep her company while I'm gone, will you, detective?" Josh slid from the booth and left before Chuck could respond.

Chuck gaped like a fish, opening and closing his mouth several times before he finally turned and said to me, "He's the manager?"

I smiled. "No. He is the owner." I took a sip of my pina colada.

Chuck put his head in his hand. "I just made a complete ass of myself."

I laughed. "No, he will actually take that sort of assessment as a good thing."

"You could've warned me." His cheeks pink from embarrassment.

"It was far more fun for me to watch, detective," I said gaily. "You have not had any more dizzy spells, have you?"

Chuck stiffened. "No, that was just low blood sugar."

I had not meant to offend him, but I needed to know if there were any lingering effects from Winters' trap.

"I am so glad to hear that," I said. "Have you made any progress on the case?"

Chuck frowned and shook his head. "We can't find the girlfriend, so she's our prime suspect."

"You do not sound so sure."

"It really doesn't fit. Whoever did this is one sadistic sonofabitch and strong. Hempstead was dragged from the bed halfway across the room. By all accounts, the girlfriend, Tessa Mickelson, was sickly and a hundred pounds soaking wet. There's no way she could have done this."

"What about with help?" I asked.

"We found no evidence of anyone else. All the prints were either from Hempstead or Mickelson."

"Perhaps the killer was just careful," I said, taking another sip of my drink.

"That's the assumption that I would like to go with. Until we can find her and rule her out as a suspect, my captain says we stay focused on Mickelson."

"What do you know about Tessa Mickelson?" I asked.

"She's from old money. Garden district family, which is probably why my captain has such a hard on for her," Chuck said and covered his mouth. "Sorry for the language. It seems I've had one too many of these, and my filter has slipped."

"I can assure you that I am not some wilting hothouse flower that is offended by coarse language or sexual innuendo," I said waving away his concern. Also, I would learn much more if the detective was candid and not censoring his language.

"Okay," Chuck continued. "So, Mickelson is 25, a recent graduate of Tulane. She got BA in art history. She's been sickly all her life, but the doctors can't decide on a diagnosis. Her parents threw a ton of money at specialists, but no two agree on what is wrong with her, other than some sort of genetic disorder."

"It sounds like she is more likely to have been a victim than the killer," I said.

"That's what I think," Chuck grumbled into his drink.

I was not sure what to make of this. It seemed odd that the department would view Mickelson as a suspect. If the genders were reversed and a male vampire died, I could see Paul letting the detectives run with the idea that the missing vamp was the killer, but not this. Something more was going on here, and I needed to speak with Paul.

Chuck looked up from his drink. "Do you think the actual killer might still have her? That she's really a missing person?"

"I think that might be a genuine possibility," I said. While I knew Tessa Mickelson was dust, as a missing person she might serve as a red herring to keep the detective busy while I figured out how to stop the actual killer. I still had not spoken to Marc about the detective and his abilities, and until I did, I needed to keep him as far from Winters as possible.

I was not avoiding the conversation with the Grandmaster; there simply had not been the time. Adding the anti-soul stealing spell to the matrix had taken almost every waking hour I'd had until tonight. Josh had joked earlier that I need a better work/life balance, and after he explained exactly what that was, I had to agree with him. There just did not seem to be a way to do that in the time I had left. Even now, at a club with tacky décor and a Tiki theme, I was sitting in a booth discussing a murder case.

Chuck seemed to sense my shifting mood and said, "You know, that's enough shop talk for tonight. Why don't I get us another round of drinks before the Bacardi runs out and we'll talk about something more pleasant?"

I smiled. "I like that idea, but there is no need to get up and go to the bar. There are perks to being the owner's girlfriend." I signal to Nathalie, who lounged seemingly casually at a nearby table with Gaetan. She came over and leaned close. I asked her to get us another round, and after a nod to Gaetan, she went to the bar.

Chuck gave me a quizzical look and I just shrugged. "Extra security. The city has a ritual murderer on the loose."

However, it was not Nathalie who delivered our drink order, but Josh. Putting the coconut glasses on the table along with another beer for himself, he slid into the booth next to me. Giving me a quick kiss on the lips, he said, "Sorry about that."

"Crisis averted?" I asked, reaching for my drink.

"Yep. Tiki night is a hit. Runnin' out of booze because the bar receipts are so good is the type of problem I want," he said with a broad lopsided grin.

"That was quick," Chuck commented.

"I own another bar, The Cowboy, just down the street. I called ahead and had the manager pull our extra stock from the back. It was ready and waiting for me when I got there. He even had manifest waiting for me, so it's all legal and stuff. I need to give that man a raise," Josh explained. "So, what did y'all talk about while I was gone?"

"The case," I said sheepishly.

Josh frowned. "Darlin', we talked about this work/life balance thing earlier tonight."

"I know. That is why Detective Spencer and I decided no more shop talk," I said lightly.

"Please, call me Chuck. Detective Spencer is so formal. Plus, I feel like I owe you an apology for earlier," he said to us.

Josh frowned slightly and then broke into a wide grin. "You mean telling me that my club isn't likely to attract bad elements? Heck, that somethin' I want to hear."

"I was tactless," Chuck said, clearly bemused.

Josh laughed. "You're in good company then because the only one at this table who has any tact at all is Juliette."

I rolled my eyes, and Chuck joined in the mirth.

"So Chuck, have you been in town long?" Josh asked.

"I was born and raised here but, left a few years ago for college," he explained.

"Where did you go?" I asked, even though I already knew the answer.

"LSU."

"That's one hell of a party school," Josh said.

"I was older than the typical freshman, so I didn't do so much partying. That's not to say I didn't have a good time. I certainly did, but I had my eye on the prize and never let myself lose sight of it."

"You graduated and came back here. Couldn't stay away from the Big Easy, huh?" Josh asked.

"Actually, I hadn't planned on coming back, but my foster father had a heart attack my senior year, so plans changed."

"I am so sorry to hear that," I said sincerely. No one that I talked to had mentioned that. "Is he all right?"

"Yes, thankfully. Triple bypass, retirement, and giving up beignets has made him right as rain—if a bit grouchy. He really loved those beignets. I stayed close anyway. New Orleans is home."

"She draws you in," I agreed.

"How about you? Your accent isn't local," Chuck noted.

"I lived here . . . a while ago, but have been away until recently," I said.

"What brought you back?" He asked.

I could hardly tell him the truth—that after two centuries my lover finally had found me and took the stake from my heart—so I contented myself with a convenient fiction.

"I have always loved New Orleans. She is the city of my soul, and it was time to come home."

"What about you?" Chuck asked Josh.

"I grew up in Texas but have been here for years. I love the music, and my sister is here."

We talked for quite a while about our pasts. Josh and I greatly editing and sometimes outright lying about ours, drawing more and more from Chuck Spencer. Finally, he said that if he wanted to function at work the next day, he needed to leave, so we said our farewells.

"What do you think of him?" I asked Josh after Chuck left.

"As a person or a possible Aether recruit?"

"Both," I said.

"He seems like a standup guy. Not crooked like a lot of NOLA cops. That's not to say he can't be corrupted, but it would take a lot."

"That is my assessment as well. I am a bit worried about his morality."

"As in he has too much of it?"

"Yes. As you know, being a vampire is very gray, and being an Aether is positively charcoal," I said.

"I'm surprised to hear you say that. You've always been very moral and humane."

"I think you give me more credit than I deserve."

"Naw. Chuck might have a problem with the morality of the Aether coven overall—as a group they are hinky—but with you heading things here in New Orleans? It'll be fine."

"Do I even have the right to consider him with everything going on?" I looked at my drink even though I knew there were no answers to be found there.

"What's the alternative?"

"Talk to Master Remy about getting Chuck some magic training from the humans. He would get the knowledge he needs without the drama." I looked back at Josh.

Josh laughed. "Do you really think the mages are without drama? Come on, you were a human mage before they turned you. You know better."

"He does not need to be caught up with the whole prophecy mess though," I protested.

"Darlin' if we don't stop that prophecy, everybody—mage, vampire, werewolf, and unsuspecting human—is going to be caught up in it. The demons are going to pour through the Gate, and they won't care if who they encounter knows about the prophecy or not. Do you think that Chuck's magic might help prevent it from coming true?"

"He is totally untrained."

"What about channeling his raw power?"

"That is mercenary."

"Darlin', this is Armageddon."

CHAPTER 21

I had questions about why the last vampire victim had not fought Winters. Hopefully, her sire could answer some of them.

Leaving Gaetan in the car, Nathalie and I approached Olivia Dupont's beautiful Greek Revival mansion. I pushed the buzzer and within seconds, I heard the clickety-clack of heels on hardwood. The door opened, revealing a middle-aged servant who politely inquired, "Mistress Grammont?"

I nodded, and the grey-clad maid led us to the opulently appointed Garden District parlor. An exquisitely dressed fortyish matron rose at our entry.

"Mistress Grammont, you honor me with your visit." Olivia Dupont gave a slight bow.

"Thank you for receiving me on such short notice, Mrs. Dupont," I said advancing into the room. Nathalie took an un-obtrusive position near the pocket door the maid slid shut behind her.

Olivia gestured at a nearby sage-green, velvet chair. "I must admit that it surprised me when the city's Steward called and said you would like to meet. Please have a seat. Can I offer you something to drink?"

I perched on the edge of the antique chair. "I am fine, thank you."

Olivia Dupont sank gracefully into a matching chair opposite me. "Sophie said you wish to discuss Tessa."

I nodded. "Please accept my sincere condolences at the loss of your progeny."

Olivia gave a delicate shrug of her shoulders. "Sophie said you were not political like the other coven leaders and I could be candid with you," she gave me a frank look. "The fact that Tessa is dead does not surprise me a bit."

I raised an eyebrow. "She was into dark magic?" I inquired. Nothing I had learned about the young woman so far had indicated that, but her sire would know such things.

"No, nothing like that," Olivia Dupont said hastily. "The manner surprised me, but not the death itself."

I frowned slightly. "I do not think that I understand."

"Tessa Mickelson was not a good candidate to become a vampire. She lacked the spark necessary to sustain the long centuries. I was honestly surprised that she survived her turning," Olivia clarified.

"May I ask why you sired her then?" I asked. The Gnome coven was renowned for its rigorous candidate vetting. It was far more difficult to become a Gnome than an Aether, and we were no walk in the park.

Olivia sighed heavily. "I did it to repay an old debt. Tessa was the daughter of James and Claire Mickelson. They are very influential in city politics. Tessa had a rare genetic disorder, and her parents hoped the turning would not only cure her but give her purpose."

"It did not?"

"Not in the least. I knew after spending five minutes with the flighty girl that she was unsuitable, but a debt is a debt. Don't get me wrong—on paper, she was an ideal candidate. She had the lineage, the connections, the money, just not the temperament. She was utterly ambivalent about becoming a vampire. I've never met any Gnome Initiate like that."

"Did this ambivalence continue after her turning?" I asked.

"Absolutely. As you know, Gnomes are leaders. We are expected to step up after our turnings. She did not. She was completely uninterested in anything and everything. Only now, she could not use her illness as an excuse."

"I read Tessa's ashes at the crime scene. She did not seem to fight the necromancer who invaded her mind at all," I said cautiously.

"I wish I could say that was atypical behavior, but I would be lying. She cared for no one—not even herself."

"Not even her lover, Aidan Hempstead?" I asked.

Olivia sniffed. "Flavor of the month. She went through men like most humans go through Kleenex. She would have never put herself out for him."

These revelations cast a completely new light on my investigation. Perhaps we were not dealing with the new drug or way to subdue a vampire. Maybe we were just dealing with an apathetic vampire who couldn't be bothered to fight. As unsettling as that was, it was far better than the alternative.

"Thank you for your candor, Mrs. Dupont. You have been very helpful," I said.

"Anything I can do," Olivia Dupont said.

"I can see myself out," I said as I rose from the chair.

NATHALIE AND GAETAN dropped me off at Gautier House after my visit with Olivia Dupont. I knew I would be ensconced in meetings with the Grandmaster and lawyers for the next several hours, and there was no reason for them to wait in boredom when I was well guarded by the Gautier House guards. Nathalie momentarily grumbled but soon saw the wisdom of my reasoning.

Sophie met me in the courtyard and escorted me inside.

"How did your meeting with Olivia Dupont go?" She asked.

"Well, I think. She said some things that have me reassessing a few of my assumptions about the last set of murders," I said.

"How do you mean?"

"I assumed that Tessa Mickelson did not struggle to regain her body because she could not. Mrs. Dupont indicated that it may have been a lack of want," I explained.

"Really?"

"Yes."

"Well, that certainly sheds a different light on matters."

"Perhaps what we were so worried about—Winters having something that would completely subdue a vampire—has not happened," I said.

"That would be a tremendous relief to everyone," Sophie said as she led me to Marc's office. Waiting for me inside was the same bevy of financial advisors, bankers, and lawyers that I had met with soon after I had returned to the city. They had been pushing to meet with me again since I had taken on the mantle of coven mistress, but because of other obligations, I had put them off.

Vanessa de Clerc, the young vampire lawyer who had assisted me with my earlier dealings, again took charge. "Mistress Grammont, thank you for agreeing to meet with us," She said politely.

"I am sorry that it has taken so long," I apologized as I took a seat at the long mahogany conference table that took up a portion of Marc's massive office.

"You are a busy woman, and the extra time has allowed for all the transfers to take place in one sitting rather than half a dozen," Ms. de Clerc said and took her own seat. She picked a manila file folder up off the top of the stack in front of her and handed it to me. "This first file is property transfers to you from your sire, Andre de la Croix. He has officially been declared dead according to vampire law and his will executed. You will need to sign where the flags indicate."

She furnished me with an exquisite Mont Blanc fountain pen, and I signed my name nearly two dozen times. More folders followed as I assumed the assets of all the abjured coven members. She explained each deed to me before I signed it. This process took several hours. The last folder in the stack was the thickest. It was the assets, mostly property, I inherited as coven mistress. I'd seen this folder before as Regent, but had declined to take them over; instead, I held them in trust for the next Mistress or Master. Honore had had almost no time to do anything with them since her tenure in that position had been so short.

When we arrived at the deed to Voodoo Royal, I stopped Vanessa.

"How is the store currently being run?" I asked.

"There are two human managers and half a dozen human store employees at the moment. I believe the managers have been there quite a while and were Frederique Deroche's servants," the young lawyer said, consulting her notes. "Most of the other store employees are new—hired since the fire that killed Mistress Deroche. They replaced coven members killed in the same fire."

I knew much of this from my own visit to the store. Soon after my return to New Orleans, I had gone to all the voodoo shops in the Quarter. Most of them had been little more than tourist traps selling harmless trinkets to the uninitiated. At Voodoo Royal, I was recognized as a fellow practitioner and invited into its rather extensive back room where the real magical implements and ingredients were kept. I had not realized then that the establishment was owned by the coven. I only discovered that when I had served as Regent.

"Honore Rochon did not replace the managers when she became coven mistress?" I asked.

"No. Mistress Rochon showed no interest in changing anything about any of the coven properties except adding this Garden District property to the collection." She handed the deed to a grand Italianate villa on Third Street to me. "I believe she meant to make this the Coven Chapter house."

I shot Marc a look down the table. The Grandmaster had sat regarding the tedious proceedings for the last several hours. Witnessing the transfer of assets was part of his job as Grandmaster, but it must have bored him to tears. His posture had subtly shifted from bored indifference to rapt attention.

"Did you know about this?" I asked.

"Not at all," he said, leaning back in his seat. "However, it makes sense. She would need somewhere to house all the foreign Aether she brought into the city. Should I have Gabe investigate it?"

I nodded and turned to Vanessa. "Please provide Mr. Gautier with the keys to the Third Street mansion," I instructed her. "I would also like to meet with the managers of Voodoo Royal at their earliest convenience—after dark, of course."

"Let me make a quick call about the keys and the security codes. Would you like them delivered here or will Mr. Gautier be picking them up?" Vanessa said pulling out her phone.

I looked to Marc.

"He will pick them up. Your office is on the way to the Garden District. Excuse me for a moment," Marc said and rose from his seat.

Vanessa made her call and waited for Marc to return. I turned to her, "Once the coven transactions are complete, I need to make a new will and set some financial provisions for my childe," I told the lawyer and banker. Both nodded their agreement.

"I believe your will is woefully out of date," Vanessa said. "Do you wish to amend it or simply draw up a new one?"

"A new one. I'm afraid that no one mentioned in the previous one still exists," I said.

"That is no problem at all," Vanessa said.

Marc returned to the room and resumed his seat. I continued signing documents. Finally, the last stack was complete, I dictated the terms of my new will leaving everything to Jaime and set up a generous bank account with a monthly allowance for her. None of my advisors batted an eye at this disposition of my wealth. They stood in unison, wishing Marc and me good evening, before departing.

I turned to Marc. "That was creepy," I said.

"What? The transfer of properties?" He asked puzzled.

"No. Their synchronized movements. They are like the Borg." I said.

Marc laughed. "Yes, they can be disconcerting at times. I am glad to see that you have made strides in your pop culture education."

"With Josh, Jaime, and your nephew as my tutors, I could hardly do less," I replied.

"This is true," Marc said as he rose from his seat. "Can I offer you a glass of wine or do you need to rush off?"

"I feel like I have taken up enough of your evening, but if you have a few minutes, I would love a glass of wine," I said, pushing back my seat.

"Come back to the sitting area. We have been uncomfortable for long enough," Marc motioned as he poured two glasses of wine for us. "You singled out Voodoo Royal earlier. Do you intend to run it yourself?"

"I would love to," I confessed. "However, that is not possible right now. Depending on what happens on the cold blue moon, I might take a more active role. The reason I inquired about it is that the shop is a good place to scout perspective new Coven members. Beyond that, I also need to make connections with the local magic-using community."

"I thought Master Remy was now their contact," Marc said, handing me the wine and sitting opposite me.

"He is, but it never hurts to make personal contact. I don't want them to see me as an enemy or a rival," I said.

"I know Frederique had a good relationship with several voodoo practitioners as well as some mages," Marc said.

I sighed, "I hope Honore has not damaged any of those relation-ships. We are going to need all the help we can get to stop Winters."

"That is a good plan. You mentioned also looking for new coven members."

"Yes. While having a passel of baby vampires would be disastrous, I want to at least start looking for possible recruits. Actually, I've already found one," I said tentatively. We had smoothed things over after I had removed Marc's hex; however I was still leery. I took a sip of my wine and waited.

Marc raised an eyebrow. "You are not thinking of poaching another Gatekeeper from Nick, are you?" He said with a trace of humor in his voice.

I smiled. "No, this one I would be poaching from the New Orleans Police Department," I said and told him about Chuck Spencer.

"And Paul isn't grooming him?" Marc asked after I had finished.

"Not at the moment. I asked. Paul actually suggested that I recruit Chuck. I think it would be quite an asset to have an Aether on the police force. Not just to the Coven, but for the entire vampire community," I said.

"I don't think there has ever been an Aether on the police force before," Marc said and drained his glass. "Would you like a refill?"

"Yes, please," I said and handed him my glass. This was nice, just sitting here talking to Marc. It reminded me of how things had been before the coup and the hex. Maybe things were returning to normal. "I would be surprised if there had been an Aether in law enforcement. Mages are usually identified early and channeled into specific careers."

"As I said before, you no longer need my permission to recruit, but thank you for discussing this with me," Marc said as he poured more wine into our glasses.

"I was serious when I said I would consult you on Aether membership. Normally, I would discuss candidates with my Council of Elders, but I do not have any at the moment. Jaime is very levelheaded but still very new. I need to make sure that I am building a solid coven."

Marc handed me my refilled glass and resumed his seat. "Have you thought about consulting Master Remy about this?"

"About Chuck Spencer? I already have. I wanted to know how we had an untrained mage in the city."

"No. I mean about possible Aether recruits," Marc clarified.

"Actually, I had not although it is a good idea. That is, if he will help me," I said, pondering the idea.

"It was just an idea," Marc said. "How are the werewolves working out as guards?"

"Very well. They do not have the daylight restrictions that vampires do and have strength that humans do not," I said, wondering about the abrupt change of subject.

"How long would it take to craft more amulets to allow the New Orleans pack access to the city?" Marc asked.

"That would depend on how many amulets I need to make and how many interruptions I have," I said. "Why? Is this a goodwill gesture?"

"Partly," Marc said. "Although I have another motive. Convocation is coming up, and I think we need heightened security. I have spoken to Beau about the pack providing that security."

Josh had mentioned Convocation in a meeting just after the first set of victims was found, but with everything else happening, it had slipped my mind.

"Do you think Honore will attack again?" I asked.

"Wouldn't you?" Marc asked.

I frowned, "It seems risky to me. Yes, you have all the vampires in one place, but you also have all the vampires in one place. The power we have in that one room would take an army to defeat," I said.

"An army of Rogue Aether, a necromancer, and a couple of demons," Marc reminded me. "And a large portion of our vampires are useless in a straight up fight."

I grimaced, remembering what we had faced during the coup attempt last month.

"Can you cancel Convocation?" I asked.

"I debated it. That was actually my first inclination, but it might be our best chance to draw out Honore and Winters. You said yourself that attacking Winters would be a suicide mission," Marc said.

"We need to draw him out," I agreed, "but do we need to put everyone at risk? Maybe something more small-scale. If Winters wants to finish his ultimate ritual—one vampire soul from each coven —he must kill again. Actually, he needs to kill three more times."

"Three? He should only need two," Marc said.

"He could not harvest the Undine soul. Catherine Day eluded him."

"I did not realize that," Marc said.

"Also, the last report that Jaime had from the Gatekeepers was that vampire attendance at the Den of Iniquity had plummeted. Younger vampires are too scared to take the chance, and the older among us find the club vulgar. Winters will soon realize that he needs a new hunting ground," I said.

"Our biggest problem is if the club is not an option, where will he try next?" Marc asked.

"With the anti-soul stealing spell in the matrix, he can no longer set up passive wards to ensnare a vampire," I said. "He can, however, still actively cast. It will be harder for him—take more time and magic, but he can do it—he is powerful enough. I hope that with him under constant surveillance, further attempts can be foiled."

"Does the matrix have any sort of early warning system included to tell you if necromancy is being attempted?" Mark asked.

I grimaced. I thought about adding an alarm to the spell too late and had not wanted to stop the spell already under way. "No. I plan to go back tomorrow and start adding that the matrix, but I thought the anti-soul stealing spell was more important."

"You are completely correct on that point," Mark agreed. "I think that you making the werewolf amulets may also need to take precedence over the early warning spell, however. Even if we can stop Winters from killing, we still have Honore and the Rogue Aether to contend with," Marc said.

There was a knock at the door, and Marc called out, "Come in."

Sophie stepped into the room and closed the door behind her.

"Sophie, come join us," Marc's voice trailed off as he noticed the grim expression on her face. I had seen that look before.

"There has been another set of murders, hasn't there." I said.

Sophie's lips were set in a grim line as she nodded. "Another Undine fledgling and his lover," she said quietly.

"Dammit," Marc cursed.

"Are the police involved?" I asked, rising from my seat.

"No. Thankfully. Mike caught the call, so he reported back that it was nothing," Sophie explained.

"Good," I said in relief. One less thing to worry about. I pulled out my phone to call Nathalie, but Sophie stopped me.

"I took the liberty of calling your bodyguards after I got Detective Angelletti's call. I hope you don't mind," she said.

"Do I mind you making my life a bit easier? Never," I assured her.

"I have not yet called Mistress St. Pierre," Sophie told Marc. "I wasn't sure if you would want to do that yourself."

"You were right to wait. I need to deliver this news myself," Marc sighed. "How did this happen, Juliette?"

I had no answer for him.

~

It wasn't long before the courtyard gate slid open, and Gaetan's Jeep pulled in. As soon as the vehicle stopped, I wrenched open the door and climbed into the back seat next to Jaime.

"Buckle up," Nathalie instructed as Gaetan swung the Jeep around and exited the parking area.

"Are you all right?" Jaime asked quietly, seeing to my tears.

"Not really. Two more are dead on my watch," I said miserably.

Jaime dug a Kleenex out of her pocket and handed it to me. "It isn't your fault, Juliette."

"Did he leave the club to go hunting?" I asked.

"I don't know," Jaime admitted.

Gaetan wove the Jeep through the French Quarter and across Canal into the CBD. He pulled up next to a converted warehouse and parked.

CHAPTER 22

I looked at Collette St. Pierre's worried and defeated posture and said, "I am so sorry. I thought the deaths would end. I do not know how this happened."

"I know," Mike Angelletti said.

"How?" it baffled me. By all accounts, Robert Winters had not left the Den of Iniquity since arriving at six this evening.

Mike was kneeling next to the body splayed on the floor, carefully avoiding the large pool of blood. Pointing to the victim's hand he said, "That's the hand stamp for the Den of Iniquity. They went to him."

"Good God, why? They know better," I asked no one in particular.

Collette answered me anyway. "The human didn't know. I'm not even sure who he is. Jordan—this is his apartment—had just broken up with his longtime partner." She shook her head sadly, "Hunter, his partner, decided he wanted out. The killings scared him. He decided he didn't want to turn and that he wanted to go back to New York where he was originally from. I wiped his memories over a series of evenings, and one of my day workers put him on a plane this morning."

"So Jordan went to the club and picked up a man to forget?" I asked.

"The best way to get over the last is under the next," Collette said dryly.

"Why that club? There are dozens of other clubs that are safe for vampires!" I retorted.

"Jordan took the breakup hard. I didn't think he would do anything this foolish, but he might not have been thinking straight. I should have kept him with me or made him stay with his sire. He swore he was alright though," Collette explained.

"I would still like to know how Winters comes to control his victims. We know it happens at the club but . . . ."

"What about the hand stamp? It looks vaguely occultish." Nathalie suggested.

"I didn't recognize the symbol," Jaime said. "But it isn't magic. I had one on opening night. I would have felt it if it was magic."

I stepped closer to the body and bent down to look at the hand. I had seen the glyph before, but I could not place it. I pulled out my phone and took a quick picture for future reference. I noticed Jaime also took a picture.

"I'm not sure, but I think this is a passive necromancy sigil. I'll need to look it up to be sure," I said.

"I don't understand," Mike said.

"Everybody gets a stamp, and it is inert until activated, right Juliette?" Jaime said.

"Josh and I didn't get stamped when we went to the opening night," I said.

"Y'all were VIPs. All us lowly peons got stamps. Since it was inactive, I thought nothing of it," Jaime said.

"What would activate the sigil?" Mike asked.

"Usually a drop of the caster's blood," I answered.

"Well, that wouldn't be obvious or anything," Mike remarked wryly.

"In a crowded club like that? No, actually it wouldn't be obvious. All he'd have to do is prick his finger and brush against his intended victim's hand. Very easy to do," Jaime explained.

"Why is this victim only partially flayed?" Collette asked. "Weren't all the rest mostly skinned?"

She was right. Winters had been in a hurry. He had flayed only the torso and legs. Both arms and head were still intact—and why the club stamp was still visible. I was sure the other victim also had stamps, but the removal of the skin had obliterated the evidence in the humans and the vampires, of course, were turned to dust.

I looked at my watch. It said 3:30. "Detective, when did the call come into the station?" I asked.

"Around 3 AM, I think. I got here about 10 minutes later and called the Steward."

"What did the initial call report?"

"Loud screams and several loud thumps. It was the neighbors downstairs. I stopped by and told them that the couple was having very enthusiastic sex. They looked a bit mortified. I radioed head-quarters the same story."

"So the human victim was still alive at 3 AM. Winters panicked when the guy screamed? He kills the hook up and then commits suicide?" Jaime said.

"I'm not sure if the human exsanguinated or not. I don't think there's enough blood for that," Mike said, examining the blood pool.

"Let me see if I can tell," I said and knelt near the man's head. "You did not happen to bring any bottles of blood with you?"

"Way ahead of you," Jaime grinned, pulling two bottles from her trench coat pocket. "I've got more if you need it."

I smiled gratefully. Jaime was turning out to be a damn good apprentice.

Placing my hand on the man's forehead, I opened my third eye.

The man's eyes flew open as the blade sent a sharp, white-hot pain through his left shin, directly below the knee. He was staring at a stark white ceiling. He tried moving. He could not. He tried screaming. He could not. The knife slid down his leg to his foot, peeling a two-foot-long piece of skin away. Why couldn't he move? Why couldn't he speak? He heard chanting. It must be that sexy Fucker he went home with. The knife bit again, sending another searing pain through the man's body. Christ, he had to pee. Way too much beer. Damn, never should've gone to that club. Another strip of skin ripped off. Shouldn't all that alcohol dull this pain? Not enough. Another stab of pain. Bladder lets loose. "God dammit!" Jordan snarled and then screamed at the top of his lungs. Something clattered to the floor. "Fuck, fuck, fuck," Jordan said. Eyes squeezed shut, willing the pain to end, but it didn't. Another cut, deeper this time, taking muscle with skin.

I forced myself to let go of the man's mind before the pain became too much for me. I was not sure exactly what had killed the man. I hated to think it, but it really did not matter if he exsanguinated or his heart gave out. Winters had ripped this man's skin from his body, reveling in his pain and fear, and then ripped his soul out.

"Do you need blood?" Jaime asked, kneeling beside me.

I shook my head. "I am all right for now. I will probably need it after I read Jordan's dust. Has anyone found it yet?" My readings could take several minutes, and I trusted the others not to waste time staring at me. Jaime would know if I were in a vision for too long, as well as how to pull me out.

"It's over here on the bed," Nathalie said. "There's also blood on the headboard. Looks like Winters cracked the guy's skull but good."

"Thanks. I will make sure to read that too."

I stood up slowly and walked to the bed. I dreaded doing this. Was it even worth it? I was not getting very many helpful answers. I pushed my doubts aside and perched on the edge of the King-sized bed. Reaching out, I touched the vampire dust.

I felt Jordan's despondence and sadness. His wish to forget the pain of Hunter's leaving. The lines of cocaine and bottles of Jack Daniels. As much as I tried, I could not get more than snippets. I pulled myself back to this plane and shook my head.

"He was upset about the breakup, but that was all I really got. He tried to dull the pain with drugs and alcohol," I said.

"Anything new about Winters?" Mike asked.

I shook my head. "I am sorry. It wasn't a good read. I will try the blood next."

I swiped my index finger through the blood on the headboard and touched it to my tongue. I snapped into the victim's mind but then seemed to get stuck. No, that was not quite right. It was more like trying to swim through molasses. This man had ingested a lot of alcohol. His thinking was incredibly sluggish, but he was hot for Jordan. As dull as his senses were, he had the single-minded determination to get the other man naked. There was a lot of fumbling and sloppy kisses, but finally the man's goal was achieved. Best sex ever—until it wasn't. Jordan got rough. The man complained. Jordan leaned over and whispered *"Tacete!"* The man could no longer speak. Strong hands gripped the sides of his head, lifted it up and drove it into the headboard. Blackness.

I jolted back to reality. I blinked a few times to clear my head, but there was no nausea.

"The human was very drunk. The sex was consensual if a bit rougher than the man liked," I said. "Almost as soon as he complained, Jordan smacked the man's head against the headboard and rendered him unconscious."

Collette nodded decisively. "We know more than we did three hours ago. That's something."

"But the cost of that knowledge . . . ." I sighed.

"Undines must be prepared to sacrifice their immortality for the greater good. That is how I am going to regard Jordan's death."

"Did anyone find anything else?" I asked scanning the room.

"Just the dead human's wallet. His name was Hector Gomez," Nathalie replied.

"Tourist?" I asked hopefully.

"Local."

I looked at Mike.

"I'll take care of it," he said.

Jaime's phone pinged, and I glanced at her in irritation. She should know to silence notifications by now.

"Sorry," she apologized as she swiped her screen. "That was Master Remy. He confirmed the handstamp was a necromantic sigil and would be activated by a drop of Winter's blood."

At least now we knew how he gained access to his victims.

~

"You do not really think that they would be stupid enough to hide here, do you?" I asked Gabe as we approached the front door of the Italianate mansion. As soon as I had found the deed to the Garden District property amongst the transfer paperwork the previous evening, I had worried that this was where Honore and the other Rogue Aether had retreated to.

"No. We didn't see any signs of recent habitation, but there were three rooms that we could not gain entrance to because of the wards," he replied.

"I should have thought about the presence of wards last night and come with you," I said.

The city's lieutenant shrugged. "Listening to lawyers drone on for hours can dull anyone's higher thinking capabilities. And anyway, Mike needed you at the crime scene," he reminded me.

I grimaced. While my logical mind knew there was nothing that I could have done to prevent that set of murders, I still felt guilty. Even Marc conceded no one could have saved Jordan from himself.

"I am tired of always being a step or two behind Winters," I confided.

"You and me both. How long do you think it will take you to break the wards?"

"It depends. If she warded them as Aether mistress, they'll come down quickly for me as her successor. If not, it might take a while."

"What do you mean if she warded them as mistress?" Gabe asked.

"If she and the other Aether elders consecrated this building as coven headquarters, then that created a magical bond between all Aether and this building. If she warded the rooms as coven mistress, the ability to unlock the wards passed to me when I became coven mistress," I explained.

"That's handy," Gabe said.

"They design it to facilitate continuity of leadership."

"Did this happen before?"

I shook my head. "When I became Regent after Frederique died, there was not headquarters to transfer. It burned."

Gabe frowned, "You aren't sure they consecrated this building?"

"No. If it was, they did it without me," I replied dryly.

"Weren't you an Elder?"

"Yes."

"Could they do it without you?"

"I think that as long as they had five Elders—from any city—they could consecrate the building."

"That would make sense since not every city has five elders."

As I placed my foot on the first stair, I felt the house's magic. I sighed in relief. The building was consecrated.

"Let me unlock the door for you," Gabe said as he pulled a set of keys from his pocket.

"There is no need," I said. Walking to the door, I splayed my hand against the wood. I let my magic flow and melt with the house's. There was an audible click and a series of beeps as my magic took down both man-made security and magical locks.

"That's pretty nifty," Gabe commented.

"Normally I would agree with you, but with the current situation, this is actually a liability."

"How so?"

"As a consecrated headquarters, any Aether can gain entrance to this building. I cannot use this building as a headquarters until we settle the current unrest."

"Can we modify the consecration?" Jaime asked from behind me.

I turned to see my apprentice and my bodyguard mounting the steps.

"It would take more time than we currently have. Besides, there are only two non-abjured Aether coven members in the city right now. We hardly need a headquarters," I reminded her.

"Just something to think about for later," Jaime said, casting an appreciative look at the house. "It won't always just be the two of us."

"You are right," I conceded. "I will put it on my list of things to deal with later." *Much later.* I opened the door and led the way inside. I let my magic flow in tendrils, searching for the magic of other Aether or the presence of others and sensing none said, "We are alone."

I felt Gabe shift into a slightly more relaxed posture. Jaime and Nathalie did the same.

"The warded rooms are this way," Gabe said, and led the way upstairs.

As we mounted the wide marble staircase, I took a minute to survey the foyer. Sparsely furnished, it soared three stories. Our footsteps echoed in the cavernous interior. Two sets of double doors were on either side of the large entry room. I would ask Gabe later what lay behind them. At the second-floor landing, the staircase split to the right and left. Gabe went left and led the way to the third floor.

"If you decide to keep this as Aether headquarters, there is room for many Initiates to live here. There are eight bedrooms on the second floor and another four for sure on the third. The carriage house has old servant's quarters that could house another half dozen or so." Gabe said.

"Honore was planning big," I commented.

"Most of the bedrooms show use," Gabe added.

"Recent?"

"I don't think since the coup attempt. Perhaps you can read the rooms to be sure."

"Let us see how much these warded rooms take out of me first," I suggested. Even though the house wards had readily responded to me, there was no guarantee that Honore set the wards on these three rooms. Considering the number of foreign Aether we had staying here before the coup attempt, I thought it more likely that one of them had set the wards.

Gabe stopped and indicated the door on the left. "This is the first one that we could not open."

I stepped up and grasped the door handle. I pushed a small amount of magic and, much to my surprise, the handle turned.

"Let me go first—to make sure it's safe," Gabe said as more of an order than request. I tried not to bristle.

Smiling softly, I said in my best diplomatic tone, "They warded this door for a reason. Chances are that whatever it is guarding is magical in nature. Your gun would be of little help." I gestured to the handgun that Gabe had unholstered when the lock clicked.

Gabe gave me a dark look but nodded. I was not foolish enough to rush in blindly. I sent tendrils of my magic through the door to check for dangers but felt none. In fact, I could feel no magic in the room at all. My heart dropped as I found the same void of aether that I had four times before.

I pushed the door open and stared at the scene in front of me. A rotting and putrefying corpse lay splayed in the blood pentagram that I had come to know all too well. Nathalie gasped and gagged behind me. Gabe took a step forward but stopped at my gesture. I quickly looked around the room. There were no other occult symbols visible besides the obvious pentagram on the floor.

"Jaime and Nathalie should examine this room. Don't touch anything with your bare hands. Gabe, you and I need to see what is in these other warded rooms," I said, stepping back from the doorway.

"Gah, that stench! Why didn't we smell anything before?" Nathalie asked.

"The ward on the room masked the smell of decomposition," I said.

"I need to call Marc and tell them now we have a fifth set of murders," Gabe sighed.

"I think this is actually the first set of murders. I will know more once I read the body, but I want to make sure that there are not more of these behind the other wards," I said.

"OK. I'll hold off on a call," Gabe said.

"You will also need to get Vinny here to dispose of the body," I sighed.

"We're gonna need to burn a shit ton of sage to get rid of all this bad juju," Jaime said as she walked past me and into the room.

"Where are these other two warded rooms?" I asked Gabe.

Luckily, both doors opened readily to my magic, and neither room contained more crime scenes. Without dead bodies, I decided these rooms could wait for closer examination.

Gabe and I returned to the first room to find Jaime and Nathalie hard at work searching for clues.

"I found the victim's purse," Jaime said. "Her ID says she's Nancy Ward from New York."

"The vampire dust is over here on the bed." Nathalie was taking short, shallow breaths to alleviate the smell.

I took pity on her. The werewolf sense of smell was acute, and this odor was overpowering. "Why don't you go downstairs and call Vinny Carlucci. Let him know what has happened," I told Nathalie.

"I'll step out too and call Marc," Gabe said.

That left Jaime and me alone in the room. It was a large space, clearly not meant to be a bedroom despite there being a bed in the chamber. I thought its original purpose had probably been the music room or perhaps the mistress's upstairs parlor. Upon closer inspection, I realize that while the pentagram was in blood, a permanent circle was laid into the hardwood floor in silver. I felt certain Honore had intended this room to be the coven's ritual room.

"Are you going to read the body?" Jaime asked.

"It is the only way to know for sure," I said and knelt next to the body.

CHAPTER 23

Several hours later, I found myself in yet another uncomfortable meeting with the city's grandmaster. While he could hardly blame me for not stopping a ritual murder that happened the night of the coup attempt, he was less than pleased to find out that Robert Winters was one set closer to completing his goal. I was none too happy about that myself.

Despite the time passage and the decomposed state of the body, it had readily told its story to me. Nancy Ward and her vampire lover, Brian McDermott, had come down to New Orleans for the promise of becoming members of the city's Aether coven. McDermott, I discovered when I read his ashes, was a moderately powerful Aether lured by the prospect of quickly rising through the coven's ranks here in New Orleans. He had willingly allowed Winters into his head, believing Honore's false promises of power and status.

While the other coven members had gathered at Honore's home a few blocks away, Winters, Nancy Ward, and Brian McDermott had stayed behind, supposedly to carry out a sex magic ritual to boost the chances of the coup's success. The sex magic performed here would work concurrently with the demon summoning at Honore's.

McDermott and Ward did not know that they were to be the first set of Winters' victims. Honore had warded the room's door before she left, and once the ritual was complete, Winters simply left the building.

"What do we do now?" Mark asked me.

"I really do not know," I answered truthfully. "He has two-and-a-half months to claim his last set of victims. To complete the pairings, he needs a Salamand. We must protect every member of the coven."

"That's easier said than done," Gabe commented.

I countered, "It is really just the same problem we had before, except now we need to protect members of one coven instead of two."

Marc grunted.

We were getting nowhere fast, and I had enough guilt about what had happened without Marc's dour looks. I decided to end this uncomfortable meeting.

"Before everything went sideways, you asked me to make werewolf amulets for the New Orleans pack. Do you still want them?" I said.

"Yes, nothing has changed on that front," the Grandmaster said.

"With your permission then, I will return home and start preparing them. I do not think that I can be of any further use here," I suggested.

"By all means, go," Marc said, waving his hand absently.

I stood, nodded my acquiescence, and left the room feeling dejected and worthless. We, or at least I, could not catch a break when it came to stopping Winters. Less than twenty-four hours ago, the outlook for our success had been much more positive.

Jaime and Nathalie stood as I entered the foyer.

"That bad, huh?" Jaime asked.

"Worse," I confided.

"Now what?" Nathalie asked.

"Jaime and I need to go home and hope Gaetan and Josh are back from the swamp," I said, leading the way to the back courtyard.

"Gaetan said they were making the trip but didn't offer any details. What's up? Is everything okay with the pack?" Nathalie asked.

"The werewolves are fine," I assured her.

Once we were in the Jeep—Gaetan and Josh had taken the Mustang to the swamp—I explained Marc's plan to the two women.

"Security for Convocation—that's big," Nathalie said.

"It is a whole new era for vampire/werewolf relations," I said.

"As long as nothing goes wrong," Nathalie said dryly.

An icy chill ran down my spine.

JOSH AND GAETAN arrived home soon after we did. I filled the two in on the evening's occurrences before Jaime and I retired to the downstairs ritual chamber to start creating another 30 werewolf amulets. I was surprised at the large number and said so.

"The pack is pretty big," Nathalie assured me. "We have a lot of territory out in the swamp. We're one of the biggest packs in the country and the largest east of the Mississippi."

"It is just that when we met with Beau for the house guards, he said he only had 12 or 13 members who could do this," I said needing clarification.

"Only a dozen or so that could work security full time. Convocation is a one-night gig. There are a whole bunch more members who can take a night and guard."

"That makes a lot more sense," I said and left to go downstairs.

Jaime and I took the neatly labeled hair samples down to the ritual room and made the amulets. We were very careful to keep the final amulet with the proper label so each werewolf got the correct one. For the rest of the evening, we concentrated on constructing the exterior structures. While that creation took magic, it cost me less than charging them. Even so, by 4 AM, I was exhausted, and my work was becoming sloppy. I sensed Jaime might not be far behind me.

"Time to stop for the evening," I declared, affixing the owners name and pushing an amulet away from me.

Jaime checked her watch. "We still have time before dawn."

"I am too tired to continue, and you could use a break as well," I said.

"But there's so much left to do," Jaime protested.

"I know, but I would rather stop now than continue working and come down tonight to find that many amulets need to be refashioned."

"I can see your point," Jaime conceded. "Remind me again why we don't just take down the anti-werewolf ward for that night?"

"Because I foolishly tied the anti-necromancy spell into its matrix. If one is taken down, the other comes with it," I sighed. "Also, we don't need a pack of man-eating werewolves in the city again. They killed so many the last time."

Jaime shuddered at the memory. "Yeah, the humans were getting suspicious with so many people going missing."

"Anyway, I need some time to think about the plan to stop Winters," I said.

"You know none of this is your fault, right? You couldn't have known about the Aether deaths. Hell, we had our hands full stopping that coup," Jaime reminded me.

No, this was not my fault, but it *was* my responsibility as coven leader to prevent more deaths at Winters' hand. I was not sure I was up to the task. Twice now, he had slid through my fingers without much of a magical fight. I had caught him unprepared—twice—and squandered my chances. Maybe I was not fit to be coven leader.

Pushing aside my doubts, I said to Jaime, "My fault or not, we cannot allow Winters to complete his series of vampire souls from each coven. It will magnify his strength far too much."

"Maybe using your focus to cast the anti-soul stealing spell wasn't such a good idea after all."

"There is no use in regretting that. It is done. We can only move forward." With that, I sent Jaime upstairs and cleaned up our work area.

As tired as I was, I found the routine of putting things away calmed my troubled mind. Although I had come to no conclusions by the time I had tidied everything up, my mind was as well ordered as my workspace was.

～

JOSH GREETED me at the top of the stairs with a mug of warmed vitae and a smile.

"How did you know?" I asked, grateful for this thoughtfulness.

"When Jaime came up a bit ago, she said you were tired. I know you fed after you read the bodies earlier, but you've been at that amulet makin' for quite a spell. I figured you'd need a pick me up. I also opened a bottle of wine for you," Josh said as he gently led me to the sofa.

Snuggling me close, he asked, "How you doing with all this?"

"Not very well," I admitted. "We are always a step behind Winters and Honore. Actually, several steps it seems. I suppose the good news is that we know for sure that Honore and Winters are working together on the murders," I said.

"Not sure that's good news, darlin'," Josh said as he replaced my mug of vitae with a glass of wine.

"It is not good news that they are working together, but it *is* one less variable we need to contend with," I clarified.

"You're sure Honore knew what Winters meant to do when she left him in the coven house?"

"Oh, yes. She gave him the Focus to drain the magic into," I said in disgust. That much I had learned from reading the blood at the latest crime scene.

"He's using a Focus?"

"Of course," I snapped and then stopped myself. Just because Josh felt magic didn't mean he understood everything about it. I took a deep, calming breath and touched his arm in apology, "I'm sorry. Yes, he's using a Focus. You remember that all of the aether has been drained from the area around the crime scenes?"

"Yep"

"It must go somewhere, and that somewhere is the Focus. He is also storing the souls he steals in there."

"So you know what this focus looks like?"

"Yes, but that hardly helps us. It will be as well guarded as Winters himself is," I pointed out.

"Yeah, I guess he ain't just gonna leave that lying around."

"Not likely," I said and sighed.

"What?" Josh asked and pulled me close again.

"I hate being coven mistress. I hate being responsible for the magical well-being of the city. I never wanted this!"

"I know, darlin'. You got dealt a shitty hand, that's for sure. You comin' back just as the Strays start attackin', then the coven fire where you lose everybody you really know. I know then you opted for Regency, hoping that another candidate would come in and fill the position, but look how that turned out."

"Ugh. Don't remind me," I said.

"I think you're takin' on too much. You and Jaime are doin' the magical work of the entire coven. Stuff that normally would be delegated to your Elders. You're also workin' with Mike on the murders. Now Marc has you makin' amulets so the pack can guard Convocation. Darlin', you're burnin' the candle at both ends and probably the middle too."

"I do not suppose you have any solutions for this. I have no one to delegate to. I am already asking Jaime to do too much. Reading blood and objects are very specialized abilities that only Aether possess, and they require training. There has been no time to teach Jaime," I groaned.

"Can you get Diana to send a couple of Aether from London to help?" Josh suggested.

I furrowed my brow. "Things are too chaotic in London, I think. Diana needs everyone she trusts there, and we do not need anyone she does not completely trust here. That does give me an idea, however. I will talk to Marc about may be some Parisian and Québécois Aether coming to help temporarily."

"Now you're thinkin' like a coven mistress," Josh laughed.

"I know there is no one else to do it, but I really hate this job!"

"That is why, as Sylph lieutenant, my primary goal is to keep Toussaint alive. Pain in the ass that man is, him doing the job of Sylph Master is way better than me," Josh said.

"Should not Em or one of the other Sylph Elders become master before you? I know you jumped hierarchy to become lieutenant because you were the only one really capable of taking the position, but will succession not revert back to proper order for the next Master?" We followed rather archaic rules for succession. If a coven leader was ousted by coup—force of arms—then whomever had succeeded became coven leader. If both the coven leader and challenger died in the attempt, or if the coven leader was killed by a non-coven member, the coven lieutenant was next in line followed by the Elders according to vampire age.

Josh shook his head. "While it ought to, none of the other elders wants the job. They're all too busy with their art, music, writin', whatever to do it. They already let me know that none of them will step up if the vacancy occurs."

"Then you better make sure a vacancy does not occur," I said firmly.

"Amen to that. Hey, could the voodoo community help with anything? Didn't you say you'd inherited Voodoo Royal?"

I thought for a moment. "I am not sure. I mean yes, I inherited Voodoo Royal, but I am not sure they can or will help."

"Can't hurt to ask and remember Delia and Owen will be here tonight. They might be able to help as well."

"Gads! I completely forgot that they were coming!" I exclaimed in dismay and sat straight up. "The guest room needs to be made up. We will need to send Nathalie to the store for food . . . ."

Josh laughed. "I'm taking care of all that. Don't worry. You got enough going on. Leave my kin to me. I'll get them squared away."

I slumped back against him. "Thank you. I would embarrass my mother with my lack of hostessing skills."

"Ain't nothing wrong with your skills—hostessin' or otherwise. Like I said, you got too much on your plate already. Let's see if we can't move some of it off."

"Thank you."

~

I AM NOT sure what I expected from Delia and Owen. All I know is that it was not what I got. First, they looked as if they were in their late 40s or early 50s even though I knew them to be much older. While mages age differently than normal humans, I knew their appearance must be magically altered.

Delia had Josh's sandy blond hair and the same piercing eyes. At 5'9, her willowy frame looked like a strong wind might knock her over. I was not deceived by her appearance, however. The magic radiating off her was formidable.

Owen was what I thought of as ruggedly handsome. Not much taller than Delia, his close-cut dark hair was just beginning to gray at the temples. His blue eyes sparkled when he laughed, and he laughed often.

Both accepted me as part of the family. I suppose that they really had no choice since I was now soul-bonded to Josh. Even so, they did genuinely seem to like me, and I truly liked them.

They also jumped right in to help Jaime and me with the massive werewolf amulet project. I still had to charge each amulet myself, but with three others to create the shells, completion within the requisite time frame no longer seemed in question. Working magically with the pair also allowed me great insight into both of their personalities. Owen had a dry wit that could catch me off guard. Delia needed to tell me several times that he was teasing. Delia's knowledge of the Craft was impressive and practically encyclopedic, so I no longer had to consult my grimoire to research things I could not remember off the top of my head; I just asked Delia. I knew that when she and Owen returned to Texas, I would miss them greatly.

The couple's presence also freed me up to take care of some coven business. I was finally able meet with the manager of Voodoo Royal. For the moment, I could not take a day-to-day interest in the business, but I had hopes that once we defeated Honore and Winters, I might be able to spend more time there. In any case, the store was in excellent hands. Esmeralda Longchamp had managed the shop for years, and with an infusion of my blood to make her my servant, she would continue for many more. I made a note to leave detailed instruction about Esmeralda's status for Jaime in case the worst happened on the cold blue moon.

The meeting had the secondary benefit of providing me with a somewhat lengthy list of candidates for Aether coven membership. Esmeralda had kept the list for Frederique. She tried to give it to Honore when she had become Mistress, but Honore showed no interest. Under Honore's leadership, we had vetted several candidates for membership, none of whom appeared on Esmeralda's list. I had voiced concerns about a few of them, and those concerns seemed validated as Honore had been looking at sketchy individuals to help her open the Gates of Hell. I had a fleeting thought to see if Honore had subsequently turned any of those individuals and decided to turn their names over to Gabe. He, as the city's lieutenant, would be responsible for the elimination of any new Rogue Aether.

When things calmed down, I would vet Esmeralda's list with both Marc and Nicholas. Even though I was fairly certain Honore had not tainted her, I would not accept these recommendations blindly. I also was not sure if this was a raw list of those who had expressed interest or those that Frederique had been watching. My guess from the length was that it was both, but wholly unvetted. I had my work cut out for me although I could delegate the initial vetting to Jaime. This seemed to be in her skill set.

I HAD THOUGHT the visit with Josh's aunt and uncle was going well until Delia approached me one evening shortly before Convocation. In a rare moment, we were alone in the house. Josh, Owen, and Gaetan were driving out to the swamp to deliver the completed werewolf amulets to the pack while Jaime and Nathalie were out in the courtyard sparring. I was on my way downstairs to the ritual room to sew protection runes on our ceremonial robes.

"Do you have time for a chat?" Never had the word "Chat" had such an ominous ring to it. I sighed inwardly. I had really been hoping to get these robes done tonight during a respite from crisis after crisis. I wanted to tell her no, that I just did not have the time, but she was Josh's aunt and had helped so much already.

"I . . . of course," I said, forcing a smile.

She patted my arm. "I won't take too long, and then I'll help with the magical embroidery," Delia offered.

Maybe this would be quick, and with Delia's help, I might get all three robes done tonight.

"Let's go sit in the living room and have a drink. Josh says that you drink whiskey?" she suggested.

"I drink whiskey when things are bad or we are at a bar and nothing else is palatable," I said, following Delia back into the living room.

She went to the wet bar and poured two glasses of Knappogue Castle 16 whiskey while I sat on the sofa. Delia had much better taste in whiskey than either Josh or Nathalie but my hopes for a quick chat were rapidly evaporating.

"Things are bad then. What is on your mind, Delia?" I asked, accepting the amber liquid from her.

"Now, you know that Owen and I like you a great deal," Delia began as she settled herself into an oversized chair that emphasized her delicacy.

"But?" I supplied for her. This was not going to be a pleasant conversation.

"We are worried about the soul bonding that has occurred between you and Josh," Delia said and took a large sip of whiskey. She shook her head. "No, that isn't quite right. It delights us that he's finally found someone—even if we don't know what a vampire to vampire and mage to non-mage bond will do. Josh is happy. Happier than . . . well . . . I've ever seen him."

"You are clearly worried about something," I said as Delia took another large sip of whiskey. I was getting the idea that the whiskey had not actually been for me.

"We're scared for him. I'm scared for him. What will happen to Josh if we can't stop Winters in time and you have to sacrifice your-self? How is he going to survive?" Delia said in a torrent.

I grimaced and took another sip of my whiskey. "I worried about this as well, so I spoke to Master Remy. He assured me that the other member of a bonded pair can survive and even survive for years."

"Normally, I'd agree with you, but this is Josh. He always seems happy because he puts on a good show, but there is an underlying sadness that's been there since he was turned. Your presence has taken that away. He is genuinely happy now—for the first time in over a hundred years."

"I worry about him too, but there is really not anything we can do. The bond is there and can only be broken with death. It is a vicious circle."

"I know. I was going to ask you to distance yourself from him, but that won't work either because you need him as much as he needs you."

"How do you mean?"

"His faith will bolster you when you begin to doubt yourself. And you *will* begin to doubt yourself. Just seeing him reminds you why you must make the ultimate sacrifice."

"Wait a minute!" Jaime angrily interrupted. Both Delia and I snapped our heads towards the doorway. Neither of us, it seemed, had heard her come in. "Ultimate sacrifice? You make it sound like it's final death. It isn't, is it?"

I winced. Even though my childe knew about the prophecy, she did not fully understand the ramifications of it. I knew I had to tell her eventually, but I was hoping for later.

Since I did not know how to soften the blow, I opted for candor. "If Winters opens the gate, or even just breaks the current seal, the only way to re-seal the gate is for me to die."

"What? You're shittin' me!" Jaime's face contorted in anguish.

I shook my head. "I am afraid not. Master Remy said the texts are clear that only all of my blood will fully seal the gate."

"Well, fuck. I thought that . . . ." My childe trailed off, blinking back tears.

I bowed my head in shame. "I know what you thought, and I am sorry I let you keep thinking that."

"Were you ever gonna tell me or were you just going to do it?" Jaime demanded.

"Of course I was going to tell you, to prepare you. I just needed time to, how do you like to say it? Wrap my brain around it? I assumed when you first told me about the prophecy that the sacrifice required would probably be total. Master Remy confirmed that."

Jaime looked at Delia. "You knew?"

"Owen and I suspected. Josh confirmed it when we arrived although he has faith that it won't come to that." Delia rose and went to the girl, putting her arms around her. Jaime shrugged her off.

"Am I the only one who didn't know?"

"Actually, there are only a few who do know. Most assume that a small amount of my blood will close the Gate, and I want to keep it that way," I said.

"What about Nathalie and Gaetan?"

"Nathalie knows. If it helps, she is even less pleased about it than you are. I assume she has told Gaetan."

"Man, I knew this sucked donkey balls, but shit," Jaime said and stomped off to her room.

"That could have gone better," I said dryly.

Delia detoured to the wet bar on her way back to her seat and grabbed the bottle of Knappogue Castle 16. She refilled both our glasses.

"I'm so sorry. I didn't realize that Jaime did not fully understand the prophecy. I never would have said anything where she could have heard if I had known." Delia seemed genuinely concerned about the upset she had caused.

I took a long drink and said, "It is my fault. I should have told her before this. I was sure she did not fully understand the prophecy and never corrected her. I just did not want to have the conversation. It was me avoiding the inevitable, I suppose."

"Will she be alright? She didn't want any comfort," Delia fretted.

"I think once she has some time, she will come around. I would not worry about her not wishing physical comfort. She says, 'she is not a hugger.' It surprised me when she allowed me to comfort her once. I will ask Nathalie to look in on her later. They have become good friends."

"She and Josh are going to need a lot of help . . . after. If the worst comes to pass," Delia said.

"Will you be here for them?" I asked.

"Owen and I will start looking for houses in the city."

"What about the ranch?"

Delia smiled sadly and took another drink. "It's a bit much for the two of us at our age. We've been talking about downsizing for a while. Plus, Josh and Emma are our only surviving kin. We should be closer."

"Thank you."

CHAPTER 24

I stopped Delia at her second glass of whiskey. I might not have the ability to get drunk any longer, but she did, and I really needed her help to embroider the robes. I hated asking her to do even more magical work, but I was desperately in need of a second set of hands. Jaime would be of no use to me in this magical endeavor. When I mentioned teaching her magical embroidery, Jaime tartly informed me it was archaic, and she had no use for it. As I had neither the time nor the energy to teach my recalcitrant childe something she clearly had no interest in learning, I dropped the subject. There were more important things to focus on. Maybe Delia could teach Jaime . . . after.

Delia and I went down to the ritual room and sat in the large protective circle that had become a more or less permanent fixture on the smooth worn wood floor—at least as permanent as chalk could be. There was so much chalk overlaid chalk that I feared nothing except a thorough scrubbing would remove all trace. I hoped one day to have a truly permanent circle etched into the wood, but there was not time now. Setting a permanent circle required days of effort on just that. Too much other magic needed to be done right now.

Delia pulled the rather loud canary yellow robe from the top of the pile. I had asked Josh earlier in the week if his ceremonial robes had protective runes sewn onto it.

"Nah, never had the need," he had shrugged.

"We have a need now," I had said firmly. "Where is your robe?"

"Hidden away in the back of the closet. I hate the damn thing. It serves no purpose. Thank God I've only gotta wear it once a year at Convocation."

I had dutifully dug out the heavy velvet ceremonial robe in the Sylph coven color. It truly was garish. Delia and I had decided earlier that she would embroider Josh's robe while I took care of Jaime's and my own. Since Josh was close family, Delia's magic would be even more potent on the garment.

I pulled the royal purple velvet robe that was next on the pile to me. Again, I owed Delia a great debt. When I had been told earlier in the week that we needed the formal ceremonial robes for Convocation, I had panicked. While the Aether put great stock in tradition and ritual, the other covens did not. No one wore robes at meetings of the Undead Synod or the Council of Five, so I assumed the Aether were clinging to the old ways only in our own coven meetings. It horrified me to learn that all vampires would be in ceremonial robes for Convocation.

Not that I minded the robe. I found all the pockets useful for spell components and such. Unfortunately, my robe had been heavily damaged during the coup attempt. All the magical protections were used up, and scorch marks marred the fabric. I had not had time to replace it. Jaime was so new to being a vampire that she did not even have a robe. Since it was just the two of us in the coven at the moment, there had been no formal meetings and thus no need for robes.

Realizing my distress over the situation, Delia stepped in and offered to make them. I had not thought there would be enough time to both make the robes and embroider the magical runes on them, but I had not counted on modern machinery. During my lifetime, it would have taken several days to hand sew the two garments. Delia put them together in just a few hours with a sewing machine. I needed to learn how to operate one . . . someday.

Delia had taken quick height, shoulder, and arm measurements and quickly set to work. I do not know where she had procured the machine or fabric, but she did so and retreated to one of the guest rooms where I heard the whirring of the machine early that morning before going to bed. When I arose after sundown, both robes were done. I could not have managed without her.

I took up my needle and white thread and began the excruciatingly dull task of chanting and stitching.

Hours later, Josh and Jaime's robes were done, and the first of two rows of runes were complete on my garment. Delia had finished Josh's robe a few minutes earlier after needing to pick out her stitches at least twice.

"I really hate magical embroidery," she said when I finally stopped chanting. "Regular embroidery is not so bad. You can talk or listen to music. This is just stitch and chant, stitch and chant."

I laughed. Those were the precise reasons that I detested the task as well. "Let's go see if Owen and Josh are back from the swamp yet," I suggested.

"I thought you wanted to put a second row of runes on your robe."

"I will. Tomorrow. I have had more than my share of stitch and chant tonight. I may start making mistakes." I tied off the last of my threads and set the robe aside.

I HAD HOPED to talk to Jaime before going downstairs to the ritual room to finish the protective runes on my robe the next night, but she was up and out before I rose for the evening. I should be glad that my childe had not inherited my sleeping late tendency. However, while she did not need my permission to do things, with the necromancer reaping vampire souls, it would be nice to know what she was up to and where she was. Even if he already had one Aether soul, I was sure

Winters would not turn down another. Nathalie mentioned Jaime had taken Gaetan with her, so there was that at least.

My stitching did not progress as smoothly as the night before, and I needed to take out part of a row and start again. I was not sure why my concentration had wavered, but eventually, I finished.

When I finally emerged from the ritual room, Jaime was sitting on the floor waiting for me.

"I didn't want to disturb you," she explained as she unfolded herself and stood.

"Thank you. I was having a hard enough time concentrating without interruption," I said as I set the mage lock on the door.

"I went to the Convocation venue tonight and checked it out. I took Gaetan with me so we could check security, and I did some preliminary warding. I hope you don't mind," Jaime said.

I could have hugged the girl. "Mind? Not at all. I was planning to have Josh stop by there after our meeting with Marc tonight."

"You'll obviously want to do more, but I put a solid foundation of wards down. I figured it was the least I could do after flaking out on the arts and crafts earlier."

"Arts and crafts?" I asked confused.

"The magical embroidery." Jaime clarified.

I shrugged. "I understand. I do not particularly enjoy embroidery myself, but I wanted us to have an extra layer of protection if something happens at Convocation. It saved me during the coup attempt."

"An extra layer of protection would've been handy," Jaime admitted. "It isn't so much that I don't want to learn it or that I think it's old-fashioned. I don't know why I said that. It's just that my Gran used to embroider. She did altar cloths for the church all the time. This just reminds me too much of her."

"That makes sense."

"I know it is silly, but I just couldn't deal with it along with all the other changes."

"It is all right. I can teach you some other time. There have been a lot of changes in your life lately. It is all right to say enough is enough."

"That doesn't sound very 18th century there, Juliette. Have you been reading hippie dippy New Age self-help stuff?"

I laughed. "Retreat and relaxation are not hippie dippy, as you call it. You modern Americans are always go, go, go. Sometimes you just need to stop and take some time for yourself or avoid a distasteful project."

"Because you are so good at that?"

"I actually used to be very good at it."

"What changed?"

"Two hundred years of enforced idleness and then the possibility of the end of the world have motivated me. Also, the responsibility of being Coven Mistress."

"Things have changed a lot for you, too," Jaime said sympathetically.

I shrugged. I did not need introspection right now. I had spent more than two centuries in torpor where my mind had been active, but my body immobilized by a stake through my heart. I'd had a lot of time to think about and examine every choice that I had ever made. And even before that, all of my decisions had been carefully calculated. My most important decisions, especially my decisions to become a vampire and a member of the Aether coven were deliberated and debated. I really need to be more spontaneous. Even my relationship with Josh was more or less plotted. He had desired me, and I had needed a protector—at least initially. It had surprised me how our feelings deepened.

"THIS IS AN ODD PLACE FOR CONVOCATION," I said to Josh as we mounted the marble steps to a newly renovated former bank. Located in the Central Business District, it had an impressive facade.

"Convocation moves around. Because it's all the New Orleans vampires in one place at one time, we don't hold it in the same place two years in a row. A group of investors bought this building a few years ago and started renovatin' it. We're actually the first group to use it."

A security guard met us at the door. He seemed to know Josh and said, "Mr. Carlucci and Mr. Roulet are already inside."

"Has Honore ever been here?" I asked Josh.

"I doubt it. The location was shifted here after the coup for security purposes."

"She and the other Rogue Aether will still know where to find us."

"Kinda hard to keep it a secret when every vamp in New Orleans is supposed to be here. Besides, I think Marc wants to draw her out. That's why Beau is handlin' security."

"I wish Marc would reconsider and cancel. I have an awful feeling about this." I was not given to existential dread, but the more I thought about this, the more it bothered me.

"Darlin', it's above our pay grade. We just gotta do the best we can."

"How many vampires are there in New Orleans?"

"A couple dozen, maybe. We're way down from where we were just two months ago. Between the devastation of your coven and the ones we lost in the coup attempt, not to mention the murderers, our numbers are much smaller. The only time I've seen this sparse a population here was in the wake of Katrina."

"The hurricane?"

"Yeah. We had an attempted coup then as well, but that wasn't why our numbers dipped. A lot of the younger vamps who didn't have decades or centuries invested here moved to Houston or Atlanta. Food got kinda scarce for us for a while."

Beau Roulet and Vinny Carlucci were deep in conversation when we walked up.

"Juliette!" Beau enveloped me in a bear hug. "Good to see you."

"It is good to see you as well, Beau. There were no problems getting through the wards?" I asked.

"Nope. I could feel 'um, but they didn't stop me."

I nodded.

"Vinny," I said by way of greeting.

"Mistress Grammont. Nice to see you when there is not an exsanguinated body to clean up."

"Speaking of that, are there any recent developments?"

"With Winters? No. Thankfully."

We spent the next several hours going over every square inch of the building. Jaime had done a wonderful job of setting the basic wards. I added another layer and wove in some anti-necromancy and anti-magic wards as well. I could not cast offensive magic in the room, but neither would anyone else.

"We'll have guards here 24/7 until Convocation. Don't worry, nothing's getting in." Vinny assured me. I just could not shake my bad feeling, but I kept that to myself.

I was very busy for the next several nights, but I could never quite get rid of my unease, so I put down another set of wards on the Convocation building and updated the city's magical matrix to warn me if necromancy was practiced anywhere in the city. I hoped it would be enough.

CHAPTER 25

While the rain did not dampen the pre-Halloween party atmosphere in most of New Orleans, it did not help my spirits. The feeling of impending doom grew as the evening of Convocation drew closer. I had checked and rechecked both the city wards and the ones at the Convocation site. They were fine, but nothing quietened my gnawing worry.

"Sumthin' bigs a brewin', that's for sure," Josh agreed when I told him of my feelings. "I feel it too. I talked to Gabe about it, thinkin' he might convince Marc to at least postpone Convocation, but no dice. They want a showdown with Honore and Winters."

"I don't think this bad feeling is about an attack; I think it is about the result."

"Hey, now. I've got faith in the Pack protecting us. Don't let Beau hear you knockin' werewolf abilities," Josh gently chided.

"I do not doubt werewolf prowess, believe me. It's just . . . ." I could not put my finger on what was causing my uneasiness.

"I know. Look on the bright side. At least it isn't snowing," Josh said, referring to the weather abnormality that had preceded the coup attempt last month.

"Bite your tongue!" All we needed tonight was Honore and her minions summoning a large quantity of demons. While I did not think she had the coven strength to do it again, I could not be sure. Opportunistic vampires who might see the lure of quick advancement in coven hierarchy could have been brought in to help again. In the past several days, I had received several calls from Aether in other cities looking to relocate to New Orleans. Everything was on hold until after tonight so that I could fully investigate each applicant and make sure that they were not Aether who wished to open the Gates of Hell.

Even though the gathering was not scheduled to start until ten p.m., I convinced Josh to take me to the venue early. I wanted to make one last series of checks before the fate of New Orleans entire sanctioned vampire community rested on the strength of my magical wards buttressed by a phalanx of werewolves and Gatekeepers. Delia and Owen would also bolster our magical ability. They were arriving later with Jaime.

Beau and Vinny met us in the building's vestibule.

"Is something wrong? You're here awfully early," Beau asked.

"Juliette wants to make another check," Josh explained.

Vinny nodded. "We can't be too careful. Gabe is here already as well. Paul called. He'll be here soon too."

"Has anyone seen the Gatekeepers yet?" I asked.

"Yeah. Master Remy and his crew showed up about half an hour ago. They're taking up positions outside."

The plan was to start Convocation at ten. If Honore and Winters showed up, the event would be suspended, and all non-fighting vampires would be protected in magical circles. The Gatekeepers and a contingent of werewolves were outside in case they brought demons with them again. Jaime, Josh, Gabe, and the other fighting vampires would join the fight outside. I would retreat to a specially prepared room and enter the spirit realm and try to stop Winters from there.

I was not in favor of this course of action. I thought it relied far too much on chance and the strength of my magical wards. While I knew my wards were strong, I also knew the amount of magical power that Honore and the Rogue Aether could possibly bring against them. They had summoned several high-level demons and not a few low-level minions from Hell during the coup attempt, after all. Add to that the strength of Winters and I would be foolish to underestimate their collective power or overestimate mine and Jaime's. Even with the Gatekeepers, as well as Delia and Owen, we could be magically outnumbered. I had argued these points during several phone calls with Marc, Beau, Nicholas, and Gabe. I was persuaded this was the best course of action—or rather overruled—by the combined power of Beau, Nicholas, and Marc.

Nicholas' ready acceptance of this risky scheme had surprised me. He simply told me it was better to meet them on our terms and in a time and place of our choosing rather than always being on the defensive. While I saw his point, I still thought far too much was being left to chance.

Despite my misgivings, or perhaps because of them, I was checking the wards on the building yet again. Jaime and I had layered anti-offensive magic, anti-necromancy, and anti-malevolent intent wards over the entire space. The anti-offensive magic ward was the same one that I had used to protect the New Orleans Museum gala last month. It did not nullify protective magic or charms but prevented aether from being drawn for offensive purposes. This ward would not stop me from casting since my magic was innate, not drawn, but neither would it stop Winters if he managed entrance into the building. The anti-malevolence ward stopped that from happening. No one with malicious intent could enter the building while this ward was active.

As a further layer of protection, Jaime and I had drawn a series of protective circles in strategic places around Convocation's main chamber. One circle was around the area where the Sylphs would sit. None of them besides Josh had any real fighting ability and would probably be more of a hindrance than a help if it came down to a battle. Another circle surrounded the pentagonal table brought from Gautier House where the Grand Council members would sit. While some council members would fight if the action started, others such as Marc, were to be protected in order to preserve 'continuity of power.' Thick carpets were laid on top of the circles to prevent smudging, but I had left a small portion of each circle accessible so that Jaime or I could quickly invoke them.

In a small room off of the primary venue, I had set a series of five circles. This was where I would retreat if I needed to meet Winters on the spirit plane. Since my body was helpless and extremely vulnerable while my soul was on the spirit plane, it needed extra layers of protection. In addition to the circles, Nathalie would stand guard with the sole responsibility of keeping my body safe. She had not been happy at all with this plan, but in the end, she too had been overruled. Josh had argued unsuccessfully that Gaetan was needed to protect me as well, but Beau and Marc deemed the werewolf necessary to the outside fight.

Josh found me pacing around the outer protective circle in the small chamber. Taking me by the shoulders, he stopped me.

"Darlin', there's nothing more you can do. What will be, will be. It's almost time to get this show on the road, so we need to robe up."

He was right. There wasn't anything more that I could do, so I allowed him to lead me out into the main chamber.

CONVOCATION WAS full of pomp and grandeur. I had not seen the like since my presentation at Versailles over two hundred years ago. I wondered if all cities' yearly events were this lavish or if Marc had ordered this show because of the coup attempt last month. He would not be the first leader to try to shore up his position through awe and spectacle.

Robed coven members were already inside waiting for Masters, Mistresses, and Lieutenants to process in. We had set convocation to start on the hour, but it was now half-past, and we were still congregated in the vestibule because of one missing vampire. Salamand coven leader, Paul Barthelmy stood off to the side on his cell phone trying to track down the newest member of his coven. In normal times, I doubt we would have noticed a missing vampire, but these were not normal times. The Salamand's were the only coven that Robert Winters had yet to cull a soul from, so a wayward fledgling was worrisome.

Paul slid the cell phone into the pocket of his crimson robe and walked to confer with the Grandmaster. Whatever he had to say, the Salamand Master did not want all of us wearing the sophisticated communications earpieces and microphones to hear.

I inclined my head to listen in, but Josh leaned close and asked, "Whaddya think?"

I tried not to glare at Josh for ruining my opportunity to eavesdrop. He had moral sensibilities that I did not. Vampire etiquette considered it rude to listen in on a conversation between a Master and a Grandmaster, but I thought the circumstances warranted it. Tamping down my irritation, I smiled saying, "I hope the fledgling still exists to regret being late. Is it possible that the importance of the occasion was not properly impressed on this individual?"

Josh gave me a look. "Ya really think Paul didn't do his job, right?"

"It is the better option," I replied.

"Ain't it though," Josh agreed ruefully.

With a significant nod from Sophie, we all fell back into line. Following the centuries old tradition, the city's Steward led the line, followed by the Grandmaster and his Lieutenant, side by side. Other Coven Masters or Mistresses next to their Lieutenants continued the processional line. Order was determined by Master or Mistress precedence, meaning that Toussaint, as the longest serving coven leader, was directly behind Marc, while I, as the newest Mistress, was last in line next to Jaime.

"Did you hear?" Jaime asked as we moved into our places.

"No, Josh interrupted. Did you?"

"Yeah, but it isn't good news. Beau sent one of the werewolves to check out the vamp's place, but there was no sign of him."

"What about his partner's residence?" I asked. All of our murders had been in pairs, so it was a valid question.

"They lived together. No dead body and no vampire dust."

"Well, then it is not bad news either," I said and fell silent as the pageantry began. I was very glad that my childe had even fewer scruples about eavesdropping than I did. I would need to give her etiquette lessons about it at some point, but this worked for now.

The double doors to the main chamber were thrown open, and the assembled hall fell silent as the city's leadership filed in. Vampires in Salamand red, Gnome green, Sylph yellow and Undine blue robes stood on either side of the wide center aisle. There was a momentary pang when the realization hit me that only Jaime and I were in Aether purple. I felt there should be trumpet flourishes or something equally pompous, but the only things punctuating the silence were the click of heels and the rustle of robes.

Gabe stopped at the last row of chairs, while Sophie and Marc walked a further ten feet—almost to the large pentagonal table. Sophie took a position slightly behind and to the right of Marc after they both turned to face us. She brought the heavy wooden mace, a symbol of her office, down on the floor three times before announcing, "Marc Gautier, Grandmaster of New Orleans and Master of the Gnome Coven."

Marc, regal as ever in his emerald green robe, was a presence to behold. As one, the assembled vampires bowed to our Grandmaster and then straightened.

"Brethren, we are gathered on this solemn occasion to reaffirm our bonds and commitments to one another and this city. I have been honored to serve as New Orleans Grandmaster for the past ninety-one years and, with your help, I will serve ninety-one more. The events of the past few months have been trying. The events of the next few months look to be even more so. Our society is in upheaval, but together we shall persevere." Marc's voice boomed through the chamber.

When he finished his speech, the Grandmaster gave a subtle nod of his head, and Sophie summoned Gabe forward to reaffirm his oath.

One by one the coven leadership made their oaths and then arrayed themselves around the Grandmaster. Eventually, Sophie called my name. I walked forward and knelt before Marc.

I reaffirmed the oath that I had taken just a month before under much less auspicious circumstances.

"I, Juliette de Grammont, Mistress of the Aether Coven, do freely swear to uphold the Traditions, be faithful to my coven, and render service to the Grandmaster of New Orleans, Marc Gautier. I will protect the city and its Grandmaster against all creatures, living or dead, until I meet final death. I will faithfully serve as Mistress of the Aether coven in this city and safeguard our existence. I place all of the talents and resources of the city's Aether coven at the disposal of the Grandmaster should they be needed. This is my solemn oath and promise."

I kissed Marc's ring of office before rising to my feet. As he had with the others in city leadership, Marc took the ceremonial dagger proffered by Sophie and cut his wrist before offering it to me. As I drank, a kaleidoscope of images flitted through my mind. This was far different from the first time I had taken the blood oath. Then, I had received a sustained scene of Marc with his father, the Grandmaster of Paris. This time I had disjointed flashes like a series of snapshots in quick succession and it took me a moment to realize what I was seeing. These were not Marc's memories, but the memories of the other coven leaders and lieutenants who had just shared blood with the Grandmaster. I filed them in the back of my mind for later reflection. There was at least one troubling image of Honore and the Undine lieutenant, but I was hardly in a position to do anything about it right now.

I slit my own wrist and offered it to Marc, thankful I was the only one in the room who could read blood. God only knew what images they would get from my blood.

After he had drunk deeply from me, Marc intoned his portion of the Oath.

"I, Marc Gautier, Grandmaster of New Orleans, do humbly accept your freely given oath of loyalty and promise to render all aid that you, Juliette de Grammont, and the Aether coven may require."

He kissed me on both cheeks, and I withdrew to stand beside the other coven leaders as Jaime was summoned to give the last of the blood oaths.

⌇

THE FORMAL RENEWAL of fealty for the rank-and-file vampires had gone quickly, if not smoothly. As was usual, some older vampires became bored, stopped paying attention, and missed their cues. There were no large snags, and no one refused the oath. I began to relax.

As we stood waiting for each vampire to individually walk up and give his or her oath, I had plenty of time to reflect on what I had read in the Grandmaster's blood. I had questions about the new Undine lieutenant, Eugene Miller. In the myriad images I received when I took my blood oath, I had seen him in a passionate embrace with Honore. This might have been an old memory, but I did not think so. He bore watching. I itched to tell someone what I suspected, but there was no way at the moment. While all the city leadership, werewolves, and Gatekeepers were equipped with sophisticated earpieces and lapel mics to facilitate communication in case of attack, Eugene Miller as Undine lieutenant was similarly outfitted. He would hear any warning I gave.

When the last vampire had taken her oath, the city leadership moved to sit around the large table. I took the opportunity to whisper to Jaime.

"If something happens, keep an eye on the Undine lieutenant. Tell Gabe if you get the chance."

"Just key your mic," Jaime said.

"I don't want him to know we suspect anything," I said, tapping my ear, indicating the communication device.

Jaime nodded her understanding.

This next portion was truly the dullest segment of the evening, with Marc giving the State of the City address followed by each of the coven leaders giving their own State of the Coven reports. At one point, Jaime leaned over and whispered, "Couldn't this have been done in an email?"

I gave my protégé a dirty look, but luckily, she had not keyed her lapel mic, and I was the only one who heard.

I did not disagree with her. This part of Convocation was tedious. Swearing fealty was archaic, but useful in these uncertain times. The blood oath taken by the city's leadership could certainly be broken, but for many vampires, especially older ones, it was a matter of honor. As long as the Grandmaster fulfilled his oath, they would uphold theirs, or at least, most would.

Two hours into the ceremony, I thought I had worried for nothing. Marc and I had already given our speeches, mostly just rehashes of everything that everyone in the room already knew. For having the smallest coven, I probably spoke the longest of the coven leaders although Toussaint was currently giving me a run for my money. He was detailing every piece of art, literature, or performance that any of the Sylph had completed the previous year. Jaime rolled her eyes and yawned. I elbowed her this time. This was boring, but there was no need to be rude. Plus, boring meant that Honore and Winters were not attacking.

I was just beginning to relax when I felt the first wave of attack hit the city's outer wards—a cold, dark magic that made me shiver. A few of the magically sensitive vampires in the room also felt it. Marc, who as Grandmaster was mystically connected with the city, also felt the reverberation of the attack. He looked confused, and momentarily, so was I. We all expected Honore and Winters to attack this building's wards, not the citywide matrix.

Keying my lapel mic, I said in a low voice, "There is an attack on the city's matrix going on."

I heard Beau and Nicholas give a series of orders over the communication system. Most of the mages were on rooftops on and around the venue. The werewolves were at street level ringing the building. Meanwhile, Marc interrupted Toussaint's long-winded speech. The Sylph leader looked mildly perturbed that the attack had begun before he finished. The Grandmaster calmly address the assembly, directing the majority to stay in their seats.

A second barrage of magic hit the matrix. This chilled my very bones. I felt the wards shudder, but they held. *Why are they wasting their strength on the anti-werewolf wards?* While I had woven the anti-necromancy spell in, it only prevented passive traps like the one Gabe had stumbled into. That was hardly worth the expenditure of power occurring—*unless opening the city to werewolves was the goal.*

The man-eating Strays had gone underground after I warded the city against them. Beau and his Pack had only tracked down a few of the killers. *Were the Stray werewolves still working with the Rogue vampires?* I had assumed that alliance ended when the Strays could no longer gain entrance to the city.

"Why are they attacking the matrix? Why not a direct attack on Convocation?" Marc asked.

"I think they are trying to let Strays into the city again," I said, standing.

The Strays were a problem not just for humans, but also for us. Vampires were vulnerable during the daytime, and most did not employ guards to protect them. We relied on anonymity. Even vampires who made it safely home from Convocation before dawn could easily be tracked and destroyed once the sun came up. All the Strays would need to do was come here, catch the scent, and follow it back to a vampire's home.

Marc looked stricken as he had the same thoughts.

"Will the matrix hold?" He asked.

Another magical barrage hit. My teeth began chattering. Dammit, cold should not affect vampires, but it was my magic they were attacking, and I felt all of it.

"Not for long with the amount of power being thrown against it," I said.

"How much longer can they keep throwing that much power? They've got to be nearly out of juice unless they've got a lot of rein-forcements," Jaime said.

"Can you bolster the wards?" Gabe asked.

"I would need to be on a ley line to do it." The nearest was blocks away on Carondolet.

Marc shook his head. "No, that's too exposed."

The city's wards took another hit, but this one was different. This was an even darker power. I trembled as I felt the wards being eaten away by the souls of the damned—souls reaped by Winters during the ritual murders.

"My god, Juliette, your lips are blue." Jaime's eyes were wide with shock.

"He used the harvested souls to break the matrix," I said as the wards fell. Much of the cold that had seeped into me dissipated, but a chill lingered deep in my bones.

I had been wrong in assuming that Winters was gathering souls in anticipation of opening the Gates. Even if it had been his original intention, at some point that had shifted, and he decided to use all the stored magic and souls he gathered in his Focus during the sex and murder rituals to breach the city's ward matrix.

"We've got movement on the street," Beau's voice informed us over the comms. "It looks like half of Bourbon Street is headed this way."

"Humans?" Gabe requested clarification.

"Mostly. There are few vamps intermingled. Looks like the Rogue Aether have shown up."

I thought the days of torches and pitchforks were behind us.

"Are they going to use the humans to attack us?" Marc wondered aloud.

"Attack ain't the vibe I get off this crowd. Seems more like a moving party. Doesn't make any sense," Beau said, obviously perplexed.

"I think it best that you invoke the circles, Juliette," Marc said quietly. "Better to be safe than sorry."

The assembled vampires were agitated. The Sylph clearly wanted to break and run while the others were sparking for a fight. Josh had his coven herded into the pre-drawn circle and was admonishing them to stay put. Toussaint showed no such leadership. The man could throw a party, but not much else. He was in a near panic—hands flapping wildly and questioning the safety of the circle.

"Are you sure those creatures can't get to us?" He asked more than once.

"Once I invoke the circle, nothing can enter it unless you or someone else inside the circle break it by stepping out," I assured him as I nicked my forearm with my athame. It never made sense to me why most mages cut their palm to draw blood. Even as a vampire who healed quickly, bleeding hands were a distraction while casting. Murmuring the proper incantation as I dropped my blood on the exposed arc, the protective circle flared to life.

"Stay put!" Josh admonished one last time before taking his position in the vestibule.

I hurried back to the central table and the city's vampire leadership. Eugene Miller was nowhere to be seen although he might be in the vestibule already.

Marc argued he should be on the front lines fighting, while Gabe shook his head.

"We have discussed this. You, Colette, and Toussaint need to stay protected in the circle. Where the hell is Toussaint, anyway?" Gabe's temper was fraying.

"Toussaint is in the other circle," I said as I joined the group.

Colette St. Pierre smiled wanly. "At least there will be no whining in this circle."

Mark harrumphed.

"All right, everyone except Marc and Colette, out of the circle," I ordered. Once the other vampires were clear, I invoked the protection.

Unsure if Jaime had relayed my message to Gabe, I looked around for him. The city's lieutenant was nowhere to be seen, and I did not have time to find him. I had to trust my apprentice had done as I asked.

At this point, Nathalie and I retreated to the specially prepared chamber. I invoked each of the concentric circles beginning with the outermost.

When we were both in the center circle, Nathalie asked me, "Human or wolf form?"

Somehow, I had never considered this. "Um, I do not know. What do you think would be best?"

Natalie quickly considered this, "I think I should remain in human form for the moment. That way I can communicate with the others via the comms if I need to. I can always transform if they breach the building."

"That is a sound plan."

"Let's see what's going on outside," Nathalie said as she pulled her phone out and tapped on an app. Beau and the others on the security team had set up cameras at various points around the building and even in the main chamber. Marc and Gabe had been uneasy about the ones in Convocation, but I had prevailed, arguing that I might need to know what was going on in there. Beau had promised not to turn those cameras on unless something attacked us. They were on now.

Nathalie scrolled through the cameras until she found one showing the street in front of the venue. There were at least a hundred people packed into the block, and even without sound, it seemed to be a party-like atmosphere. Unfortunately, I could not read auras over the camera feed and could not tell who was human and who was vampire.

"Is Rob Winters somewhere in the crowd?" I asked Nathalie.

She moved her fingers over the small screen several times and swore. "There's no zoom feature on this camera! I can't get any close-ups."

I needed more information than this video feed was giving me. "Has anyone spotted Rob Winters?" I asked through my lapel mic.

"Everybody's in costume out here. Kinda hard to tell," Beau said.

"I detect no necromancy," Nicholas Remy supplied.

"You won't until he casts. He shields his magic," I replied.

"I've got him, Gaetan said "He's here. There's a void in the crowd where there should be a person. Winters is right in the middle."

"What are they planning?" Nathalie wondered aloud.

As if that was their cue, pandemonium broke out in the street as the vampires in the crowd outside began killing the humans. I blinked in horror as body after body hit the ground, throats torn out by vampire fangs.

"I'm going to the spirit plane," I said as I sat down. I quickly pulled the comms piece out of my ear and put it in my pocket.

"Be careful," I heard my bodyguard say before I opened my third eye and entered the spirit plane. Physical barriers were transparent here, so I had an unobstructed view of the magical commotion on the street. It was even more active than I had imagined with Necromantic magic flaring as Winters harvested the souls of the dead. More to my surprise was the fact that Winters and I were not the only two mages on this plane. I should have expected this since I had attacked Winters twice while he had been unprotected in spirit form. He had finally learned his lesson and brought guards. It took normal casters a great deal of energy and magic to enter this plane, so most usually did not bother. They had bothered today.

Where in the world are they getting all of this energy and magic?

I had my answer when I saw Winters reaping the souls of the fallen. In a masterfully choreographed dance of death, the necromancer touched each victim as their throat was torn out. He collected dozens of souls in a matter of moments and stored them in his Focus as the vampires outside frenzied at the overwhelming scent of fresh blood. On the spirit plane, I was unaffected, and luckily, the coven vampires were behind a thick bank of windows in the vestibule, or they would have been drawn into the melee. I quickly realized there was nothing I could do here. There was a phalanx of Rogue Aether standing ready to stop me. I could not defeat that many. I stepped back through the door I had just opened and returned to my body.

"What is happening?" Nathalie demanded as soon as I sat up. "This damn camera isn't giving me much, and Dad has commanded everyone stay put—not attack!"

"Winters is reaping souls. I wanted to stop Winters from gathering enough, but he is too well protected," I explained quickly.

"Enough souls for what?" Nathalie asked.

The dark magic hit the building's wards in a series of heavy waves that made the earlier attack on the city's matrix appear amateurish.

"To take down the building's wards."

I started to spool aether to bolster my wards but stopped. It was not worth wasting my energy. I would need it for the coming battle. I shook with silent frustration. My wards would fall in a matter of minutes under the onslaught of dark magic.

"Why aren't the Wolves and the Gatekeepers attacking?" Nathalie asked.

"They don't want to give Winters anymore souls," I answered.

"Looks like he's taken a bunch as it is!"

"Magic user and werewolf souls are more powerful than a human soul. It takes a half dozen or more human souls to equal the power of a single supernatural soul."

The slaughter continued on the screen, and with each death, the wards flickered. As soon as a person died, the power of their soul was added to the onslaught against my wards. There was nothing for us to do except wait. Unfortunately, we would not need to wait very long. I did not know how many human souls it would take to break the wards, but I knew that the Rogue Aether would kill as many as it took.

The Stray werewolves appeared just as the wards fell. Pack werewolves and Gatekeepers poured from their hidden positions on rooftops and in nearby buildings. Our vampires held rank inside the vestibule.

I always thought that frontal assaults were suicide missions. For many of the man-eating Strays and Rogue Aether, it was, but eventually some made it into the building. Magic and bullets flew. Claws slashed and fangs descended.

I made a split-second decision and broke the five circles. I quickly redrew the innermost circle changing several key glyphs transforming it from a protection to a containment circle. I dropped my shields and allowed my power to act as a beacon for Honore. She would not resist challenging me again.

"What in the world are you doing, Juliette?" Nathalie demanded.

She was not happy when I told her.

"Remember, once we initiate single combat, you cannot interfere," I said.

Nathalie growled, having finally transformed into her werewolf form.

"I mean it. She's challenging me for coven leadership. If I can't defeat her without my bodyguard, I don't deserve the position." Even though it would tip the scales in her favor to attack me in concert with Winters or another Aether, Honore would never do it. It would undermine her claim to leadership after my death.

I knew Nathalie wanted to argue, but in her current form she could not. I counted that as a blessing.

I did not have long to wait. Honore, dressed as she had been during the coup attempt in leather pants and a royal purple bustier, found me as I knew she would. Instead of going after the Grandmaster, she came for me. If I could neutralize Honore, perhaps we could end this sooner rather than later.

Flanked by two henchmen that I did not recognize, Honore entered the room as if she owned it. There was no stealth for her. All three appeared well fed and ready for battle.

Nathalie, at my side, growled low in her throat and took a step forward.

"Call off your dog," Honore sneered. "This is between us."

"Yes, it is," I said glaring at her. "Let us end this." Before the words were even out of my mouth, Honore threw her first spell.

I was ready for it and dodged the ice ball. I had actually thought she would enter the room attacking and was not fooled by her brief parlay.

I was not a trained battle mage and even though Jaime had promised to teach me, there had simply not been enough time. All I had managed was to memorize two last resort spells. I was not sure if either of them would work or what toll they would take on me if they did.

Much like the last time Honore and I met in magical combat, I was not at full strength. The near constant casting to make the werewolf amulets and wards was draining. Even when I was at full strength, Honore and I were fairly evenly matched. While I had the slight magical advantage of being able to use both drawn and inborn magic, Honore had more battle spells and was unafraid to use dark magic. I was also hampered by the fact that I could not use deadly force in this battle. As much as I hated her and it was well within my rights to kill her, we needed Honore alive. We needed to know what the plan was for opening the Gates.

Honore spooled lightening in her hand and threw it at me. I cast dispersion and watched her spell fizzle mid-air. I followed that with a volley of small fireballs—more distractions than anything that might hurt her—that bounced harmlessly off her shield spell.

It went back and forth like this for quite a while, both of our strengths dwindling in this grinding war of attrition. I was trying to use just drawn magic, but that was not always possible. Rapidly tiring, I knew I needed to somehow shift the balance to end this fight. Before I could act however, Honore did. Finding an extra reserve of magic, she became a magical berserker, throwing magic in rapid fire sequence with little care to where it went. I threw up the most powerful shield I had, hoping she would exhaust her magic before I exhausted mine.

At least I did until one of those wild spells, a blast of frost, hit Nathalie square in the chest, taking her down. My bodyguard had been waiting off to the side for the outcome of the battle. I was not sure if it was really a stray spell or if Honore had harmed Nathalie to provoke me. Her intentions did not matter because she did anger me.

I came out from behind my shield and threw one of my new spells at her. Five blood shuriken flew from my fingertips. It was only after they were whirling towards her, I remembered we needed Honore alive. Luckily, Honore managed to shield herself in time, but the effort cost her.

That spell, using my inborn magic, also cost me dearly. Both of us were flagging, and I knew it was time to end things. I retreated to the far end of the room, drawing Honore to the center. As soon as she had crossed into the innermost circle, I invoked it. Her next spell rebounded off the containment shield and back at her. Whatever Honore cast must have been powerful, because she collapsed in a heap.

My brain had not even registered my triumph when Honore's

henchmen hit me with spells in quick succession. They would have taken me down if not for the protective runes on my robe.

I turned and sent ten blood shuriken toward the two men. They were brutal, efficient, and took far more of my strength than I had anticipated. Her minions dropped instantly, blood pouring from their eyes, noses, and mouths.

❧

I DROPPED to my knees beside Nathalie, praying she was still alive. I took the fact she was still in her wolf form to be a good sign. Usually dead werewolves revert back to human form. A thick crust of ice coated her. When I placed my hands on her, I could detect shivering. Still alive but fading fast.

I called my fire magic to gently warm her. It took longer than I wanted, but eventually the ice melted, and the scent of wet wolf filled my nostrils when I breathed a sigh of relief. Only Nathalie's heavy pelt had saved her from the savage attack.

Slowly, she opened her eyes.

"Nathalie, can you hear me? Blink once for yes," I said.

She closed her eyes and slowly reopened them.

"Can you shift back?"

Another slow blink.

I turned my back to give her some privacy and fished the earpiece out of my pocket. Once inserted, I heard Nicholas call for all mages to converge in the main hall.

Without looking back, I said, "Stay with Honore. I'm needed in the Convocation Hall."

CHAPTER 26

I was not prepared for the carnage that I encountered in the main room. The siren call of fresh blood, both werewolf and human, beckoned me. I ruthlessly clamped down on the Hunger that rose in me and concentrated on the problem at hand. Dozens of bodies littered the floor. Chairs were strewn wildly about. Several vampires and werewolves were engaged in fang to claw combat. The circle I had constructed around the Sylph coven was broken. The protective circle around the Grandmaster and Undine mistress still held, but Rob Winters was doing his best to break it. Half a dozen Rogue Aether formed a protective barrier around him, fighting off five Gatekeepers and Jaime. Battle magic flew fast and furious between the mages, but they were equally matched. I was watching the equivalent of magical trench warfare. This was a stalemate that could go on until dawn.

I angled myself between Jaime and one gatekeeper and spooled my fire magic. I was hoping to get my spell behind one of the Rogue Aether's shields and turn the battle in our favor. I was horrible at geometry but threw the tiny fireball where I thought it should go. The ball was so small that the mage did not notice it until it ignited his sleeve. Fire is one of the few things guaranteed to kill a vampire, and soon the Rogue Aether was nothing more than a pile of ash.

Jaime threw a quick glance over her shoulder and turned her attention to the next Rogue Aether. I now had a clear shot at Rob Winters. I spooled another fireball—this one much larger—and threw it at his back. As I expected, it dissipated when it hit his shield. It served its intended purpose, however, by breaking his concentration. The necromancer stopped hammering at the protective circle. He whirled, throwing lightening as he did. Only my preternatural reflexes saved me from a direct hit. Another fireball hit his shield but did nothing. He was so powerful, and I was weakening fast. My earlier battle with Honore and her minions had taken a huge amount of my energy even though I was using drawn magic. I was not sure how long I could last in a straight up fight with the necromancer. He seemed no longer to be using stored magic from the Focus, but rather his inborn magic. Lightening flashed from his fingertips, and my shield spell barely deflected it.

Winters threw more lightening at me, battering my defenses. I managed a quick succession of fireballs, hoping to catch him off guard. That did not happen, but his shields did falter. Using the last of my inborn magic, I let fly ten Blood Shuriken. All ten stars found their target, seeming to pierce his flesh, but instead of dropping to the ground dead or at least mortally wounded, he exploded into a flutter of ravens.

I stared stupidly, unsure of what had just happened. One thing I knew was that Winters was not dead. I could still feel his cold death magic. I sat down hard on the marble floor as my knees buckled. My vision dimmed, but I fought to stay conscious. Jaime was at my side in a moment.

I shook my head to clear it. "I am alright," I assured her. "That last bit took more out of me than I expected. Just give me a moment."

"Winters split his soul, didn't he?" Jaime asked, scanning the room for threats.

I gathered what strength I had to answer her, "I think so. I have only read about it, but the dark magic can allow for a mage to split himself into many pieces."

Now that Winters was gone, the remaining Rogue Aether scattered, realizing the battle was lost.

My vision dimmed again, and I heard Jaime call for Josh. I fought the torpor that threatened to overwhelm me.

I felt Josh pull me into his arms. "Juliette, darlin', open those beautiful brown eyes for me," he begged.

I forced my lids open, and Josh's face swam before me.

"Come on, darlin', focus," he said.

We were still not sure what keyed the energy and magic transfer of our soul-bond. It did not happen every time we kissed or even just when needed. Owen and Delia had not been helpful with that either. Despite their nearly two centuries long marriage, they were unsure what triggered theirs. Only that it always worked when need was desperate, and right now the need was desperate.

Concentrating hard, I pulled my vision into focus and looked into the depths of Josh's green eyes. Almost immediately, I felt the transfer begin. I drank him in as if parched from a desert journey.

"Holy shit," I heard Jaime say.

When I was full, the energy flow reversed itself. Back and forth the energy and magic flowed until there was just a steady hum between us. Finally, he pulled me into a tight hug.

"Oh God, Juliette, I thought I'd lost you," Josh whispered in my ear.

I smiled. "I'm harder to get rid of than that."

"You gotta quit scaring me like this. If I had a beating heart, it would have stopped."

"I am alright now." I pulled back and took in the room. It was frightful. Magic was not going to fix this or the carnage in the street. "We need to help with the clean-up."

"Are you sure you're ready?" he asked.

I nodded, and Josh helped me to my feet. Slowly, we made our way to where Marc Gautier stood giving orders. A look of relief passed briefly over his features before they once again became an inscrutable mask.

"I am glad to see you both survived," the Grandmaster said.

I dropped my eyes and bowed my head. "I am sorry my wards failed, my liege."

Marc shook his head. "What happened here was not your fault. That power was . . . I have no words for what that was other than dark and overpowering." The Grandmaster shuddered, remembering what he had felt through his bond with the city. "Am I correct in assuming Winters isn't dead and that flock of ravens was him escaping?"

"Yes. I would guess that he and any Rogue Aether will regroup somewhere. The silver lining is they will be doing that without Honore," I said.

"Did you kill her?"

"No, just incapacitated her. She is in a containment circle in the other room being guarded by Nathalie. I thought you would want to question her."

"I will have Gabe take care of her," Marc said and gave a series of orders to his brother via the comm microphone.

"What do you need us to do?" Josh asked when Marc was done.

JOSH STARED PENSIVELY out the window at the rain. I joined him, twining one arm around his waist. He embraced me, pulling me close. We stood looking at the empty, wet street for a long time, each lost in our own thoughts. We were finally alone again; everyone else in the house had wisely already sought their beds. Josh and I would soon need to retreat ourselves since dawn threatened, but we both needed a few minutes to reflect on the night.

The clean-up had been a brutal race against time and was still not complete. Everyone worked for hours to erase all traces of the attack on the street outside the venue. Human bodies were loaded into vans that would be driven by pack members when they left the city. There were dozens of bodies but thousands of acres of swamp. The wolves knew to leave no more than two bodies in the same place and to space the sites out. Hopefully, the local alligators would obliterate the remains.

Beau and other pack members were tracking down the remaining Strays. Jaime, along with the newly promoted Undine lieutenant and several Gatekeepers, had gone after the remaining Rogue Aether. When she had returned earlier, my apprentice reported that they had killed several of their quarry.

The Convocation site was locked tight and glamoured to appear normal until Vinny Carlucci and his crew could return at sundown to complete the cleaning. He, along with many of the Sylph, had done an incredible job of removing all the blood from the street. The rain had come at the tail-end of the clean-up, helping to wash the final traces into the storm drains. One of the Gatekeepers was a cyberwitch—I had not known such a thing existed—and she altered all the security camera footage.

"How are you?" I asked quietly.

He hugged me tighter and kissed the top of my head. "I should be askin' you that. You went toe to toe with Honore and Winters tonight."

"Just part of my job," I said.

"Yeah, the job." He visibly winced.

We in the vampire world had come through Convocation relatively unscathed—except for the Sylph coven. Sophie had pulled me aside during the clean-up and assured me privately that my ward had not failed. Toussaint had panicked when the Rogue Aether entered the hall and broken the circle himself. As a result, the Sylph master and three other Sylph had perished. That made Josh coven leader—a job he emphatically did not want.

"I understand your trepidation about becoming coven leader," I said.

"What? Oh, that. Well, I sure as hell ain't excited about it, but that isn't what's on my mind?"

"Then what?"

"Us."

"Us?" *Was he having second thoughts about our relationship?*

"Yeah. Seeing you layin' there on the floor scared me, Juliette. Like I ain't ever been scared before. I thought I was gonna lose you."

"I had just done too much magic," I assured him. While I had taken some hits and suffered some damage, all of it was minor enough that I would be fully healed when I rose after sundown.

He nudged my chin with his hand so that I looked up at him. "I know, but it got me thinkin.' I want to spend the rest of our time here on earth together." He hesitated a second before continuing, "Juliette, will you marry me?"

"You know that I may not have much time. The prophecy…"

"All the more reason not to wait. Let's not waste the time we know we have."

I looked into his green eyes and saw the earnestness there, and I made my decision. "Yes. Yes, I will marry you."

BEYOND THE STORY

The Supernatural Community

Vampires: Undead creatures made by ingesting the blood of another vampire at the moment of death. Most belong to one of the five covens. Those who have been abjured are **Rogues.**

Werewolves: Creatures that appear to be human but that can shift into wolf form. They belong to numerous packs throughout the world. Non-pack werewolves are **Strays.**

Mages: Those who can wield magical elemental power.

Gatekeepers: Mages who belong to a secret order tasked with keeping the Supernatural community secret from humans and guarding gates to other realms.

Vampire covens:

   Aether: Mages and other magic using vampires
   Sylph: Creative types, mostly artists and musicians
   Gnome: Leaders within the vampire community
   Undine: Intelligence gatherers and spies
   Salamand: Warriors and protectors

Hierarchy:
    Grandmaster/mistress: vampire leader of a city
    Master/Mistress: leader of one of the five covens in a city
    Master Gatekeeper: leader of the Gatekeepers in a city
    Alpha: leader of a werewolf pack

ACKNOWLEDGMENTS

Under the Harvest Moon has been a four-year labor of love, but I did not do it alone. I had a lot of help along the way. First and foremost, I'd like to thank my mom, Diane, for putting up with all of my musings and bolstering me when I wanted to quit. My fabulous Beta readers—Crystal O'Leary-Davidson, Mert Gareis, and Lisa Bro—gave me insightful feedback that streamlined the plot. An extra shout out goes to Mert for her fabulous editing. Special thanks to Andy Davidson who gave helpful publishing advice and Kelly Saderholm for being an overall cheerleader when I needed it most. Thanks so much, each and every one of you!

ABOUT THE AUTHOR

Tracie Provost grew up all over the US, rarely staying in place for more than a year. She dreamed of becoming an author but decided that career path was not secure enough so she got a Ph.D. in European History. Despite the odds, that actually was more secure, landing her a job at a small southern university. Tracie never forgot her dream, however, and began to write again.

Still teaching full time, Tracie divided her time between academic and fiction writing. There is a surprising amount of carryover between the two. Vampires, werewolves, and witches make regular appearances in both her classes and Urban Fantasy novels.

facebook.com/tracieprovostwriter
twitter.com/drtracieprovost
instagram.com/drtracieprovost